To his surprise, she melted into his arms.

"You're quite strong for a Sassenach," Fia murmured.

Thomas tried to ignore the sensations her warm body ignited in his own. *Sweet Jesu, she is a snug armful.*

"Och, I think . . ." Her breath was ragged, her gaze fixed on his mouth. "I think you mean to kiss me." Her lips parted, and the edge of her tongue moved slowly across the fullness of the lower one.

It was almost more than he could stand; the stirring of excitement grew stronger yet. *She should be terrified, damn it.*

Instead, she tilted her face to his as if to accept a kiss he'd not thought to offer. He knew he should try to scare her more, to frighten her into submission, for there was far more at stake here than the desires of a Scottish wench.

He should have.

But he didn't.

All he could think about was the promise of Fia's lips, the warmth of her in his arms, and the delicate fragrance of heather that drifted from her hair.

Turn the page for rave reviews of Karen Hawkins . . .

Much Ado About Marriage is also available as an eBook

Also by Karen Hawkins

The MacLean Series

How to Abduct a Highland Lord
To Scotland, With Love
To Catch a Highlander
Sleepless in Scotland
The Laird Who Loved Me

Contemporary Romance

Talk of the Town
Lois Lane Tells All

Available from Pocket Books

KAREN HAWKINS

Much Ado About Marriage

Pocket Star Books

New York   London   Toronto   Sydney

Pocket Star Books
A Division of Simon & Schuster, Inc.
1230 Avenue of the Americas
New York, NY 10020

This book is a work of fiction. Names, characters, places, and incidents either are products of the author's imagination or are used fictitiously. Any resemblance to actual events or locales or persons, living or dead, is entirely coincidental.

For information about special discounts for bulk purchases, please contact Simon & Schuster Special Sales at 1-866-506-1949 or business@simonandschuster.com.

The Simon & Schuster Speakers Bureau can bring authors to your live event. For more information or to book an event contact the Simon & Schuster Speakers Bureau at 1-866-248-3049 or visit our website at www.simonspeakers.com.

Cover illustration by Craig White, hand lettering by Ron Zinn.

Manufactured in the United States of America

10 9 8 7 6 5 4 3 2 1

ISBN: 978-1-4391-8760-9
ISBN: 978-1-4391-8762-3 (ebook)

Acknowledgments

I would like to dedicate this book to Hugh Jackman,
who inspires each and every one of my heroes.
(Hugh, if you're reading this, call me!)

Dear Reader,

Congratulations, you have found my secret book! *Much Ado About Marriage* is the first book I wrote, but like many first books, it was hard to sell. Various publishers said it was set in a difficult time period (Elizabethan Scotland and England), was too long (126,000 words), or didn't have enough conflict (which is Very Bad).

By the time I figured out how to correct the book, I'd already sold the next book, *The Abduction of Julia,* which was a Regency set historical. The book did very well and my publisher asked for more books set in that time period.

This left *Much Ado About Marriage* languishing in a box under my bed. Later, on a whim, I sold the book to a different publisher on the condition that it would be printed under another name. It came out with very little fanfare, sold fairly well, and then disappeared. I regained the rights some years later. After that, the book was once again relegated to a box under my bed.

Last year, as I wrote the MacLean Curse series and developed the idea for the Hurst Amulet series, it dawned on me that *Much Ado About Marriage* could be rewritten as a prequel for both series. And so I set to work.

The book is now quite different from the original in many ways. However, I worked hard to leave my heroine's unique spirit intact. Fia MacLean is one of my favorite heroines and I hope you feel the same way about her after you've read her story, *Much Ado About Marriage*.

Thank you for reading my lost book!

Love and laughter,
Karen Hawkins

Much Ado About Marriage

Chapter One

Duart Castle
Isle of Mull, Scotland
May 2, 1567

*I*t was one thing to fall—it was quite another to be shoved from the ledge of a second-story window.

Thomas Wentworth landed flat on his back with an ominous thud, his head saved from the rocky ground by a thick patch of herbs. Light exploded before his eyes as the breath left his body in a whoosh, and blessed blackness beckoned.

For several long moments, he fought for breath. Just as sweet air swept in to reassure him that he wasn't dead, a lilting voice exclaimed softly, "Och, I've killed him!"

Low and husky, the voice flowed over him as rich as sweet cream. The grass rustled as someone knelt beside him. "I'm cursed for certain," she murmured. "'Tis an ill omen to kill the finest man you've ever seen."

The luscious voice demanded his attention. Wincing, Thomas forced his eyes open and focused on the figure kneeling above him.

"Blessed Mother Mary, you're alive!" She smoothed the hair from his forehead with a feather-soft touch.

The moon made a nimbus around the thickest cloud of hair he had ever seen. Luminous in the moonlight, her hair streamed in waves and curls, frothing in abandon across her shoulders.

The end of one persistent curl brushed his ear and he weakly swatted it. "Aye, I live," he muttered, struggling to rise.

Before he could do more than lift his shoulders, the wench pressed him back to the ground. "Don't get up 'til we've certain you've no injuries." Warm hands slid lightly over his arms and legs.

He caught her wrists and pushed her away, the rough wool of her sleeves telling him her position within the castle was menial. He forced his aching body upright. "Leave me be," he growled unsteadily. "I am well."

There was a long pause and then she said, "You're a Sassenach." A faint note of accusation hung in the air.

Thomas silently cursed. His throbbing head had made him forget to disguise his voice with a Scottish accent.

"You, sirrah, are no simple thief." She brushed a hand over his shirt. "Your clothing is too fine."

A flicker of annoyance increased his headache. He had chosen his dark garments with the utmost care to blend with the shadows should anything go awry.

The thought brought a twisted smile. In truth, little had gone right with this venture. From the second he'd crossed into Scottish waters, the famous Wentworth luck had been tested to the breaking point.

First his ship had run into a gale off the rocky coast and had barely managed to get to safety. Once in port, Thomas had discovered that his horse had been severely bruised by the rough crossing and it had taken several days to find a suitable replacement.

And now this: shoved from a window and accosted by a saucy wench. 'Twas yet another delay in his carefully laid plans.

Delays caused risks, and risks were something he rarely took without exquisite preparation and consummate attention to detail. Hurried plans inevitably ended in failure. Thomas Wentworth never hurried, and he never failed.

The woman rested back on her heels, her head cocked to one side. "What are you doing so far from your home, Sassenach?"

"'Tis no concern of yours," he returned curtly.

"I cannot agree. 'Twas me who opened the shutters and bumped you from the ledge. I have a responsibility for you now."

He frowned. "Who are you? A housemaid?"

"I belong here, but the same can't be said of you, Mr. Thieving Knave—or whatever you are."

Her lilting voice tantalized even as her words challenged. Thomas leaned forward and sank his hand in the silken softness of her hair. Ignoring her surprised gasp, he tilted her face until the moon slanted cold rays across the smoothness of her cheek.

He glimpsed a small, straight nose and a pair of very kissable lips before she shoved his hand away, her voice full of breathless outrage. "Stop that! What were you doing, perched on the window ledge like a big chicken?"

Despite his aches and irritations, he couldn't help but grin. "I prefer to think of myself as a more noble bird, like a hawk."

"I'm sure you do. But you flew more like a chicken than like any hawk I've seen."

He chuckled. "Point taken."

"You still haven't answered my question, Sassenach. Why were you on the ledge?"

"I don't remember." For emphasis he rubbed his head, which still ached a bit.

She stood, her skirts rustling. "Aye, 'tis known that Englishmen have delicate heads made of eggshells."

"No doubt you heard that from some heathen Scotsman wielding a claymore the size of a tree."

"Testy, are you?" She patted his shoulder in a kindly way that was more insulting than spitting at him would have been. "I daresay that's because your soft English head is aching."

It was tempting to challenge her, but he couldn't allow himself to get distracted from his real purpose. He put a hand on his pocket, the reassuring crackle of paper calming him.

She eyed him and said in a voice tinged with disapproval, "You were a fool to try to enter the castle through the upper window. 'Twould have been easier to climb in through a lower one."

Though she didn't know it, he had been climbing out not in, when she'd knocked him from the window. "I suppose a Scottish thief would have walked in the front door and not taken a craven entry like a window?"

She chuckled, the sound husky and warm like good Scots whiskey. "I've known one or two as would. There's more gold and silver to be had in the lower floors, too."

"You seem to know a lot about the castle."

"I should. I'm the laird's—" The silence was as complete as it was abrupt. "That's not important. What is important is that you need to improve your thieving ways before you attempt such a fortified castle."

"I appreciate your assistance, Mistress Saucy Wench. I suppose you are a master thief, to offer such advice?"

She shook her head, moonlight flowing across her hair like firelight on a rippled pond. "Not a master. Tonight was my first effort at reiving, and 'twas not near as exciting as I'd hoped," she said wistfully.

She was a thief? Had he heard her right?

"'Twas dull work indeed 'til I knocked you from the ledge. 'Tis amazing, but you didn't make a sound on the way down. You fell like a great rock, with nary a cry 'til you landed in the garden. Then you went 'oof' like a—"

"For the love of Saint Peter, cease your prattle," Thomas hissed, casting an uneasy glance at the looming castle.

"Pssht. Don't fash yourself about being heard. There's no one home but the servants; Laird MacLean's gone."

"Aye, he's been traveling these last two months."

"Nay, he returned last week."

"What?" *Damn it, my sources were wrong.* According to the information Thomas had been given, the laird wasn't to return for another fortnight.

"Aye, but then that witch sent him a letter that crossed him. He stormed out immediately to enact vengeance."

Thomas frowned. "MacLean left again because of . . . did you say 'witch'?"

"Aye. The White Witch Hurst. I've never met her, but she's cast her spell over MacLean until he doesn't know if he's coming or going. She gave the local magistrate some ancient documents that lay claim to half of the MacLean lands."

"Good God. No man would stand for such."

"Especially not the MacLean." She shook her head, her mane of hair fluttering about her. "But I think 'tis lust as draws him to her. I hope he has a care. She's a powerful witch, though Duncan claims that she's but knee high to a goat."

"I don't believe in witches or curses."

"I do," she said simply. "I believe in all sorts of magic."

"I'm quite aware of the Scots' love of all things mystical."

"And I know of the English love of coin." She shrugged, an elegant motion that dismissed him. "We both have our weaknesses."

He clambered gingerly upright, his head swimming as he spaced his feet far apart to balance the swaying earth. Bloody hell, he felt as though he were on the deck of the *Glorianna* in a full gale. A warm hand tucked into the crook of his arm. "Are you well enough to be walking?" Concern filled her voice.

"I'm fine," he said curtly, shaking off her hand.

"Very well."

Thomas wished he could see her expressions. Since the moon was behind her, her face was in shadow. On impulse, he grasped her arm and turned her so the moonlight spilled across her.

For a moment he could only stare. His earlier glimpse had suggested she was comely, but he had never seen such beauty as he now faced. Her dark eyes sparkled, surrounded by a thick tangle of lashes, and her full lips begged to be tasted.

Perhaps I believe in magic after all, he thought numbly.

She yanked her arm free and hefted up a large bag that clunked and clanked. "I've wasted too much time here. If you're of a mind to get caught, Sassenach, then stay where you are. The laird could return any time and I, for one, will not be here to greet him."

Some foolish part of him wanted to feel her honey-smooth voice a little longer. "You surprised me when you thrust open the shutters at this time of the night."

She'd already turned away but now paused. "I was trying to decide if I should climb out the window like a proper thief or take the stairs. After watching you fall, I thought 'twas very possible I could have dropped my bag during the climb down and broken and dented my reivings, and then all of my efforts would have been for naught."

Her casual attitude toward her less-than-honorable profession made him smile. "You are a saucy wench," he said with grudging admiration.

She laughed softly, the sound curling inside him and heating him in unexpected ways. "That's exactly what Duncan says."

For a second, Thomas envied the unknown Duncan. "What's your name, little thief?"

"Fia." She shifted the bag to her other shoulder. "I just took the best candlesticks. I think they'll be easier to sell than heavy plate, don't you?"

She turned and made her way down a faint path that led toward the black forest, saying over her shoulder, "We should hurry, for Duncan returns this morn."

Thomas accepted the unspoken invitation and fell into step beside her. "Who is this Duncan?"

"Why, Duncan MacLean, the Earl of Duart and laird of his clan." She quirked a disbelieving brow his way. "Surely you knew whose castle you were stealing into?"

"Of course I knew. I just didn't think of him as 'Duncan.'" This woman knew MacLean well enough to use his given name. Who was she, then? She'd said she was "the laird's"—and then hadn't finished the sentence. *She must be the laird's mistress, then.*

Refusing to examine the irritation that swelled at the thought of such beauty being sullied by a possible traitor, Thomas tried to focus on the return of his good fortune. Since Fia was within MacLean's inner circle, she would be privy to valuable information.

He stepped into the shadows of the forest, pulling her into his arms.

"Stop!"

Though she struggled, he held her easily. "I've a wish to know more about you . . . and this Duncan."

"Why should I tell you anything?" She twisted, attempting to stomp his feet with her muddied boots, her bag clanging noisily.

Thomas pushed aside the wild abandon of her hair, his fingers encircling her neck. "Hold still, comfit," he whispered. "I want to know everything about Duncan Mac-Lean. If you tell me, I'll release you."

She stopped struggling. "You wish to know of Duncan? Why?"

"That's none of your concern."

Her mouth thinned into a stubborn line. "Everything about Duncan *is* my concern."

"I can't imagine that you care too much, to steal from him the minute he's out of sight." His mouth was but a whisper from hers, his thumbs resting suggestively at the delicate hollow of her throat. "Just tell me what you know; I ask for nothing more harmful than information."

She dropped her bag with a noisy clank and, to his surprise, melted into his arms, her lithe body flush against his. "You're quite strong for a Sassenach."

He tried to ignore the sensations her warm body ignited in his own. *Sweet Jesu, she is a snug armful.*

"Och, I think . . ." Her breath was ragged, her gaze fixed on his mouth. "I think you mean to kiss me." Her lips parted, and the edge of her tongue moved slowly across the fullness of the lower one.

It was almost more than he could stand; the stirring of excitement grew stronger yet. *She should be terrified, damn it.*

Instead, she tilted her face to his as if to accept a kiss he'd not thought to offer. He knew he should try to scare her more, to frighten her into submission, for there was far more at stake here than the desires of a Scottish wench.

He should have.

But he didn't.

All he could think about was the promise of Fia's lips, the warmth of her in his arms, and the delicate fragrance of heather that drifted from her hair.

Thomas kissed her with every bit of passion that welled inside him, possessing her mouth as he cupped her rounded bottom through her skirts and molded her to him.

She clutched at his loose shirt, her soft, yielding lips drinking hungrily from his.

His body flamed in response and all thought fled. He slipped an arm about her waist and pulled her firmly to him, brushing aside her entangling hair to taste the sweetness of her delicate neck. He traced the contours of her back and hips, stopping to pull her bodice from the waistband of her skirt. Sweet Jesu, her skin was so deliciously warm and inviting. He pulled impatiently at the ties at her waist, his mouth now ruthlessly possessing hers.

Through a haze of raw passion, something hard and cold intruded harshly into his awareness. Suddenly he realized that a razor-sharp point, cold and deadly, was pressed against his side.

Thomas opened his eyes.

Fia regarded him with a cool smile. "'Tis time you were on your way, Sassenach." She moved away and he saw that she held a knife that shone wickedly in the moonlight. And in her other hand, she held his purse.

Damn the wench! He had played right into her hands. "Why, you little thief!" He ached with frustrated passion and harsh disappointment.

She brightened. "I *am* a good thief, aren't I?"

Cold fury raced through him. Should he lunge for the knife? No; a bloodcurdling scream would awaken the servants.

Thomas swore. "You common, thieving—"

"Och, spare me your wild words. 'Tis your own fault, laddie."

"Do you know who I am?"

"Nay, and it matters not."

"I am Thomas Wentworth." He waited. Even here, in the wilds of Scotland, the Wentworth name had meaning. His family was the wealthiest and most powerful in all of England.

But apparently someone had forgotten to mention that fact to this particular maid. Fia tucked his bag of coins into her bodice. "Well, Master Thomas, 'tis nice to meet you, but 'tis your own fault 'tis come to this."

"It's *my* fault that *you* robbed me?"

"I had no notion to take aught from you 'til you tried to seduce me."

He laughed bitterly. "One does not seduce a trollop. One pays."

Her hand tightened on the knife; her delicate brows lowered. "Have a care, Sassenach. You may have a tongue as sharp as a knife, but I hold a real one."

"You wouldn't use it."

To his astonishment, she quirked a brow, cool and proud. "Why should I fear a poor Sassenach who can't even climb into a window without falling on his head?"

He stepped forward and the knife flashed wickedly in the moonlight.

She eyed him warily. "Now, I shall go my way and you will go yours. If you're as smart as you'd like to think you are, you'll leave before Duncan arrives."

"I will find you, wench," he warned.

"That's not likely." Still holding the wicked-looking knife before her, she grabbed her bag of loot and slowly backed toward the shelter of the forest, her eyes fixed warily on his.

He smiled with cold menace. "Tell me why his lordship returns in such haste, and perhaps—just *perhaps*—I'll allow you to leave in peace."

"As though you had the choice of it," she mocked, but her gaze darted toward the castle, the roof faintly agleam as dawn crept stealthily into the sky.

"Come," he urged, forcing his voice to a calmer level. "A little information for the gold you've stolen. 'Tis a fair exchange."

Fia regarded him soberly. "You won't chase me into the woods?"

"Not if you tell me what I seek."

After a moment, she nodded. "Fine, then. 'Tis only fair. MacLean is returning to marry."

Damn it, his sources hadn't mentioned a marriage. "Who is he marrying?"

She smiled, and he knew her answer before she even spoke.

"Me, Sassenach." Her lilting voice taunted. "He comes to marry me."

And with a rattle of stolen candelabras and a mischievous smile, she turned and fled, disappearing into the woods.

Chapter Two

$\mathscr{F}$ia hurried through the brush, glancing over her shoulder. The Sassenach would surely follow; he'd been too angry not to, but she had a goodly lead on him, so she was safe.

She crested a low slope and paused behind a thicket for a final glimpse of Duart Castle. The morning sun tossed pale streamers of light across the grassy slope around it. If she were there now, she would be rising to the familiarity of her own comfortable chamber with its red velvet hangings, heavy oak bed and bench, and thick carpets. She would be snug, warm, and safe—not hiding in the damp, cold woods from an irritated Englishman.

But Fia had had her fill of comfort and safety. She wanted excitement, the thrill of the uncertain, and the chance to prove herself without her cousin's overbearing "assistance."

She almost laughed out loud. She couldn't imagine a more fortuitous beginning for her adventure. And what an adventure it was, too! At this very moment, tucked into a leather pouch and tied to the back of her horse deep in the woods, were her treasures—the plays she had painstakingly written over the past six years.

Fia patted her sack of silver, a bubble of excitement humming through her. Already she'd met with such good fortune. Soon she'd be in London and, if fortune continued to smile, she'd be a playwright. All she had to do was escape before Duncan returned.

Her smile faded and she turned into the woods ahead. The sad truth was that Duncan had indeed decided to marry her. "Aye," she muttered with distaste, "he's decided to marry you to the first qualified man as stumbles through the castle gates."

Her cousin had spent the last two years searching for a man he deemed worthy of her hand. Fortunately, Duncan's idea of a deserving husband was a man of proud birth, possessing great wealth and capable of wielding both sword and pen.

With such a lengthy list of qualifications, Fia had felt sure that she would never be shackled.

But lately the political situation had changed, and Duncan had grown dark and quiet. The Scottish throne was at risk as Queen Mary made error after error, aligning herself with men believed to have murdered her husband.

No one liked the thought of such men holding the strings to the throne, which they would, once they held the capricious Mary under their complete power. The whispers had grown, and some of the clans were openly aligning themselves against their own queen. The rumblings of war had grown to a near-deafening level and some of the more powerful clans were only waiting to see where Clan MacLean stood before they declared. No one had more resources or trained men than Duncan, and few lairds were as well regarded.

But Duncan remained stubbornly mute on his position.

Lately more and more men arrived under cover of night, demanding and pleading that he take a stand.

Fia didn't know where Duncan's thoughts rested, since he refused to discuss it even with her, which hurt her feelings mightily. But her cousin was a wily leader of their clan, and whatever was holding his tongue, 'twas for the good of them all.

Still, lately she'd caught him eying her with a considering gaze, and twice he'd said plainly that she would be safer elsewhere than Duart Castle.

Fia feared she knew the reason why; Duncan wished her away from Duart should there be war. And if that were the case, he might become far less exacting in selecting her a husband.

She grimaced. *Who needs a husband? Unless the man can sponsor my plays, I would be no better off than I am now.* She hurried deeper into the woods, the woody scent of the forest tickling her nose. She knew the path well and didn't hesitate, pausing only once to pluck ripe berries from a nearby bush and pop the sweet morsels into her mouth.

Her plan was to go down the path to the shore, where maid Mary and her husband would be waiting with the skiff. Then to the mainland, and on to London.

Ah, London! She shivered with excitement, her resolve firming even more. To take control of her own fortune, that was where she must go. Queen Elizabeth was a strong patron of the arts, especially the theater. Any playwright worth her salt would head to the queen's court, where opportunity awaited.

It was a pity she hadn't thought to question the Sassenach about the English court. As pompous and arrogant as he seemed, 'twas possible he'd visited it. She grimaced at her lost opportunity—though she knew from the Sassenach's kiss, she knew that there'd be a cost to such questioning.

She touched a finger to her lips, marveling at how they still tingled. Perhaps she wouldn't mind paying such a cost. She'd shared kisses before, but none had sent her heart racing like the Sassenach's.

Sadly, 'twas a waste of time to think of the Sassenach, for she'd never see him again. She hurried along the path, the damp leaves muffling her booted steps. Yet still, the memory of that kiss slipped into her thoughts.

'Twould be good fortune indeed if the Sassenach were a real lord, and knew Queen Elizabeth, and could ask her directly to—

But no. 'Twouldn't help her one jot even if he *were* a real English lord. 'Twas easy to see he was too self-involved to bother with a mere playwright like herself. And even if he were not so clutch-hearted, 'twas highly unlikely the man would forgive her for knocking him out of a window *and* stealing his purse. One or the other, perhaps, but not both, and especially not both on the same day.

She sighed wistfully. The handsome thief was probably a very pleasant companion when his head didn't ache and his coins were still safely tucked in his belt.

"Och, Fia, you've gone daft," she said sternly. "For all you know, there could be a soul as black as the bottom of a kettle beneath that handsome exterior."

Something flickered at the corner of her vision and she paused and looked about, but nothing moved in the thick woods. A faint twinge of disappointment went through her. The Sassenach hadn't even attempted to follow; she'd thought he had more spirit than that.

She settled the heavy bag on her other shoulder and glanced at the sky, where a growing brightness crept through the trees. The tide would be rising by now. She continued on, stepping lightly over thick ferns, fallen leaves, and broken tree limbs. Her leather boots made very little noise on the moss-covered path, each step stirring sweet pine scent into the air. A swirl of morning mist crept along the ground and the grove looked as if it had been touched with an ancient magic.

It would have been easy to believe she walked through an enchanted forest. The entire scene would have made a wonderful setting for a play, perhaps one about a fairy queen who'd fallen in love with—

A band of steel clamped about her arm. Fia gasped as she was yanked against a newly familiar broad chest.

A deep voice murmured into her ear, "Where are you off to now, my little thief? Looking for another fool to fleece?"

"Nay, I've reached my limit of reiving for the day."

"I'm surprised a wench like you has any limits." His warm breath brushed her cheek. "What? No sharp retort? No hidden knife?" The lazy voice was cutting her to shreds.

Desperation whipped her into action. With a lithe twist, Fia shoved her bag into Thomas's broad chest and whirled to make her escape as she fumbled at her waist for her knife.

She took only three steps before his body crashed into hers, tumbling both of them to the ground. Her knife, knocked from its sheath, came to rest under a bush.

He lay atop her, his breath warm on her cheek, his huge body pressing her into the soft earth.

Fia gasped, struggling for air.

"I daresay you wish for your trusty knife, but alas, I can't allow you to have it. Not until we've reached an understanding."

"I . . ." She struggled mightily with each word. "I . . . cannot . . . breathe—"

Immediately, he raised himself on his elbows.

She gulped in the cool morning air, the spots before her eyes disappearing. *Ah, much better.* The only trouble was that now she was freed from his weight, she was far too aware of his warm body over hers, his thigh pressing between her legs in the most intimate way.

She drew a shuddering breath. "You nearly killed me."

"Don't tempt me." Thomas's hands slid over her throat, pushing aside her hair in what seemed more a caress than a threat.

Her panting increased at the feel of his warm skin on hers. "'Twould be a grievous error to murder me. The women of my family have a tendency to go a-ghosting if they are done away with in a foul manner."

His gaze locked with hers. "A-ghosting?"

"Aye. I'd be dressed in flowing white and keening at the top of my lungs. 'Tis not a sight you would enjoy." She couldn't help but give a wee grin at his expression.

To her surprise, he smiled warmly. "I can do without the keening, comfit, though the thought of you dressed in a flowing white gown is quite another matter." His gaze boldly lingered on the fullness of her breasts, which pulled the thin fabric of her dress taut. "Especially if your ghostly gown showed off your impressive attributes in a more seductive manner."

Fia flushed. She had bought this dress from the village laundress, a gown someone had forgotten and left behind by the river. Plain and homespun, it was the perfect disguise. She hadn't expected the garment to fit so snugly.

The heavy purse nestled between her breasts did little to ease the strain on its lacings. The thought of the Sassenach's gold brought her grin back in full measure. "I'm sure I'd be a pleasing ghostie, dressed in a fashionable sort of way just to tempt your fancy." She snorted inelegantly and wished he would rise. It was difficult to converse at such a close distance, especially with a man who had such warm brown eyes flecked with amber. "I might wear ghosting white, but 'twill be a thick fabric, and ragged—so you can stop your wishful thinking."

"Well, then, rags it is. On a wench like you, though, rags might not be so unattractive." His breath was warm and sweet near her ear, and she shivered.

"Attractive?" She regretted the wistful tone of her voice instantly. "Just what do you mean by 'a wench like you'?"

A smug smile settled on the Sassenach's face. "What do you think? And don't tell me the laird is coming to marry you, for I'll not believe it. While 'tis possible the MacLean is on the verge of finding himself wed, he would never marry a common maid."

"Och, you—!"

"I'm just speaking the truth. I think you are angered to be losing your protector, so you stole away with a small fortune in your sack."

"How wise you are, my Lord Lackwit." If sarcasm were gold, she would have just made her fortune. "Though I took some silver from MacLean, 'tis more in the line of a loan."

He chuckled. "And I suppose you were sneaking out at dawn merely for the fun of it."

"And to keep the servants from knowing which direction I took. I have my own silver, but cannot access it." She'd have taken silver candlesticks from her own household goods, but they were stored in trunks deep in the castle hold, awaiting her eventual marriage.

"You are a foolishness, but a sweet one." He ran a finger over the rough fabric that stretched across her breasts. "This, milady thief, is neither silk nor brocade."

The sensations his wandering touch created were unbearable. Fia bit her lip to keep him from seeing her weakness, but her breasts were not so easily tamed. Her nipples hardened and peaked, as though eager for him to repeat the touch.

His grin widened. He captured one of her hands, running his thumb over her ink-stained fingers. "And this is not the hand of a lady."

She clenched her fist. "If you wait much longer, Duncan himself will come and tell you exactly who I am. Neither of us would benefit from that."

"I'd enjoy seeing MacLean's face when you explain how you came to possess his best candlesticks," he retorted. "But I suppose you're right and I shouldn't tarry."

"Then leave. I'm not stopping you."

"Oh, but you are. I came for my gold, little thief. Hand it over and we'll part ways." His gaze drifted over her, lingering on her bottom lip.

Fia noticed with rising trepidation and excitement that Thomas's eyes glimmered with the heat of sun-drenched moors. She couldn't let this go any farther. As muddled as he made her feel, if he attempted to kiss her or more, she'd not have the strength to refuse him. She'd never seen such a handsome man, and his touch instantly turned her bones to butter.

It had taken every bit of her resolve to halt his kiss in the garden, and she doubted she could do it again. She simply hadn't had much experience with kissing and such; Duncan had seen to that. Even now she grimaced at the memory of what her cousin had done to the Duke of Argyll's youngest son when he'd stolen a very brief kiss. But not even the handsome son of the Duke of Argyll had left her aching and breathless the way the Sassenach's touch did.

She couldn't allow him to kiss her again, or it would prove her undoing. Still, she wasn't about to hand over her hard-won gold.

To buy time while she found a solution, she blurted out, "My great-grandmother is a real ghost, you know." She could tell by the flicker of interest in his eyes that she had his attention, so she quickly pressed on. "My mam flitters across Loch Buie, howling and a-moaning, scaring the people of the village nigh to death. She wears a gray gown, I think. Or perhaps 'tis brown—"

"Cease your prattling, comfit." His eyes glimmered with humor as he flicked a careless finger over her cheek. "I won't be distracted from my gold."

"Och, no. I just thought you might wish to know what the blurry figure is who waits for you when you go to sleep at night. She's a tenacious ghost, she is, and not for the unwary."

"I don't believe in ghosts."

"I do, for I've seen many." She lifted her brows. "Do you believe in fairies?"

"No."

"Pixies?"

"No."

"Banshees? Stiths? Witches?"

His mouth began to form the word "no" yet again, and she burst out, "Och, there must be something, Sassenach! Have you never lost something and then found it in the place where you already looked? Or come to a place you'd swear you'd seen before, but 'twas impossible? Surely, you believe in magic of *some* sort!"

He regarded her for a long moment. "How did your grandmother die?"

Fia had to hide a grin. She could tell he wished the question back as soon as he asked it, so she hurried to answer. "'Twas rumored my grandfather killed her with his own hands."

"Did she tell senseless stories?"

"Nay, she didn't have the gift. To be honest, Grandmother was as demanding a woman as ever lived. Poor Grandfather could neither drink nor fight without her harping from dawn to dusk."

"A harpy, eh?" He murmured, tracing feather-light circles on her jaw with one thumb.

Fia steeled herself against his touch. "Aye. 'Twas said her voice could freeze a running river in the height of summer. Grandfather finally lost his temper and slammed his mug upon the kitchen table, smashing it to pieces, and ordered her to leave him and ne'er return. And she did."

The Sassenach's brows snapped together. "That's a bit harsh."

"So everyone thought. When he realized what he'd done, he wept for twenty days and twenty nights."

"He must have loved her after all."

"Och, nay! 'Twas just that he could never drink from a mug again as it reminded him too much of the whole affair. He said 'twas enough to sour even good whiskey."

Thomas laughed, his laughter rumbling in his chest. Fia's breath caught in her throat. He was beautiful, all black hair and golden skin. A subtle heat spread through her and made her move restlessly.

His laughter died and he regarded her through suddenly heavy-lidded eyes. "You are nothing like your grandmother, my sweet. You have a voice like pure honey. Indeed, I would like to hear you moaning in pleasure with that luscious voice of yours."

It was all she could do not to twine her arms about his head and pull his firm mouth to hers. But the pressure of the bag of gold between her breasts reminded her of her purpose.

"You should be worrying about the MacLean and nothing else," she admonished desperately. "We have no time for this."

His eyes gleamed and he gave her a smile of such incredible sweetness that her heart lodged in her throat. *'Twas almost a crime to make such a handsome man and loose him on the world without warning.*

He shifted to one side, his warm hands sliding to her shoulders and then to her breasts. All coherent thought fled her mind.

"The laird be hanged," he murmured. "My sources say he is not to return so soon, and besides, I begin to think you might well be worth the risk." His mouth lowered toward hers, and Fia felt herself drawn toward his lips— beautifully carved lips that would taste as sweet as warmed honey. She closed her eyes and waited . . . and waited . . . and waited . . .

She opened her eyes and saw his mocking expression. She flushed.

His grin was irritatingly smug. "I will have my purse." His gaze locked on her mouth as he slipped a finger under the front of her gown.

She gasped, fighting a maelstrom of shivers. "I'll give it you! Just let me up!"

For one agonizing second she didn't think he'd agree, but then he stood and pulled her to her feet. "My purse, Fia. Now. Else I will come and get it."

Flushed from head to toe, Fia reached into her gown, halting as she saw his obvious interest. "Turn your back."

"Modesty?" *From a woman like you?* The unspoken words hung in the silence, loud and bruising.

Fia bared her teeth in the semblance of a smile. "Very well, Lord Thomas. Watch if you must."

He was tall and handsome beyond belief, with a smile that could drop one's heart into one's shoes, but he was no gentleman. Had she written this scene, Thomas the Handsome would have fallen to his knees and promised to take her to London. He would have found a sponsor for every one of her wonderful plays and would have fallen deeply and desperately in love with her.

Alas, this was not one of her plays.

She yanked open the front of her dress, her fine lawn chemise on display for the world to see as she removed his purse. Fia tossed it to the ground and pulled her bodice closed, tying the laces as quickly as she could.

In the quiet of the glen, his breath sounded almost labored. "You tempt me, wench, but I dare not tarry." He glanced about the clearing. "Where is your horse? Or were you going to steal one on the road?"

Fia shot him a baleful glare and picked up her bag and knife. "Of course I have a horse. Only a fool would travel by foot when a mount is available, and—" She frowned. "Where's *your* horse?"

"Now, there's the rub, comfit. Some damned hound has chased it away, so I need yours."

Some damned hound? *Sweet Saint Catherine, let it not be* . . . "Ah, and just what kind of dog chased away your horse?"

"'Twas an ugly cur." His face showed suspicion. "Why do you ask?"

"No reason. Was . . . was this cur brown in color, with only half an ear?"

His gaze narrowed. "Aye."

She winced. "Was his tail slightly bent at the end?"

"Aye," Thomas stated grimly.

"And his left eye . . . was it but half-open?"

"'Tis a dog well known to you, I see." His tone was grim.

"Och, no! I have never seen such a dog, though I must admit he sounds like a poor, sad little beastie. I daresay he's very sweet . . . when not chasing off horses."

"God's blood, you are the unluckiest wench I've ever encountered." He sounded thoroughly disgusted. "You owe me a mount, milady thief."

"The dog isn't mine!"

"No?"

Fia became intensely interested in rubbing an ink stain from her fingers. "Not really. 'Tis possible I may have seen him in the garden once or twice." She glanced at him from under her lashes. "And I may have fed him a mite now and again."

She could hear his teeth grinding. He would have naught but stubs left if he made it a habit to abrade them so often.

"I will have your horse," he stated.

"Hmph. 'Tis unfortunate you are forced to become a horse thief because of a poor, abused pup. A good thing we have no wayward cows about, else you might commit murder or worse."

"I've had about enough of you for one day, mistress."

"La, how high and mighty! What are you, a prince?"

"Nay, I am but an earl." He gave an insultingly brief nod. "The Earl of Rotherwood, at your service."

An earl. An English *earl. He must be a member of the court, then!* Fia said a short prayer of thanks to the saints for delivering such an Englishman. She could already see her name written in flowing script across the playbill.

"Why did you pray for an Englishman?" Thomas demanded in an outraged tone.

Fia winced. 'Twas her greatest fault to speak every thought out loud. "I-I've just always had a liking for earls. Duncan is one and . . . I am just. . . used to having one about."

Thomas rubbed his temple. "Sweet Jesu, you make my head ache. Just give me your mount."

"You'd regret taking her. She's a Scottish horse, and she'll have naught to do with an Englishman."

"I can handle her. Where is she?"

Fia decided Lord Thomas's attractiveness faded even as they spoke. While he was blessed with beauty of face and form, 'twas obvious his Maker had been forced to scrimp when it came to the man's temperament. That was the real tragedy—he would have made a wondrous character for one of her plays had he possessed but a measure more charm.

She nodded her head toward the clearing. "Thunder is tied to the big tree in the glen. Just follow the path."

"Excellent. Meanwhile, I suggest you hie yourself back

to replace the candelabras before it's discovered that both you and they are missing."

That would never happen. She'd decided on this path and one way or another, she would take it to the end. Still, she was loath to lose her horse, loath to lose her newfound gold, and, strangely enough, loath to see Thomas leave. "You're off to London, I suppose."

He paused. "Aye."

"You'll need a guide through the Scottish countryside. I could lead you, and—"

"Rob me the first time I look elsewhere than my pockets? I think not, my little Scot. Though the idea of having you warm my blankets makes the offer most attractive."

The pig. "I'll be warming no man's blankets, thank you." Fia sniffed. "'Tis time you left, for I've tired of you."

Thomas's mouth hardened into a harsh line. "No doubt you expected to wrap me about your little finger as you did MacLean. I am not such a fool. Good-bye." Disapproval evident in his every move, Lord Thomas the Proud turned and strode into the shadowed woods.

For several long moments, Fia stood where she was. Had she been a heroine in one of her plays, perhaps Rosalind, the banished duke's daughter who'd bravely dressed as a boy to make her own way in the world, she might have followed Sir Thomas into the forest and tried to trick his gold from him once again. But she wasn't Rosalind, and the thought of facing Thomas once again seemed a dangerous proposition.

She kicked a rock down the path. "Well, arrogant sir, you'll not get far on Thunder. That much I'm sure of." That would be worth seeing, too. All Fia had to do was wait.

With a smile, she shouldered her burden once more and began to walk.

Chapter Three

Whatever image the name "Thunder" conjured up, this was not it.

Thomas had never seen a more pitiful horse. Its dull, pale brown coat was rough and completely bare in places. A straggly mane hung in limp strands on a gaunt neck.

Worse, some romantic fool had plaited the sparse mane with colorful wildflowers that drooped piteously, as if hanging their heads in shame.

He regarded the thin, knobby legs and the swollen body with a disbelieving eye. 'Twas a wonder the horse could even stand, much less walk. "Excellent. I've stolen a horse not even fit for a tannery."

The beast slowly turned her head and measured him with a look of acute dislike.

"God's blood, *everything* about that wench is cursed." Thomas wanted nothing more than to turn and walk away, but he needed this ugly mount to reach his ship by nightfall. "Easy does it, old girl." He patted her neck, wondering if she could bear his weight.

Encouraged, she attempted a spirited snort, only to end up wheezing and coughing so hard, Thomas felt obliged to thump her soundly on the back.

The relentless ache in his head increased. He could only be thankful Robert wasn't nearby. One of Thomas's closest companions, Robert MacQuarrie enjoyed a jest more than life itself and wasn't above exaggerating common circumstances into a tale of mirth. If Robert ever saw Thomas on this broken-down old nag, he would hear about it for the rest of his life.

He sourly rubbed the lump on his head. Robert wouldn't have to exaggerate to make a mockery of this particular foray. Everything had gone awry that could go awry, and it had all been made worse by a fey Scottish wench.

Thomas glanced back at the forest with a sharp sense of regret. The thought of her made him burn, which surprised him. He wasn't a man to linger where fate did not wish him, but . . . damme, she was lovely. Full lips and mysteriously dark eyes were indelibly etched in his memory, and he feared her luscious breasts would haunt his dreams for many a night.

He reminded himself grimly that she was naught but a beautiful thief with a penchant for causing trouble. She had already shoved him from a window, stolen his money, and she and her mystery mongrel had been indirectly responsible for the loss of his horse.

"Well, Thunder, 'tis just the two of us. If you carry me well, I promise to put you out of your misery and sell your hide to the first tanner we meet."

Thunder yanked her head about and glared at him.

Thomas eyed her with growing unease. *Surely the stupid horse didn't understand me. God's blood, I'm becoming as fanci-*

ful as that wench. But as much as he tried to deny it, events were teetering on the verge of disaster. He *had* to get back to his ship, and quickly.

He didn't relish the situation. He was a Wentworth, and, as his father had told Thomas countless times during his brief childhood, Wentworths never failed. His father would have died alone and bootless before throwing a single leg over such a decrepit animal.

But he wasn't his father, overly focused on appearances and pedigree. If Thomas wished to succeed, he was going to have to ride the pathetic beast. Gathering his resolve, he collected the reins and swung into the saddle. There, he set his heels and urged Thunder on with a click of his tongue and a gentle nudge of his heels.

The mare twitched nary a muscle.

Thomas tightened the reins and tapped the horse's sides more firmly.

Again, nothing.

This time, Thomas planted his heels as firmly as he could.

Thunder bolted forward, only to come to an immediate halt, jerking Thomas forward in the saddle. "You bedeviled, worthless bag of bones—"

She swung her head around, showed her teeth, and lunged for his leg.

He yanked his legs tighter to her sides and out of reach.

She glared at him.

"So that's the game you play, eh?" Thomas smiled grimly. "You don't know who you're dealing with, you scourge-ridden old nag. I'm the most powerful earl in England, and I'll not be denied."

The words hit his own ears flatly. He sounded far too much like his father, blast it.

Thunder apparently agreed, for she bared her yellowed teeth and flattened her long ears, suddenly looking like a donkey.

That was it. Grasping the reins tightly, Thomas planted his heels into Thunder's bloated sides and yelled, *"Hie!"*

The mare hunched her shoulders and began to swell.

"What the—"

In a swift move, the mare dropped to her knees and threw herself onto her side.

"Oof!" The wind flew from his lungs as Thomas went down with a bruising blow to his hip and an incredible pressure on his leg.

It took him a full moment to realize what had happened. He was trapped beneath a fat, hide-bare nag, his leg held as securely as though shackled in iron.

"Move, you ill-begotten, mangy bag of bones!" he roared.

Thunder bared her teeth over her shoulder and lunged. Thomas stared at his torn sleeve in amazement, then bellowed in rage.

He placed his free foot squarely on the horse's back and pushed with all his might. The horse grunted, but the shaggy head didn't even move. He tried yet again, but his efforts elicited only a heaved sigh from the horse.

Thomas lay back panting, his struggles leaving him as breathless as the fall from the window. It was unbelievable. He, Thomas Henry Wentworth, the fifth Earl of Rotherwood, scion of a long line of immaculately bred, impeccably comported, and extremely dignified English nobility, was pinned in the cold mud beneath a fat, wheezing nag.

Things could get no worse.

A sudden noise had him straining to see over Thunder's

heaving sides, and Thomas found himself gazing at the mangiest, most flea-bitten mongrel ever to put four paws to earth.

It was *that* dog. *Her* dog. Which meant—

"Och, imagine that." The honey-rich voice was laced with amusement. "Here's a horse just a-lying about the wood with nary a rider to be seen."

He should have strangled her when he had the chance.

Fia peered over Thunder's side, her hair a riotous mass about her shoulders, her lips parted in feigned amazement. Peeking from the safety of her skirts was the scrawny, ugly dog. Half of one ear was gone, the jagged edge pointing straight into the air, while his narrow muzzle was adorned with a ridiculous grin.

Thomas looked about for a good-sized rock.

"Why, 'tis Lord Thomas! You poor man, have you gone and hurt yourself yet again? Scotland's not been very kind to you, has she?"

Thomas clamped his mouth shut. He'd be damned if he'd let her see how angry he was until he was in a position to do something about it. Like putting his hands around her lovely neck and choking the grin off her face.

"Och, 'tis a pity. First you hit your head in the garden, and now your backside is like to be just as bruised." Husky and inviting, her voice quivered with laughter.

Strangling was too quick. *First,* he would lock her in a dungeon and starve her. *Then* he would strangle her.

"If you've come to gloat, be gone," he ground out. "I've no need of your company, nor of that hellhound of yours."

"Sweet Mother Mary, is that the way you speak to someone who has come to help you?"

"Help me? Like you helped yourself to my gold?"

"You can keep your gold."

He scowled at her. "Oh? Have you found some other innocent to fleece?"

"No, though I have to wonder that you call yourself an innocent. You were climbing into MacLean's castle through a window; I'd say that was evidence that your intentions were hardly pure."

He sent her a sour look. "I refuse to engage in a debate with you. I've other, more pressing issues at hand."

She quirked a brow, and he noticed how the morning sun lit her hair to a deep, rich brown. He reflected with satisfaction that he had never liked brown hair, especially unruly brown hair.

Thunder reached out and pushed her nose against her mistress's hand.

"There, you sweet beastie. You are the best horse in all of Scotland, are you not?" Fia crooned as she lovingly stroked the horse's nose.

"That is the most disgusting untruth I have ever heard," Thomas stated flatly.

Fia patted Thunder's neck. "Thunder, don't mind the Sassenach. Some of his manners must have leaked from his head when he cracked it in the garden."

"I have perfectly good manners, when they're warranted."

"Hmm." Dropping to the forest floor, Fia maneuvered herself so Thunder's head lay comfortably in her lap. *Her* horse, Thomas reminded himself grimly. Which was lying on *his* leg. Her dog padded to the other side of Thomas and sat regarding him with what could only be described as a huge grin, his long tongue lolling out one side of his muzzle, his ragged ears perked in interest.

Thomas wished his leg would simply rot off so he would be free of the whole lot of them—lackwits, every one.

"You're not helping matters, Sassenach. If you're nice to Thunder, she'll be nice to you. She's had a hard life, the poor bairn. Her master beat her and made her work from dawn 'til night, so she tends to hold a grudge." Fia's silky voice crept into his ears and tried to lull away his anger, but Thomas would have none of it.

As a child, he had endured his share of beatings. It hadn't affected him in the least, other than to make him determined never to treat any child of his with such sternness.

"You really should stop that," she said.

He glared at her. "Stop what?"

"Grinding your teeth so. It can't be good for them. I had an uncle once who had nary a tooth in his head. 'Twas piteous; he could eat naught but pap." She frowned. "Or soup; he could eat that. And he did take bread soaked in milk for his Sunday supper. I once saw him try to eat a piece of manchet, but it took him two hours just to gnaw down one bite. Even then he couldn't eat mo—"

"Forget your toothless uncle, and get this damned horse off my leg!" Thomas snapped.

The dog growled, and Thomas snarled back.

Fia raised her eyebrows. "You've the devil of a temper, haven't you? 'Twas a simple observation that you seem addicted to grinding your teeth." She nodded wisely. "I think you should see a specialist when we get to London town."

"*We?*"

"Aye." She met his gaze, calm and cool. "If you wish Thunder to rise, you must promise to take me to London."

It was a ludicrous idea. He was on a *mission*, for God's sake, though she didn't know that. "No."

Fia shrugged, her lovely eyes shadowed with disappointment. "Fine. Do it your way, then. But be aware that MacLean may arrive any moment, and we have yet to make our escape from the main grounds of the castle."

"I don't—"

"Meanwhile, Thunder here has quite a temper. I've seen her lie this way for hours when she gets into one of her moods, never moving though 'twas snowing or raining buckets." Fia stroked the horse's neck. "Didn't you, poor beastie?"

Thunder snorted her agreement.

Thomas rubbed his pounding temple. Sweet Jesu, he would give all he possessed to be gone from here.

Fia regarded him from beneath her lashes. "Of course, if you would be willing to assist me to London . . . and make one or two other small efforts once we arrive, I might be willing to get Thunder off your leg *and* show you a shorter path to the shore."

Try as he might to resist, the velvety voice laid a steady assault against his anger. With great reluctance, Thomas admitted that he might indeed need Fia's help to reach his ship before dark.

Some hint of his thoughts must have shown, for she flashed him a saucy grin. "I make a merry traveling companion, I do. I can even sing a wee bit."

"Please, no singing!" He sighed deeply. "I know I'm going to regret this, for I've always heard it said 'tis better to be alone than in bad company."

"Och, my mother used to say the same thing!" A wistful smile curved her mouth. "She died when I was but eight."

"She had to warn you about the company you were keeping when you were that young? From what little I know of you, I'm not surprised."

She chuckled. "I was forever sneaking off to play with the animals. I had a partiality for pigs. My mother would always find me in the barn, covered with hay and dirt."

He felt an unexpected surge of envy. His memories of his own childhood weren't nearly as happy.

Younger than his father by almost fifteen years, Thomas's mother had been undeniably beautiful, with black hair and cool, distant brown eyes. When Thomas had been a small child of six, she had run away with a man of no fortune and less breeding. After that, Thomas's father had become obsessed with proving to everyone that the legendary Wentworth luck—a family myth that had followed the head of the family through wars and famines—still existed. More, he was determined to prove that it was even stronger after his young wife left.

"You look sad," Fia said softly.

"'Tis having this damned horse on my leg," he snapped, irritated at her close scrutiny.

"Do you agree to our bargain? You will take me to London and—" She stopped and regarded him uncertainly.

"And what?" he asked.

She flushed, and a horrible suspicion crossed his mind. He eyed her narrowly. "You aren't asking me to help you steal the crown jewels or the like, are you?"

"As though I would do such a thing!" she answered hotly.

"Then out with it, plague take you! My leg is likely to wither off before you finish a sentence. Whatever duty you have for me, 'tis apparently so horrendous you cannot even ask it without stammering and blushing."

She drew herself up with regal pride, and Thomas had to fight the unexpected desire to grin. Her queenly air was strikingly at odds with her appearance; bits of straw stuck out from her wildly disordered hair, while the morning sun added a healthy golden glow to her skin. She had the look of a milkmaid just tumbled in the hay.

"There is nothing horrendous in my request at all. 'Tis just that if I wish to make my way in London, then I will need a patron."

A patron. He couldn't say a word.

"I thought perhaps you could sponsor me." Her voice was all forced unconcern, but the trembling of her hand as she stroked the horse's nose told another story.

For a moment, he was tempted to refuse her. Surely the horse would get up of its own accord. But Fia's eyes caught his attention. As dark as the rich peat that covered the forest floor, they shimmered with determination.

God's wounds, she wants a patron? His gaze wandered, lingering on her mouth and coming to rest on her tight bodice, and he realized with shock that he would have been willing to fill that position without having been caught beneath this damned horse.

Perhaps the Wentworth luck hadn't completely abandoned him after all. He met her anxious glance with a warm smile. As soon as he got her to London, he would take great pleasure in tying back that frustrating mass of hair with yards and yards of silk ribbon. "Don't fret, comfit. You had only to ask. I will be your patron."

Her relief was evident. "Och, I was so worried you wouldn't like the idea. Though I'm surprised you didn't ask for proof of my abilities."

Thomas burst out laughing. "You're a forward piece, even for a Scot. Now is not the time for evidence of your skills; I can scarcely appreciate such a display while weighted down, can I? The world looks vastly different from the underside of a horse."

He was rewarded with such a laughing look that he began to tingle in places not being pressed into the dirt. "I hate to rush you, sweet, but my leg is numb."

"Of course." She stood, her skirts swaying about her narrow hips.

He admired her lithe, graceful movements with new awareness.

"Up, Thunder," Fia commanded softly. Wheezing heavily, the horse clambered to its feet.

"That's it?" Thomas managed to get the words out through the rush of pain that flooded his leg. "You just say 'up' and she gets up?"

Fia blinked. "What else should I say?"

He rubbed his leg, trying to force the blood back into it. "I won't tell you what you *should* say to that horse, for we've wasted far too much time as it is. So come, let's get off this cursed isle of yours. My ship awaits."

She led the horse beside Thomas. "I had best mount first, to keep Thunder from nipping at you."

He nodded curtly. He would get out of this abhorrent land if it killed him.

Fia tied her bag to the saddle and nimbly climbed onto the horse's back, her skirts sliding up to expose rounded calves and delicately trim ankles above small, muddy boots.

His body responded instantly. *I must have injured my head to be so affected by the sight of a pair of ankles.* "Your boots are muddy."

"Aye, 'tis the rainy season. Your boots didn't fare much better."

He glanced at his boots, which they were just as caked with mud as hers.

Her chuckle instantly made Thomas's mouth go dry. "I dislike wearing shoes of any kind, and often forget to wear them. Duncan swears he'd nail them to my feet, would it do any good."

Thomas scowled at the mention of her old lover. *He* was her patron now, and as soon as he got up on the horse, he would remind her of that fact. As he lifted his good leg to the stirrup, he stifled a moan as his bruised leg protested. He doubted he would be able to move it at all when the day was over.

Setting his jaw, Thomas threw himself onto the horse, the pain wiping out every other ache in his abused body. It took a moment before he could speak; then he said through clenched teeth, "My ship is north of here."

"I know." She sent him a smug smile over her shoulder. "There's only one safe harbor on the isle other than the one by the castle."

"Let's hurry."

"Aye, Duncan is not known for wasting time, and we have to stop for Mary and Angus."

"Stop? For whom?" he demanded.

"Mary is my maid. She has worked at Duart Castle since she was a child. Angus is her new husband and knows the harbor like no other." Fia looked over her shoulder, the trees casting long shadows across the silk of her cheek. "Mary has been like a mother to me. 'Twill take no time at all to fetch them."

Thomas looked into her uptilted face. Common sense urged him to say no, but something about her pleading look made him hesitate. She'd been so fearless up until this moment, yet now true concern darkened her gaze. "How old are you, comfit?"

Her lashes dropped over her gaze, shielding her expression. "I'm old enough, Sassenach."

Hmm. She didn't look more than seventeen, but her self-assurance told him she had to be older. Still, she wanted this Mary and Angus to be with her . . . Why should he argue? As long as she was right about Angus's talents as a guide, of course.

"Very well. If this Angus is as knowledgeable as you say, then we'll take both him and Mary."

She smiled, and it was as if the sun had broken through a rain-darkened sky. With a gentle click of her tongue Fia urged Thunder on, and the horse began to make its way down the path with amazing sure-footedness.

"Come, Zeus!" Fia called. The ugly dog rose from where he'd been sitting. Panting happily, he loped along behind them, his gait uneven like a cart with an oval wheel.

"Must he come with us?" Thomas grumbled.

"But of course. No one else would feed him."

Thomas thought of a thousand answers, none worth saying aloud. Besides, the horse was moving steadily down the path, much faster than he could walk.

Thomas wrapped his arms more securely about Fia. He was a solid mass of bruises, aches, and lumps. The only thing keeping him upright in the saddle was the thought that if anything could speed his recovery, it would be her lush, naked body lying in his bed, her incredible hair spread across his pillows. His loins tightened uncomfortably and he called himself sharply to order. The last thing he needed was to spend his entire time in the saddle fighting his own lust.

Safety beckoned. All they had to do was reach his ship before MacLean returned home. Thomas glanced at the sun to estimate their arrival time. By late afternoon he and Fia would be safely ensconced on the *Glorianna,* sailing to London and away from the nightmare of the last few hours.

He relaxed in the saddle, and Fia snuggled back against him as if she'd always ridden within the circle of his arms. The sweet scent of heather filled him with the inexplicable desire to grin like a complete lackwit.

And for the briefest moment, despite his aches and pains, Thomas was warmed by the hope that the Wentworth luck was once again shining.

Chapter Four

"Och, Thunder, what have you done now?" Fia rubbed her cheek against the horse's rough mane.

Thunder's answering whicker sounded suspiciously like a laugh.

"Lord Thomas was right about you," Fia chastised the mare. "'Tis poor sport to pretend to be lame just as we're nearing the coast. Mary will be wondering where we are, too. I told her we'd be there by supper time, and 'tis at least an hour past that now."

The mare hung her head and lifted one foreleg.

"Don't try that with me, you silly nag. As soon as Thomas stomped off into the forest to find something for us to eat, you forgot all about limping and started scrounging for clover, as healthy and well as a young colt. I saw you myself."

The horse swished her tail and stared off into the distance.

Zeus whined at her feet.

Fia frowned at him. "Don't you play the innocent, either! 'Twas ill mannered to gobble up all of our food when our backs were turned."

The dog wagged his tail and Thunder snickered again.

Fia threw up her hands. "There's no speaking with either of you. 'Tis a wonder the Sassenach hasn't washed his hands of the lot of us."

And oh, had he ever been angry. After cursing for an entire five minutes at their predicament, Thomas had finally admitted they were stuck for the night. Growling about being too hungry to think, he'd stomped into the woods to find some food.

Fia sat on a small log, her stomach protesting noisily as she cast a disparaging look at the dog curled up beside her. Zeus met Fia's condemning gaze and whined pathetically. Even stuffed with all of their food, he looked ravenous.

"I hope you get a stomachache," she said.

Zeus cocked his good ear and wagged his tail.

"Don't try to cozen me; I know your tricks."

He sighed heavily and threw himself back onto Thunder's discarded saddle blanket. His sad eyes pleaded for forgiveness.

After a long moment, Fia gave in and patted him. He was such a sweet beastie and only doing what was in his nature.

She rubbed his ear and the dog wiggled about so that his chin rested in her lap, his eyes slowly closing. She hugged him, shivering slightly in the wind. 'Twas cold and damp this evening, the breeze carrying a hint of rain.

As the darkness deepened, the wind turned every shrub into a shadowy threat. Fia's imagination began to simmer. She was used to facing the dark from the inside of a well-fortified castle. It had never dawned on her that the world would look so different from outside, every bush a possible wolf, every looming tree a potentially hungry giant.

She shivered and rubbed her chilled arms. Perhaps she should light a fire; Thomas had suggested she start a small one, making sure to diffuse the smoke so it couldn't be detected.

Fia gently pushed Zeus's head from her lap and set about gathering sticks and several large branches. When she had enough, she used her flint on some dried pine needles and soon had a merry blaze. "There," she said with satisfaction, comforted by her efforts to keep the night at bay. She settled onto the saddle blanket and snuggled up to the heat, Zeus resuming his place by her side.

Fia wondered how Thomas was doing. As he'd marched into the woods, it had been obvious that he was both stiff and sore, favoring his leg. His clothing hadn't fared well either, covered in mud, the fine cloth ripped thanks to Thunder.

Though the old nag had agreed to carry Thomas, she'd taken great delight in snapping at him every chance she'd gotten. The poor man's sleeve had been in tatters by the time they'd arrived.

Fia stirred the fire and wondered how long it would take him to return. "I'm hungry," she announced.

Thunder's ears flickered.

Fia rubbed Zeus's good ear, and he gave a heartfelt sigh. "Enjoy the heat whilst you can. Once Lord Thomas returns, 'tis back in the cold you'll be."

Zeus gave a disdainful yawn and rolled onto his side, promptly falling back into a deep sleep.

Fia pulled out her knife and whittled aimlessly at a stick, her gaze wandering to the gathering blackness. Where was he?

"He said he'd be back soon," she told Zeus. The words sounded hollow in the darkness.

He would come back. He had to; he'd promised. But . . . how much was a vow worth when one was pressed into the cold mud beneath a huge horse? The thought held her fast as she stared into the forest.

Night crept into the campsite inch by inch, bringing dampness and uncertainty. Thomas had warned her not to build the fire too large, for fear Duncan might see the smoke and discover them.

But now Thomas was gone, and she feared—nay, she *knew*—he would not come back. Why should he? She'd forced his cooperation. She wouldn't blame him for making his own way.

An uncomfortable lump rose in her throat, and suddenly the forest seemed alive. Fia's imagination began to tickle her thoughts, adding sinister meaning to every wind-brushed shrub, every crackling tree limb.

The shriek of an owl made her jump. Heart pounding, she grabbed the biggest piece of wood from her pile and threw it on the fire.

The flames blazed, and she tried to calm herself. "I don't need the Sassenach's help to get to London. Once I arrive, I'll find another patron, and he'll be better than His High and Mighty Lordship, won't he, Zeus?"

Zeus rolled onto his back, a deep snore emitting from his slack mouth.

Fia looked at him in disgust. "Some guard dog you are. Here I am, alone in the midst of the great forest filled with dangerous creatures, and all you do is snore fit to wake the dead. Lord Thomas was right about you being a la—"

The forest crackled, the bushes swirling mightily as if a great bear had stirred them to life.

Thunder shied, prancing frantically as Fia whipped out her knife. Zeus bounded to his feet and snarled viciously.

Thomas stumbled from the bushes, a bag over his shoulder, his temper as frayed as his horse-nipped sleeve. He regarded his arm sourly. 'Twas yet another pain in a long and painful day. "Damn all of Scotland! You can't go anywhere in this land without stepping into a bog or being punctured by a thistle. God only knows why anyone would want to conquer such an unsightly, ill-favored land. Once we get to London, I'll never step foot in this—"

Fia launched herself into his arms, her small body flattening against his broad chest. He reflexively closed his arms about her, sinking his hand into her cloud of hair and holding her cheek to his chest. Her heart thudded so hard that he could count each beat.

Surprised, Thomas stood completely still. The woman was plastered to him like wet silk, her arms wrapped uncomfortably tight about his waist. He could feel every soft curve of her, every warm bit of skin.

She lifted her face to his. "I-I'm sorry. I don't know why I—" Her lips quivered.

He grinned. "Hello, poppet. Miss me?"

Her cheeks colored and she moved as if to step away, but it was too late; he had her tight and wasn't about to let her go. An uncertain laugh passed through her soft lips. "I-I thought you weren't coming back."

"You thought wrong, then."

"So it seems." Her eyes, as black as the night sky in

the midst of a storm, seemed mysterious in the uncertain light.

Thomas was as fascinated with her eyes as with her long lashes; they were so tangled and luxuriant. He lifted a finger and brushed it over her cheek, which glowed with vibrant color and health.

And her body . . . he almost groaned. He was stirred beyond thought by the warmth of her curves pressed against him.

He had to taste that lush mouth. He already knew the honey-sweet flavor of her lips, and nothing was going to stop him from tasting them again. Her face flushed rosily in the light of the roaring fire as he—

The fire?

The roaring *fire?*

"Damn it!" Thomas pushed Fia away and kicked dirt onto the smoking branches. "Didn't I tell you to keep the fire small? Woman, what were you trying to do, alert the whole isle?" He kicked more dirt onto the crackling flames, and the light dimmed as the fire sputtered. "What in hell were you thinking? If you wished Duncan to find us, all you had to do was sit upon your arse and he'd eventually appear! God knows the laird doesn't need a beacon to find us, you fool!"

No sharp reply met his tirade. The fire damped, he turned to find Fia behind him, her head bowed, her arms crossed over her chest as though warding off the chill breeze. Even without seeing her eyes, Thomas knew there were tears in them.

Weariness flooded through him. He was too tired and battered to deal with this most difficult of all tasks—a woman's tears. Especially *this* woman's tears.

He'd known Fia but a day, yet it was obvious that she was a spirited lass, not one to cry lightly. She had to be just as aching and exhausted as he was.

He sighed. "Fia, please don't cry."

She immediately wiped her face with her sleeve, her bottom lip quivering like a child's. He grimaced. Until he had run over her with his sharp temper, she had been genuinely glad to see him. There hadn't been many times in his life when his arrival had been greeted with such unabashed pleasure, and like the clumsiest of fools, he had crushed her spirits.

He had a fleeting memory of his father returning home to their manse after months in London, serving the king's court. A mere child of nine at the time, left alone for those long months with a strict tutor and uncaring servants, Thomas had heard the coach and had run to the window to see his father's entourage approaching.

It had been an unusually cold and dreary winter, and for a lonely boy confined to endless Latin, Greek, script, and other dull subjects, Father's arrival had been beyond exciting. Ignoring his tutor's shout, Thomas had dashed down the stairs and had run to meet the coach.

Frowning at Thomas's exuberance, Father had climbed from the coach, flicked a cold glance at his son, turned his back, and entered the house. Thomas didn't see his father for three days, a punishment for his unrestrained behavior. In the earl's world there was no room for emotion, unless it was fealty or fear. Thomas had promised himself to do better, to treat others with more consideration.

Now Thomas looked at Fia's downcast face, a tear trailing down her cheek. "Forgive my temper. I'm in a horrible mood because of the horse and that damn dog, and then I grew hungry and—"

The bag slung over his shoulder wiggled, and Thomas grinned. Supper. *That* was how he would make his little Scottish thief smile once again.

He sat on the saddle blanket, placed his foot on Zeus's back, and shoved the mongrel to one side. Zeus staggered to the other side of the fire and collapsed in a boneless heap.

Thomas patted the blanket next to him. "Fia, come and sit." He flashed his most winsome smile, one that rarely failed him. "Please?"

Fia dried her eyes, then went to stand beside Zeus. Across the fire, Thomas met the dog's grin with a hard look that made the dog drop his head in submission.

The old nag snorted indignantly and shuffled around until her rump pointed directly at Thomas.

He fixed his gaze on Fia. "I brought you something, but you can't see it from way over there." He held up the bag, which shook as something struggled within.

Fia's eyes widened in reluctant fascination. "What is it?"

"Come and see." He held the bag toward her. It had taken an hour of laying traps and praying faithfully to catch some dinner, and he was as proud of this plump rabbit as if it had been his first successful hunt.

Her gaze locked on the bag, she moved toward him. "Och, let me have it!" Her rich voice settled about him as rich and warm as a thick, fur-lined cloak.

She dropped to her knees on the blanket beside him, her face abeam alight with curiosity. "Is it very large?"

Every ache Thomas possessed melted into insignificance under the warmth of her smile. She was as lovely as a morning mist, even with leaves in her hair, her eyes bright with tears, and her nose reddened by the cold. He handed her the bag. "Open it, Mistress Impatience, and see what I've caught."

She tugged on the tie and yanked the sack open. "Och! 'Tis a rabbit!" She pulled out the plump animal and held it from her. The animal immediately stopped struggling and stared at Fia, his little nose quivering furiously.

Thomas could almost smell the roasting meat. *Should we skew it on a stick and—*

She turned toward his. "Thank you."

He shrugged. "'Tis naught."

"Nay, this is the loveliest present anyone has ever gotten me."

Something about the tone of Fia's voice gave Thomas pause. "Present? I wouldn't call him that, exactly."

"What would you call him?" Fia cuddled the rabbit close and cooed softly, "He's such a sweet little bunny."

Thomas's smile faded completely. *Bunny?*

She rubbed her cheek against the rabbit. Across the soft brown fur, Fia's eyes met Thomas's, their softly glowing light telling him all he had to know. *Bloody hell, the wench thinks 'tis a pet.*

He looked at the way she cradled the rabbit, her cheek pressed to its soft fur, and his heart sank. *Damn. I'm getting no supper tonight.* His stomach immediately growled in protest.

Fia apparently heard his stomach, for her gaze grew concerned. "Thomas?" She glanced from him to the rabbit, and then back.

Thomas read her thoughts as clearly as if she'd spoken them aloud. She realized the probable truth of the rabbit's appearance but was loath to believe it. She liked the rabbit, which was curled into her arms as if recognizing his one and only path to freedom.

It was rather odd to see the wild animal turn tame just by her touch. How had she done that?

"Thomas? Is the rabbit . . . did you mean us to—"

"He's yours," Thomas blurted. "He was caught in a trap and I rescued him to, ah, bring him to you." That much was true . . . more or less.

"You *saved* him?" She positively beamed at him.

Normally Thomas was completely unaffected by approbation. But it had been a long time since someone had looked at him with such unadulterated admiration. "I didn't do much. I merely removed him from the trap."

"Poor bunny! Was he hurt?" Fia's dark head bent over the rabbit, delicate fingers carefully looking for injuries. "Och, look, the poor dear has an injured leg."

Thomas winced as his stomach growled again.

Fia smiled. "'Tis not as bad as I thought; he'll recover without any permanent damage."

I wish I could say the same for myself. I've never been this hungry.

Fia settled the rabbit in her lap and stroked it, her long fingers graceful as they trailed over the soft fur. "He's so tame!"

Thomas frowned, thinking of the struggle he'd had getting the creature into the bag. "Aye, 'tis unnatural."

"Mary says no one has a way with animals like I do." She peeped at Thomas through her lashes. "'Tis magic, you know. From my mother."

"I don't believe in magic."

"I do." She spoke calmly, without a hint of braggadocio. "I understand animals." She frowned. "I wish I understood people as well."

"Together, we would rule the world, for I understand

people well enough. If they don't do what I wish, I crack their heads together."

She chuckled. "Duncan has the same manner about him. 'Tis effective but doesn't allow for much warmth."

Thomas felt the rabbit's accusing gaze, and he stared determinedly back at it. He'd be damned if he would let a hare make him feel uneasy.

Even though he could do nothing about it, he imagined how the plump rabbit would taste, basted with honey, turning slowly on a spit over a crackling fire—

He watched morosely as Fia made a soft bed for her new pet out of the blanket. The *only* blanket, Thomas reminded himself.

As she tucked in the wounded rabbit, she lifted shining eyes to his. "Thank you, Sassenach."

The soft words curled into the hollowness of his stomach and filled it. As he gazed into Fia's fathomless eyes, something inside his chest shifted and warmed.

Drowning—that's what he was doing. He was drowning in the eyes of a wench who brought him the devil's own luck. He ached for the taste of her, the sweet fragrance of her hair and the lushness of her rounded body.

His gaze dropped to her lips, which were delectably moist. He couldn't look away from that tempting mouth.

He had to have her.

Now.

Thomas reached across the small space that separated them and buried a hand in her hair, pulling her to him. She leaned into him, offering herself so sweetly that his lust burst into flames.

With every ounce of the desire that burned through his body, he kissed her, devouring her sweetness. Fia didn't hesitate, returning his ardor as passionately as he could have wanted. Her fingers tangled in the folds of his shirt as her soft moans sent him spiraling toward heaven. *God's wounds, she is a hot little piece.*

She made him as addlepated as a youth, but oh, what a delectable madness it was. He sank his hands deeper into her hair and tasted the smoothness of her cheek as he feathered sensual kisses over her face, her eyes, her sweet neck, making her gasp with pleasure.

She clung to his shirt, pulling him closer. As he nipped at her ear, he impatiently tugged at the lacings on her bodice. With a soft pop, the tie gave way and the material gaped open, revealing the silken white chemise that barely covered the mounds of her breasts.

Thomas rained kisses down her throat to the hollow of her neck.

She gasped. "Duncan!"

Thomas froze. *She couldn't have said another man's name.* His ardor cooled, he pulled back. "No, comfit, 'tis not Duncan. 'Tis Thomas. My name is Thomas Wentworth."

Deep and rumbling, a masculine voice filled the small clearing. "That is useful to know. 'Twould bring my clan ill fortune were I to kill a nameless man."

His heart thudding sickly, Thomas met Fia's pleading gaze.

She gave a weak smile and pointed over his shoulder. "Thomas, 'tis Duncan. I fear he's found us."

Chapter Five

"Where is he?" Fia demanded.

The guard remained solidly in front of the great oaken door.

She stomped her slippered foot, wincing as her heel met the stone floor. "MacKenna, I asked you a question. Did you not hear me?"

The large man simply stood, booted feet wide, kilt hanging below his knees, his bulging arms crossed over his wide chest.

She crossed her arms and set her feet apart, too. "MacKenna, don't make me lose my temper."

MacKenna's gaze finally flickered, a look of unease crossing his red-bearded face. "Now, lass, dinna be threatenin' me. I'm only doin' the laird's biddin' and ye know it."

"Where is he, then?"

"Ye know where the laird is, or ye wouldn't be a-standin' there tappin' yer foot."

"I wasn't speaking of Duncan. I want to know where the Sassenach has been taken."

"The Sassenach is with the laird, and the laird dinna wish to be disturbed."

Fia squared her shoulders. "He is about to be disturbed whether he wishes it or not."

Concern flickered in MacKenna's blue eyes. "Settle down a mite, lassie. The MacLean is as mad as a bear with a sore paw. Ye had best wait 'til—"

The huge door slammed open. "MacKenna!" Duncan bellowed. "Send for my daft cous—" His dark gaze locked on Fia, his mouth tightening. "There you are."

"Aye, and I want to see the Sassenach."

Duncan glowered down at her. If MacKenna was huge, Duncan was a giant. Tall, broad-chested, and as dark-haired as the night, he filled the large arched doorway. His arms bulged with muscles that made MacKenna look like a lad.

Yet for all that he was as big as a house, his face held a beauty rarely seen in such a large man—something she didn't often notice, since she thought of him as a brother. Duncan had taken care of Fia since she was but a wee bairn; he treated her with the fondness and exasperation of natural-born sibling, and she returned the favor. She'd been mildly surprised when she'd begun to notice how many maids succumbed to his flashing black eyes, strong jaw, and dark hair, like grass before a roaring brushfire.

Duncan stood to one side and jerked his head to indicate she was to precede him. "We must speak."

"Yes, we must." Fia lifted her chin to a lofty angle suitable for one of the many princesses who populated her plays and swept past him into the great hall.

As she did so, she cast a considering glance up at Duncan through her lashes. He was angered, there was no doubt of that. His mouth was a bleak slash and his eyes burned with suppressed fury.

"I take it by your expression that your quest to find the White Witch came to naught?"

His dark glower did not abate. "I didn't call you here to discuss that."

"You didn't call me here at all; I came myself. What happened with the White Witch?"

Duncan shrugged, his gaze shadowed. "I found her."

"And? What was she like?"

To Fia's surprise, a deep red flush rose over Duncan's face. "She was infuriating and damnably proud."

Fia lifted her brows. "Was she as beauteous as they say?"

He didn't answer for the longest time. "I did not notice."

Ha! "I would wager you did."

He shot her a hard look. "It matters not. I have declawed that particular cat." He touched a heavy silver chain around his throat, pulling a magnificent amber amulet free from his clothing. The chased silver work that held the jewel depicted an odd mixture of flowers, grass, and a sinuous snake.

Fia blinked at the seductive beauty of the amulet. "Is that *hers?*"

"'*Twas* hers." Duncan's face held a sense of exquisite satisfaction. "Now 'tis mine."

"Good God. Won't she come to get it back?"

Duncan's smile was pleased and secretive. "Perhaps."

"But she's a witch! She'll not tamely sit by and—"

"Enough." Duncan's smile was gone. "That's *my* concern and no one else's. I wish to speak about your behavior with the Sassenach."

"Fine. Where is he?"

Duncan nodded to the far side of the great hall, and she saw a tall chair facing toward the fire. She knew the arm that rested on it was Thomas's by the ragged fringe of his sleeve. As she drew closer, she realized his head was bowed.

That was odd. Was he praying, perhaps? Or— She frowned. He wasn't moving. She hurried her steps. *What's wrong? Is he—*

Her heart ached as she realized he was unconscious and bound to the chair. "Duncan, what have you done to my Englishman?"

"Nothing he did not deserve," Duncan said, walking behind her.

She knelt beside Thomas, noting the trickle of blood running down one cheek. One eye was swelling, while the other was a telltale red.

Fia smoothed back Thomas's thick, black hair and carefully examined the large lump on his forehead. "Och, you've beaten him to a bloody pulp!"

"He's an intruder on my land. I could have rightfully killed him and no one would have said a word."

"He says he's an English earl. I don't know that I believe that, though."

Duncan gave a grim smile. "I know exactly who he is."

"Aye, he's a Sassenach. Queen Elizabeth's not one to greet with a smile the news that someone has beaten one of her subjects."

"My men wouldn't have done so much if he'd talked. The damned fool wouldn't say a word."

"Ha! You were looking for an excuse; I know you too well." Fia gathered a pitcher of water and a cloth from the sideboard and returned to Thomas's side. She carefully bathed his bruised face.

"Let the man be," Duncan grumbled. "You'd think he was made of glass, to be hurt by a few light taps."

"Light? And who among your men is given to delivering 'light taps'?"

Duncan scratched his bearded chin. "Well . . . young Fitzgerald has a light fist."

"I should hope so; he's only twelve." Fia pinned Duncan with an exasperated glare. "You had my Englishman trounced soundly, and not by young Fitzgerald."

Duncan rubbed his ear, a sheepish look on his face. "Aye, but—"

"I'm ashamed of you, Duncan MacLean, for causing harm to an innocent man!"

"Innocent, my ass."

"Innocent. And if you weren't such a hothead, you'd know it for yourself." Fia dabbed at the cut on Thomas's mouth. She hoped it wouldn't leave a scar.

Duncan took a chair and watched as she tended the wounded Englishman.

"I cannot believe you'd treat a man such, and for nothing more than giving me a kiss. "

"'Twas more than just a kiss. I saw it. If I had not arrived when I did, there is no telling what might have happened."

True. Still . . . "He didn't deserve this."

"If you hadn't put yourself in the most damnable position, I wouldn't have been forced to take such an action."

"No one forces you to do anything, Duncan."

His jaw tightened. "Life forces us all to make decisions we dinna like. For example, I returned home and found you gone. Then I discover you wandering about in the middle of the night with an Englishman, like a common—" He snapped his mouth shut and glared. "What were you thinking?"

Fia rinsed out the cloth and dabbed at a bruise beneath Thomas's eye. "I was on my way to London."

"Och, London again."

"Aye, where my destiny awaits. I've told you that time and again."

"So you have." Duncan regarded her grimly. "But not with an Englishman you didn't even know."

"That was a stroke of good fortune."

"Lass, you're daft, you are."

"No, I'm not. I had everything planned."

"Really?" Duncan scoffed. "What were you doing with the candlesticks? A house full of valuables, and all you could think to steal were some paltry candlesticks?"

"Borrow," she corrected as she rinsed out the cloth. "My household goods are all locked away."

"Where they'll stay until you marry."

"So I borrowed some of your house goods. If I'd sold some of my jewels or silver plate, you'd easily have tracked me down. The candlesticks were nondescript; I doubt you'd have even missed them."

Duncan looked sour at this calm assertion. "How did you propose to sell your loot? Just walk into some crofter's hut and flash it before their amazed eyes?"

"Angus's brother is a tinker. He was going to sell the silver and take us with him to London."

Duncan's brows lowered. "Angus?"

"Angus Collins, the man who helps in the stables. He is Mary's new husband. They are waiting for me at Crenahan." Fia wondered if Thomas would need stitches for the wound on his cheek.

Duncan looked thunderous. "Mary knows about this?"

"Of course."

"By the rood, I pay Mary well to be your companion and to *stop* just such nonsense!"

"'Tis not nonsense, Duncan. One way or another, I *will* go to London."

He crossed his arms over his chest. "Over my dead body."

She clenched her fists. "Don't tempt me."

They glowered at each other.

Finally, Duncan scowled. "I thought Mary had more sense than to encourage you. Has she gone daft, too?"

"She thinks I am wasting away on this isle." Fia smiled through gritted teeth. "She loves my plays and knows I will be famous."

Duncan groaned aloud, but Fia continued undeterred. "And as Angus is her husband, it only made sense that once Mary agreed to come, he wouldn't stay behind."

"Addlepated, the lot of you." Duncan scowled down at his boots before shooting her a sharp glance. "How did you plan on getting off the isle?"

"Tam MacCrea's father has a boat."

"MacCrea?"

"The sheepherder."

"God's wounds, have you recruited all of my servants to plot against me?"

"Pssht. Don't be so dramatic; I asked them to help. No one's done a thing against anyone." She gave Duncan an admonitory frown. "You should make more of an effort to get to know your retainers, Duncan."

"Why should I bother? You know them all much too well as it is."

"They are good people. Tam's father agreed to take us across the firth to Carnorvah. The tinker's cart is waiting for us there. He was to trade the candlesticks for silver, and we were to travel in stages to London."

Duncan looked astounded. "Bloody hell!"

Fia rocked back on her heels. "'Twasn't such a foolish plan after all, was it?"

"Nay," he said, his voice somber. "And that scares me more than anything else." He frowned at Thomas's bent head for a long moment. "Where did you find the Sassenach?"

"Perched in the library window like a great bird."

Duncan's gaze warmed with interest. "Was he, now?"

"Aye, I think he was climbing in to steal some of your worthwhile items."

"An earl was climbing into my window? I am honored."

She blinked. "Wait . . . he's truly an earl? I didn't believe him."

"Aye, he's an earl; one of Elizabeth's court favorites."

"How do you know that?"

He shrugged. "So 'twas mere coincidence you met the man as he was climbing through the same window?"

"Nay, Duncan—'twas fate." He grunted and she added, "Of course, none of this would have occurred had you taken me to London as you promised."

"Once you are married—"

"By the time I am married I will be a hundred years old, too bent and gnarled to hold a pen in my hand, let alone reach London. I'm twenty-four now and I've yet to see a single road into London."

Silence filled the room as Duncan glowered at her. With a disgusted noise, Fia turned back to Thomas, brushing his dark hair from his forehead. He looked like a prince, she thought wistfully, tracing the bruise on his cheek. A beaten and muddy prince, but a prince nonetheless.

Duncan watched, his brow lowered. Finally he spoke, his voice loud in the quiet. "You're right, lass. 'Tis time and then some that you were wed."

Her hand froze, curled about a strand of Thomas's hair.

Duncan leaned forward, resting his elbows on his knees. "I've found you a husband. He's not exactly who I'd have for you, but considering these uncertain times, he's the best—"

"*No!*"

He frowned. "You were just complaining that you weren't wed."

"I was complaining I'd not yet been to London! I wish to go there—but not with a husband."

Duncan's brow lowered. "London is a great morass, lass, 'twould not be safe to go there on your own. 'Tis past time you were wed. Let your husband take you there."

Fia recognized the iron-hard sound of Duncan's voice. *He is decided, and there'll be no changing his mind.* She clasped her trembling hands in her lap. "Who . . . who have you chosen?"

Duncan shifted in his chair. "Malcolm Davies."

"He's but seventeen!"

Duncan's face reddened. "He just turned eighteen and his mother says he is mature beyond his years."

"Pssht! What else would she tell you? That he's never left the walls of Dunvena Castle? That he has no chin and less manly parts? They say his mother rules both Malcolm *and* the clan, and keeps them both under lock and key."

"Malcolm's been ill," said Duncan bracingly.

"Ha! Faint of heart is more like it."

Duncan gave an exasperated sigh. "'Tis not easy to find a bridegroom for you, lass. You want the impossible—a well-made man who will allow you to write *and* take you to London. There's not eight men in all of Scotland who'd do so much."

She gave Duncan a disbelieving gaze. "Malcolm the Maiden would leave Dunvena Castle and travel all the way to London? Has he promised to do so?"

Duncan's color rose even more. "Who calls him Malcolm the Maiden?"

"You did, just last year. After the gathering at Lochvie, you said he was a maggoty light skirt of a man who—"

"That was before," Duncan interrupted hastily. "Let anyone else say such now, and I'll have their liver in my haggis." Fia raised her brows and he waved a hand. "Malcolm will go to London. He has pledged it."

"With or without his mother?"

Duncan shifted in his seat. "'Tis possible his mother will wish to accompany him on such a long journey."

"Sweet Jesu, Duncan! The man is a babied lackwit. I want a *man* to husband—a *real* man. Worse than his lack of backbone, they say he is cruel to the maids in his house. That he forces himself upon them and then, when they get with child, he sends them away to—"

"Who told you such drivel?" Duncan snapped.

"Everyone knows it."

A concerned look settled on Duncan's brow. "'Tis not true. 'Tis only servants' gossip."

"But—"

"Nay." Duncan crossed his arms over his wide chest, his jaw set. "I'm your guardian, lass, and I know what's good for you. Malcolm will not dare hurt you; he knows he'd have to deal with me if you come to harm. His mother's skirts wouldn't protect him then."

Fia started to argue again, but then thought better of it. She could see the telltale signs that Duncan's calm humor was already wearing thin: his mouth was white about the corners, his jaw set like a rock. His irritation was bubbling to the surface and if she continued, it would explode.

She'd wait until later to make her point, when he wasn't so tired. He might be made to see reason then.

Heart heavy, Fia returned to her Sassenach, regarding Thomas's fine broad shoulders and well-muscled arms with new admiration. Why couldn't Duncan have chosen a man like this? One who was tall and handsome and dashing—not to mention his kindness while they were attempting to escape the island, even after she'd stolen his gold.

Instead of a worthy companion like this, she was to be married to a hunchbacked, addlepated, cruel lackwit.

She sighed and leaned her forehead against Thomas's arm, suddenly feeling painfully lonely.

"Lass, dinna look so forlorn." Duncan stood restlessly and crossed to stir the fire with a long iron poker. The fire gleamed along the hard lines of his face and reflected on the amber amulet until it shone with a fire of its own. "You must understand; these are dangerous times. Things have come to a head and I must act. And you've given me no choice, with your desperation to go to London. I won't have you alone and unprotected in that hellish city."

She regarded him somberly, noticing for the first time the heaviness that sat about his dark eyes. He wasn't just tired; he was worried. A chill touched her heart. "What's happened?"

He leaned against the mantel and kicked aimlessly at

the sputtering fire. "I fear Queen Mary will soon marry that fool Bothwell."

"*What?* But he murdered her husband, Darnley!"

"So many believe. Bothwell isn't trustworthy and will not be accepted as her consort. The lairds are talking war."

"Bothwell will be surprised at such resistance."

"Nay, I think that has been his plan all along. But the fool doesn't understand that such a move will enrage Elizabeth, perhaps to the point of sending her own army to put down what can only be seen as a revolt."

Fia's chest ached. War would mean fighting and death. Duncan was not a man to fight from the back of the field; whatever happened, he would be at the forefront. "What can be done?"

"If the Scots band together and support Prince James, Mary's son, then we stand a chance. Elizabeth's fears will be soothed."

"James is but a babe, barely a year old."

"Aye—a babe who can be molded into a real king and ruler, rather than one left to spoil within the French court, as Mary was. If we renounce Mary and join behind the babe, then Elizabeth will leave us alone."

"Mary is such a fool! Why did she align herself with Bothwell?"

"She says she's in love." Duncan shrugged. "Bothwell attempted to stage it so that she could claim rape and thus not be to blame for the hasty wedding—but I know differently. She was a more than willing participant."

Fia didn't ask how he knew; Duncan was a man of many secrets. "You are attempting to gather the other lairds behind the prince, then?"

"Aye. We shall see if 'tis true that as the MacLeans go, so

goes Scotland." Duncan's face was bleak but set. His gaze flickered to Fia. "As you can see, I can't leave you unwed. If I am killed in battle, or assassinated beforehand—"

"Assassinated?"

"It could happen. I'm not invincible, and neither are you. Look at what just happened: our castle broken into in the dead of night by an English earl."

"You knew of him before, didn't you?"

Duncan crossed his arms. "Aye. Thomas Wentworth is the Earl of Rotherwood. The greatest of his estates marches the border between Scotland and England. He has lands in Northumberland, Devonshire, and Yorkshire. He possesses an ancient and respected title and is of good birth. Furthermore, he is reputed to be one of Queen Elizabeth's favorites. All that, and he's a bloody Sassenach and not fit to step foot in Duart Castle."

Fia returned her gaze to Thomas. That explained the man's arrogance. She reached out and touched Thomas's ragged shirt, the quality still evident. "What else do you know about him?"

Duncan's gaze rested on Thomas's bent head. "His closest companion is Robert MacQuarrie."

Fia raised her eyebrows. MarQuarrie was the laird of his clan and had once resided in glorious Balmanach Castle. As a young man of sixteen, MacQuarrie had disappeared with his five sisters following the murder of their parents by a rival clan. At first it had been assumed that the children had been slain as well, and the young laird had been a figure of great sympathy—until rumors began to circulate that he had suddenly appeared at the English court and was well on his way to becoming a favorite of the English queen.

Few Scots thought well of a laird who slunk away in the dark of night and refused to accept his responsibilities.

Fia frowned. "'Tis hard to imagine such a proud man having a friend like Robert MacQuarrie."

Duncan shrugged. "All I know is that the Coward of Balmanach is never far from your Sassenach."

Fia regarded Thomas's face for a moment. "What else do you know?"

"Wentworth works closely with Francis Walsingham, Queen Elizabeth's most trusted counselor. Walsingham is reputed to be like a father to him. They say your English-man dons the guise of a spy on occasion at Walsingham's behest."

Fia looked at Thomas as if she had never seen him before. "Is that why he came here?"

"Perhaps. Your Sassenach is known as the luckiest man in England. Perchance he came to—"

Thomas stirred, and Fia dropped to her knees beside his chair. He moaned as he lifted his head. At first, his blurry vision found nothing more remarkable than a nimbus of dark red-brown hair curling about a piquant face. He blinked rapidly, his eyes swollen and pained, his mind too fuzzy to remember how he'd gotten here.

A pair of fascinating dark eyes came into focus and made him momentarily forget his aches and pangs. *God's wounds, she's lovely.* Below an adorable nose, a lush mouth curved in wanton invitation. He smiled in return, his lips stiff. Whatever dream he was having, it would be complete once this angel touched him.

"Welcome back, Sassenach," rumbled a hard masculine voice.

Thomas blinked and turned his head, wincing with

the movement. Leaning against the mantel stood a giant. Though Thomas was several inches over six feet, this man would tower over him by a hand's span. But it was more than his height; it was also his shoulders, which appeared capable of holding up the entire castle.

The giant grinned, white teeth flashing in a darkly bearded face. "Are you comfortable, my feeble little Englishman?"

Remembrance hit Thomas like the slam of a fist. The giant was Duncan MacLean, the Earl of Duart, laird of Clan MacLean. And the angel . . . he looked at Fia. The angel was not an angel at all, but MacLean's woman.

"Duncan, untie him," she said softly.

Thomas looked down at his arms. He was indeed tied.

"Nay, lass. He'll stay trussed like a pig until I say so."

Fia was on her feet before the giant stopped speaking, marching to stand toe-to-toe with the laird. "Release him! He's done naught."

MacLean glared. "Among his *other* sins, his hands were on you. 'Tis a wonder he's even breathing."

Fia flushed. "'Twas dark. You don't know what you saw."

The laird quirked a disbelieving brow.

Fia turned to Thomas, whose hair she softly stroked. "Can you at least loosen his ties? Just until we have settled this?"

"He's not a guest but a prisoner. And that's that."

Fia's full lips pressed into a straight, unhappy line.

Thomas disliked that Fia was pleading for his life with a man who was obviously her lover. The idea soured his stomach and he sent her a hard glare. "I can speak for myself."

Fia shook her head. "Duncan, he looks fevered. If he falls ill, 'twill be your fault."

Duncan's brow lowered, though his gaze took on a considering air. "I suppose it would look bad if one of Queen Elizabeth's favorites were to die in my care."

"I'm not going to die," Thomas snapped.

Fia stroked his arm in a way that made him think of the way she'd petted her damned rabbit. "Duncan, 'twould be a most generous gesture if you were to send a hale, hearty Lord Rotherwood back to the queen."

Duncan's black gaze hardened. "No. I cannot forget that he touched you."

"Just look at the poor man. He's already been punished. Your men beat him, I took his purse, poor Thunder fell upon him after Zeus chased off his horse, and then we'd no food and he was nigh starving to death while—"

MacLean burst into deep, roiling laughter. "Poor Sassenach! I had no idea your beast of a horse had already been at him. And you took his silver, eh?" Still chuckling, he shook his head. "The luckiest man in England, eh?"

Thomas fought to keep from glaring at them all.

"Which," Fia added, "is why we should take care of the poor man and not treat him ill. He's been through enough as 'tis."

"Whilst I feel pity for the man, he's no innocent puppy needing your tender care."

"Duncan, you shouldn't jump to conclusions. You were woefully unfair."

"If you took more care, cousin, I would not have had to act at all."

Cousin? This wasn't the laird's wench but his cousin. Thomas had been caught fondling a *lady*.

He closed his eyes, his irritation growing by leaps and bounds. Of course the damned wench hadn't seen fit to mention that. Not that he'd have believed her, seeing as how she was dressed in the veriest rags and carrying a sack of stolen silver.

Fia shook her head sadly. "Duncan, I vow on my mother's grave that the Sassenach's been nothing but fine and honorable."

"Is it fine and honorable to take advantage of an innocent lass?" MacLean demanded.

"Is it honorable to attack an unarmed man?" She crossed her arms and frowned fiercely. "You owe him an apology. The man did naught to merit such treatment."

"Apology?" The laird looked at Thomas with an incredulous gaze. "You can't expect me to do such a fool thing!"

"Pray, do," Thomas said, forcing his split lips into a grin. "I need a good laugh."

Two pairs of wrathful eyes pinned him to his chair, but Thomas didn't allow his grin to slip.

MacLean spoke first, his disgust plain. "Lassie, 'twould take the sharp end of a claymore pricking that man's neck before he acted in an honorable way." The laird's hand rested on his sword as he spoke.

"Duncan, that just goes to show what a poor judge of men you are. The Sassenach is *twice* the man Malcolm the Maiden could ever hope to be."

"Leave young Davies out of this," growled Duncan.

Who the hell is Davies? Thomas wondered.

Fia sniffed. "I am more than willing to leave young Davies out of *everything*."

Thomas stared from one to the other. Was young Davies another laird? Elizabeth's chief adviser, the wily Lord

Walsingham, would rub his hands in glee to find out what alliances were being offered to the powerful laird of Duart. Perhaps Davies was a code name for some of the supporters of Queen Mary. Was it possible that—

Fia lifted her chin. "Duncan, I think you should know all. His lordship promised to become my sponsor once we were in London if I would help him reach his ship."

Thomas stifled a groan. The wench was going to get him killed. Catching MacLean's black eyes on him, Thomas gave a vague shrug.

MacLean rubbed his bearded chin, a genuinely quizzical gleam in his gaze. "Now why would you do such a thing, Sassenach?"

Because she's damnably beautiful? Because she asked me in such a way that no man could have refused?

Thomas glanced at Fia and caught her encouraging smile. "Tell him," she urged.

He supposed he might as well. Fia was going to blurt out the whole, anyway. "Aye, we agreed to some such arrangement. I did it because she seemed to wish it very much."

MacLean looked puzzled. "Have you ever sponsored a lass before?"

Thomas's mouth went dry, and he shot an uneasy glance at Fia. "Once or twice," he managed to croak.

"I knew it!" Fia cried, evidently happy at this news. "'Twas fate that sent you to me."

MacLean rubbed his neck, his brows knit as though the answer to some puzzle still eluded his grasp. "What did you hope to gain?"

Thomas didn't know where to look. What could he say to such a question? That he found the laird's cousin to be

an incredibly sensual and delectable woman? That there
was something about her sparkling eyes and the way she
smiled that heated him beyond measure? That he lost what
little sense he had whenever she pressed those full, silken
lips to his? That just the sight of her here, kneeling beside him, was enough to make his aching and abused body
strain against his bonds?

Fia patted Thomas's arm. "Duncan, let the poor man be.
Can't you see he is still befuddled? Lord Thomas agreed
to sponsor my plays in exchange for help in getting to his
ship."

Thomas blinked. "What plays?"

Fia's brows lowered. "But . . . if you didn't know about
my plays . . . what did you mean by 'sponsor'?"

The voice curled around Thomas's neck and tightened
into a noose. He didn't need to look at MacLean's way; he
could feel the fury coming from that direction.

Sweet Jesu, she writes plays.

It was the last thought he had before the hilt of a claymore slammed into his head and blessed darkness wiped
out the sight of Fia's white face.

Chapter Six

The three men yanked Thomas's inert body from the chair. His head dropped back and thudded against the table edge.

Fia gasped. "Be gentle with my Englishman! Though he's an arse, he's suffered enough at the hands of the Mac-Leans without bumping and thumping him all the way to the bedchamber."

"Bedchamber?" Duncan snapped, his black gaze cold. "Where else is he to go?"

"To hell for all I care; he's done naught but offer our family insult." He jerked his head toward the door and ordered his men, "Take that pox-ridden swiver to the cellar."

"Och, Duncan, you can't just—" Fia began.

"Yes, I can. MacKenna, you, Berwick, and Talent see to it the Englishman is well bound, too. I'll not have him escape."

Fia whirled to face MacKenna. "Don't you dare take him to the cellar! The dampness will kill him."

MacKenna gave an apologetic shrug. "Sorry, lass, but the laird is the laird."

Fia crossed her arms, her gaze locked on the laird's men. "Douglas MacKenna!"

The large guard shifted uneasily from one foot to the other. "Aye, me lady?"

"Who nursed you back to health last winter when you were moaning and crying fit to shame a priest?"

He shifted uneasily. "'Twas ye, me lady."

"And who sat by your Katherine's side when she was giving birth to little David?"

The grizzled face softened at the mention of his youngest son. "Bless ye, m'lady. Ye stayed with her the whole night."

"And who gave you the silver to buy that new horse you are so fond of?"

A dull red stole across MacKenna's cheeks. He cast a miserable look toward Duncan before replying, "'Twas ye, me lady."

Fia raised her brows. "Then tell my cousin how dangerous 'twould be to put a puny Sassenach in the cellar. How the man could easily die, which no one wants since he is a favorite of Queen Elizabeth's."

MacKenna swallowed noisily and laid down his burden. "Ah, me lord, if ye'll forgive me fer sayin' so, 'tis a bit cold in the cellar."

Thick black eyebrows rose slightly. "Cold?"

MacKenna nodded miserably. "Aye. And . . . and damp, me lord."

Duncan's smile made his men pale. "'Tis *damp* in the cellar. By all means we can't have such for our wondrous guest, can we?"

MacKenna fidgeted but managed to say in a reasoned tone, "Me lord, if this was a Scotsman I wouldn't hesitate, but with an Englishman . . ." He shook his head. "The littlest thing could do him in."

Berwick nodded. "Aye, me lord, 'tis true."

Duncan regarded Berwick sourly. "I suppose Lady Fia sat with your wife whilst one of your sons was born, too."

Berwick looked shamefaced. "Nay, but she brought me soup every day fer two weeks when I had the ague and was shaking fit to fall from me bed. I think I'd have died if no' fer her."

Duncan turned to Talent. "And you?"

Talent shifted uneasily from foot to foot. "Lady Fia helped me poor sister when she cut her foot and it swelled until we thought the skin would split and smelled as if—"

"*Enough*. The three of you are worthless!" Duncan's face darkened until Fia thought he would explode.

Fia was relieved when he finally let out his breath in a long, drawn-out hiss. "Take the damned Sassenach and place him in a bedchamber. Post a guard—nay, post *two* guards. And by the saints above, MacKenna, stop looking like a witless sheep!"

MacKenna sighed his relief and gestured to the men to resume carrying their burden from the room. As he passed Fia, she murmured, "I owe you."

His shrewd blue eyes twinkled somberly. "That ye do, me lady. Don't think I'll let ye be forgettin' it, neither."

Fia grinned. "I won't." She slanted a challenging glance at Duncan from under her lashes before saying loudly, "Take him to the blue bedchamber. I'll be up shortly with some medicines." The men moved with exaggerated caution as they maneuvered the Englishman out of the doorway.

Fia followed them to the door.

"Hold, cousin," Duncan growled. "I'm not finished with you."

She sighed. "I was afraid of that."

"Sit."

She reluctantly came to perch on the edge of a chair near Duncan. "Very well. What else have you to say?"

Duncan crossed his massive arms over his chest, the amber amulet gleaming against his dark clothing. "You will not go near the Sassenach without a chaperone."

"For heaven's sake, Duncan, who will nurse him—"

"Mary. She's not worth one whit as a chaperone, but she's a good nurse."

"Duncan, I'm not a child who—"

"Furthermore, I am inviting Malcolm Davies and his mother to attend us at their earliest convenience."

She leapt to her feet. *"No!* Duncan, please don't—"

"You will marry as soon as Lady Davies and I agree on the contract."

"I don't want to marry that babied lackwit!"

Duncan's expression gave her no hope. "'Tis for your own safety. The Davies clan is powerful and will see to it that you're well cared for."

"Duncan, I can't—"

"You will be married by Sunday a week. Earlier, if I can arrange it."

"You cannot force me in this," she warned.

"Oh?"

"Nay. They say Lady Davies is as proud and haughty as a queen. What would she think to see me kicking and screaming all the way to the altar?"

Duncan's eyebrows lowered. "This is no laughing matter, Fia. I'm serious."

"So am I."

His jaw tightened. "If that's the way you wish to do this, then so be it." He crossed to the door. *"Fitzgerald!"*

A flurry of rushing footsteps followed and a redheaded lad slid into the room. "Ye called, me lord?"

"Aye. Go find MacKenna and tell him to throw that damned Sassenach in the cellar after all."

Fia gasped. "Nay! 'Twill kill him!"

Duncan's flat gaze answered her. There was a tense pause as she struggled with her temper.

"Och, to the devil with you," she snapped. "I'll meet this bridegroom of yours."

Duncan nodded once and Fitzgerald, looking as if he'd received a reprieve from the devil himself, raced from the room.

Duncan arched an eyebrow at Fia. "You'll do more than meet young Davies, lass; you'll wed him."

"But I—"

"Nay, no more. I've explained to you all that I'm willing. Now I've letters to write that must be sent before the day is out." With that, he turned toward the large desk that sat in a corner of the room.

She watched him take his seat and pull a sheet of vellum forward. "Duncan, I—"

"Nay." His broad shoulders seemed bowed, as if the weight of the world pressed upon him. He flipped the inkwell open and dipped a silver-tipped pen into the bowl. "No more of this, lass. Not tonight."

She couldn't ignore the tiredness of his voice, so she slowly went to the door, pausing once to look back. He was still seated at the desk, his face bleak as his pen steadily crossed the paper. Her anger melted at the strain she saw upon his dark face, the amber amulet resting on his chest among his leathers and plaid.

Poor Duncan. He carries so many responsibilities. So many cares. She started to say something but then thought better of it. He was the laird of the clan and, wish what she would, she couldn't release him from that burden.

She sighed and quietly left the room, softly closing the wide oak door behind her.

Fia smoothed the blanket for the hundredth time. "The Sassenach's still asleep and it's been more than fifteen hours." She couldn't keep the worry from her voice as she placed her hand upon his forehead. "His fever has not yet broken."

Mary came to stand beside her. "'Tis not unusual fer a person to have a low fever and sleep fer hours—even days—after facing such calamities as this one did."

"But he'll get better?"

"He'll be fine, lass. Weak as a kitten, but other than that, no worse fer the wear."

Fia wished he'd sigh in his sleep or move in some way; this deathly stillness was nerve-wracking. "Duncan says I may not visit the Sassenach without a chaperone, though the man's so tired he can't even awaken."

Mary's blue eyes twinkled. "I told the laird this morn that if he truly wished to see ye married, then the less chaperonage ye had, the better."

"I'm never going to get married," said Fia sharply.

"'Never' is a big word, lassie."

"In some cases, 'tisn't big enough." She turned from the bed and began straightening the room, pouring fresh water into the pitcher on the washstand and dusting a small pile of books that hadn't been moved in weeks. The morning light from the mullioned window streamed across the stone floor and turned the dust motes to glittering fairy dust.

She returned to the bed. "His poor eye is black and blue. And that welt on his cheek—tsk."

Fia lightly traced a bruise on his cheek to the corner of his mouth. She should have been glad he was having such a restful slumber, but she wanted him to waken and look at her the way he had when he'd kissed her in the forest. The passion in his brown eyes had melted her into a puddle of desire. Even now, just looking at his handsome profile made her stomach tighten.

"Lassie, are ye ill? Ye look a might heated."

"Nay, I'm fine," Fia said, though her neck and face prickled with warmth. Mary eyed her suspiciously and Fia hurried to change the subject. "I hope Duncan hasn't been harsh on you for helping me on my journey to London."

"Och, don't ye worry 'bout me, my lady. Jenny Dow used to be Duncan's nurse when he was a babe, and she's my third cousin." Mary grinned. "Nothing can hush a man quicker than a good memory, especially when it involves the changin' of swaddlin'."

Despite the feeling of hopelessness that had begun to seep through her, Fia had to laugh.

"Do ye know what is really surprising? " Mary asked. "That the laird hasn't put a stop to these sickroom visits of yers. Chaperone or no, the man is fine to look upon." She squeezed one of Thomas's finely muscled arms. "Hale and hearty, and as tasty as fresh-made pottage."

"And he's an earl," Fia said proudly. "A favorite of Queen Elizabeth's. They say she loves a good play."

"'Tis a pity the laird caught ye afore ye could escape."

"Aye, a great pity." Fia perched on the side of the bed. "'Twas a higher power that caused an English earl to fall into my lap just as I was setting out for London, and so I told Duncan at breakfast this morning."

"What did he say?"

"Och, he will hear none of it."

"The laird has a hard head, he does. My second husband, James Brodie, used to say 'twas an ill wind as blows 'gainst a storm. If anyone would know of ill winds, 'twould be the Brodies. Horrible short on good fortune, they were."

Fia traced a finger down Thomas's fine arm. "Duncan says war is coming."

"Pshaw," Mary scoffed, tossing her short red curls. "There's naught but a thimbleful who'd support the queen."

"Aye, but that thimbleful will pull the rest into the fray—including the English."

"If the English come onto Scottish soil, 'twill unify the clans. I dinna think Queen Elizabeth will be wantin' that."

"Do you think we could beat the English?"

"O' course we could! One or two bouts and we'll rout those spalpeens like the dogs they are." Mary reached over and smoothed Thomas's hair from his brow. "Yer Sassenach is a hearty sleeper. The sign of a clear conscience, milady."

"'Tis a sign of a good drubbing, too."

Thomas stirred in his sleep, one long, beautifully muscled leg shoving aside the covers. Fia's breath caught in her throat.

Mary examined the huge bruise that covered his thigh. "La, the laird's men must have used a tree branch to make such a mark."

Fia inwardly cringed at the colorful weal. It was a perfect imprint of Thunder's shoulder.

Mary clicked her tongue. "I wonder why they trounced him so thoroughly. Did he try to hurt ye, lassie?"

"Nay, he just kissed me."

"That's no' so much. Why, I'd been kissed two dozen times by the time I was yer age."

"I've not had your opportunities."

"More's the pity, lass."

Fia had to grin. "To hear Duncan tell it, 'tis a wonder I'm not with child from such a seductive kiss."

"The laird o'erspeaks at times. I've noticed it now and then." Mary shot Fia a sharp look. "Tell me about this kiss. Did ye kiss him in return?"

Fia shrugged. "Perhaps."

"I wouldna blame ye a bit. This man was made fer kissin'."

"He gave me a present, too—a wee rabbit."

"Nay! Not the one that's fallen in love with the laird's right shoe?" Mary chuckled, her girth shaking like pudding. "I never saw Lord Duncan so discomforted. There he was, meetin' with an envoy from clan Davies, when the rabbit hopped up and started humpin' his foot like—"

"The Davieses? Here?" Fia asked, her heart pounding so loudly she could barely hear herself. She'd thought to convince her cousin to give up his plan once he was in a better mood, but he'd refused to speak about it again.

Mary sent Fia a sly glance. "I know a bit about the message, if ye care to hear."

"Yes?" Fia asked eagerly.

"Caroline Davies, the iron fist of the Davies, sent the message that she and that rat-faced son of hers are within a week's ride."

"Och!" A band of fear tightened about Fia's stomach. "What . . . what did Duncan say?"

"He ordered Cook to prepare a banquet fer their arrival and told me to see to it that more bedchambers were made ready."

Fia's heart sank.

Mary wrinkled her nose. "If ye ask me, 'tis a waste of good spice to feed the Davies, although the laird looked pleased enough to spit gold."

"That's because Duncan's made up his mind that I am to wed Malcolm Davies."

"*What?* Ye canno' be serious!"

"Aye. I tried to dissuade him, but he was adamant."

"But the laird hisself called the lad Malcolm the Maiden!" Mary shook her head. "Meanin' no disrespect to yer intended, lass, but they say he's a childish boy and a fumblin' fool to boot."

"Duncan thinks I'll be safe with the Davies clan."

"Phsst. Ye need a strong man—not some snivelin' weasel who hides in his mother's skirts."

Fia's spirits sank even lower. "It can't be all bad. I-I've heard it said that Malcolm's fluent in languages, philosophy, and history."

Mary snorted. "How wondrous fer his tutor."

Fia rubbed her temples. "Aye, I'd rather die than marry such a mealworm, but unless we can think of something to change Duncan's mind, I will be wed whether I wish it or not."

She leaned against the bedpost and regarded Thomas's sleeping form. "I don't know what Duncan is thinking. For so many years, he looked for far too high and mighty a husband, and now at the mere suggestion of war, he settles on one who's less than half a man. It makes no sense."

"Och, lass, men ne'er do."

Fia absently traced the pattern that adorned Thomas's pillow. It was one of her favorite designs, colorfully embroidered with leaping unicorns. The fanciful pattern belonged on the bed of such a handsome man, she thought wistfully. They both looked as if they had sprung from an ancient fairy tale. "There's only one bright spot in this for me. Duncan said he has a promise from Malcolm and his mother to take me to London."

Mary snorted again. "They'll take ye to London, but if ye think they'll sponsor yer plays, think again. Caroline Davies will allow no slight to her noble name, and havin' a playwright as a daughter-in-law will not sit well with her. 'Tis not respectable in the eyes of some."

Fia's threatening headache began to thrum in earnest now. "That's what I am afraid of. That I'll be worse off than I am now."

"Ye *should* be worried. I've buried four husbands, so if anyone would know about what makes a good one, 'tis me. Malcolm is a horrible choice fer any woman, but especially for a headstrong lassie like ye."

Fia sighed. "It would be better to be married to the Sassenach. A pity Duncan would never agree."

Mary looked thoughtfully at Thomas's still form. "I wonder if the Sassenach is already married?"

Married? God's breath, surely not! The idea burned in Fia's stomach like a live coal. "He can't be," she said stiffly.

The maid sent her an amused glance. "A pity ye didn't take the time to find out before ye cavorted with him in the forest. Och, now, don't glare at me. We'll find a way out of this mess. Have a seat by the bed and make sure his lordship does not try to climb from his bed if he awakens, fer he'll no' have any strength at first. I dinna want him fallin' and bruisin' yet more of his fine self."

"I'll make sure he stays in bed."

"Good. I'll fetch a bit of soup fer us both and some extra fer the Sassenach, should he wake. We'll eat here, where we can keep an eye on him."

"But Duncan said—"

"That ye were not to be left alone with the Sassenach. I know, I know." Mary gathered some folded bandages and tucked them into her pockets. "There are guards in the hallway should the Sassenach miraculously awaken wit' enough strength to sit."

Fia nodded and settled into a chair as Mary whisked her wide girth out the doorway with surprising grace.

When the door closed Fia leaned forward and placed both elbows on the bed, rested her chin in her palms, and stared intently at Thomas.

Mary was right; his color was better today. Fia noted his even, steady breathing, which relaxed her even more. He was going to be fine.

He looked so peaceful. With a sigh, she leaned forward and gently rested her head on his broad shoulder. A deep sense of peace immediately drifted through her.

She could feel his warmth through his sleep shirt, his heartbeat comfortably strong and steady beneath her ear.

Life seemed so uncertain lately, with the pending war and the dreaded arrival of the Davies. Worst of all were Duncan's unexpected actions. For the first time in her life she felt distant from her cousin and alone.

What could she do to stop the swiftly turning events? She turned her face into the Sassenach's shoulder, hiding it in the clean shirt Mary had dressed him in. She rubbed her cheek against him, savoring the feel of his muscled shoulder. If Duncan could have seen her he would have been furious, but that did not frighten her. Far more than Duncan's anger, she feared her own weakness where the Sassenach was concerned.

The mere memory of their kiss in the forest was as warm and real as if it were happening again, at that very instant, and it took all of her strength not to lift her head and place her lips upon his once again.

She shut her eyes tightly and kept her head upon his chest. *I am becoming bewitched. But how can I forget this man and content myself with the boy my cousin has chosen?*

She opened her eyes and sighed. It seemed so spiritless to do as she was told, to follow the well-worn path of all womankind since the beginning of life.

Well, she was certain she'd think of something.

She had to.

Chapter Seven

Thomas paced in front of the fire in his bedchamber, wincing every time he put his weight upon his bruised leg. It hurt, but he knew the only way to work out the stiffness was to walk.

He scowled. His mission was foiled, for not only had he been caught, but when he'd awoken, the letter he'd come to fetch had been removed from his tattered clothes.

He ground his teeth at the thought. It had been tempting to ask after it, but that would only have exposed him more thoroughly, if that was even possible.

He limped on, glancing around the pleasant room. Laird MacLean must be more financially set than Walsingham realized. Thick, richly woven rugs covered the polished flagstone floor and complemented the large ornate trunk and a pair of fine red-cushioned oak chairs. A cheery fire warmed the smooth stone walls and lit the rich red velvet hangings that hung about the huge bed.

As prisons went, this one was grand enough for royalty. But even more impressive had been the number of visitors he'd been allowed. Not only had Mary, Fia's troublesome maid, visited him, but so had Fia and Laird MacLean.

He saw Fia the least, which irked him. She darted in and out, always in the presence of Mary. While Fia's gaze assessed his well-being, she never remained long enough for a genuine conversation. Thomas found it exasperating; the tantalizing glimpses only fanned the attraction he felt for her.

And he did feel an attraction; he couldn't deny it. But what man would not? The woman was beautiful, her dark eyes mysterious and warm, her movements graceful, her voice rich and seductive—he ached just thinking of her.

He found himself hoping that every step in the hallway outside his door might be hers, though far too often it was not.

Where Fia refused to linger, her cousin surprisingly seemed to have too much time upon his hands. When the laird came to visit, he stayed talking of this and that, carrying on a conversation of a depth normally reserved for close compatriots.

MacLean asked as many questions as he answered and seemed determined to take Thomas's measure, though to what end, he would not say.

Thomas soon discovered that MacLean was very well-read and could discuss politics, religion, travels, philosophy, even music and plays with great ease. If nothing else, the visits made the days pass.

Today, though, something was happening. For one, he'd been left alone for most of the day; even Mary's visit this morning had been rushed and distracted.

For another, the courtyard bustled with people arriving hourly, the hallways noisy with the call of servants. Something—or someone—had arrived.

Thomas paused by his door and listened. Though he could hear the calls and murmurs, none of them told him anything. He grasped the handle and slowly turned it . . . to no avail. He was still locked in, a prisoner.

Cursing under his breath, he resumed pacing. *Damn it, what does MacLean have planned? And where is Fia? Do these visitors have anything to do with her?*

I shouldn't be thinking about her. I should be thinking about escaping. He glanced at the fine clock that adorned the mantel. It was nigh on three in the afternoon. Perhaps this commotion was just what he needed to escape. If he could twine his bedsheets into a rope that could reach the top of the second floor, at least, he might be able to—

He paused, hearing the unmistakable sound of footsteps approaching down the hall, followed by the murmur of someone greeting the guards. Then the oak door opened and Mary entered, her arms full of clothing. "Och, ye're up! Good, fer I've ordered a nice hot bath fer ye."

Every morning for the last week, Thomas had awakened to the sight of the maid's wide, dimpled smile and freckled, weathered face. Until this week, he hadn't realized how wearisome habitual cheerfulness could become.

Mary smiled brightly and placed the clothes in a chair, but there was something different about her, a squaring of her jaw that bespoke a decision of some sort.

Hmm. I wonder what's toward now? "'Tis kind of you to bring me better clothing."

"'Twas no' my idea. Lady Fia sent this."

"A pity I won't see her to thank her myself. I noticed the commotion in the courtyard. Visitors have arrived, I take it."

The smile on Mary's face dimmed. "Aye, we've visitors."

"Who?"

Mary didn't meet his gaze but began to straighten the clothing she'd brought, sorting through them to pull out a very fine lawn shirt with lace cuffs. "Clan Davies has arrived."

"The whole clan?"

"Many of them; their laird and his mother will come soon." She held out a shirt. "Do ye think ye might fit these? They may be too large."

He accepted the shirt, noting that while 'twas of obvious quality, 'twas far too large for him. Fia must have pilfered her cousin's wardrobe, probably without his knowledge. "'Twill fit well enough."

"Good. I'll tell Lady Fia; she was worried it might not."

Thomas absently rubbed the finely woven cloth between his fingers. While he'd been unconscious, he'd dreamed of Fia—of her sitting beside him, regaling him with tales, her soothing voice sending him into a deeper and yet deeper sleep. He'd been so involved in his dreams that when he'd finally awakened, his first thought had been of her.

A large clang sounded in the hallway, and Mary said, "Ah, yer water." She went to open to the door as the sound of voices rose in the hallway. "'Twill be good fer ye to soak in some hot water." She opened the door and a group of men carried in a huge tub. More followed with buckets of steaming water.

Mary bustled about the room, straightening as she went. "Ye won't believe what a flutter the whole castle's in. Lady Davies and her son are to arrive on the morrow. They sent almost two hundred men to secure the way. They've set up camp outside the castle walls."

He hobbled to the window, unlatched the shutter, and

threw it open, grimacing as his sore muscles protested. He leaned out the window, the waning afternoon sun unable to hold back the chilled wind. His room was on the third level, the surrounding wall across the courtyard almost even with his window. Lines of tents had been erected on the fields outside of the castle gate. *Bloody hell. The entire place is surrounded.*

His heart sank and he closed the shutters. "That's a large number. Do they always travel with their pennants flying?"

"'Tis a very important visit. The laird has had Lady Fia with a seamstress fer the last day, sewing pearls upon her best gown. She will be presiding over the banquet."

He shrugged. "As is usual for the lady of the castle."

Mary shook her head, her smile dimmed. "Nay, fer the laird would never allow it before. He's very protective of her."

"Why is she to be at this banquet, then?"

Mary glanced at the servants filling the tub and said in a low tone, "The laird's decided 'tis time fer Lady Fia to do her duty."

'Twas obvious there was more to it than that, but Mary would say no more in front of the other servants. Thomas waited impatiently until the men left, swinging the door wide as they did so.

Thomas took the opportunity to count the men posted as guards. One, two, three—ah. Five of them, and all burly men equipped with swords and knives.

He rubbed his black beard. Even if he did manage to overcome the guards, he would be lost in the maze of hallways. He needed a guide, someone who knew the castle and could find a way past the encampment outside the walls. Someone like Fia.

Mary closed the door and returned to place some thick towels by the tub. "Get in the tub, me lord. 'Twill help those aches and pains of yers."

The clean, steaming water beckoned and he undressed as fast as his aching thigh would allow, Mary assisting as she could.

He soon slipped into the water with a thankful sigh. He had to find a way out of this predicament. Though the letter had been the ultimate prize and he'd lost it, he'd still managed to collect some good information that would benefit Walsingham and England. If he could just make it to his ship, his efforts would not have been wasted.

Mary placed the rest of the clothes upon his bed. "I dinna know if the clothes will fit, but they're better than what ye had."

Thomas slid deeper into the hot water. "So tell me more of clan Davies."

Mary's face darkened. "There's not much more to tell. 'Twill be a grand banquet and the kitchens are cooking all sorts of fine dishes—ten geese, a roasted pig, and lamb stew."

Thomas's stomach rumbled and she nodded. "Aye, ye'll get a portion, too. Lady Fia will see to that." Mary pulled a small stool to the side of the tub and sat, then took a small cloth and a cake of soap and began to lather it. "I worry fer Lady Fia, I do. Ye should worry, too."

"Me? Why?"

"Because once she's gone, no one will stand betwixt ye and the laird. 'Twill be the dungeon wit' ye then."

Thomas didn't like the enthusiasm Mary was displaying as she lathered her hands, her expression determined, as though she were getting ready to attack an especially crusted and greasy pan.

"'Twill be a fine banquet, indeed. There's to be raspberry tarts, savory turtle soup, bread pudding—"

"I'm sure 'twill be a fine feast." He eyed her narrowly. "Mistress Mary, is there a reason you keep bringing up this banquet? I cannot help but notice that you are upset."

The maid's lips quivered, and for a horrible moment he thought she might burst into tears. She gave a great sniff, wiped her eyes with the back of one hand, and then began to scrub his shoulder as if her life depended upon it. "I'm upset because the laird's decided 'tis time to marry Fia off to Malcolm Davies."

"The laird of the clan?"

"Pssht. His mother rules that clan, and everyone knows it. He's the laird in name alone."

"God's wounds, you cannot be serious."

"Aye, the ceremony is to be held before the week's end."

"That's rather sudden, isn't it?"

"In some ways, aye. The laird wishes his cousin to be safe. The Davies are a powerful clan and should be able to withstand any number of attacks, even in these coming times."

"Coming times?"

"Aye. The troubles have come to Scotland. The queen—" Mary's lips folded together in a straight line. "Howe'er 'tis, the laird's decided Fia's to marry Malcolm Davies and will no' listen to reason."

Thomas couldn't shake the thought of Fia getting married. Not that he wished to marry her himself, for he didn't. Fia was not the type of woman one married; she was too impulsive, too wanton, too everything. When he married, it would be to a properly raised Englishwoman who would benefit his name and knew how to control her spirit. Nothing led to ruin faster than marriage to a woman of passion; his own history told him that.

Still, he couldn't help damning the fates. First they put that maddening Scottish wench in his path, with her tempting mouth and lush curves, and then they expected him to sit idly by while her giant cousin married her off. "When's the wedding?"

"Sunday."

"At one time, I thought Duncan and Fia were to be married."

"Whist, now! Shame on ye fer thinkin' such a thing. The laird treats Fia like a sister, he does. And now he's marryin' her to that Malcolm Davies."

"And Fia is not pleased?"

"She'd rather eat rusted nails."

Thomas frowned. "I do not hold with forced marriages. They benefit no one."

The maid looked at Thomas speculatively.

"What?" he asked.

"Oh, nothing," she replied in a tone that said the opposite. The maid rubbed his shoulders with the warm cloth, her touch brisk and impersonal. "So . . . it seems that both ye and Lady Fia are in a mite of a fix. Once Lady Fia's away with her new husband, there's no reason fer the laird to keep ye alive. 'Tis only because of her that ye're not restin' in the damp cellar, trussed like a Michaelmas goose."

Many times in the last four days Thomas had heard from Mary the story of how Fia had intervened for him with her cousin, so he wisely didn't say a word.

"'Tis a good thing she put her foot down and demanded ye be given this chamber," Mary continued. "Ye'd have not lived long in the damp cellar. Not to mention the laird's been a bit distracted this week, and 'tis possible no one would have thought to feed ye."

So Fia had that much influence over MacLean. It was strange that Walsingham, with his endless web of information, hadn't mentioned the laird's taking cousin before now.

"Aye," Mary continued, "the laird loves only two things: Scotland and his cousin. Fia has been his charge since she was a wee mite. Lord MacLean had just begun to scrape the whiskers from his chin when the little lass was brought here at her parents' deaths and placed in his care. I was a scrub maid at the time and I took to her right away, as we all did. She's brought light and happiness to the household 'til we canno' remember what 'twas like without her. Now she's to be wed to a weak-kneed brute and I—" Mary wiped her eyes on her sleeve. "Och, now. Look what ye've made me do! I was goin' to offer ye a way to escape from certain death, and instead ye got me weepin' like a babe."

Thomas straightened in the tub. "Escape? Do you know a secret way out of the castle? One that would avoid the men camped outside?" Many castles had such passageways; it was how their inhabitants restocked their stores or escaped when under seige.

The maid nodded, her graying red curls bouncing along. "Aye, I know the secret way. *But*"—she eyed him with a somber expression—"there's a price fer such help."

"Name it."

"Ye have to take the lass with ye."

"You mean Lady Fia?"

"Ye heard me. Ye *and* the lass must escape, and soon. She canno' marry Davies, and ye're wantin' to return to

London, which is where she wishes to go. 'Tis the perfect solution."

"Mary, I can't take Fia with me. The laird would come after us—perhaps all the way to London."

"Then ye'll have to protect her," Mary said stoutly. "Ye've no choice, me lad. Ye'll be a dead man the minute Lady Fia sets foot outside the gates. Ye *must* to take her to London with ye or ye'll die here—alone, a failure, yer life wasted."

A failure. The words echoed with the bitter salt of truth. He was damned if he did and damned if he didn't. Though if he did take Fia to London, she might prove useful to Walsingham. If she was as close to her cousin as Mary suggested, then it was entirely possible that Fia knew MacLean's position on the coming uprising.

That could be very valuable information indeed. "Very well; if you will help me escape, I'll take Lady Fia."

"And me and Angus, too."

"What? I can't—"

"Yes, ye can. I canno' allow Lady Fia to go unchaperoned."

Thomas scowled. "Very well, but you'll have to travel light."

Mary beamed. "Of course, me lord. Angus and I dinna own enough to fill a sack."

Thomas relaxed. "Very well. How many men does the laird have?"

"MacLean put five of his best men to watchin' ye. He has a hundred or more here within the castle walls, with the remainder of his men and those who came with the Davies clan camped without. Over three hundred in all."

It was worse than he'd thought. "Where's the secret passageway?"

"Lady Fia will come to ye when she can and 'tis safe to leave. She knows the way, she do."

"When will that be?"

Mary frowned. "I dinna know. As soon as she can do so wit'out the laird knowin' her intention."

"Mary, tell me the way out of this blasted castle. The sooner I know the route, the better."

"Lady Fia will tell ye," Mary repeated more firmly. "I'll not have ye leavin' without her."

"I give you my word I will not do that—though 'twould be easier to escape without her."

Mary scrubbed with vigor. "Lady Fia may be a mite different from the fancy women ye're accustomed to, but she's a rare one fer all that."

"Aye. Rarely properly clothed, rarely where she ought to be, rarely thinking before she speaks, rarely anything other than cursed infuriating."

Mary's lips thinned and she began scrubbing his arm with such effort that it made his skin red. "The mistress is as proper a lady as any!"

Thomas winced at the strength of her touch. "If it weren't for your mistress, I wouldn't have been captured," he stated. "She's too flighty by half. I don't mind taking the lot of you with me, but I won't leave the details of this endeavor in her hands. *I* will be the one in charge of the escape."

Mary threw the washcloth into the tub, splashing sudsy water in Thomas's face. "Fine! Ye can be in charge, but dinna be a fool and forget that the lass grew up in this place and knows every nook and cranny."

Thomas wiped the water from his face. *God save me from all Scots,* he thought. *They're all cursed lackwits. 'Tis a won-*

der the country exists at all. "Fine. I'll listen to Lady Fia, so long as you both know I'm in charge of this venture."

Mary looked slightly mollified. "Ye promise?"

"Aye. I promise." Thomas lifted his shoulders and winced in exaggerated pain. "My back is sore; I would appreciate it if you'd scrub it for me."

She nodded stiffly and then grasped his shoulder and shoved him forward until his head was but inches from the water. He managed to swallow his grunt of pain, holding himself at the ready for her not-so-gentle touch. But to his surprise, Mary dropped the cloth and began to knead his back with exquisite thoroughness, every movement easing his sore muscles.

A warm lassitude seeped through him. "You are washing away every ache."

"The mistress will have more bruises than this if she's made to wed Malcolm Davies."

Frowning, Thomas lifted his head. "What do you mean by that?"

"He's evil," Mary said in a tight voice, her gaze direct and unflinching.

"You think he will hurt her?"

"He's been known to beat the women servants."

Thomas's jaw tightened. "Surely he wouldn't do such a thing to Fia. MacLean would kill him."

"If he knew, aye. But after she marries it may be months before the laird sees her again, and by then—" Mary shook her head, worry darkening her blue eyes.

"What sort of an animal is this Malcolm Davies?"

"He's a wee, mean, shallow youth protected by a doting mother who thinks he's too important to be corrected." She leaned closer. "Only male servants are allowed in Malcolm's rooms, fer fear he'll kill the next female he puts his hands on. He has a terrible temper, he do."

Thomas's jaw ached at the thought of Fia—winsome, fey Fia, who could not walk past a half-dead animal without adopting it as a pet—at the hands of such brutality. "That would kill her spirit, if not her body."

Mary's lip quivered. "Sassenach, she *must* escape."

Thomas nodded. "I will take her to London with me and put her under Queen Elizabeth's protection."

A smile burst upon Mary's face. "Ye're many things, but ye're not a wee, mean-hearted man."

"Thank you," Thomas said drily.

She had the grace to look slightly embarrassed. "Och, I'm sorry to speak so bluntly, but this is Lady Fia we're talkin' about. She has to go to London and produce her plays. 'Tis what she was born to do."

Ah yes, the plays. He'd almost forgotten them. "Are these plays so important to her, then?"

"Have ye ever wanted somethin' so badly ye were willin' to give up everythin' ye had to possess it?"

In the flicker of an eye, Thomas remembered when he'd been but a child of six, the agony of the days after his mother had fled. His father had been a madman, stalking about the house, screaming at the smallest of things, raging loud and long at everyone, including Thomas.

Thomas had been devastated by his mother's desertion. He'd ripped apart her room, looking for a note, a letter, some sign that she would return, but he'd found nothing.

His father's reaction had frightened Thomas, but he understood the feelings behind it better than anyone else. He became determined to show his father that he would never leave, and he had stopped at nothing to please his remaining parent.

Much later, he realized that he had taken on an impossible task, but at the time, oh how he'd yearned for his father's approval.

Gruffly, he said, "Aye, I know how it feels to want something badly."

"Then ye understand that she's made it her goal to reach London and see her plays upon the stage. Mistress Fia has a gift fer writin'. 'Twould be folly not to pursue her dreams."

Thomas sighed. "It is a bigger folly to pursue them. No woman of good birth would allow her name to appear on a playbill. 'Twould be an enormous scandal."

Mary clambered to her feet. "I dinna care what society thinks, and neither should you." She collected the washcloths and put them over the edge of the tub. Then she placed the large towel near the tub and made her way to the door. "Lady Fia will come fer ye as soon as 'tis safe, so be prepared anytime. 'Twill be soon; a day or two at most."

"Very well. I will be waiting."

Mary whisked herself out the door, closing it solidly behind her, and the rattle of a key told him the guards had once again secured the lock.

Chapter Eight

Two days passed and still no Fia. The wait was maddening, made worse since he was tortured by the unmistakable sound of her voice floating up from the courtyard, ordering the servants to various duties as more of the Davies clan arrived.

Each time he heard that lilting voice, Thomas rushed his sore body to the window, but to no avail: he never caught sight of her. It was infuriating.

Now 'twas late at night. Thomas piled another log onto the fire as the clock struck two.

He leaned against the mantel, rerolling the sleeve that had fallen over his hand. The clothing Fia had sent was laughable. The doublet was so large that it was more like a cape with sleeves and the hosen so loose that they threatened to fall to the floor. He'd twisted the waist and tied a knot to keep them from slipping over his hips. Bloody hell, Duncan was a giant.

Damn it, when will she come? He ground his teeth and paced his way about the room.

What was she waiting for? Was she attempting to procure supplies for their escape? Or had something happened? Was it possible that Duncan had discovered the plan?

Surely not. Surely she'd have sent someone to tell him. And if Fia had been caught, would her cousin take his ire out on her? Thomas could only hope not, though his jaw clenched at the thought.

He shook his head. God's wounds, but he was tied in knots over a mere slip of a girl with a penchant for collecting mangy animals like most women collected jewels. *She's an unruly, undisciplined, disheveled, impulsive, un—*

Voices rose in the hallway, followed by the sound of Fia's voice. She was chuckling, the guards laughing with her. He heard her say, "Aye, 'tis late; I should be abed. Good night, gentlemen. 'Til the morrow."

Then there was only silence. He curled his hands into fists, unable to believe that she'd left. Why hadn't she at least tried to see him or—

Several thuds in the hallway sounded, like heavy bodies falling down. After a long moment, the door slowly creaked opened. "Sassenach?" came Fia's low whisper.

Thomas took an eager step forward just as Zeus stuck his head into the room. Fia glanced down at her dog and held the door wide. "Stand guard."

The dog cast a longing look at the fire but walked into the hall, his crooked tail sagging between his legs, and Fia shut the door. "He'll bark if he sees anyone."

"I wouldn't count on it," Thomas said drily. "Where are the guards?"

"Sleeping like babes. I gave them a wee dram of whiskey with their dinner, and I mixed a good dose of sleeping draught in it to make sure they'd sleep heavily."

"Mary says you know a way from the castle."

"Aye, I do." Her gaze flickered over him, resting on the knotted hosen. She grinned.

"I'm glad you're amused; I am not. I've been waiting for two days to leave this godforsaken place and my temper is thin."

"I couldn't come while the Davies clan was still arriving. The last few came this evening, so now the focus will be upon the banquet hall and kitchens." She tilted her head toward the door. "Mary's down the hall, serving lookout. Are you ready to leave?"

"I've but to pull on my boots." Thomas limped to retrieve them, pushing his stiff leg to one side as he bent over. As he did so, he lost his balance.

Fia was there in a trice, pressing a bracing shoulder to his, and in the space of a shocked second, Thomas found himself staring into the her eyes, surrounded by a wildness of sooty lashes. His body came alive with a burning heat.

Thomas couldn't tear his attention from the curve of her lips, wondering if she remembered the kiss in the forest as well as he did.

"We . . . we must go," she said huskily. The richness of her voice swirled through his stomach and below. He shifted restlessly, and Fia's gaze locked onto his thigh.

He knew she was wondering about his bruises, but some imp of mischief made him flex the muscle. She wet her lips with the tip of her pink tongue and his body tightened with desire. He ached for a touch, a kiss. *Just one,* he told himself. *A very quick one.*

So he kissed her—this fascinating, frustrating, innocently wanton woman-child who'd captured his imagination far too much. He kissed her with a thoroughness that allowed for no thought beyond the feel and taste of her. All of his earlier arousal returned in triple force and he caught her against him. She twined her arms about his neck and pressed against him, instantly as aroused as he.

He wanted more. He parted her lips and gently ran his tongue across the smooth edge of her teeth. She moaned into his mouth, pulling him closer, and Thomas knew she was his. Then Zeus scratched at the door.

It took every bit of his self-control, but Thomas freed himself from her luxuriously sensual embrace, panting as he said, "Mary awaits."

Fia flushed, stepping back even farther. "Aye. That wasn't— " She bit her lip.

He captured her hand and pressed his lips to her fingers. "As soon as we reach London, comfit, those plays of yours will have their sponsor. I swear it."

Her embarrassment fled before a visible wave of happiness. "Thank you." She looked delightfully, sinfully mussed, her black eyes awash with passion.

"In return for assisting me in escaping, you may have anything that is in my possession to grant you." *I only hope one of the things you desire is me.* He cupped her face between his hands and ran his thumb over her swollen bottom lip.

Her eyes closed, a deep shiver going through her. He could feel her passion-heated skin beneath his fingers and see her nipples peaked against the fabric.

God, she is beautiful. Beautiful and as intoxicating as the whiskey the Scots produce.

"Come," she said huskily, shaking her head as if just waking from a deep sleep. "The guards will only sleep an hour, no more."

"Where are we going?"

"In the kitchen storeroom behind the flour barrel, there's a small trapdoor that leads down some stone steps into a natural cave that leads to the creek. It's far behind the Davies encampment."

"Excellent!" Thomas scooped up his boots and crossed to her side. "I'll carry these; 'twill be quieter."

"Very well. First we'll stop by my room for Lord Thomas, and then we'll—"

"Lord Thomas?" he said, stopping by the open door.

"The wee rabbit you gave me." She smiled almost shyly. "I named him for you."

"I don't give a damn who you named him for; we can't take your animals. 'That got us captured last time." Irritation washed over him. "I vowed to help you, not those decrepit animals."

Her chin lifted. "I am not leaving without them."

"And I am not leaving with them," he ground out. "We cannot escape with those animals slowing us down. We tried that once."

"I have Angus and Mary to help with them now. You won't even know they're there."

"No."

She jutted her chin. "Either we take the animals or you'll stay here by yourself, and Mary and Angus and I will go without you."

"I know the secret escape route now so I don't need your help. I will just go on my own." He'd find his own way to the harbor where his ship was waiting.

"You can't just go!" She stood there like a mast, straight and immovable. "You *promised*."

"Fia—" He took a steadying breath. "We'll send for your pets as soon as we arrive in London."

"*No.* They come *now.*"

A rumble of anger streaked through him like an arrow. "You had your chance. Now I'll take mine." He made a quick bow. "Thank you for the information on the escape route. I shall be forever in your debt." He strode down the hallway, refusing to look back.

Her footsteps sounded in the passageway behind him. "Thomas, wait!"

Finally, she is seeing reason. He smiled to himself and turned to face her, ready to be magnanimous. "Yes, my—"

She snatched his boots from his hands and ran, her skirts flying, her boots slapping on the flagstone.

Thomas lunged for her, but the dog was in the way, making him stumble as Fia flew on. He regained his footing and bolted after her, his loose hosen slipping down one hip. He jerked them back into place as he raced on.

Damn the woman! He reached the corner and tried to turn, his hose-covered feet slipping on the smooth flagstone. He scrambled madly and slid right into Fia, who had stopped dead in the center of the hall.

She grabbed at his arm, trying to remain upright. Thomas's boots went flying and they both flailed wildly, struggling to keep their balance.

Zeus, who'd loped after them unnoticed, decided to join in the fun. With his tail wagging furiously, he gave a joyous bark and leapt against them. Thomas and Fia crashed to the floor, arms and legs tangled in a tumbled heap.

When Thomas's breath returned to normal, he realized he was lying on the floor with Fia on top of him, her knees straddling his head, her skirt covering his face. Worse, his hose were now about his ankles and he could feel her cheek pressed against his bare thigh.

Thomas shoved skirts out of his face. "Fia, move your—"

"*Damnation!*" rumbled a deep masculine voice. *"What is the meaning of this?"*

Thomas looked up and saw Duncan's scowling face. Beyond that he saw a bejeweled older woman who smirked like a cat with a bird, and behind her was a thin, pale youth dressed in a manner befitting a prince.

And in that moment, Thomas knew his fate. He closed his eyes and cursed.

Chapter Nine

Thomas urged his horse to a faster pace, ignoring MacLean's men doing likewise at his sides. In a few moments he would be back on his ship, casting off from this cursed Scottish isle. He tried to forget that he had failed in his mission. Failed like the veriest of fools, and even worse, he'd fallen into the oldest trap in the world. Somehow, some way, he'd landed at the altar, an unwilling groomsman.

Damme, how did I allow myself to be put in such a position? He'd fallen for Fia's painfully obvious plan like the veriest schoolboy.

At first he had wanted to blame MacLean, but who could do so when Lady Davies and her gawking mealworm of a son had been there, snickering at his predicament? MacLean had done the only thing a sane man could have done—he'd demanded Thomas and Fia wed at once.

And they had.

Thomas ground his teeth and urged the horse on.

Bloody hell, this sort of thing wasn't supposed to happen to him. He was Thomas Wentworth, the famed Earl of Rotherwood, known for his great fortune and brilliant future. Now, in a mere week, he'd been bitten, bruised, dismissed, captured, and worst of all, forced to marry the most unconventional, the unluckiest, the most ink-stained Scottish playwright to ever grasp a quill.

Married to a ragamuffin of a chit who thinks more of her mangy animals than she does of the proprieties. She will be a disaster in court, and the one thing I've sworn to prevent with my dying breath—seeing the Wentworth name humiliated yet again—will happen without fail.

Thomas couldn't seem to wrap his mind around it. If only they'd left his bedchamber a few moments earlier. If only he hadn't paused to kiss her.

Truthfully, that kiss—like all of the ones before—had done nothing to satisfy the hot, frustrated lust that burned inside him. It was a sickness of some sort. A yearning like no other he'd ever experienced. Was this what his mother had felt for the man she'd left his father for?

Guilt tightened about his heart. If it *was* something his wild, undisciplined, selfish, and shallow mother had felt, then he needed to fight it with every ounce of his being. He would *never* embarrass the family name for something as transient and insignificant as mere lust. He owed his father and his family name far more than that.

But now he was stuck with the woman who caused him such a surfeit of feelings. He had to fight the way Fia made him lose control. Fight it for all he was worth even though it seemed that the harder he fought, the more deeply he was ensnared in her net.

For the first time in his life, Thomas wondered if the chit had put a spell on him. He could make no sense of his reaction otherwise.

The sound of the sea lifted from the haze-shrouded trees around them and he took a deep breath of the fresh, tangy air, pulling his thoughts from such treachery as spells and magic.

Things will be different once I return to the sanity of London. Here in the wild Scottish countryside, Fia shines like a rare gem against a streambed of pebbles. That will all change once we reach the English court and are among the sensual and accomplished women who surround the queen. Fia will fade into the paneling like a knot on a pine plank.

MacLean's voice boomed out, ordering his men to keep a closer eye on "the damned groom." Thomas favored the laird with a sour gaze. The laird rode in front of Fia's coach, looking as dark and forbidding as Thomas felt. *Damn the man. If I ever get the chance, I'll—*

Fia leaned out the window of the coach and her dark gaze locked with his. Thomas's thoughts flew away as if blown by the wind that caught her hair and swirled it behind her, a banner of rich russet brown. He could almost feel the silken curls and smell the heather that twined through them.

She smiled with all of the beauty of the sun breaking through the a clouds, and suddenly the gloomy day seemed brighter, warmer.

God's blood, it is a spell. His heart sank into his boots.

Just then the path opened onto the shore, the mist blown away by the joyous sea breezes. As the *Glorianna* burst into view, Thomas's heart swelled with pride. She was so beautiful; he'd never seen a prouder ship.

MacLean pulled up his horse. "Wait here, Sassenach. I wish to speak to Angus before you leave."

"Angus?"

"Mary's husband. He's escorting Fia to London." Mac-Lean's gaze narrowed. "He will be sending me missives every two weeks, so have a care how you treat my cousin."

Thomas shrugged. "He may write every day, should he wish it."

"He may. I shall send some men to serve as runners, too." With a dark smile, MacLean turned and rode to where a small group of men stood by the quay.

Fury rippled through Thomas. He dismounted, tossed the reins to a nearby Scot, then stalked across the beach toward the ship. Damn all Scots, every last one.

He strode to the natural rock quay where the *Glorianna* was moored. Soon he'd be on his way. Although he'd be saddled with a wife he did not want and an escort of unofficial guards/runners, at least he would be gone from this cursed place.

Each step toward his ship restored his calm. As he reached the gangplank, he scanned his ship with expert eyes. She was in fine trim. His first mate, Simmons, had kept the men busy cleaning and polishing every surface during their wait, for she gleamed. A swell of pride lifted in his chest.

Behind him someone shouted at him in a gruff voice, "There ye are, ye lazy Sassenach! Turn and face yer accuser!"

There it was—a vent for his anger, a challenge so direct that Thomas could retaliate. He turned on his heel, hands fisted to deliver a message to the rude dolt who dared speak to him so.

There, his blue eyes sparkling in a handsome face framed by a trim black beard, feet planted firmly apart, his hand resting casually on one hip near a jeweled sword, stood Robert MacQuarrie.

"Robert!" Thomas hurried forward, aware that the Scots were muttering and looking black. *Let them, the paltry fools.*

Engulfing him in a hug, Robert slapped Thomas upon the back and then held him at arm's length. "How fare thee, *mon ami*?" Robert's blue eyes took in every scratch and bruise, his merriment fading, though the smile remained steadfastly in place for those who watched from the shore.

"I prosper, now you have come." Thomas returned the back-slap with a bit more vigor than necessary.

"Careful! You'll damage my ruff."

Thomas chuckled. Few others knew the quality of the man behind the foppish exterior of the lean and elegant Viscount Montley. "Your neckwear has always been in keeping with your person, Robert. 'Tis overdone and too damn frippery to stomach." Even now, positioned to take to the sea, Robert wore a fine Italian doublet of plum velvet shot through with silver, complemented by exquisite woolen hose and ornate leather boots, his cuffs and ruff of the finest Belgian lace.

Robert ran a critical eye over him in return. "Look to yourself, man. Where *did* you get those hosen?" He shuddered. "As good to be out of the world as to be out of fashion."

"'Tis but clothing."

"I would hesitate to call that clothing. God's blood, what's afoot? I came prepared to fight my way through a welter of angry Scotsmen at yon castle to free you by sword or ransom, only to find you escorted to your ship like an honored guest, although dressed like a court jester."

"Trust me; I am no honored guest."

"Aye, I can see it in the lumps you have acquired."

"'Tis naught. What's this of ransom?"

"Hearing of your predicament, I brought a chest of Spanish gold to win your release, should the edge of my sword have no effect." Robert smirked. "I know their weaknesses as my own; there's nothing a Scotsman prizes more than the gleam of gold."

"Your own money? I am touched."

Robert shrugged. "I'm certain Walsingham would have repaid any loss I suffered. After all, 'tis his arse I pull from the fire as much as yours." Robert brushed a bit of dust from his sleeve. "So, how did you come to be captured?"

"'Tis a story for another time." Thomas could not, would not, explain how a tiny mite of a wench had summarily disposed of him, the greatest instrument of Walsingham's secret network. "How did you find out I was here? When I left Simmons, you were not on board this ship."

"When you failed to appear, Simmons came after me posthaste. Luckily I was nearby."

"And why was that? You rarely come this far north."

Robert's smile was that of a cat with the cream. "I happened to be rusticating in a small Scottish village in a nearby harbor."

"But how did Simmons know where you—"

"Your ship is a beauty." Robert gestured toward the *Glorianna*. "I was glad for the chance to sail her; she's as steady as they come, light and responsive to the touch. If you ever wish to sell her, let me know."

"That will never happen."

Robert stroked his trim beard as he turned back to Thomas, a glint in the bright blue eyes. "I hate to plague you with questions, but MacLean sent a most curious missive. He said that not only would the Earl of Rotherwood be gracing us with his presence, but the *countess,* as well."

Wonderful. "I'll explain after we sail. I want to get under way as soon as possible."

"So are you wed or not?"

"Aye," Thomas said grimly. "Forced to marry the laird's cousin at the tip of a sword." Even now the memory singed.

"Thomas, I am sorry to hear that." Robert looked around. "Where is she?"

"In the carriage."

"I'm truly sorry, my friend. Is she short and fat, too plain to mention?"

Fia, plain? Infuriating, bothersome, maddening—yes. But plain?

He caught Robert's quizzical gaze and forced himself to shrug. "She's an ill-dressed, ill-mannered, ink-stained chit who wants nothing more than to take her mangy animals to London and become a playwright."

Robert blinked, a slow smile spreading over his face. "*Mon ami,* she sounds delightful! Where is this paragon? I must make her acquaintance *immediately!*"

The queen had always held that it would be easier to turn the Thames than to stop Robert MacQuarrie from being a useless fribble.

Thomas turned toward the shore, where Fia's coach had just come to a halt. "There she is now."

Thomas refused to watch as MacLean's men opened the carriage door.

Robert murmured a heartfelt "Sweet Jesu!"

Scowling, Thomas kept his gaze fixed on his ship. He knew what Robert was seeing—Fia, cheeks pink from the ride to the harbor, her reddish-brown hair flowing about her shoulders, her full lips parted in a smile—

He ground his teeth as his body tightened. "Well?" he demanded as Robert's silence stretched.

"She's, ah . . . very . . . *rounded.*"

"Rounded?" Thomas turned toward the coach. There beside MacLean stood Mary, her broad face damp with perspiration, her reddish-gray hair curled riotously, her rotund form shaking with laughter.

"That's not her," snapped Thomas. "That's her maid, Mary. There—MacLean is assisting Fia now."

Her hair tumbled as Thomas had predicted, Fia stepped from the carriage, the wind ruffling her skirts and hair even more. On another woman such a ruffling might have been disastrous, but on Fia it merely made her appear more like a windswept fairy.

"God's breath! She's—" Robert opened and closed his mouth and, for the first time in the fifteen years Thomas had known him, fell silent.

A slight sense of relief washed over Thomas; he was not the only one she affected. "She's handsome," he said grudgingly.

"Are you *blind*? She's—" Robert clasped his hands over his heart. "I would brave a thousand dangers for a glance from those dark eyes. I would fight the fires of hell with my bare hands to receive a kiss from those dewy lips. I would—"

"She is *my* wife." Thomas's voice was so harsh that it surprised both him.

Robert raised a brow. "I'faith, you're possessive. Though 'tis no wonder—you won her, after all."

Thomas managed a shrug. *Good God, where did that flood of possessiveness come from? I do not wish her to be in my life at all.*

Do I?

Robert sighed heavily. "You have proven the Wentworth luck once again, *mon ami*. You come to Scotland to procure a mere piece of paper and walk away with a bride worth a fleet of *Glorianna*s. You make it difficult for the rest of us to stomach our mundane lives."

MacLean approached them, his arm about Fia's shoulders, his black gaze narrowing at Robert. "Well, well. If 'tisn't the Coward of Balmanach."

Robert made a graceful bow. "So 'tis. And you are the Black Laird of the MacLeans, known for your spitting temper and hamlike fists."

MacLean's gaze narrowed, but he turned to Thomas and said in a rough voice, "You'll miss the tide if you tarry."

Thomas nodded, itching to be at sea. Once he was back on English soil, the odd feelings that had overtaken him on this isle would leave, and he would once again be in complete command of himself.

He turned to Fia. "Come. We leave."

Fia swallowed a sudden burst of intense loneliness. The cool brown eyes that met hers were impersonal; they held no emotion, no welcome. They were the eyes of a stranger, not a husband.

Duncan took her hand. "Write often, poppet. At least once a week." He glared over her head at Thomas. "If she's not happy, I'll come for her."

"I'll write," Fia said, collecting herself. "Though I'll be hard-pressed to think of something to say. I rarely see you more than once a month now, what with all your meetings and the like." She stood on tiptoe to deliver her kiss, and he swooped down to hold her tight.

Thomas stepped to one side, pulling MacQuarrie with him.

Thankful for the privacy, Fia tightened her hold on Duncan's neck. "I'll miss you."

"Och, as will I you, lassie," he replied, his voice husky. With a final hug, he gently set her on her feet. "I've done what was best for you, but if you find you're not happy, you've only to tell Angus and he'll bring you home."

She tried to smile. "I know."

Wiping his eyes in a suspicious manner, Duncan turned to MacKenna. "Where is it?"

MacKenna withdrew a small velvet bag from inside his doublet. "Here, me lord." The Scotsman handed it to Duncan, then went to oversee the loading of Fia's trunks onto the ship.

Fia looked at the heavy velvet bag that Duncan had placed in her hand, an odd warmth creeping into her fingers. "What is this?"

"'Tis the amber amulet from Maeve Hurst."

"The White Witch?" Fia looked at the bag. "But . . . won't she want it back?"

The ghost of a smile touched his hard mouth as he crossed his arms over his broad chest. "She is already on her way to fetch it now. My spies tell me she'll arrive any day."

"Duncan, she'll be furious! Aren't you afraid she might—"

"Nay, I am not." Before Fia could respond, he added gruffly, "Give that cursed thing to the English queen as a gift from the MacLeans. 'Tis the sort of trinket Elizabeth loves, and she'll think well of us for it."

Fia started to open the bag, but he closed his big hand over hers. "Be careful. It—" He clamped his mouth closed.

"What? What's wrong?"

"The amulet makes a person dream." Oddly flushed, he released her hand. "And don't be asking me about what, for I'll not say. The White Witch cursed it just to outwit me. The closer she gets, the more I dream, and the more I—" He caught Fia's fascinated gaze and his jaw flexed. "Take that damned thing with you and never let it see the sun of Scotland again."

"Och, Duncan, you're angry at the Hurst woman for getting the best of you, but you're just going to make things worse. Please think about this—"

"I have thought about it, and that's the way it's to be." Duncan's jaw was set as hard as a rock.

Fia sighed and tucked away the heavy velvet bag, the links on the silver rope chain clinking. "You'll live to rue this day."

"Why? For teaching a lesson to a tiny white witch? Her head doesn't even reach my shoulder."

"Her powers won't be measured in mere inches."

"Mine can."

She frowned. "How—"

"Never mind," he said hastily with a sheepish grin. He gave her a quick hug. "Ask no more questions, lass. You leave the Hurst woman and her confounded powers to me, while you take care of the English queen. The amulet could turn her favor in our direction, and we may have need of it before Queen Mary's done with us."

A call came from the ship, and Thomas approached them.

Duncan sighed. "The tide's turning." He cupped Fia's cheek with one of his big, rough hands, his voice suddenly gruff. "Remember to write often, lass."

Thomas cleared his throat. "I'm sorry to intrude, but we must go."

"Sassenach, take care of my cousin. If you don't, I will come for you and—" MacLean rested his hand on his broadsword.

Thomas met MacLean's gaze with a cool one of his own. "As of this day, she is mine and thus protected."

Fia caught MacLean's hand and pressed it to her cheek. "Duncan, I—" Her voice broke and, his own eyes wet, Duncan enveloped her in a hard hug. For a long time, they stood thus, the huge highlander and his tiny cousin.

Thomas didn't know where to look. The two were obviously close—even closer than Thomas had realized, more like brother and sister than cousins. He was oddly relieved by that.

Finally, MacLean gently set Fia back on her feet, his dark eyes suspiciously bright. "Good-bye, lass."

Her face wet with tears, she choked out, "Good-bye, Duncan."

"Off on your adventure." With a final warning look at Thomas, MacLean called his men and tromped back up the hill to the horses, his kilt swinging about his powerful legs, his cape swirling behind him. Thomas noticed that the laird swiped an arm over his eyes, though he didn't look back.

Mary bustled up, carrying the items she deemed too precious to let another touch. MacKenna was hard on her heels, cradling a bundle of brown fur.

"There he is!" Fia's smile broke through her tears like the sun through a bank of clouds. "I thought the wee rabbit was already on the ship."

MacKenna looked disgusted. "He's been on the ship twice now and keeps escapin'. Thunder and Zeus are already sleepin' in the hold."

"Damned nuisance, the lot of them," Thomas said.

Fia started to retort, but then Robert MacQuarrie strode up, his lace-bedecked appearance causing MacKenna to eye him with distaste. Though Fia didn't know the fashion at court, she had the impression she was seeing the best of it right here.

He swept a bow, his blue eyes merry, his teeth flashing white in his trim black beard. "Robert MacQuarrie, Viscount Montley, at your service."

Fia dipped a curtsy. "Lady Fia Mac—" She flushed and cast a glance at Thomas, who didn't seem to notice.

"Oh, I know your name, Lady Rotherwood," Montley said gallantly, hooking his thumbs in the wide, silver-worked black leather belt that set off his plum-colored velvet doublet and silver-edged short cape. "Pray tell, where *did* you procure such a fine rabbit?"

Fia had to smile. For all of the horrible tales she'd heard about Robert MacQuarrie, he didn't *look* like a coward. Indeed, the boldness and merriment in his blue eyes warmed her heart.

She held the rabbit aloft so he could see the animal better. "Lord Thomas came from Mull. He's an islander."

"Lord Thomas?" Montley asked, a quiver of laughter in his voice.

"Aye. I named him after—" Fia inclined her head toward Thomas. "He saved the poor rabbit, you know."

Montley turned an incredulous stare on his friend. "*You* saved a *rabbit*?"

"Mind yourself, Montley." Thomas took Fia's arm and firmly marched her up the long, wide plank that led onto the ship, leaving Robert to assist Mary.

"Yes, but . . . a *rabbit*?" Montley called after him.

But Thomas was already boarding the ship, where he was greeted by a welcoming cry from the crew.

The feel of the ship beneath her boots helped to lift Fia's spirits. *Finally, I go to London!*

She stood to one side, watching as Thomas, looking dashing despite his ill-fitting clothing, set the crew to putting the ship to sea.

Mary took the rabbit and headed belowdecks to their quarters to help Angus in storing their numerous trunks, Montley following to offer his assistance.

The wind rose as Thomas stood on the foredeck, his feet planted wide, his arms crossed over his chest as he roared instructions at his men. There was a flurry of movement as the ropes holding them to shore were removed and coiled back on deck.

Fia's heart swelled as the ship began to move out to sea. The great sails unfurled as the wind ruffled Thomas's hair and swished Fia's skirts about her legs. The sails caught the wind, snapping loudly as the billowing canvas filled, and the ship strained eagerly toward the sea.

It was glorious. Fia leaned against the railing, the salty windy blowing her hair and streaming over her, calming the beat of her heart. The island faded behind them, a misty green slash in a deep blue ocean as the ship sped along. She turned and met Thomas's gaze, and offered a tentative smile.

He almost returned it, but then turned away and resumed shouting orders to his men.

Fia turned back toward the sea. She would find a way to reach this obstinate man she'd been forced to wed. Perhaps with time, they could at least develop a friendship.

She couldn't help but be glad she was married to

Thomas and not Malcolm. Thomas had potential. He didn't yet possess the noble qualities of the heroes of her plays, but who knew what might happen?

Meanwhile, her entire life stretched before her! A sudden grin lit her face and she lifted it to the wind and sun, letting the roll of the ship raise her spirits.

Chapter Ten

The Glorianna
Sailing for London from the Isle of Mull
May 10, 1567

I'll be a loose-limbed Greek, Cap'n! Is that salted pig?" The first mate, Henry Simmons, peered into the open barrel.

Thomas glanced up from the supply list. "'Tis a whole side of pork." Unfortunately for Thomas's wishes to make haste to London, the ship had needed supplies, so they'd gone straight to the closest safe harbor on English soil. Simmons was a force to be reckoned with and he'd managed to complete the task in a little under three hours.

Now, with the hold freshly stocked, and the winds lifting, they were under way once again. If the weather held, they'd be in London in three weeks' time, maybe less.

Thomas sent a quick glance at the ladder down to the hold. The lower deck held the deckhands and the ship's storage; it was also the home of Fia's nag and her ragged dog. The upper level held the officers' cabins, the galley, and an area for the crew to eat in. And now it also held one other item of interest—Fia.

Thomas tried not to think about it, but as darkness fell

it was becoming more and more difficult *not* to. She was his now. His for the taking, as was a husband's right. But if he did so, that would make their marriage permanent. There was still a possibility that he could enlist Queen Elizabeth to set the marriage aside if Fia remained a maid.

The first mate began issuing orders to a sailor about the repair of a sail stored in the hold, and Thomas took the opportunity to step away and enjoy the beauty of the day. He faced out to sea and leaned back against the mast, a feeling of deep satisfaction slowly rising through him. Whatever troubles the future held, he was once again back on ship and in charge of his own destiny. For now, Fia was safe belowdecks, and Scotland was merely a place of memories. He could almost feel the fetters dropping off as the wind filled the sails and carried him home.

His relief was overshadowed by the fact that he'd failed in his mission. *Damme, I wish I'd managed to keep hold of that letter. Walsingham will be disappointed.*

Watkins, a lanky, red-haired bos'n's mate, scrambled to the deck. "Cap'n, I bring ye word from Lord Montley. He says to tell ye that now we're under way, he's going to allow the women from their cabin." The freckled brow puckered. "Least, I think that's what he was sayin'. 'Tis hard to tell."

Simmons snorted. "Montley is a coxcomb. He was the devil of a trial to abide on the way here."

"Full of spirits, was he?" Thomas asked.

"He walked about spoutin' enough poetry to sicken a man." Simmons spat over the rail.

Thomas laughed.

Simmons cast a sardonic glance at Watkins. "Don't mind the cap'n. He's been sort of giddy since he took hisself a wife. Sad that we're cursed now, but I suppose it can't be helped."

"Simmons, that's the biggest untruth I've ever heard from you. 'Tis a foolish myth."

"Cap'n, everyone knows women on board ship is bad luck, and a Scottish wench— "

"Wench?" Thomas asked softly.

Simmons flushed. "Lady, I mean. A Scottish lady is twice the ill luck of an English one."

Thomas shot a hard look at his first mate. "I'll not have it said that having either the countess or her maid aboard is ill luck. If I hear such again, that man will find himself keelhauled."

Simmons swallowed noisily. "Aye, Cap'n. Watkins, tell the men."

Watkins nodded and scurried off, looking a bit pale.

Thomas usually preferred to captain through respect rather than fear, but he also knew the way of the uneducated and highly superstitious crew. If they came to believe Fia was a danger, they'd blame her for every mishap that occurred—and there were plenty of mishaps to be had on the wet, slippery deck of a ship crisscrossed with ropes and brass rings, men running hither and yon and climbing upon the rigging in their bare feet.

Simmons rubbed his neck sheepishly. "Cap'n, I hope ye know I didna mean to say anythin' ill toward yer lady."

"I know. But such loose talk can break down the order on ship." Before the first mate could apologize again, Thomas said, "Tell me something of more interest: how did Lord Montley come to be upon my ship? I heard that you fetched him yourself."

"Aye, Cap'n. When ye didna return as planned, I knew we'd a situation on hand and that lace-ruffed arse was the closest thing to an Englishman I was like to find so far north." Simmons added grudgingly, "The man's a sissified braggart, but he do know his way around both ship and sword. The man can handle both gale and attack; few cap'ns other than yerself can say that."

"He'll be moved to tears by such a declaration."

Simmons flushed. "Now, Cap'n, don't ye be repeatin' what I said! He'll come spoutin' some nonsense at me, and I'll be right back to not likin' him again."

Thomas chuckled. "Your secret is safe with me. Well done, Simmons. He may be of use yet. Come, let me set the course; then I'll inspect the rigging." He consulted with Simmons, then left the wheel.

The weather was cool and clear, perfect for sailing, and for just one moment, he wanted to think about nothing but the pleasure of being off that cursed isle.

Rumor would spread that the famed Wentworth luck had taken a beating. Thomas knew it wasn't really luck that had supported his family for so many successful decades, but hard work and careful planning. Somehow, he'd allowed his desire to assist Walsingham in protecting the queen to interfere with his usual calm thinking and strong common sense. He should never have ventured onto the island without some assistance.

It was odd. He could usually count on Lord Walsingham's advice on covert missions, but this time Walsingham's spies had failed to detect a number of things.

Thomas leaned against the railing that lined the high deck, the waning sun warming his face. The sea jauntily rolled along, the sun dancing across the glistening water.

Riding high and tight, the ship cut through the white-topped waves.

He wondered what Fia thought of the *Glorianna*. Her obvious delight at being at sea had lightened his mood. She might not have been the bride of his choosing, but at least she understood the joy of a sailing ship.

She was a rare one for adventure, which he found surprisingly appealing. He loved a good adventure, too, which was why he continued to assist Walsingham, but one did not marry a woman who yearned for adventure. One married a woman who yearned for hearth and home and an orderly house. That was the sort of woman he planned to make his countess, once he'd gotten his current predicament resolved. He wouldn't call this a marriage—not something done under the shadow of a sword.

Queen Elizabeth would take it very unkindly that one of her subjects had been forced to the altar in such a manner. With Walsingham's support, Thomas was certain an annulment could be arranged. That one thought kept him calm.

All he had to do was deliver Fia to London still a maiden. His gaze returned to the ladder leading down to the hold, and he remembered the feel of her against him, the taste of her. Temptation always tasted better when denied, he told himself wryly.

Still, there was no reason not to be a welcoming host. He should look in on her and her maid and see if they were well settled. The sea was rougher now, and it was possible she might not be feeling well.

Thomas made his way down the ladder. Robert was probably entertaining Fia with some improbable tale, flirting outrageously and noting how the soft wool of Fia's gown outlined her lush body—

Grinding his teeth, Thomas hurried his steps. Serviceable wool was *not* seductive, though he'd have been lying if he didn't admit that on Fia, wool took on qualities he'd never thought it could.

Perhaps it wasn't ordinary wool, but a special Scottish weave that was impossible for an English loom to create. The wool hugged and molded every delectable curve with a loving familiarity that made a man's mouth water.

And now that he considered it, the thinness of her gowns drew attention to her shocking lack of underskirts. He would bet his finest horse that she purposefully refused to wear proper clothing in order to vex him.

He strode down the passageway, his steps determined. Once he had Fia in London, he would see to it that she possessed more petticoats than the queen. He would purchase them in green, blue, red, purple—every color imaginable. She would have an entire wardrobe devoted just to the underskirts he would buy her—and she would wear them.

He reached Fia's cabin and paused to listen at the door, expecting Robert's deep voice.

All was silent; no voices could be heard.

They must have retired, exhausted from the events of the last few days. He was exhausted, too. Yawning mightily, Thomas turned toward his own cabin, unlacing his shirt. A refreshing wash and the familiarity of his own bunk called to him. He reached his cabin, flung open the door—and came face-to-face with *wool*.

"Och, now," came Fia's rich voice as she muttered to herself from where she was bent over the edge of one of her trunks, her feet almost off the ground, her rounded ass covered with that damnably fine wool. "Where did I put that box? I know 'twas in here when we left." She struggled to reach deeper into the trunk, her ass wiggling with her efforts.

An immediate onslaught of hot, burning lust hit Thomas.

"What in the hell are you doing?" he snapped.

Fia jerked upright, her head hitting the trunk lid. "Ow!" The rabbit scampered from behind the trunk and began to race wildly around the room, skidding under the bed. Zeus announced his presence on that very bed by emitting a low growl.

Thomas scowled at the dog, who showed his scraggly teeth in a weak snarl. "Bloody hell! Get that mangy hound off my blankets!"

Fia, flushed and breathless, turned to the bed. "Zeus, come!"

The dog slowly ambled to his feet, then came to stand at the edge of the bed, swaying back and forth as he eyed with misgiving the jump to the floor.

"Oh, for the love of—" Thomas strode to the bed, scooped up the dog, and placed him on the floor. *"Out!"*

Zeus wagged his tail, shuffled off to a corner, and plopped down with a huge sigh.

Fia noted how Thomas's gaze narrowed on the dog, and she hurried to distract him. "I'll never, *ever* find it," she announced loudly.

Thomas's gaze immediately turned her way. "Find what?"

"My writing desk. I think 'tis in this trunk." She peeped at him through her lashes and noticed the weary lines around his eyes. *Poor man, he must be as tired as I am. It's been an eventful week.*

"Shall I look in the trunk for you?" he asked courteously. "I'm a bit taller and it might help."

Her heart flooded with warmth. "Yes, please."

He pushed the trunk lid higher and began to search through it, glancing at her as he did so. "Forgive me if I startled you upon entering the cabin. I didn't expect to see you here; you were to be placed with Mary in the cabin next door."

"But Lord Montley said I was to stay here."

"He did, did he?" Thomas said grimly. "Montley's sense of humor is odd."

Fia realized she should have known. "He's quite charming, as well. That always bodes ill when it's paired with a sense of humor."

Thomas's lips quirked and she felt a stab of longing to feel those lips on hers once more.

"I don't see your writing desk in this trunk. Are you certain this is the right one?"

"No," she answered truthfully. "I thought 'twas so, but I'm not certain. If 'tis not in these two, then it could be in some of the trunks in the hold."

Thomas closed the first trunk and opened the other one. "How many are there?"

"Too many. Duncan was far too generous; I don't even know where he found some of these treasures. There are lengths of silks and brocades, spools and spools of silver and gold thread, and boxes of jeweled pomanders and necklets, bracelets and rings. I feel as if I'm a princess."

"'Tis obvious he cares about you very much."

She smiled almost shyly. "He raised me since I was a child, when my parents died of smallpox."

"He was certainly generous with your bride clothes."

"Yes." She looked at the large trunks. "Not all of them would fit in the smaller cabin, so these two were stowed here. Do you wish them moved to the hold?"

"They may stay here. We can slide them against the far wall and . . ." He continued on, telling her how he'd secure them to the rings bolted to the cabin walls.

Fia tried to listen, but her mind was elsewhere. She'd been imagining what Thomas might be like away from Duncan's ominous presence, once he wasn't being held prisoner, beaten, or having horses fall upon him. She'd imagined that he would be relaxed, talkative, perhaps even charming. More like Lord Montley.

She eyed her husband. He was more at ease now but talkative? Nay. He answered questions, explained things, but no more. Now that his explanation about her trunks was over, he merely continued his search for her writing desk.

"I don't see it in here," Thomas finally said.

Partially bent over the trunk, he was at eye level with her. Dark, rich brown, flecked with amber lights, his eyes made her feel warm and shivery at the same time. *No man should have such beautiful—*

"Are you well?" His brows quirked down.

Fia realized that she was holding a bolt of velvet to her like a shield. Heat rose in her cheeks, and she tossed it back into the trunk. It had been a long day, and she was stretched as taut as a bowstring. "I don't need the writing desk this very moment. I—I'll just take Zeus and my wee rabbit to my own cabin."

He straightened, rubbing his back. "That dog belongs in the hold with Thunder. There's hay there and he'll be warm enough."

"Perhaps."

"You don't agree?"

"No." Fia walked past him and pulled a lawn night rail from the trunk, tossing it over her arm. "But I'm too weary to argue."

Thomas leaned against the bedpost and crossed his arms over his broad chest, and Fia's attention was caught by the ripple of muscles under his shirt.

Her mouth went dry. *This is my husband.* The thought sang through her mind and washed away some of her tiredness. Why *shouldn't* she look at his fine chest? He belonged to her now.

She eyed him more boldly. His white shirt was unlaced all the way to his breeches, and she was fascinated by the crisp curls of black hair that were sprinkled over his broad chest and then narrowed to a tantalizing trail that pointed straight to his belt. Her breath quickened in her throat.

"Fia?"

Fia couldn't look away from that muscular chest or those beckoning curls. How would they feel beneath her fingertips? Would they feel crisp or soft? Would they be warmed by his skin? Would she?

"Perhaps I should remove my shirt?" Amusement laced his deep voice and finally drew her gaze to his face.

His look of arrogant satisfaction told her that he knew what she'd been thinking as clearly as if she'd spoken every thought aloud. Her face heated and she stammered, "Y— your cabin is quite large." It was a stupid comment but all she could manage at the moment.

His lips quirked. "Are you certain you're referring to my cabin, and not my—"

"*Nay!*" Her cheeks burned even more, though she

couldn't help but smile a wee bit. "I meant exactly what I said. Your *cabin*."

He looked around as if regarding it for the first time. "'Tis a grand one, for this is my home when I'm away for months at a time."

"Och, that must be lonely for you."

"No, 'tis far too exciting to be lonely." His grin turned wolfish. "When I go to sea, 'tis to fetch things for Her Majesty."

"Fetch what sorts of things?"

"Spanish galleons loaded with gold and silver, French merchant ships returning from China with silks and teas, Dutch ships loaded with furs and spices." His eyes crinkled in the most attractive way. "'Tis amazing what you can find at sea."

She leaned forward, mesmerized. "You're a *pirate*?" It seemed so at odds with his proper demeanor, and she realized how little she knew about him.

"Nay, my lady. I'm a *privateer*, my ventures condoned by the queen's decree and perfectly legitimate. Pirates are outlaws."

"King Philip might disagree with that."

Thomas chuckled. "So he might. But since his own ships do the same, it matters not."

She shook her head. "You enjoy a dangerous game."

His warm brown eyes gleamed. "Aye. My family is known for its luck, and I like to test it."

"My family is known for having a short temper, as Duncan has already proven."

Thomas's amusement faded. "So he has." He paused a moment, then said in a far more serious tone, "Fia, I know you're tired, for neither of us had any sleep last night, but we should speak about our circumstances while we have the opportunity."

Apprehension caught her, but she managed to say, "Aye?" in a steady voice.

He paused, as if choosing his words with care. "I think you will agree that this marriage cannot stand."

Her heart sank, though she forced her lips to smile. Somehow, in her imaginations of their first conversation as man and wife, she hadn't thought of his explaining why they shouldn't be.

But he was right, of course. The marriage couldn't stand. If not because of the complications it could cause, then because of the determination she saw in Thomas's gaze.

She refused to be an unwanted wife. "Of course we cannot allow this union to stand."

That's what she wanted, wasn't it? A life without the fettering bonds of a husband. Still, she was stung by the flicker of relief on his face.

"As soon as we reach London, I will ask Walsingham to approach the queen for permission to seek an annulment."

Hearing him say it aloud pinched her pride, and in some inexplicable way, she felt . . . rejected. Hurt. Dismissed.

She tossed her head. "I wish we could undo the marriage before then. I dislike waiting so long."

His smile faded. "It will take but three weeks, perhaps less, to reach London."

"Three *weeks*?" Three weeks of being on ship with this man, finding out more things about him that fascinated her? Like that he had a streak that craved excitement just as she did? That he had a gentle sense of humor? That his smile crinkled his whiskey brown eyes and made her stomach do the oddest flips? She didn't know if she could maintain her spirits being around Thomas for such a length of time, only to give him up when they reached shore.

But I don't want a husband! I've told Duncan so a thousand times before, only . . . somehow, now that I have this one, I don't wish him to go away. I want— She bit her lip, suddenly beyond exhausted. *I don't know what I want.*

Thomas's frown deepened. "Trust me, my lady, I am in as much of a hurry as you."

She doubted it but managed a stiff nod. "Good."

His jaw tightened. "I will do my best to make our trip quicker. You are not the only one anxious to end this farce."

She had to look down to keep him from seeing the sudden tears his words had caused. *What's wrong with me? Isn't this what I want?*

Fia blinked away the tears before she shrugged and said, "Aye, 'tis a pity we were forced to wed, but there's no discouraging Duncan. Once he sets his mind to a path, he's like a great rock, rolling over everything and everybody."

"I noticed." Thomas's gaze narrowed on her and he said in a silken voice, "I find it oddly convenient that your cousin caught us not once but twice, and both times in most compromising positions. I can't help but think 'twas a bit *too* convenient."

She stiffened, snapping her gaze to his. "Are you accusing me of trapping you into this marriage? For 'twas *you*, Lord Lackwit, who fell from a window whilst trying to break into the castle. I had no notion you were arriving."

"Perhaps."

"There is no 'perhaps' about it. 'Twas also *you* who brought such a silly mount that was scared by a poor mite of a dog with no teeth. Had you brought a proper mount, no one would have prevented your departure."

His face reddened. "The horse might have been high-strung, but he was also fast."

"I am also not the one who decided to run through the castle with my hose falling about my ankles. I hear not coincidences but the decisions of a fool!"

He shoved himself from the bedpost, his mouth pressed into a forbidding line. "I wouldn't have been running at all had you not stolen my damned boots!"

"Look, Sassenach, I wouldn't have taken your boots except you were threatening to leave without us!"

"I'm not 'Sassenach'; I am Thomas Wentworth, Earl of Rotherwood, and you'd do well to remember that."

She plopped her hands on her hips. "Whatever your name, you have no right to suggest that your misfortunes were caused by anything more than your own behavior. You're fortunate that I calmed my cousin when he was calling for your head!"

"I never asked for your help!"

Fia's shoulders tightened and she stomped forward to jab a finger into his chest. "You dolt, if it hadn't been for me, your body would now be floating out to sea with fish nibbling your toes!"

His eyes flashed. "If you'd wished it, you could have convinced your cousin to free me without this marriage. Not once did you suggest such a thing."

"Which shows how little you know Scottish ways. My cousin is laird first and foremost. You're fortunate he didn't determine that your presence was dangerous to the clan, or there would have been nothing I could have done to save you."

"Really?" he jeered. "You certainly were quick enough to agree to the ceremony."

"Fool! Duncan was determined that I wed, and soon. If it hadn't been you, I would have had to marry—" She stopped, her face heating.

"Exactly," Thomas said in a quiet voice that was more condemning than any shout. "But for me, you would have wed Malcolm Davies."

Even to Fia's ears, Thomas's reasoning sounded damning.

He continued, his voice deep and even. "You and I both know that clan Davies would have never allowed you to go to London. You had plenty of reasons to spoil those plans by presenting another suitor, no matter how unwilling he was."

"I would never do such a thing!" Fia's eyes stung with unshed tears. "With you or without you, London is my destiny."

"London may well be your destiny, my lady—but I am not."

Fia's pride was stung. "Lord Rotherwood, allow me to explain something. I never thought you were my destiny, which is why I'll be *happy* to get an annulment the second our feet touch London soil."

The events of the day suddenly seemed more than she could bear. She'd never felt so lonely in all her life, and the bite of it filled her throat with a lump the size of a pillow.

She lifted her chin. *Let Thomas rant and rail. Let him decry our marriage and wish to be free of it. I will not cry in front of him.* "I am done here. I will retire to my cabin now, if you'll show me the way."

For a long moment, he merely scowled at her, but then he rubbed his chin, his expression softening. "I'faith, Fia, don't look so. I'm sorry if I've allowed my temper to get the best of me, but this marriage cannot—"

"I agree. We will do what we can to get an annulment and we'll both be the happier for it. How do we do that?"

He hesitated. "I will ask Lord Walsingham to approach the queen."

"And?"

His face reddened. "We cannot—" He looked as if he could not say the word.

She frowned. "We cannot what?"

His gaze met hers, and he turned an even deeper red. "You know what I mean but cannot say."

She shook her head uncomprehendingly.

"You must be a maid," he burst out.

"Ah. Of course."

"Which means you must be willing to vow it before the queen."

Ah! So he needed her cooperation, did he? He might *try* to toss her out like a discarded shoe, but when the time came to leave, it would be on *her* terms. *Good.*

"Which leaves us with one matter to address," she said.

"Which is?"

"Once we are no longer married, I do not wish to return to Scotland. London is where I have always wished to be."

His gaze grew suspicious. "So?"

"So I will need a sponsor for my plays."

He shrugged. "*I* will sponsor your plays."

"Nay. I wish someone else to do it."

His brows snapped down. "Why?"

Fia wished his eyes were warm with laughter, as they'd been a few minutes ago. More than that, she wished that the two of them were back beside the fire that first night, before Duncan found them. Thomas had kissed her then, in a way that had left her remembering that moment over and over. What she wouldn't give to feel his arms about her now.

God's wounds, what is wrong with me?

She'd always yearned to be in love, but only with someone who enjoyed life as she did, someone who loved theater and animals, the thrill of a brisk canter through the moors, and the joy of a good book. These simple things made up her life. Thomas was not that man.

"Fia, answer. Why can't I sponsor your plays?"

Because I want a sponsor who believes in them and me. She shrugged. "'Twould cast suspicion if we continued to have a connection after the annulment." She straightened to her full height. "The truth is, I'd prefer to find a more *artistic* sponsor. One who understands the theater."

"But I—"

"Lord Montley said that you don't enjoy the theater at all. Not even a little." She fixed her gaze on him. "Do you?"

He shifted awkwardly from one foot to the other. "I occasionally attend a play."

"Don't count the ones that are performed at court; you're forced to attend those."

He grimaced. "Very well, I don't often attend the theater."

"Then you will not do."

"But I—"

"When you look for a sponsor for my plays, not only must he be well funded and trustworthy, but he must possess an artistic nature. Montley mentioned several possibilities: Lord Leicester, Lord Essex—"

"Essex? That philanderer?"

"I didn't ask for moral recommendations, so I don't know. Let's see, also Lord Steeleton, Lord Montjoy—"

"Montjoy!" Thomas snapped the name as if it burned his tongue. "He's a lecherous old man who has twelve by-blows from twelve different maidservants."

"*I* am not a maidservant and would never allow someone to treat me that way."

"You allowed me to kiss you in the forest."

Fia's face heated. "That was different."

"Why?"

For an instant, he thought he caught a glimpse of an answer in her remarkable eyes, but then she lowered her lashes and said in a cool tone, "I had no intention of ever seeing you again after that night, so what was the harm? Besides, I didn't consider you as a potential sponsor, so there's no comparison."

"Yes, you did. I promised to sponsor you and you thought it was for your plays and you *kissed* me." He still warmed to think of that kiss. Had her cousin not arrived when he did—

She waved her hand through the air. "Och, do not make more of a mere kiss than there was, Sassenach. We Scots are simply a passionate people."

Thomas found that he couldn't swallow. How could he allow a woman so full of passion that she kissed strangers on a whim loose upon the world? And what would happen when he found a patron for her plays and she became grateful to the wretch, or simply found she enjoyed his presence? Would she kiss *him*, too?

Thomas's jaw ached, and his chest felt like an iron band had tightened around it. He gazed down into Fia's fathomless eyes and wondered why he felt such a strange hollowness at the thought of her kissing another man. All he wanted was his freedom . . . didn't he?

But no. If he was honest, he wanted more than that. He wanted more of Fia—but not at such a price. She was unlike any woman he'd ever met. She tantalized and teased without the least knowledge, and that, added to her beauty and wit, intrigued him more than any powdered and perfumed court beauty ever had.

But it wouldn't last; passion never did. Even his mother, who'd run away for love, had eventually been thrown aside by her new lover. Love—passion—didn't last.

Duty was all one could count upon, all one needed. And duty had nothing to do with the lush woman who stood before him, her chin raised in challenge, her mouth begging to be tasted.

"Fine," he said harshly, irritated at his reaction to her impudence and spirit. "I'll find you a damned sponsor for your plays, and we'll have our annulment."

She flashed him a smile. "Excellent."

Thomas found himself looking at her full bottom lip, and suddenly the air grew thick with desire. It was all he could do to keep from reaching for her, holding her against him, sinking into her softness.

She must have felt the change, too, for her breath quickened, her lips parted, her skin flushed. He could see where her heartbeat pulsed in her slender neck, and his gaze traveling down to her full breasts where they were so warmly displayed by her wool gown. *God bless Scottish wool. Thin Scottish wool. Soft Scottish wool.*

And then somehow he was no longer looking at that wool but feeling it. That wool filled his hands as he hauled her against him, capturing her mouth with his. She melted into his arms, her sweet curves pressed to his.

Thomas ran his hands down her sides to the gentle

swell of her hips, and then on to cup her ass, her gown clinging to his fingers.

She gasped against his mouth, murmuring "Och, Sassenach!" in such a sweet, husky voice that his passions fanned into a blazing flame.

He held her tightly, plundering her mouth as ruthlessly as he plundered Spanish galleons. Fia eagerly accepted his embraces, sliding her hands over him in return, seeking and touching until he couldn't think or breathe.

He slipped a hand through her long hair and her curls clung to his fingers like silken kisses. God's blood, she was as sweet as fresh snow, yet warmer than a summer day. He slipped both hands around her firm, delectable ass and lifted her against him. To his bemused delight, she parted her legs and clung to him, her skirts riding up to her thighs.

He couldn't take her. *Could not.* The knowledge made the kiss wilder, the embrace more daring. Desire flared fiercely through Thomas, filling his sails with a hot gale so suddenly, he feared he might capsize. He knew he needed to stop the embrace, but his mind was no longer functioning beyond the immediate sensations that crashed over him.

Fia grasped at his shirt, her legs clutching him tightly, as desperate as he was. He slipped his hands from her ass to her thighs and walked the two steps to the wall, pressing her against it. She arched into him, squirming with desire.

It was almost more than he could bear. He shifted her until his turgid cock rubbed between her legs. His breeches and her chemise were the only barriers, the only protection, but it was enough.

Though Thomas ached with the need for her, for the

taste of her, for the feel of her, he knew this was as far as they could go. As far as they dared to—

The door flew open. "Thomas, Simmons says the course to—" Robert's voice stopped short.

Fia's eyes shot open, and she looked over Thomas's shoulder with a horrified gasp.

Damn you, Montley!

Her face red, Fia squirmed free of Thomas's embrace, frantically trying to pull down her gown.

Thomas turned to glare at their intruder, but all he faced was an open door. Montley was gone. Left boiling with desire, his cock achingly erect, his heart still thundering in his chest, Thomas yearned to punch his friend's face.

An adorably mussed and red-faced Fia had gathered her rabbit and was trying to pull her snoring dog to its feet. "I-I really must go—Zeus, wake up! I'll just return to my cabin and—blast it, Zeus, get *up*!"

A twinge of conscience caught Thomas. "Fia, I'm sorry Montley—he acts as if this is his ship. Still, this is my fault. I shouldn't have imposed upon you."

"Imposed? I'm as much to blame as you."

He frowned, suddenly realizing that her cheeks weren't rosy from embarrassment. Instead, they appeared sunburned, as if . . . He lifted a hand to his chin, which was rough with stubble from the days inside Duncan's castle. "Damn it! Fia, I fear that my whiskers have scraped your skin. I'm sorry."

She touched her cheek and winced. "Whiskers will do that?"

"Aye, they can."

She is such an innocent, he told himself fiercely. *But she won't be if I keep finding her alone.* "I must admit something, Fia. I have trouble resisting you."

She sent him a surprised look. After a moment, she said quietly, "And I have trouble resisting you."

"That bodes ill for our decision to remain chaste. For the safety of our plans, we should make sure Mary is present whenever we meet."

"I can do that."

He turned toward the door. "I'm needed on deck now, so I'll leave you."

"I—yes. Thank you." She nodded, her motions jerky, her gaze averted.

A million words crowded to Thomas's lips, but not a single coherent sentence. With one last glance, he turned and left, leaving the door open behind him.

Scowling, he strode down the passageway to the ladder. *Damme, how did I allow myself to lose control in such a way?*

The wind whipped across him as he reached the deck, cooling his ardor even more and calming his thundering heart. He began to pace the length of the ship, hands clasped behind his back, the wind whipping his hair as he locked gazes with the white-crested sea and wrestled with his thoughts.

There was something about Fia MacLean that befuddled him. She was such an intriguing mixture of innocence and sensuality, guile and beguilement. And he could not be in the same room with her without yearning to taste her.

He thought of their conversation in his cabin and had to shake his head. She was a cheeky wench, he'd give her that. She'd accepted his demand for an annulment but had added the price of finding her a sponsor. She was never at a loss for words, and he'd do well to remember that.

She was from a different world than his. She didn't care or know that his family name was tied to the ancient Norman conquerors or that he was from one of the purest bloodlines in England. All she cared about was seeing her plays upon the stage.

Oddly enough, after working so many years to maintain and build his reputation, it was intriguing to find someone who didn't value it at all. And if that was the case, then her interest in him wasn't caused by his position or wealth, but in him as a man. That, too, was unique.

Shaking his head, he paced faster, ignoring the sideglances from the men as they went about their work, the cool air calming him. Over and over, he relived the scene in his cabin, lingering over the new memories: the scent of her hair and how it had clung to his hands; the sweet taste of her skin beneath his lips; the way her voice had deepened and grown husky as passion had overtaken her, too.

Then he remembered her embarrassed air when he'd left, and he winced. Whatever her flaws, she hadn't intentionally led him into temptation. He'd done that all by himself.

She needed to know that she was safe upon this ship and that he'd never again cross the boundaries of good behavior. He owed it to his own good name as captain of the *Glorianna*. *It's what I'd do for any woman aboard ship, not just Fia.*

He gazed at the ladder that led below deck. He should reassure her of his intentions, yet that would mean facing her again, and he wasn't certain he could. Not while his body still ached for the feel of her.

A shiver ripped through him at the memory of her strong legs gripping his hips. His body ached anew, and he had to stifle a groan. *Damn it all, but she's too sensual for a wife. As a mistress, though . . .*

He gripped the railing and stared unseeingly out to sea. *How can I even think such a thing? She is an innocent. Am I like my mother, so governed by primal urges that I cannot even perform my duty to my family and queen?*

Scowling, Thomas pushed himself from the railing and resumed pacing, vowing to never again succumb to temptation, no matter how often she smiled. No matter what it took.

Chapter Eleven

The door slammed, startling Robert, whose whiskey sloshed onto the table.

"Where in hell have you been hiding, you cur?" Thomas snapped.

Robert winced and took a delicate sip of his whiskey. "Pray speak quietly, for I have a tender ear whenever I venture upon the sea."

Thomas threw himself into a chair, his face as dark as a thundercloud. "I'll see that more than your ears are tender if you don't explain why you put Fia in my cabin."

"I was being chivalrous. There are few places on the ship to house guests, and your cabin seemed the most suitable to a lady. Besides, she *is* your wife." He frowned at the whiskey that had spilled; he still had a Scotsman's dislike of wasting good drink. 'Twas but one of the many inherited traits he seemed unable to remove, try though he might.

"She will not be my wife for long."

Robert sat up straighter. "What's this? Do you plan a murder? Shall I help you toss the body from the side of the ship? Before you carry out your nefarious plan, be sure to learn Lady Fia's handwriting. Her painfully expressive cousin is expecting a letter every week and if he doesn't get it, he will have no hesitation in marching to London to fetch it."

"I am not afraid of Duncan MacLean."

"You should be. In fact, you're fortunate he didn't realize why you were attempting to crawl into his castle."

"Oh, he realized it soon enough. I found the missive without problem, but then MacLean found me and I awoke unlettered."

"Did he say aught?"

"Nay, but I'm certain he knew." Thomas frowned. Though he and MacLean had never spoken of it, the laird's smirk had told its own story.

"So you risked life and limb for naught." Robert's jaw tightened; his gaze flickered over Thomas. "When I saw you on shore so bloodied and beaten, I was almost ready to kill him. Tell me of this letter you came to fetch."

"Walsingham wanted the missive and knew 'twas in MacLean's desk in a hidden compartment." Thomas added darkly, "That's *one* thing the arse bothered to tell me. He certainly never mentioned MacLean had a lovely cousin that he was guarding like a prize jewel."

"I wonder why Walsingham didn't mention Fia? The castle was more heavily fortified because she was there; MacLean would not leave her unprotected."

Thomas frowned. "That's true." He'd had much the same thought over the last week. Why *hadn't* Walsingham told him about Fia? It was unfathomable that Walsingham would miss a major development like that.

In fact, the man had said that with MacLean gone,

none but a few elderly servants would be at the castle. "Something happened, but I don't know what." Thomas shook his head. "Anyway, as I was saying, I had that damned letter in my possession. I wish I'd made it to the ship with it."

"'Tis a miracle you managed to escape alive. You are the luckiest bastard I ever met."

"No, I'm not. I lost the letter, and I wonder if 'twas worth a wife."

"*I* wonder that you follow Walsingham's commands like a puppet. He uses you most hard and yet you care not."

"He does no such thing," Thomas said, annoyance clear in his tone. "He offers me adventures, excitement, and ways to set the Wentworth name with the queen."

"He places you in danger every chance he gets." Robert's blue eyes blazed. "Walsingham is a maggot on the underbelly of the earth, yet you are determined to think well of him."

"Walsingham has done more for England than you admit. One day, you will understand."

Robert had to bite his tongue to keep silent. It would do no good to rail against the minister. In the dark days after the death of Thomas's father, Walsingham had slipped into Thomas's good graces. As a new earl, Thomas had been grateful for the older man's quiet support. Robert had to admit that Walsingham had been an invaluable source of advice to Thomas during those hectic and sad days when Thomas had struggled to set his father's estates in order. During those weeks, he and Walsingham had forged a deep bond that now often put Thomas in grave danger.

Thomas didn't shy from that danger, for he'd been raised

to put duty above all else. But that Walsingham would ask so many dangerous tasks from a man he professed to care about did not ring true with Robert.

No, Walsingham was the sort of man to find one's weakness and play to it—all the way to the gory end, if it suited his purposes.

Robert took a sip of whiskey to wash away the bitter taste of his thoughts "Speaking of monsters, have you seen the creature your lady wife has secured in the hold? I think 'tis a horse, though I wouldn't swear it." He leaned across the table for another mug, poured a stately measure of whiskey into it, and slid it across the table to Thomas.

"Aye, I've seen it." Thomas took a sip of the whiskey. "And it's seen me."

Robert shuddered. "The men were talking of it, so I went to have a peek and . . ." He lifted his arm and a straggle of lace drooped from his sleeve. "It tried to eat me!"

"You're fortunate it didn't get your arm."

Robert smoothed his sleeve. "I'd rather have given up a finger than my lace. 'Tis Italian, you know."

Thomas grunted.

Robert regarded him for a moment. "Well? Tell me by what foul manner you plan on ridding yourself of your lovely wife. Shall it be by knife? Sword? Pistol? Poison?"

"No, we are to get an annulment from Queen Elizabeth. I was forced at sword's end to wed the chit, and the queen won't enjoy hearing how one of her own was so cruelly abused. With Walsingham's help, she will agree to set the marriage aside."

"And what of Fia? She will have to agree to the petition as well."

"She agrees it must be done."

Robert caught a hint of sharpness in his friend's voice. "Oho! The web tangles! She is glad to be rid of you!"

Thomas gazed at him with a considering look. "As usual, you act the virgin, yet there is something of the harlot in your gestures."

Robert's grin was swift. "A minor talent. I have others."

Thomas knew better than to argue with this piece of impertinence. For all his foppish ways, Robert MacQuarrie was the most gifted swordsman and navigator of any man Thomas had ever met. He sighed and rubbed his chin, wincing when he touched a lingering bruise.

Robert regarded him over the lip of his mug. "You certainly took a beating at MacLean's hands."

Thomas tossed down the whiskey, welcoming its burning warmth. "It could have been worse. I was to be consigned to the dungeons, but Fia intervened."

"She saved you? Then 'tis love. What other reason would she have to go against her own kith and kin?"

Thomas frowned. "Cease your jesting."

"'Twas no jest," protested Robert. "Now that I think on it, you have all the symptoms of being in love, as does she. Do you find Lady Fia attractive?"

"She's a beautiful woman. Every man on this ship would agree to that."

"Ah, but no other man on this ship is feeling the cut of jealousy."

"Jealousy? When have I been jealous?"

"When have you not been? You glare at everyone when she is about, including her own cousin. And then there is your attraction to her—" Robert grinned. "Forgive me for mentioning it, but I couldn't help but notice it when I accidentally walked into your cabin yesterday eve."

Thomas's face heated. "You should have knocked."

"However I came to interrupt you, you had the look of a jealous husband. I know, for I've witnessed it many a time."

Thomas was hard-pressed not to answer Robert's grin with a fist. "I admit Fia has an effect on me, and I'll be well rid of such a troublesome wench. London cannot come too soon."

"And then?"

"And then the maid is free."

"Free to do what?"

"Whatever she wishes." Thomas took a deep draught of his whiskey. "There's only one thing I must do. In order to gain the lady's cooperation, I promised to find a sponsor for her plays."

"You *had* to promise? Or you made this gesture out of the munificent generosity of your own heart?"

Thomas didn't answer.

"Ah." Robert took a long sip of his whiskey. "Tell me something, *mon ami;* why seek an annulment at all? Why not keep the beauteous Fia as wife?"

"What sort of a question is that?"

"A practical one. Isn't she of noble birth?"

"Aye."

"And pleasant to look upon?"

"More than pleasant," Thomas said grudgingly.

"Quick of wit?"

"*Too* quick of wit for my tastes."

Robert quirked a disbelieving brow. "You prefer a witless woman?"

"No, of course not. Just one who isn't so prone to speaking out of turn."

"Hmm." Robert nodded thoughtfully. "And I know that you find her physically appealing."

Thomas stirred in his chair, assaulted by memories. "Aye," he admitted reluctantly. "I can scarce look at the maid without becoming as ready as a ship in a full wind."

Robert looked delighted. "She torments you, eh?"

"In a manner of speaking, yes."

Robert counted on his fingers, "So she's wellborn, beauteous, filled with wit, blessed by passion and character, and you cannot keep your hands from her . . ." He threw up his hands. "Explain why you should not be on your knees thanking the stars to have been gifted with such a wife!"

"She's also untamed and half-wild; she says what she thinks when she thinks it, regardless of the appropriateness of it; would rather be with her animals than people; runs about with her hair tumbled to her shoulders and her skirts clinging to her; wears muddy boots like some stable boy—" He shook his head. "Damn it, Robert, I don't have to explain this to you. You know how brutal the court can be; she'd be scorned and ridiculed."

Robert shrugged. "I hear naught that could not be fixed. She could be taught comportment."

"Robert, the woman doesn't even own a petticoat. And then there's the *wool*."

Robert blinked. "Wool?"

"Aye, it clings and is far softer than any wool I've ever touched and—" He clamped his mouth closed as he noted the twinkle in Robert's eyes. "I've already admitted that I lust for her, you pestilent cur. What more do you want?"

Smiling smugly, Robert took a considering drink. "So you think this is lust and not love. You are ever the cynic."

"I prefer the term 'realist.'" Thomas took another draw

of his whiskey. There might be no answers for him in Robert's company, but at least the whiskey was melting some of his tension. "It's a pity, I admit, for she's certainly comely, but she's not the woman for me."

"'Tis a sad case," Robert said, his gaze faraway, as if he could see the solution. "There is only one thing to do, then."

"What's that?" Thomas looked at the bottom of his mug. 'Twas already empty. He found the bottle and refilled his mug. At this rate, he would soon be unable to stand. Part of him welcomed the idea of a few hours of blissful unawareness.

"You must take her. Make her yours. Woo her and—"

"*What?* How am I to do that and leave her a maid? Elizabeth will not grant an annulment if I so much as touch the wench."

"Then there is no hope. From what I witnessed in your cabin, that woman will not touch the shores of London still a maid. Your blood is too high."

As much as Thomas hated to admit it, Robert was right. There must be something he could do to lessen the tension. Seeing her in such close quarters, her silken hair flying, her mouth soft and begging for kisses . . . He shifted in his chair. The chit stirred his blood just as he knew he stirred hers; her kisses could not lie. Indeed, she'd scarce been able to look away from his bared chest last night.

It was gratifying that the attraction he felt was shared. Too gratifying.

All he had to do was outlast this yearning until they reached London. Once there, he'd allow the wiles of the perfumed court beauties to douse his lust. If only there were some diversion here, aboard ship, at least for Fia.

Thomas set his mug on the table.

Why not? It wouldn't hurt Robert to do something worthwhile.

Thomas eyed his friend. "Perhaps there is something *you* can do to help with this situation."

"*Me?*"

"Aye. The queen herself says you'd as soon talk a woman out of her petticoats as pull the laces yourself."

Robert beamed and tilted back in his chair, placing his booted feet upon the table. "I must admit to owning some address."

"Then *you* will keep Fia busy during our voyage home."

Robert's boots and the front legs of his chair hit the floor. "*What?*"

"You heard me. You'll keep her busy and well escorted. I'll not have her out of her cabin without a proper chaperone."

"Just how am I to keep her 'busy?' We're on a ship. It's not as if there are amusing places we could ride to, or people to visit, or—"

"I don't know and don't care; just do it. Perhaps you can play cards or chess, or read books aloud—you know better than I how to entertain a fanciful woman. Better yet, tell her you've always wished to be an actor, and offer to act out her plays."

Robert was silent a long time before he let out his breath in a long sigh. "I cannot. She's a MacLean."

"So?"

"The MacQuarries have been pledged to the MacLeans for centuries; I can't forget the allegiance of my clan. They may have abandoned me, but I'll never abandon them. 'Tis a matter of honor."

"Since when has honor been a concern of yours? You would as soon cheat at cards as take an honest loan."

"Cheating a Sassenach at cards *is* a matter of honor among Scots," said Robert gently.

"I never realized just how much of a Scot you are. I'll not forget it."

"Thank you, *mon ami*. I'll stand at your side in any venture you care to undertake, be it pirating, fighting, or else. But I'll not lift a hand against a MacLean."

"I never said anything about lifting a hand," Thomas said irritably. "I merely asked you to keep her busy so she's not wandering alone on deck, tempting me to—interfering with the crew as they go about their duties."

Robert frowned. "Why can't you simply order her confined to her cabin?"

Because she'd refuse. "For three weeks? Robert, you have ever been good at weaving stories. Tell her . . . tell her you've no skill at sailing and are of no use on deck, and so are bored and wish for a merry companion to pass the days. 'Tis only for three weeks, at most."

Robert stroked his trim beard. "I cannot believe you'd ask me to dally with your own wife."

Thomas stiffened. "I did not ask you to *dally* with Fia."

"Dally, entertain—what's the difference?"

Thomas's jaw ached from clenching it. "Robert, don't make me—" Robert chuckled, and Thomas realized he'd been teased. He managed a grudging grin. "I suppose I ran into that full sail."

"Head-on." Still laughing, Robert said, "Very well; I will keep Lady Fia company, *if* that's all you're asking."

"That's all."

There. Now he would reach the banks of the Thames with his wife's virtue intact. Relief filled him and the tiredness he'd held at bay returned in full force, accompanied by the effects of the whiskey. He yawned and stretched. "I'm exhausted. Therefore, I must now request you leave."

"But this is my cabin."

"Nay, this is *my* cabin. *You* placed Fia's trunks in mine, and she will most likely rise before me and will need access to those trunks, so I'll use your cabin, instead."

"But—"

"No buts, my friend." Thomas stood, stretched again, and went to the bunk. He sat down, pulled off his boots, then climbed in and pulled the blankets over him.

Robert corked the whiskey bottle and gathered the mugs with an offended air. "I plan and plot to help you, and this is the thanks I receive. Very well. I'll share the cabin with you, but—"

"Nay," interrupted Thomas as he fluffed his pillow and settled into it. The bed wasn't as fine as the one in his cabin, but it was better than naught. "You may have my cabin if you need to nap before I arise."

"But I—"

"Or if you wish, you may bed down with the crew. But *I* have no wish to hear you snore."

"I do not snore."

Thomas didn't answer.

After a great deal of huffing, Robert finally left, slamming the door behind him.

For the first time in two days, Thomas relaxed. He yawned and settled deeper into the blankets. His eyes grew heavy and his breathing deepened. Soon he was sound asleep, his peace interrupted only once, when he dreamed of a black-eyed Scottish wench dressed in his best captain's coat as she sailed his ship across a racing sea, laughing at him where she'd tied him to the mast.

Chapter Twelve

*R*obert squinted and slowly lowered the mug to the top of the leaning stack. He had managed to pile fourteen mugs of varying sizes into a complex tower. 'Twas a record, he was sure—and Simmons had sworn it could not be done!

The most difficult part was adjusting for the constant shifting of the deck. He would have sworn that the first mate was sailing against the wind just to make his task more difficult.

As his hand lowered with the fifteenth and final vessel, he became aware of someone standing just beyond his range of vision. He forced himself to stay focused on his task. If he could just get this mug atop the pile without it falling over, Simmons would have to pay up. And since there was little else to do for entertainment, this offered considerable amusement.

The person moved and Robert became aware of a generously rounded bosom, full and plump.

The mug tower wavered and then toppled with a rousing chorus of thunks and thuds.

Simmons gave a shout of laughter from the foredeck. Robert sighed. Well, it had been worth it. 'Twas a truly magnificent bosom, and over the course of the last week, he'd had to fight the urge to look at it more than once.

His assignment to keep Lady Fia busy had turned out to be a delight. The lady was educated, well-read, and sweet natured, facts Thomas had failed either to report or to realize. She was a charming companion, unexpectedly witty and possessing a lightning wit that left him gasping for laughter.

Another reason his assignment was a delight was the effect it had on Thomas. The earl was never beyond earshot, his expression growing more dark and brooding as the days wore on, apparently unable or unwilling to completely trust Robert in his task.

He grinned and turned toward the bosom that had disturbed his concentration. "Lady Fia! How fare thee this beauteous afternoon?" He rose to his feet and made an elaborate, if unsteady, bow. 'Twas perhaps unfortunate he had felt the need to drink out of each mug before adding it to the stack. It hadn't been precisely necessary to win the wager; 'twas more a question of style.

"Och, 'tis a lovely day. The wind is fresh and free today."

The voice drew a shiver from him. *God's breath, as soon as we land I'll write a sonnet to that voice.*

The ship rocked upon a wave and Robert's lack of balance caught him unawares. Grabbing at the barrel, he quickly lowered himself to his makeshift seat.

"Lord Montley, you've been drinking." The lush voice carried a touch of reproof and he was instantly apologetic.

"Aye, but I'm lucid and bored with my own company, so pray do not leave me to mine own devices. I can only hope that you'll forgive me for my state."

Her lips quirked into an irrepressible smile. "Actually, your 'state' might help me in my quest."

"Which is?"

"Information, my lord. That's all."

She spoke so innocently that his guard was instantly up. Had one of his sisters spoken in such a tone, he would have immediately known she was up to something. "For you, fair lady, I am an open book. Ask what you will, but first, pray take a seat." He raised his voice so Simmons could hear him. "Whilst the *Glorianna* is a fine ship, her crew is inexperienced and frequently heads into the sea like an unrestrained horse gallops over the moors."

Lady Fia, who didn't seem to notice the first mate's sputtering presence, said, "I would indeed like a seat. The ship's rocking badly today."

She gathered her skirts and perched upon the barrel, looking magnificent as the wind tugged at her skirts and hair.

Robert decided that he would have kissed her, had he not been so lamentably drunk and she so damnably innocent . . . and married to his best friend, of course.

God's wounds, how could he have forgotten that?

One of the mugs rolled to Fia's feet and she hopped off her barrel, retrieved the mug, then found her seat again, all without staggering on the rocking deck. She was innately graceful doing even the most awkward of things, and the roiling ship never gave her pause. She seemed a born sailor.

"Lord Montley, I—"

"Pray, how many times have I asked you to call me Robert?"

She pursed her lips, her eyes twinkling. "Twenty-one.

Twenty-two if you count the time Mary interrupted you yesterday."

He waved a hand, his fine lace cuff drifting about his wrist. "Allow me to make it twenty-three. Lady, pray call me Robert. There can be no formality between us, as we are nearly family. Thomas is as a brother to me. Thus, you are my sister." *More's the pity.*

"Very well . . . Robert."

His name rolled off her silken tongue and made his heart grin.

Unaware of her effect, she smoothed her skirts over her knees and regarded him from beneath her lashes. "Since you are almost as a brother to Lord Rotherwood, you must know his lordship very well."

Aha, so that's it, is it. If there was one thing his sisters had taught him, it was to beware a woman who asked a question about another man. He answered cautiously, "We've been close these past fifteen years."

She slanted him a look redolent with doubt. "Only fifteen? Then there is probably much you do not know about him, then."

Her eyes were the velvet black of midnight with the veriest tinge of amber in their depths. *Such eyes. No wonder Thomas feels he must avoid her like the plague. He could fall victim to eyes like those and—*

"Lord M—I'm sorry. Robert, you don't answer."

He blinked. "Forgive me, Fair Damsel. I was lost in wonder at thy beauty."

She frowned impatiently. "Pray listen. I asked a question."

Robert's lip twitched, but he replied meekly, "Forgive my impertinence. What did you ask?"

Her cheeks pinkened, but she said with an air of great determination, "I was saying that I—" She straightened as if facing a mountain. "Robert, I want to know what a man such as Lord Rotherwood might require of a wife."

God's wounds, she's serious. "I am a bit befuddled."

"Why?"

"Because I'm not used to women asking my opinion of other men when they're basking in the sunshine of my companionship."

Her lips quivered. "No one basks in the sunshine of your companionship as oft as you."

Robert found himself chuckling with her. She reminded him of his sister Aindrea. Like Fia, Aindrea was a dreamer, yet very practical when occasion demanded. "That is a very short but very complicated question. What men *think* they want in a wife and what they *actually* desire are two very different things."

Fia grimaced. "Och, 'tis so complicated."

His blue eyes warmed. "Do not despair yet, lass. Let me think on it for a moment and see if I can put it into an understandable form."

She nodded and waited, grateful yet again for Robert's attentions this last week. Without him, there would have been no one to talk to but Mary. After the first night on ship, when Thomas had surprised her in his cabin and kissed her as if he couldn't kiss her enough, he'd avoided her as if she had the plague.

At first, she'd just assumed he was busy. But twice now upon leaving her cabin, she'd chanced upon Thomas coming down the passageway. On seeing her, he'd come to a sudden halt and glanced at the closest venue of escape. Then, after mumbling a disjointed phrase, his face as red as fire, he'd turned on his heel and marched back the way he'd come.

She wondered if he thought her forward for kissing him so passionately that first night. *And that wasn't the first time I kissed him, either. Perhaps he thinks me loose.*

"Fia?" Robert was regarding her with a puzzled air. "Your expression. You look as if—"

"'Tis nothing. A fleeting thought is all." Pasting a smile on her lips, she said, "Robert, perhaps I ask too much. 'Tis obvious I'm not the sort of woman my husband prefers as wife. I was just—" She shrugged, her heart unexpectedly pained at the admission. "I don't know what I was hoping for."

Robert waved his hand. "Pssht. Ask what you will. The trouble is this: the question is as big as the sea and best answered by the man himself."

She plucked at her skirt with restless fingers. "'Tis not a question one can easily ask. He would feel bound by politeness to try to encompass me in his answer, though that is not how he feels."

"Hmm. I can see where 'twould be awkward." Robert stroked his trim beard, his expression thoughtful. "I can only tell you what I think, not what I know, for men do not discuss such things with the passion and frequency of women."

"I understand."

"I think the problem lies not so much in what you aren't, but in what you are."

"And what am I?"

"His wife. Thomas doesn't believe good can come from any marriage. His father soured him on the idea when his mother ran off with a stable hand."

"No! Did Thomas go with her?"

"Nay, she left him with his father—a stern, unlikable man who treated his son with a coldness that I cannot begin to describe."

How sad. Fia thought of her own childhood, during which she was cherished and loved.

That went a long way in explaining why Thomas immediately demanded an annulment and didn't consider attempting to make the marriage work. "I think he believes 'tis possible I or my cousin trapped him into this marriage, too, though the truth could not be farther from that."

Robert shrugged. "Did he love you, it wouldn't matter."

A shaft of pain shot through her as surely as if Robert had loosed an arrow at her heart.

Fortunately, Robert's gaze was now fixed on his fine Italian leather boots. After a moment, he began to speak in a low voice, his blue eyes darker than usual. "Since he's taken on the title, Thomas Wentworth has known nothing but success and good fortune. 'Tis a family inheritance, of a sort." He pursed his lips thoughtfully. "You could call it a curse and not be far wrong."

"Being blessed with success is a curse?"

"Do you know what it's like to be known as the luckiest man alive? The whole world begins to plan your downfall. Oh, not intentionally. 'Tis just that one success must lead to another. Thus, the more luck you have, the more daring the wager you are expected to take. The more successful you are, the more dangerous your next assignment must be."

"Assignment?"

A shadow crossed Robert's face. "Assignment, or wager, or queenly request—it matters naught. It just matters that you win yet again. Thomas has worked since childhood to become an excellent rider, a master tactician, an outstanding swordsman, a sea captain without rival—he is driven to be superior in everything he does. His father drove him mercilessly, and Thomas became what his father wanted— a man as near perfect as could be. His accomplishments would earn any other man esteem and praise, yet for Thomas, he is only doing what is expected."

"That is weighty, indeed."

"That is but half of it." Robert's smile twisted with bitterness. "Thomas was raised to believe the worst of his mother—of all women, really. She's the blight on the family name, the one proof that the Wentworth luck may not be what all believe it."

"How sad for him."

"Aye, his father was determined that no Wentworth ever be subjected to such humiliation again. He taught Thomas to trust no one lest he, too, would be made a fool." Robert's blue gaze rested on her gently for a moment. "Can you understand now why he has never thought of marriage? Or, when he did, 'twas distant, far away from today."

Fia nodded, a lump in her throat. She could almost see the bereft young boy as he lost both his mother and the love of his father in one fell swoop. "He seems to see you as his brother. Surely he trusts *you.*"

Robert smoothed a hand over his sleeve, though no smile touched his lips. "He tries."

Fia wondered at the emotion in Robert's voice.

"I accept that his trust is only conditional because I owe him more than I can ever repay." Robert stared out at the ocean, beyond the white-capped swells. After a moment, he turned to her. "Do you know why some call me the Coward of Balmanach?"

Though she had heard tales, she shook her head.

He read the truth in her face. "Aye, you do. When I was a youth of sixteen, my parents were murdered."

He faltered over the word and she said quickly, "Robert, you don't need to tell me this if you don't wish to."

"If you want to understand Thomas, then you must know this." Robert adjusted the fine lace on his cuffs across his elegant hands. "When I was scarcely into my adolescence, my parents were murdered while returning from my uncle's house. My uncle himself gave me the news. He could scarcely contain his triumph, for their blood still glistened on his sword."

"But . . . I thought the MacDonald clan ambushed them."

"That's what my uncle wanted everyone to think." White lines of tension bracketed Robert's mouth. "I was just sixteen and barely a man. My uncle told me of his deed and gave me a choice. I could either stay and fight for my right as laird, or I could run as far from Mull as my feet could carry me."

There was a pause, then he said, "I chose to run. I had five sisters who looked to me. If I perished in the contest of wills, who would take care of them?" Robert's lips thinned, his eyes blazing.

Fia drew back, almost not recognizing her previously merry companion.

Robert saw her concern and he immediately lifted a hand. "I'm sorry. It was a damnable situation and I still harbor anger toward my uncle."

"I don't blame you. It makes *me* angry just hearing about it."

His lips quirked into a reluctant smile. "You've a good heart, my lady."

"What did you do, since you couldn't fight your uncle?"

"I walked away from him, though my fingers ached to feel his neck beneath them. It was the hardest thing I've ever done. In the space of an hour, I was forced to become man enough to know when I was beaten, yet I was still child enough to taste the full bitterness of defeat."

"You did what you had to."

"Aye. My oldest sister, Aindrea, was only eleven. The rest were babes—the youngest were the twins, and had just turned two." His face hardened, and once again Fia caught a glimpse of the iron hidden beneath Robert's silks and laces. "My uncle allowed us to leave into the icy night with only what we had on our backs and one horse among us. I suppose that was a sop to his conscience."

"That—that—*bastard*!"

Robert chuckled, the lines about his eyes easing.

Fia's face heated. "I'm sorry. That slipped out before I could stop it. Pray continue with your story."

His smile faded, but her outburst seemed to soothe him in some way for he said in a calmer tone, "It was freezing cold the night we left, the snow blowing until we couldn't see. I put the smaller ones on the horse, just strapped them on and bundled them with every loose rag Aindrea and I could spare, and then . . . we walked. And walked. And walked. It was bitterly cold, the wind harsh. Each step grew more and more difficult. We were spent, tormented by the loss of our parents, and fearful for our lives; I can't express how horrible it was.

"Just as I thought we could go no more, Aindrea cried out. I turned and she was gone . . . but not because she'd stumbled into a drift, as I'd feared. Instead, her sharp eyes had found a cave."

"She sounds very resourceful."

"Aye, she is. Without that fortunate find, we wouldn't have survived the night. We managed to scrape together enough wood for a small fire, and that saved us. The cave was damp and cold, small and rock strewn, but it was safe and for that we were thankful. As soon as it was morning, we began walking again."

"You came to England?"

"Aye. My uncle's reach wasn't long enough to cross his own borders, so we headed south. It grew warmer with each step. My sisters and I made it as far as the border, begging for food and stealing what we could. We were doing well, considering all things, when once again, the winter weather returned. Only this time it was a deep cold like no other I'd ever seen before, or have seen since."

"And that's when you met Thomas?"

"It was by pure chance. My sisters and I were desperate for shelter and had stumbled onto Wentworth land. We crawled into the stables and huddled in the hay, thankful for the warmth. The next morning, one of the stable hands found us and raised a cry. Thomas was home alone, as usual, his father off to court. Without a care for his father's reaction, Thomas brought us to his house and treated us as guests."

"Eventually, though, his father returned?"

Robert nodded. "Two months after Thomas allowed us into the house. The old earl was livid to find strangers under his roof. He ranted about what a fool Thomas was, how we were taking advantage of him, how we were using him and his good fortune and how we would desert him and bring shame onto their house once again."

"Like his mother."

"Aye, but Thomas wouldn't listen. I think he had always wanted someone or something to prove his father wrong, and finally, there we were. I've spent years proving that he didn't make a mistake in helping the MacQuarries. Sometimes I think he believes it; other times, I'm not so certain."

The wind blew a strand of hair over her cheek, she brushed it aside. "So . . . Thomas is caught between what he was taught and what he wants to believe."

"Aye, but his heart is where it should be and will one day save him. I am sure of it."

Fia considered this and for a long time, neither spoke.

Finally, Robert sighed. "Over the years, to protect himself, Thomas has developed a faraway concept of the perfect wife. She is calm, perfectly behaved, and devoid of emotion. She will never embarrass him, nor fall passionately in love with the stable master—or with Thomas, for that matter. She will represent him and his family with ease and a cool bearing. Above all other things, she will bring no shame on his family name."

Fia curled her nose. "I would never bring shame upon his house, but I could not be cold and controlled."

Robert chuckled. "No one could, and there he is safe from ever having to wed."

Fia looked down at her hands, which were clenched in front of her. "Robert . . . I need your help."

He turned his gaze to her. "Does it involve helping Thomas?"

"Aye. I think it does. Would you teach me what I need to know to win over the English court?"

"Why?"

"If Thomas wishes for an annulment, then so be it, but

I will not have him putting me aside because he thinks I will embarrass him."

"I suppose I could teach the basics, had we time, but . . . how would that help Thomas?"

"If I can conquer the English court, then I can prove to Thomas I'm not a liability against the Wentworth name. Then he will see that he is wrong in his vision of me."

Robert looked amazed and then amused. "Fia, my love, that's a damned good idea! If you were to charm the court, every objection Thomas could possibly have against your marriage would disappear."

"Except that I am not passionless," she pointed out.

"Except that one," Robert agreed.

"Do you think I could learn what I must within the two weeks we have before we reach London?"

Robert looked as if his ruff had suddenly been drawn too tight, but after a moment, he nodded. "'Twill be difficult, but . . . very well, lass. We'll *make* it work. You'll have to promise to pay attention. There are dances to learn, titles to memorize, proprieties to master, and all manner of things."

She nodded, her excitement growing. For the first time since Thomas had kissed her she felt the warming presence of hope. "We will work at it night and day if we must."

His eyes gleamed with excitement. "Excellent! When I'm finished, you'll have manners fit for a queen."

"Thank you. I—I wish I could pay you for your assistance."

"Do you, now?" His brows lifted in a waggish gesture. "Then pay me you shall. I know exactly what payment I would want, and 'tis not money."

"What is it?"

"It's . . . no, I'll not tell you as yet. Just know that you owe it to me, and you are pledged to pay when this scene is played out."

"Robert! I cannot agree to such a mad promise."

"Not even if I vow that my payment will compromise neither your virtue nor your honor?"

She bit her lip and looked at him uncertainly. "Perhaps."

He leaned close. "You will be the desire of every man at court, the most accomplished woman since Elizabeth to walk through Hampton Court Palace! Thomas will be awed by your grace and talents. How can you say nay?"

The picture he painted was almost too appealing to be true, but his confident words, combined with the absurdity of his grin, reassured her. He was as impish and naughty as a child, but there was no harm to him and she knew from the light in his eyes that he cared about Thomas, too.

"Very well," she agreed. "I pledge, but only on the understanding that if your requested payment seems too harsh, then you will forfeit."

"Done!" He stood and pulled her to her feet. "Come, we've no time to waste. You must learn the most important skill of a lady in the queen's court."

"Curtsying? How to address the queen?"

"How to use a fan."

She blinked. "What use would I have of a fan?"

"Oh ho, what lady of the court *doesn't* use a fan? Once that's accomplished, we'll learn dances. The queen loves dancing like life itself and she also . . ." Robert went on and on, the list of what he needed to teach her growing until it was too much to follow.

Fia allowed herself to be swept along by Robert's enthusiasm, her excitement building. It was a gamble, but the whole marriage had been a chancy venture since the beginning.

But now, she was realizing that there was much more at stake than mere dreams. Now there was the matter of her pride. If Thomas Wentworth thought he could set her aside, he would at least do it with a powerful sense of regret and wonder at what might have been. She deserved at least that much.

Chapter Thirteen

$\mathcal{A}$ week later, Thomas realized he'd made a complete and utter mistake in asking Robert to keep an eye on Fia. Everywhere Thomas looked, *there they were*. Either the pair was in the comfort of his own cabin, exchanging exaggerated compliments and sallies with enough wit and archness to mock the most jaded of the queen's court, or else they were seated on deck, deep in some card game or a discussion of the merits of linen to silk, of silk to lace, of lace to brocade. And all with enough laughter and merriment to lead Thomas to believe they spoke of some scandalously naughty topic other than fashionable court gossip.

It wouldn't have mattered except that it had dawned on Thomas that, lately, Fia no longer paid him any heed. She was focused solely on Robert, her expression intent as she hung on his every word.

Damn that bounder!

Thomas ground his teeth. Despite his best intentions, he found himself hovering nearby, straining his ears to find out what was bewitching Fia so. Robert knew it, too, and was beside himself with mischief. At least once he'd purposefully caught Fia's hand and brought it to his lips for a much-longer-than-necessary kiss, glancing Thomas's way with a mocking expression. Thomas could have cheerfully killed him.

The music from a lone flute drifted through the air to tickle his ears, then a barrage of rhythmic clapping told him the likely location of his entire crew. *And Fia*, his treacherous mind whispered. *If there's merriment, Fia can't be far away. But . . . dancing before my crew?*

He shouldn't have been surprised, for within six short days, Fia had bewitched them all. No doubt every man on ship was now admiring her trim ankles as she whirled about on Robert's arm, practicing all of the latest Italianate dances so favored by Queen Elizabeth.

The sooner he put a stop to this nonsense, the better. The only problem was how to do it without appearing a fool. Every time he attempted to complain to Robert of Fia's sudden frivolity, his friend would expound on the sin of envy until Thomas was ready to explode.

He was *not* jealous. He was merely concerned about the spectacle Robert was making of an innocent maid. *What in hell was I thinking, to ask such a bounder to keep watch over a beauty like Fia?*

If she fell victim to Robert and his flowery ways, then Thomas was as much at fault as that damned Scot. She should be warned of Robert's low purposes.

Damn it, I should have seen this coming. If Fia could lavish affection on a broken-down nag and a half-blind dog, 'twasn't difficult to imagine her response to Robert's wit. What if she came to actually *care* for Robert, or to at least think she did, which was as bad?

Thomas's blood chilled. *I will not allow my wife to embarrass the family name.*

Fia's laughter drifted above the clamor, and Thomas was as drawn to it as a moth to flame. He reached the railing and glared down to the lower deck at the dancing duo. Fia's skirts flew higher with every turn she made on Robert's arm, her bare feet skimming over the deck. The sight made Thomas as queasy as a cabin boy on his first voyage. *God grant I live long enough to buy that Scottish hoyden a decent number of petticoats and at least one pair of slippers.*

She looked up at Robert and laughed, her eyes shining. *She once looked at me that way, but I discouraged her.* The thought burned into his heart. Damn it all, he would make this ship fly. The less time Fia spent in Robert's worldly presence, the better.

Thomas looked about for Simmons. The portly first mate was nowhere to be seen. In fact, Thomas was alone on the foredeck. He leaned farther over the railing.

Simmons, his stomach peeping from beneath his too-tight shirt, was now holding Fia's hands. Under Robert's close tutelage, Simmons pranced through the intricate steps of a French dance. His round face perspired freely, his chin to his chest as he stared at his feet. Robert stood to one side and shouted instructions as the couple passed near.

"*Simmons!*" Thomas bellowed.

There was a satisfying and abrupt halt to the mewl of the flute. Simmons made a quick, awkward bow to Fia and scurried to the ladder.

Thomas was about to order the men back to their tasks when the flute began again. The merriment resumed as Fia began to whirl about on Robert's arm, her skirts flying once again. There was such joy, such happiness, in her expression that Thomas held his breath. *By the saints, she is lovely.*

"Ye yelled fer me, Cap'n?" The first mate's face was red from his exertion.

"Call the crew and turn eastward. We'll draw more sail and speed."

"East?"

"'Tis a shorter route and will let us reach London two, perhaps three days sooner."

"But we'll have to navigate the reef along—"

Thomas glared.

"Aye, aye! Ye know about the reef, o' course." Simmons squinted up at the rigging as he scratched the seat of his loose breeches. "I'll turn her if ye wish it, though I doubt we'll catch a swifter wind—"

Thomas raised his eyebrows.

"I mean, aye, Cap'n!" The first mate bawled the orders, and the flute once again ceased. Thomas eyed his crew as they scrambled to obey. He would have all of them scrubbing and cleaning and so tired that not a one of them would remember having seen his wife's ankles. Now, all he had to do was find something to busy Robert, too.

"Amazing, the effect marriage has on some men."

Thomas turned on his heel to face Robert.

The Scotsman was leaning against the railing, his rich wine-colored doublet half-open, his white shirt unlaced at the throat from the physical exertion of dancing. "Well, *mon ami*? Why did you call the entire crew to stations? Are we under attack?"

"Need I remind you that we are upon a ship, sailing through the sea? The crew needs always to be at attention."

"So we are, but you didn't need to—" Robert looked up

at the sails. "We're turning." His brow lowered. "We're to take the shore route?"

"Aye, 'tis faster."

"And riskier."

"I've done it many times. Besides, 'twill give the crew something to do other than leer at my wife's ankles." He pinned Robert with a stare.

"Oh-ho! Now we reach the crux. You're jealous again."

Thomas's eyes narrowed, tension crackling through him. He was spoiling for a fight. He thought a good thumping might turn Robert's thoughts away from Fia. If nothing else, Thomas could make sure the libertine was in no condition to dance for the rest of the voyage. "Say no more, Montley, else I'll consider it wrongly. We're turning now and will make London by midweek, one, perhaps two days sooner than if we continued on this route."

"Sooner?" Robert's brow lowered. "Surely we don't need to hurry so—"

"But we do," Thomas interrupted abruptly. There was only one reason Robert would wish more time at sea, and that was to flirt with Thomas's wife. "I've an annulment to procure."

"I'faith, you weren't thinking of your annulment when you turned the ship, and you know it. You ordered the men back to work to keep them from looking upon the fair Fia."

"That 'fair Fia' is *my* wife."

"For now."

Thomas's blood boiled and he strode to Robert until they stood toe-to-toe. "I asked you to keep her busy, not to teach her to make a spectacle of herself."

Robert's jaw set. "Allow me to point out that the fair Fia is only yours until you gain an audience with the queen. After that, she's fair game to anyone who wishes to pursue her."

"Do not speak such gibberish!"

Robert's smile mocked. "Once you cast her aside, she won't be alone for long. There will be others hard upon your heels."

"Like you?"

"Perhaps." Robert shrugged. "Perhaps not. Best you get used to the idea of another now."

Red anger ripped through Thomas. Without thought, he seized Robert's doublet and hauled him forward until but a hair's breadth separated them. "Fia is *my* wife until the queen says otherwise, and you will keep your distance or face the consequences."

Robert's eyes blazed. "Unhand me!"

Thomas released Robert so quickly that the Scot stumbled, though only once. With a lithe twist, he was poised, hand on his short sword, his face a mask of icy fury.

The crew, who'd been watching the altercation, gaped openly.

Their shock returned reason to Thomas's fury-addled brain. *God's blood, what's happened to me? This is what comes of passion.* He rubbed his jaw. "Montley, this is not the place for a fight. We should take this belowdecks."

Robert glanced about and slowly, reluctantly, released his grip on his short sword. As captain of his own ship, he clearly recognized the importance of maintaining order. At sea, organization and discipline often meant the difference between life and death.

Still, 'twas obvious it took all of Robert's control to tamely nod, though he managed it. "Belowdecks, then." He turned on his heel and left, his back stiff with anger.

Thomas turned to the crew. "What's this? None of you have work to do?"

The crew scattered instantly, obviously disappointed. Soon Thomas was alone on the top deck, wondering how he'd been brought so low.

The truth burned in his stomach. He *was* jealous. Jealous beyond reason for a wife he didn't even want. Somehow, some way, he would fight his burgeoning passions and he would subdue them.

He clasped his hands behind his back and paced the short length of the top deck. His feelings for Fia were purely proprietary. He'd never had a wife before, and because of his mother's poor behavior, he was merely more sensitive to slights than the average man.

Aye, that was the problem. Perhaps he was going about this the wrong way. Perhaps, instead of avoiding Fia completely, he should spend time with her, grow more used to her presence and thus less fascinated.

He stared out at the ocean with unseeing eyes. That made sense. Avoiding her had done nothing more than increase his fascination and stretch his emotions as taut as a drawn bow. Nothing would cool his lust better than discovering all of her faults and foibles. Surely she had some. Perhaps she cleared her throat all during dinner, or sang off key or . . . or . . . He couldn't think of more annoying habits, but he was certain she had some and he'd be sure to find every one.

Thomas smiled grimly. By the time they arrived in London her spell over him would be broken.

"I said," Robert repeated with exaggerated loudness, "'tis your turn. However, should you need more time to stare out at yonder sea, I will continue to await your pleasure, for God knows I've naught to do but sit here and stare at my own cards and—"

"Pssht, Lord Montley, leave the mistress be," said Mary, her red curls ruffled by the wind. "She's thinkin', she is. Ye wouldn't have her play the wrong card, would ye?"

"The wrong card would be better than none at all," grumbled Robert. "I age as we sit."

Fia glanced back at the foredeck, where she could just catch a glimpse of Thomas's dark black hair as he paced, his expression austere, his firm mouth framed by his trim beard. He looked so—

"Fia?" Mary eyed her mistress with a stern gaze. "'Tis your turn."

Fia flushed, selected a card from her hand, and tucked the discard under the mug that weighted the loose cards and kept them from blowing across the deck.

The sea surged green and blue as white-capped waves rocked the ship. The wind licked at the cards on the barrel, trying to pull them free. Fia lifted her face to the sun. Perhaps she would write a play about a pirate. A pirate with black hair and honey-brown eyes. A pirate whose cool, calm gaze held a hint of sadness.

"'Tis my turn." Mary plucked a card from her hand and started to lay it down. She hesitated, her hand hovering a scant inch above the barrel, her face puckered in thought. After a moment she returned the card to her hand, only to draw it forth again a second later and repeat her actions.

"Are you playing that godforsaken card, or aren't you?" Robert demanded, his gaze never leaving Mary's hand.

"I'm puttin' it down now, ye cankerous maw worm." Mary slapped the card onto the barrel.

"Praise Saint Peter," Robert said fervently. He stared at his cards, absently chewing his lip.

"Go!" Mary ordered.

"I'm looking at my cards."

"If 'tis against the rules fer me to take a second to look at me cards, then 'tis against the rules fer ye, so don't just sit there like a lump. Play yer card."

Fia swallowed a giggle. Since their conversation over a week ago Robert had been true to his word, working ceaselessly to teach her the ways of the court. He had shown her the proper way to curtsy and address the queen. Over the last few days he'd described in detail the many men and women who were court favorites, explaining their alliances and their positions within the court, and drawing up a list for her to study.

Though Mary fussed and fumed at Robert's exaggerated ways, Fia thought the maid was slowly softening to him. Just this morning, Mary'd watched him stride across the deck in his puce short cape trimmed with silver thread and said doubtfully, "He's a mite too French fer my taste, but he does know his way with fashion."

From Mary, that was high praise indeed.

Now, from where he sat on a barrel across the small table from them, Robert slid a card under the mug. "I vow, this jack of hearts plagues me. Your turn, Fia, my sweet."

She regarded her cards for a moment and then discarded an eight of diamonds.

Robert nodded his approval. "Excellent."

"Thank you." She stifled a yawn.

"Tired, my love? You—"

"Lord Montley," Mary interrupted, her back stiff. *"Must*

ye call Lady Fia yer love and yer 'sweet' and all of yer silly names?"

"*Must* I?" Robert's blue eyes gleamed with humor. "But yes. 'Tis quite the fashion at court to parlay the language of love whenever possible."

Mary didn't look convinced. "The English court sounds mighty ramshackle to me."

"Oh, it is, but in a deliciously well-done way." Smiling, he glanced at Fia and caught yet another yawn. "Perchance you need a nap?"

"That would be lovely. I couldn't sleep last night, so I'm a wee bit sleepy today."

"Oh? Was your berth lumpy?"

"No. I was just thinking." Every thought had revolved around her triumphant appearance in court and the successful reception of her plays, and at the end of each dream had been Thomas.

Lately, her dreams were always about him, and often she'd awake panting, her entire body a-tingle as it had been after their last kiss. Of course, it had been far more than a kiss. She shivered to think of how real her dreams seemed.

Could the Hurst amulet have caused her dreams? Duncan had said that it—

"'Tis your turn again, my sweetest of the sweet." Robert ignored Mary's glare.

Fia absently plucked a jack of spades from her hand and placed it on the barrel.

"I win!" Robert threw his remaining cards onto the barrel.

"Ye did not!" protested Mary.

Fia leaned forward to stare at the cards on the barrel. "How could you win from that?"

He waved at the cards. "Look."

Mary's brow lowered. "Who played the knave?"

Fia bit her lip. "'Twas me."

"Humph. Ye need to pay more attention." Mary shot a hard glance at Robert and added, "Though if ye were to ask me, I'd have to say Lord Montley's cheatin'."

Robert blinked. "Me? Cheat such beauteous women? Never!"

Mary's scowl softened. "Don't play off yer airs on me, Robert MacQuarrie. A no-good lazy wastrel is what ye are."

"Words fall from thy lips like rubies, sparkling in the sun with blinding truth."

A reluctant smile tugged Mary's mouth, her cheeks suddenly pink. She cocked a brow at Fia. "He's a blithering idiot, but a charming one fer all that." She placed her cards on the barrel and stood. "As much as I'd like to stay and waste away the mornin', I need to work on yer gowns. Ye should have at least one good one fer when you reach London town."

"Thank you, Mary, that would be lovely."

"I've already a bodice pinned together. I'll need yer help once I get ready to pin the skirt to it."

"Just say the word and I shall assist," Fia replied with a smile.

Mary patted her charge on the shoulder. "Ye'll do me the best favor of all if ye'll learn this wretched card game so I don't have to play again." She leaned forward and whispered loudly, "Watch yer spares." With a warning look at Robert, Mary made her way back into their cabin.

Robert gathered the cards and shuffled them with an elegant twist of his wrists. "Come, there's another game I would teach you. Perchance this one will hold your attention better."

Fia looked at the cards Robert dealt, listening with half an ear as he explained the rules. 'Twas difficult concentrating on such a glorious day. The ocean rolled with a joyous motion while the sky was a clear cerulean blue. Best of all, just over the edge of the upper deck, she could see Thomas.

"Fia?"

Fia caught Robert's amused gaze and resolutely turned her back to the top deck. "I'm sorry. I was just thinking. Every day, we get closer to land. I worry what will happen then."

"Hmm. Seems a common ailment. Your husband suffers the same illness. In fact . . ." Robert's gaze focused over her shoulder. "Here comes the mighty prince now."

Fia turned, her heart thudding as she saw Thomas striding toward them. His white linen shirt hung in graceful folds over his powerful chest before it disappeared into snug breeches that were tucked into soft black leather boots.

Robert waited until Thomas was almost upon them before saying loudly, "While 'tis true, Lady Fia, that the married women of the court are not the most discreet of lovers, 'twould be an error to allow the queen to become aware of any dalliances."

Thomas came to freezing halt, choking audibly, and it was all Fia could do to keep from laughing at Robert's guileless expression.

The Scotsman laid a card on the barrel and gave her a sweet smile. "'Tis your draw, beauteous maid."

Fia drew a card as she stifled a giggle at Thomas's shocked expression.

"Montley, I have been looking for you," Thomas said shortly.

"And you have found me. I trow, 'tis a wondrous life."

Thomas scowled. "You are needed on the foredeck."

"But I cannot leave, bold captain of the seas. I'm pledged to Lady Fia and we are deeply in play."

Fia kept her gaze firmly fixed on her cards.

"She'll live without your presence. 'Tis time you earned your keep. Simmons thinks there's a storm brewing. We need to ready the ship."

"I am but a guest!" Robert protested. "Why should I overtake duties befitting a member of your crew?"

"If you don't like it, then leave."

"Leave?" Fia asked. "But . . . we're at sea."

Thomas's eyes glinted with amusement. "Precisely."

Robert seemed to consider this. "Whilst a swim would be pleasant, I fear 'twould ruin my new doublet."

"Most likely," said Thomas, devoid of sympathy. "The choice is yours."

"I vow, you're unreasonable," huffed Robert.

"And Simmons awaits you."

Robert sighed heavily. "Very well. As soon as Lady Fia and I finish this one hand, I will go."

"For the love of God, Montley. Give you a deck of cards and all the world may go to hell with your blessing." Thomas raked a hand through his hair and Fia yearned to smooth it back into place.

"Just one hand, Thomas. Come and watch." Robert indicated the barrel seat that Mary had just left.

Thomas regarded the barrel much as one might a snake. "I don't wish to play cards."

"Then Lady Fia and I will play without you." Robert smiled at her. "'Tis your turn to deal, my love."

She took the cards, but before she could do more than

turn them over in her hands, Thomas sat on the barrel Mary had just vacated. "This had better not take long." Legs firmly set, he crossed his arms with the air of a man determined to see some unpleasant business through. "Make haste. We've work to do."

Fia sent Robert a glance beneath her lashes and he embarked on a lengthy description of the game they were to play. Fia obediently dealt the cards and they began.

Robert did not cease prattling, which was a relief, for Fia's heart was thundering far too hard to allow her to engage in casual conversation. She stole glances at Thomas. His eyes were weary looking. Had he been having trouble sleeping, as well? What had—

Robert cleared his throat. "My sweet, do you discard?"

Fia dragged her gaze back to her cards. She chose a card at random and slid it under the mug.

"Ah, Lady Fia," Robert said. "I begin to suspicion you harbor unexpected depths. *Gutta cavat lapidem non vi sed saepe cadenda.*"

Thomas's brows lowered as he silently mouthed the words.

Fia arranged her cards in a more organized manner. "He said, 'The drop hollows the stone not by force, but by falling often.'"

"I know what he said," Thomas replied curtly. "I just didn't see how it applied."

"He thinks I'm pretending to lose merely to catch him unawares."

Robert blew her a kiss. "You have explained me better than I could have myself."

Thomas sent Robert a disgusted look. "I don't understand why you couldn't have said that in simple English."

"Ah, the burdens of genius! Understood by so few." Robert sighed and stared at the sea as if beholding some invisible sign of his greatness.

Thomas snorted. "Crackbrained fool."

"You see what I have to contend with?" Robert asked Fia. He made a great show of choosing a card. "'Tis a difficult decision when there's so much at stake."

"At stake?" Thomas asked, suspicion lowering his brow.

"Aye, Lady Fia and I wagered on the outcome of this game."

Fia slanted an astonished look at Robert, who gave her a quick wink.

"What's the wager?" Thomas snapped.

"Why, Thomas," said Robert sweetly, "Lady Fia and I play for kisses."

"*What?*" Thomas roared. In a second, he was on his feet, pulling Fia with him. Her cards flew into the air, were caught by the wind, and tumbled across the deck. "Return to your cabin!"

"No." Fia pulled her hands free and dropped back onto her seat, her jaw set. "Stop ordering me about! I will not be treated so."

Had Thomas politely asked her, she might have agreed to return to her cabin, but to be yelled at in such a manner irked her no end. "I am staying where I am. Robert and I have a game to play." She gathered the fallen cards, brought them back to the game, and took her place back on the barrel. "Robert, 'tis your turn."

"So 'tis," Robert said, calmly playing another card.

There was a moment of silence while Thomas glared down at Fia.

"Fine," Thomas finally said. He sat down, his jaw taut. "Deal me in."

Robert eyed Thomas with an interested gaze. "Are you also playing for kisses? For if you are, you'll have to shave that face of yours before I pucker—"

"Not from you, arse," Thomas snapped. His gaze flickered over Fia, lingering on her mouth. "I play for *her* kisses and she for *mine*. You will have to satisfy yourself with less. *Far* less. Now deal the damned cards." He sent a burning look at Fia as he spoke.

A shiver traveled over her and extinguished her irritation.

"But—" Robert sputtered. "What if I win?"

Thomas slapped a card onto the makeshift table. "You'd better hope you don't. In fact, if you wish to spare yourself a lumped head, I'd suggest you lose as hard as you can."

Robert sniffed, looking offended. "'Tis ill-mannered to threaten a man while playing cards. You break my concentration. Fortunately for you, I thrive on challenges. Shall we sweeten the pot?"

Thomas's gaze lingered on Fia. "I think the pot sweet enough."

Fia's cheeks heated, and she pretended to organize her cards.

"Well said, *mon ami*," Robert said with grudging admiration as he settled back into the game.

"Of course 'tis well said," Thomas returned calmly. "You are not the only one who delivers compliments where they are deserved."

"Oh, you deliver compliments with ease, just not as often with such *eloquence*."

Naturally, Thomas returned with a witty sally, which Robert immediately answered.

In their determination to win the game, they completely

forgot about Fia. When they twice missed her turn without noticing, Fia threw her cards on the barrel. Neither did more than glance up until the wind tried to carry the cards away. For a moment, they were occupied in gathering and placing the lost cards into the discard pile. Then, with the air of men achieving greatness, they settled back on their respective seats and lost themselves to strategy and counter-strategy, mocking parry and return.

She was forgotten while the two fools competed for her. 'Twas ludicrous! Finally, she could take no more. With a muffled exclamation, she rose. "I'll take my leave. Mary needs me below."

"Very well, my sweet," answered Robert absently.

"Anon," answered Thomas, his regard solely for the card Robert slid under the edge of the mug. "A-ha! Now I have you! You play like a damned novice, Montley."

"Aye, but at least I *play*. You merely toss random cards and hope one will take."

Fia marched away. As she reached the steps to descend into the hold, she looked back.

Robert stared at his cards with a rapt expression, lost to everything but the game, but Thomas met Fia's gaze with a knowing smile. *That bounder had acted thusly on purpose!* He had cut her out of the game as cleanly as a knife through warm butter. For some reason, the knowledge sent a trill of warmth through her and she found herself smiling back before she turned and went to seek out her maid.

Och, 'twas a fine madness, indeed. Fia could no more untangle her thoughts where Thomas was concerned than she could fly. All she knew was that when he was close, she felt as alive and free as if she were on a stage before a wildly appreciative audience.

Yet the reality was much different: if she entered into a real marriage with Thomas, the last thing she'd feel was free. His views on the correct comportment and place of his wife within the confines of his life were harsh and narrow, and she knew she'd fret against such restrictions.

It was a maddening conundrum, and she feared there was no real answer. The best thing she could do was enjoy her time with Thomas, for when they reached London, all would change. And sadly, it would not be for the better.

Chapter Fourteen

Fia flipped the fan open and turned it toward her, admiring the rich colors of the painted silk. A pastoral scene decorated one panel. It presented a man asleep in the golden grasses of a sun-drenched field, his long, bare legs peeping through the wheat. A covey of young, buxom nymphs admired him with wandering hands, their nudity barely covered with garlands of flowers.

She held the fan before the window and examined it more closely. The man lay naked, and the grass was very inadequate to cover his nether areas. She gazed anew at his face. "Sweet Saint Catherine, 'tis Robert MacQuarrie!"

She shut the fan with a snap, her face burning. Only Robert would own a fan so daringly painted with his own likeness. She had to laugh, though, at his audacity.

Fortunately, she grew up in a castle filled with men, and she knew how to deflate even such a high and mighty personage as Robert.

Hmm. Perhaps she would wonder aloud why the nymphs were so enthralled with such a plump little man?

Of all things Robert abhorred, to be thought plain or ordinary burned him the most.

Grinning to herself, Fia danced around the cabin, an imaginary partner clasped in her arms. She was just beginning to understand the more complicated steps that Robert had been teaching her. It had been pleasant to whirl around the deck, her feet moving with the music. It had been even more pleasant to have Thomas staring at her with such interest.

'Twas a pity he hadn't won the card game. She had waited impatiently for the outcome, pacing the cabin until Mary had sent her away. Robert had met her in the corridor, and there was no mistaking the triumph in his blue eyes.

"You won." She hadn't meant to say the words with such a lack of enthusiasm, but disappointment weighed her down like a heavy, wet blanket.

Robert laughed. "Do not look so put-upon, my love. The game ended just as it should have and—"

Thomas's deep voice bellowed down the passageway from the deck above. *"Montley!"*

Robert sent a good-humored glance toward the deck before he grinned back at her. "I must go. When I return, we'll practice the art of conversation. The queen is an intelligent woman and she is most impatient when bored. 'Tis important to be able to turn a phrase, tickle her wit, make her laugh or—"

"Montley! Before the hour passes, if you please!"

Robert chuckled. "Adieu, my lady." With that he left, his short cape swirling behind him.

Fia had frowned and returned to her cabin. Her husband was a mite high-handed. 'Twas probably for the best that he'd lost the game.

Mary always said fate was what you made it, and Fia was beginning to believe that more and more. Perhaps she should take her fan and go practice her wiles on some of the sailors on deck? Simmons would be a good beginning. He was a kindly old man and always grinned when she came about.

She approached the ladder leading up to the deck just as a shadow darkened the opening. She fluttered the fan. Robert had vowed there was little so entrancing as a pair of feminine eyes peering over the edge of a fan. Not only did it draw attention to the beauty of one's eyes, he had explained, but it screened the rest of the face from view, and there was not a man alive who could withstand a mystery.

She peeped over the edge, lowering her lids to give a sultry expression. Robert had specifically taught her this trick to render her admirer speechless.

"God's blood! Where did you get that?" Thomas did not sound admiring.

Her smile froze into a grimace behind the fan. "Lord Montley was most kind in allowing me the use of it."

"Return it to him. I don't like such frippery nonsense."

"I am told 'tis all the fashion."

His brows lifted. "Perhaps I don't care for fashion."

She lowered the fan and closed it with a practiced flip of her wrist. "Perhaps you'd be more enjoyable if you did."

After a surprised moment, he chuckled. "I suppose I deserved that."

"Trust me, you did." Fia couldn't help but feel a bit piqued. Thomas was supposed to be charmed by the fan. He should have bowed and flattered and responded in turn, not chuckled at her as though she were a child playing dress-up.

Perhaps she had not plied her fan correctly. She tried again. "My lord, I look forward to hearing what you have to say. May I suggest that we go somewhere more . . . private?" She gave him a languishing glance through her lashes.

Thomas's smile disappeared and his face turned red. "Sweet Jesu, what has that devil's spawn been teaching you? You sound and look like a—" His mouth opened and shut, but he seemed unable to continue.

She dropped her hand and drew herself up to her full height, disappointment rumbling through her. "You cannot tell me that the ladies of Elizabeth's court do not ply fans and flirt."

"They might, but that's no reason for you to—" His gaze narrowed. "Wait a moment. Why do you care what they do in Elizabeth's court?"

"Once our wedding is annulled, I could very well join the queen's court as a lady-in-waiting. Robert said 'tis a possibility, given my position."

"You will spend your day running errands for a woman known for her ill temper and shrewish nature."

"I've been living with Duncan for years now; I'm used to ill tempers. It might be nice to have some female companionship. Robert says 'twould suit me well and he's been teaching me some of the ways of Elizabeth's court."

"Damn Montley! I knew this was his doing. He's trying to irk me."

"No, he's trying to help *me*."

"Montley knows the court is infested by the vultures who constantly encircle the throne. 'Tis not the place for a tender-skinned halfling like you."

Fia stiffened. "A tender-skinned halfling? Must you act

as if I am a mere child and not a grown women well over the age of twenty?"

"I have never treated you like a child."

"You're doing so now." She flicked the fan open and shut to show her irritation.

Thomas regarded the fan with distaste. "Whatever nonsense Lord Montley has been teaching you, you are to forget it forthwith. I'll have that blackguard's head for his arrogance in attempting to transform my wi—" He caught himself and snapped his mouth closed.

"You will not say a word to my Lord Montley. I *asked* him to teach me how to present myself."

"Mistress, let me remind you that at this moment you carry *my* name. And as long as you do, you will do as I say."

"Oh?" She lifted her chin and gazed directly into his eyes. "And who will make me obey? *You?*"

Irritation flickered through his eyes, followed just as quickly by interest. "You don't even come up to my shoulder and yet you dare challenge me." The tiniest flicker of humor warmed his brown eyes. "I'm nonplussed, my lady."

'Twas the humor that was her undoing. With his expression softened, his brown eyes warm with laughter, she couldn't say him nay. The realization frightened her no end.

As if he sensed her weakness, he leaned closer and placed his hand on the wall over her head until she was partially caught between his chest and the wall, the delicate fan her only barrier. "So that there will be no confusion, comfit, when it comes to my wishes I *will* make you obey. Only I will not use sharp words and a heavy hand. I will use one like this." He lifted his hand and brushed her temple and cheek with a feather-light touch, his warm fingers causing her heart to thunder.

Fia shivered, though she tried to hide it. "I-I don't need anyone to make me do anything. I am not a child."

"No, you're not." He leaned forward yet more, until his cheek brushed her temple and lingered there. "Far from it."

His deep voice rumbled against her ear and warmed her head to toe.

Fia's skin tingled and she had to fight to keep from leaning against him.

"Fia?" His voice was deeper now, almost lazy sounding.

"Yes?"

"I wish to ask something."

"What?" *Anything. Right now, I'd give you anything. Ask me for an embrace, or a kiss, or a—*

"Leave this preposterous idea of becoming a lady-in-waiting."

Why couldn't he have asked for a kiss? "Why should I? I must have a plan for when we're no longer married."

He pulled back and smiled into her eyes. "Comfit, I never planned to throw you out into the streets, annulment or no."

"I know you'll find a sponsor for my plays, but I will need more than that."

"Aye, and I will see to it that you receive it—funds, servants, a house."

"You'd . . . you'd give me a house?"

"Aye, a fine manse on the river. I don't wish you to be destitute."

"I . . . I didn't know."

"Aye. But until then, I must ask that you behave with more decorum than Montley is wont to teach you."

She stiffened. "I have done naught but act with decorum."

"Aye, but you're far too beautiful to—" He hesitated, his face turning faintly pink.

"Too beautiful?" she prompted hopefully.

His face fairly flamed now. "Never mind. I meant only to say that there are circumstances that can make even normal actions seem scandalous. Like your presence on this ship."

Fia blinked at him. "Thomas, I don't know what you're asking. You must speak more plainly."

"Fine." He straightened, his face definitely redder. "I must ask you to cease visiting the deck so often. It distracts the men."

"The men like it when I visit the deck; Simmons has told me so."

"I'm sure they do, but I do not. And I am the captain."

"Not of me."

"*Especially* of you. Furthermore, there will be no more dancing on deck. Your skirts were flying about, your ankles exposed to one and all to see."

"Your own queen dances in just such a manner."

"But when she does so, it doesn't—" He shook his head and then leaned forward, pressing his warm length against her, cupping her cheek with his large, warm hand. "She's not my wife."

Fia didn't answer, equally irritated and mesmerized. 'Twas just like the scene she had written in her play *The Merry Maids of Azure*. Ramonda, the warrior queen, was being seduced by Thelius, the handsome hero intent on stealing her birthright.

What was it Ramonda had said? Oh, yes . . .

Fia tossed back her head and held her hands up to ward off his advances. "Do not try my will, man of my heart! Though you tempt me with chosen fruits and forbidden caresses, I will not turn from—" She paused. "My people" didn't exactly fit. "—dances."

Thomas blinked. *"What?"*

She grinned, pleased she had remembered the whole passage. "'Tis a passage from *The Merry Maids of Azure,* one of my plays."

"Oh yes."

He spoke as if her plays had no importance at all.

The realization that Thomas—her husband and the man who, with a mere touch, could make her knees quiver like jelly—could so cavalierly dismiss her plays irritated her greatly. "Fine. You don't enjoy the theater. I'm sure it doesn't matter though it shows 'tis a paltry marriage we have."

His smile faded. *"Paltry?* I am the wealthiest man in England!"

"Oh, are you? I wouldn't know. I'm your bride and yet I have no ring." She wiggled her hand in his face.

He stared at it, his brow lowered. "I didn't have the chance to—"

"Pssht. As if you tried. Admit you never thought of it until now."

"Perhaps I hadn't, but as this is no real marriage—"

"If 'tis no real marriage, then why should I listen to you at all? I will flirt with Montley, learn the ways of court, and dance upon the deck. I'm my own woman and belong to no man."

His brows lowered. "Damme, I came to warn you, and this is the thanks I get to—"

"Hold. You came to *warn* me?"

"Aye. You may think Montley is earnest in his attentions, but he's merely amusing himself with the only woman available. He will feed on your regard and then leave at the first flitter of another skirt, forgetting you."

"He sounds quite callous."

"Nay, nothing so intentional. 'Tis just his way." Thomas frowned. "Fia, you've been protected by your cousin and haven't faced the guiles of a sophisticated soul like Montley, who charms simply because he can. You are a passionate woman and so you must have a care."

"Thank you for the warning. I will make certain to protect my heart from Montley's flirtation." *Not that it needs it, for 'tis you who have captured my thoughts.* The realization lowered her spirits. Why couldn't she have developed thoughts of Montley, instead? He may have been a flirt, but at least he would have welcomed some interactions.

"Good. We will both benefit if you do so."

Fia wondered if Thomas was thinking back to his mother's elopement and its horrible effect on his own life. Suddenly, looking into his eyes, she could see him as the small boy who'd waited desperately for his mother to return, who'd vowed to find a place for himself in his father's affections, only to be denied over and over.

Behind the bravado and strength, she thought she'd caught sight of flashes of sadness, but it was more. It was deep and abiding loneliness.

Fia's heart caught in her throat and she turned away, blinking rapidly to keep the tears at bay. *How lonely was he as a child that it eventually became a permanent part of him?*

Tears blurred her sight and Fia realized that in fighting her emotions, she'd clenched her fan too hard. With fumbling fingers she attempted to open the delicate silk, but the bent and wounded spines refused to part. The once glorious fan lay like a broken bird in her hands.

To her horror, Fia felt her lip quiver.

"Fia?" Thomas's voice sounded strange.

She swallowed with difficulty. "I—it's nothing."

He cupped her chin with a warm hand and lifted her face to his. "You are crying. I didn't mean— God's blood, I've made a mull of things. I just wished to warn you and—" His gaze dropped to her bottom lip and he paused as if unable to continue speaking.

Fia's heart tripped and then sped up, her body tingling. *Please let him kiss me. Please let him.*

He slowly bent toward her, his gaze locked upon her lips. She leaned toward him, lifting her face to his as—

"Aye, Simmons!" Robert's voice drifted down the hold opening. "I'm going belowdecks now. I've set the course and that's the last thing I'm doing."

Thomas pulled back, sending a dark glare at the ladder. "Damn Montley's hide."

"And don't think you can send someone to wake me every hour as you did last night." Robert's voice was closer this time. "You were merely trying my patience and I won't have it. If someone knocks upon my door this eve, they'd best expect a blunderbuss to be their answer."

Thomas gave a muffled curse and, without warning, swept Fia into his arms.

She gasped and clasped him tightly about the neck as he stalked down the hallway. "What are you doing?"

"Trying to finish this conversation without that damned fop getting in the way." With one well-placed kick, Thomas opened his cabin door and carried her inside. He placed her upon the bed, then turned away to bolt the door. "If that knave is foolish enough to knock, don't answer."

Fia sat up and scooted to the edge of the bed, adjusting her skirts as she sent him a sour look. "I had no desire to speak to Montley right now. I spent all morning in his presence and 'twas enough."

Thomas turned a surprised look her way. After a moment, he said in an odd voice, "Aye, 'tis said Montley would make conversation even with the dead, given the chance."

"While I am grateful to him for his assistance, he wears my ears out." She bit her lip. "I shouldn't have said that, for he's been so kind and I'm most grateful for his assistance."

"'Tis not treason if you speak the truth." Thomas leaned a shoulder against the door. "Now, my lady, we were talking."

"Were we? I thought we were about to kiss."

His gaze became hooded. "You mistake."

"Nay, you were thinking about kissing me. I could see it in your eyes."

"About why *not* to kiss you, more like."

She smiled smugly. "Be that as it may, I am glad that you are at least speaking to me. You've been very distant since we came on ship."

He was quiet a moment. "I was. I thought it safer for the both of us. We'll not win an annulment unless you remain a maid, and I have difficulty remembering that when you are near."

Put that way—especially when combined with his grudgingly admiring glance—'twas quite a compliment. She peeped at him from beneath her lashes. "And now?"

"Now I've decided that anything is better than leaving you to fall prey to Montley's tutelage." He regarded her for a moment, absently rubbing his chin. "Milady, I think what we need are rules."

"Rules? For what?"

"For your behavior. Something simple, yet useful in knowing where to draw the line with knaves such as Montley. You are a scribe; why don't you write these rules down? Once we have them fixed, we will all breathe easier." He motioned for her to sit in a chair by the windows that kept the cabin bright and airy.

"Hmph. I don't know if I agree to your idea of rules, but I'm willing to listen." She sat, noting that while the chair was bolted to the floor, the cushions were snuggly and soft.

Thomas took the chair opposite, the sun glistening off the tanned skin of his throat. "If we know what we expect of each other, then there won't be any more misunderstandings. Four or so rules should suffice."

It was obvious that he already had some specific rules in mind. She nodded. "Then there will be two for you and two for me."

"For me? That's not what I was thinking."

"Surely you didn't expect me to have rules whilst you have none?"

"God's breath, woman! There's no need to make this complicated."

"I have no wish to make this complicated, but I do demand that it be *fair.*"

He scowled. "'Twould be easier were you less fair and more agreeable."

"Alas, the fates did not bless me so." She held her pen over the paper. "Begin."

"I'm trying to decide how to word this."

"Then I shall go and—"

"Nay, give me a moment!" His lips twitched. "I begin to fear what rules you have in mind."

She grinned. "I think you're going to dislike them."

He chuckled and leaned back, more at ease than Fia could remember seeing him. "Rule one: no dancing on the deck."

"None?" she asked, her humor fleeing.

"Nay."

She nibbled on end of the quill. "What if we just write 'No Italian dances.'? Robert says they are more lively than the others."

"No. None."

She sighed and wrote the phrase. 'Twas inconvenient to her plans, but she supposed she could work with Robert on some other area of her instruction. "Very well."

"Rule number two: no com—"

"Nay!" she interrupted. "'Tis my turn to make a rule."

His gaze narrowed, but he inclined his head. "So speak, Mistress Impatience."

"Very well: no more shouting." She wrote it in her elegant scrawl.

"Shouting? I don't sh—" He must have realized that his voice was lifting with each word, for he grimaced. "I don't shout. I merely make my requests in a firm voice."

She waved the quill in his direction. "Be that as it may, now you must use a more reasonable voice. We are now to rule three; 'tis your turn."

"No more conversing with Lord Montley," he answered promptly.

"I see. And just what should I tell him? That you've forbidden me to see him?"

"Nay, not that. He'd pester me until my ears bled and my stomach burned."

"If you forbid me to speak with Montley, I'll have to tell him why. 'Twould be rude otherwise. Perhaps you should think of a different rule?"

For a moment she thought Thomas might disagree, but then he nodded. "Fine. You may talk to Montley. So long as you know the man's a bounder and a scoundrel."

"'Tis rather obvious, I think."

"Aye, well, there are many ladies of the court who have yet to realize it." He rubbed his chin. "For my next rule I think I'll say, no parading about the deck flirting behind your fan, no giggling, and no wearing clothes that"—he gestured vaguely—"fit."

"That is more than one rule."

"No, it's not. 'Tis a broad sweep, but 'tis still just one rule."

She lifted her brows.

He sighed. "Fine. How about we simply say, 'No public displays.'"

She rolled her eyes. His new rule actually encompassed the no-dancing one, but she wasn't about to point that out. The fewer rules she had to follow, the better. She made a show of writing the rule across the page.

"Now 'tis my turn," she pronounced.

He nodded and eyed her warily. She rested her chin on her hand and stared out the window, her mind awhirl. She would have liked to add "More kisses." She wanted to feel the pressure of his lips sliding across hers. She cast a quick glance at him, only to see those warm brown eyes fixed on her with unnerving regard. She blushed and hurriedly dipped her quill into the ink.

"What have you decided?"

She flashed a grin and wrote in a large, firm hand, "More smiles."

"Smiles?"

"Aye, I'd like to see a bit of merriment from you. 'Tis unnatural, the way you glump about."

"I don't 'glump.' I'm not even sure what that is."

"Mary says 'tis a sign of an ill liver, but I'm more inclined to think 'tis a sour stomach."

"Neither my stomach nor my liver is ill," he said, his brow furrowed.

Fia looked at him and pointed to the fourth rule.

He grimaced but, after a moment, bared his teeth in a false smile. "There."

"Much better," she said with an encouraging nod. "That doesn't hurt, does it?"

"Yes, it does, but I shall do it anyway, if only to keep you from displaying your ankles before my crew."

She peeped up at him, her lips quirking. "I had no idea my skirts were cut so short."

"'Twasn't your skirts but your decorum that was lacking."

"I can only be glad my husband was there to offer correction," she said in a prim voice that was patently false.

Thomas's stiff smile softened. "You are an impossible chit."

"Och, that is exactly what Duncan says, too." She examined the paper. "Should we sign this to make it official?" She held out the quill.

He took it and the paper and signed his name with a flourish. "And now you, my lady." He handed her the pen.

She dipped it back into the ink and then went to sign her name. Just before the nib touched the paper, she paused. "We've not listed a forfeit. What if one of us doesn't follow this agreement?"

He smiled, then rose and stood behind her. Leaning over, he closed his large, warm hand over hers and guided the quill slowly through seemingly endless loops. She stared in wonder where he had written in an exaggerated script, *If either doth forfeit, then their virtue is at risk.*

"Virtue? But . . . do you have any left?" She blinked up at him, her eyes wide.

He chuckled. "You had better pray, my little Scottish thief, that you never find out."

Chapter Fifteen

Robert watched as Thomas strode across the deck. "Forsooth, I don't know what's come over Rotherwood. He's been acting odd the last three or four days."

"Odd?" Fia asked from where she was sitting decorously on a barrel by his side. "How so? I think he's been more pleasant of late."

"Exactly. He's been pleasant, even charming. I wouldn't recognize him, except that he occasionally reverts to his usual surly disposition. *Then* I know him."

Fia was most pleased with Thomas's efforts to follow their rules. He moderated his tone when speaking to her and they'd had several very pleasant conversations. It strained him, but no more than it strained her to behave like an old woman.

It chafed her very soul. If it weren't for the fact that she had to behave thus only for the time it took to reach London and perchance a day or two beyond, she might have exploded. Whenever she felt too caged, she'd take Zeus for walks through the hold, wending through the crates and barrels and ending in Thunder's makeshift stall.

For his part, Thomas not only moderated his snappish tone but, as he'd promised, was making an effort to smile. Judging from the strain in his gaze, Fia suspected it cost him dearly, and she did what she could to encourage him. Sometimes she was able to tease him until a genuine laugh overtook his false one.

It was in those moments, when they were both grinning ear to ear, that Fia's heart gave that odd jump that was becoming familiar whenever Thomas was around. She did what she could to fight that warm, breathless feeling, though she feared 'twas larger than she.

It was a good thing Thomas had no idea how devastating his true smile was. Had he realized it, he'd have flashed it more often.

"And you," Robert continued in a grumpy tone, "have refused to learn any new dances."

"My ankle is sore."

"Yet you do not limp."

"It only aches when I spin upon it, not when I walk."

Robert clearly did not believe her.

She pulled a card from her hand and attempted to tuck it beneath the mug, but the wind whistled, ruffling the cards. "The sea is high today."

"There will be a storm before the night's out." Robert frowned. "We're taking the shore route to London so there's more of a chance for storms." He frowned at the racing gray clouds that streaked the sky overhead.

They played a half hour more until the wind made it impossible to use the cards. Thomas appeared briefly to escort Fia belowdecks, ordering two of his men to secure all of the trunks to the metal rings set into the walls and the plank floors.

He then ordered Mary to escort Fia to his own cabin, where they would be more comfortable. Large shutters had been fastened over the windows, and Fia's two extra trunks were already lashed to the walls.

After hooking an astonishing array of netting about the bunk and telling her and Mary to climb inside it when the storm grew more violent, he'd left. When the waves grew wilder, it became impossible to sit in a chair even while gripping the arms. They'd staggered to the bed and had just been ready to climb inside the netting when a crew member had appeared to inform Mary that Angus had fallen and hit his head, and Mary had left.

On the bunk, Fia listened to the wildness of the storm, both excited and fearful. The heavy netting kept her securely on the mattress and she clung to it, saying prayers for their safety and absorbing every moment of the experience to use in a future play.

For what seemed like hours, she stayed in the bunk as the ship rose on the crest of one wave and then slammed downward into the base of another. Over her own fear, she worried about Thomas until her stomach tied in knots. The thought of him on the deck, exposed to those huge waves, made her almost ill. She wondered if Robert was on deck, too, assisting Thomas. Earlier, Robert had helped her secure Zeus and Thomas the rabbit in the hold with Thunder. She had piled up a mound of hay so that all were snugly ensconced in a comfortable nest. Robert had promised that once the ship hit rougher seas, Thunder would lie down and serve as an anchor for the others. *Please, God, let my wee animals be well, too.*

There was nothing to do but lie there and wait. Fia tried to sleep but she couldn't rest, wondering if the ship might sink and if Thomas was in danger. Restless and worried, she found herself holding the pouch that contained the amber amulet. Had the White Witch arrived at Duart Castle by now? What might she do when she discovered her prized jewel missing? Fia shivered, glad she wasn't Duncan. He might scoff at the old magics, but she would never dare.

She pulled the amulet out of the pouch and examined it in the flickering light of the lamp bolted to the wall by the door. The amulet felt oddly warm and she pressed it to her cheek, the long chain draped about her arm as she settled back on her pillows. Oddly, the warmth of the amulet soothed her fears, and though the ship seemed to creak louder and the waves beat even more ferociously, she soon slipped into a deep slumber.

In her dream, she was walking through a house she'd never seen—large, impressive, decorated with rich tapestries and mahogany furniture heavily embossed with gold, the tables covered with gold plate embedded with jewels. Through large open windows she could see a slow-moving river, the green grass rolling down to the shore, where ships and barges moved with majestic pride.

She looked about her in wonder, at home and yet not. Where was this place? And why did she feel such a connection that—

A door opened and Thomas appeared. He was dressed as if for court, in a deep-purple doublet shot through with silver threads, a neat but expensive pickadil about his neck. Hose decorated with dark panes stretched over his powerful thighs, complemented by a pair of rich canions.

He appeared powerful and relaxed, that engaging smile of his upon his lips.

She loved that smile and returned it, walking toward him, holding out her hands as if sure of a welcome.

He grasped her hands immediately, chuckling deeply as he pulled her close. "Lady wife, you look surprised. Did I not tell you I'd be but a half hour?"

"If I look surprised, 'tis because you're early."

He pressed first one and then the other of her hands to his warm lips, his gaze never leaving hers. "I could not keep away."

A shiver traced through her at the deep timbre of his voice. "Thomas, I . . . we're happy, aren't we?"

His smile widened. "Aye, we're happy. Happy and content and well, and everything we deserve." His expression darkened with concern. "But why do you question that? Do you not remember what I told you when we had our second ceremony?"

"Our *second* ceremony?"

"Aye, to replace the one your cousin forced upon us. I told you then, and I'll tell you the same now. No matter what was, or what is, or what will be, I am your—"

The ship pitched fiercely and Fia rolled hard against the netting, the amulet tumbling into the tangled bedding. She searched hazily about her, her fingers closing over the amulet once more, and she tucked it back into the bag and slipped it into her pocket.

Though wild, the seas were calmer than they had been, the howling wind coming only in brief fits now. Fia found herself wide awake, oddly refreshed by her short nap and ready for a new adventure. How she wished she could have been on deck to see the ocean come alive like an infuriated dragon, thrashing and writhing enough to sink an entire ship. The thought thrilled her.

Staying so still irked her, and she decided to rise since the ship's pitching had softened. She undid the netting and stumbled to the writing table, where she found her small lap desk tucked into the locked drawer. *Bless Mary for being so organized.* Fia clasped the desk to her and staggered back to the bunk. Perhaps she could begin a play with a shipwreck. That would be exciting indeed!

Fia absently rubbed the amulet as she looked about the cabin for further inspiration. This would do for a pirate's cabin. The handsome furnishings would serve well with just a few embellishments.

She looked at the desk. Would a pirate have a desk? Aye, Thomas the Pirate would. No doubt he would keep detailed records of his exploits. She would put a big lock on it to keep all of his maps, charts, and treasure inventories safe from prying eyes.

And perhaps, she thought, nibbling on the end of her quill, she should put a secret drawer in it. For the next several moments, the retreating howl of the wind and the scratch of her quill were the only noises in the room.

Sighing with satisfaction, she finished her description of the desk and looked about the room again, her eyes falling on the intricately carved chest at the foot of the bunk. She scooted over to regard it. It was so small, she had scarce noticed it before.

There was no need to embellish the description of the trunk. Made of sinister, dark carved wood, it looked for all the world like a pirate's possession. *What would be inside a pirate's trunk? Gold? Jewels? Swords? Coins? Or something more sinister . . .*

She shivered. She *had* to know what was in the trunk. She could relock it once she'd looked. And it wasn't as if Thomas had told her not to look. Indeed, he'd never mentioned the trunk at all.

Within moments, she was on her knees, the end of her knife in the lock. It took but a few twists before the lock gave and the chest opened with a satisfyingly gruesome creak.

Taking a deep breath, Fia peered inside and saw . . . folds and folds of pale blue silk. It shimmered like water as it rippled through her hands. 'Twas of such a light, pale color, 'twas obviously meant for someone of a fair complexion.

That is odd, she thought. As she pulled the silk from the trunk, a small leather pouch fell into her lap. For a moment, she could only stare at it. "Gold?" she whispered to herself. "Or jewels?" Her heart pounded as she lifted the bag. 'Twas too light to be either.

She untied the lavender ribbon that cinched the pouch, opened the bag, and poured the contents into her lap. Light yellow, deep purple and amethyst, bloodred, pale blue, azure, and every shade of green imaginable lay twined across her lap. "Embroidery thread," she said in a hollow voice. "He keeps blue silk and embroidery thread locked in a trunk."

Her heart began to sink. These were not pirate treasures but gifts. "The kind a man might bring to a woman he loves," she whispered aloud.

At sea it had been easy to pretend that only the people on board the *Glorianna* existed, but the truth was there were many other people waiting for the ship to dock so that they could make their presence known. Was a beauteous lady waiting on Thomas? Were the gifts in the trunk for her?

Like a woman possessed, Fia dug into the chest, heedless of disarranging the contents. A pair of women's shoes, the heels painted a pale blue to match the silk, flashed into view, and Fia halted to compare the shoe to her foot. It was inches too long. "Och, Thomas, you are dressing a giant."

Fia could almost see the mystery woman encased in pale blue silk and lumbering about in the blue heels. The troll-like image faded into that of a beautiful fairy queen and Fia's heart sank even lower.

Aye, a man of Thomas's looks and position would have a woman with long, blond hair and pale blue eyes to match the carefully stored silk. She would be tall and beautiful and practiced in all of the feminine arts. No doubt such an accomplished woman already resided at court and was fully accepted within that closed circle. Perhaps that was why Thomas was so eager to return to London and annul their marriage.

Fia slumped against the trunk, a shoe clutched in one hand and the packet of tangled embroidery threads in the other, and wondered why she felt so . . . betrayed. He'd never pretended to care for her and yet, somehow, she'd been secretly hoping that he might come to do so. In the few weeks she'd known him, she hadn't been able to shake the thought that they were somehow meant to be. That fate had brought them together.

Now, looking at the lovely shoe, she wasn't so certain. She was so lost in her unpleasant reverie, she almost didn't hear the footsteps coming down the hallway until they were almost at the door. As the knob turned, Fia gasped and leapt to her feet, shoving the fabric and scattered threads into the trunk.

She slammed the lid shut only to see the tip of a pale blue shoe peeking beneath the bed just as the door began to swing open. With a kick, she sent the shoe sliding farther under the bed just as Thomas stepped into the room.

He offered her a tired smile. "You're awake. I hope the squall didn't frighten you."

Fia's irritation faded completely. He was wet from head to toe, as if he had been swimming in the ocean and not sailing upon it. His clothing clung to him as lovingly as ever ivy had clung to a castle wall, his white shirt open to reveal his tanned throat and clinging to every well-defined muscle. She'd known he was a powerful man, but to see his arms ripple as he moved, the way his broad shoulder tapered to a stomach lined with muscles, made her knees go curiously weak.

"Fia?" Concern had deepened his voice. "Are you well?"

She hurried to find her voice. "I'm fine."

"Good. Where's Mary?"

"Angus hit his head. She went to see to him."

"I hope he is well."

"I'm sure he is or we would have heard from her."

"So we would. Did you bear the storm well?"

"Aye. I was just— After the sea calmed, I didn't have anything to do so I—ah, I was bored." Her voice was breathless with the need to keep his attention away from the trunk. The loosened lock creaked with every move of the ship, loud enough to be heard all the way to shore.

By some miracle, he didn't seem to hear the creaking iron. He leaned against the table, a mere arm's length away, and Fia had to curl her fingernails into her palms to keep from staring. "'Twas quite an exciting experience. I thought to write a scene with a shipwreck in it," she said.

"A shipwreck?" He grinned, and she felt the force of that devastating smile all the way to her knees. "Such is your faith in my skill as captain."

She chuckled. "I have complete faith in your skill, but I know nature to be an unforgiving mistress who cares naught for such things."

"Aye, she put on an impressive show this night." He sighed wearily and rubbed his neck, water dripping from his arm. "I came to find dry clothes and perchance some sleep."

"You can leave the deck now?"

"Aye, we're through the worst of it. Simmons will send for me if things change."

His drenched shirt hung in almost transparent folds about him, the wet curls on his broad chest glistening. She wanted nothing more than to run her fingers through those crisp hairs and watch the water drip down his chest, past the flatness of his stomach and on to—

"I don't know what you are staring at, comfit, but perhaps you'd like to come and help me into a dry shirt." His smile was wicked and angelic at the same time.

Her breasts tightened at the images all too quickly forming in her mind. "A shirt. Where do you—"

He pointed to a chest of drawers bolted to a far wall.

"Of course," she said, hurrying to it and finding a clean shirt. "What of a towel?"

"There's a cloth hanging in the wardrobe."

The large wardrobe was directly beside the chest, so she opened it and found the towel, then brought them both to Thomas.

He took them and smiled. "Thank you."

"Nay, I should thank you. It was quite comfortable here in your cabin. The bed in ours would not have been so comfortable."

"I shall add it to the bill."

"Bill?"

"You already owe me a kiss."

"A kiss?" Understanding came at once. "*You* won the card game and not Lord Montley?"

"Aye."

"But you said nothing and that was days ago!"

"I would have said something sooner, but we had other things to discuss."

"Our rules."

"Aye. I believe you said I should smile more often."

She nodded mutely.

"A kiss would bring a smile quicker than anything else. Perhaps I should claim it now whilst I am too tired to do more." His gaze flickered over her, resting on her lips, her neck, her breasts.

Fia shivered as he undressed her with his eyes.

He laughed softly, and a wave of longing swept through Fia with such intensity that she nearly sank to the floor. She needed to look away from those torturing eyes and that bared chest. With a supreme effort she dropped her gaze to the floor and saw . . . the lavender ribbon.

A cold hand clutched at her heart. She knew only a little of Thomas's past, but she knew he needed to trust and would do so only reluctantly. Why oh why had she allowed her imagination free rein with the trunk?

Fia took a casual step toward the ribbon. If she could just keep his attention off the floor . . . It was a pity she was not Argyll, the great seducer of men, from her play *Tempest at Sea*. Argyll knew how to draw a man's attention and keep it.

Fia closed her eyes, imagining the way Argyll would approach this.

Opening her eyes, she locked her gaze with Thomas's, she allowed her fingers to trail lightly down the high neckline of her dress. Surprise at her own boldness mixed with a hot flush of pleasure when Thomas's eyes followed the slow movement as her fingers reached the cleft between her breasts. His breath quickened to match her own, and she knew that she had his complete and undivided attention. A crate of ribbons could have been spilled at her feet right then and he'd never have noticed.

Fia took a casual step toward the center of the room, and Thomas's heated gaze followed her. He seemed to have forgotten about changing his wet clothing, forgotten they'd been talking, forgotten everything but her.

Just one more step and the ribbon would be safely hidden by her skirts.

She lifted her foot but couldn't move. Her skirt held her as securely as if it were nailed to the floor. She pulled on it, but to no avail. She glanced down and had to swallow a grimace; her skirt was caught in the hastily shut trunk. She tugged at it with a desperate hand, but it didn't budge.

"A-ha," intoned a deep voice. "I see you're back to your reiving ways."

Fia bit her lip. "Och, nay! 'Twasn't reiving. I was bored."

"So you mentioned before."

"There was naught to do, so I decided to write a new play, and the storm made me think about pirates and so

I was trying to imagine what a pirate might keep in his trunk, and I saw this one and—" She gripped her hands together. "I didn't take anything."

Fia expected anger, outrage, a loud and violent reaction. What she saw was Thomas's beautiful mouth curving into a reluctant smile. "What did you hope to find?"

She prayed the slight pitch of the ship wouldn't send the blue shoe sliding into view. "Gold," she confessed.

His lips quirked. "I take it you didn't find any."

She eyed the trunk regretfully. "Nay, though I wish there had been." *Anything other than clothes for your lover.*

Thomas crossed to her, his gaze trailing a heated path down her body. "'Tis your misfortune, little thief, that you're not very good at hiding things. I saw the shoe under the bed when I arrived, so I knew you'd been visiting places you hadn't been invited."

"*Och!* And you didn't tell me! I was so worried you'd be angry and—" She plopped her fists on her hips. "You had to know that!"

"I can only wonder what you would have done if the trunk *had* been filled with coins."

"*Real* gold coins? Like Spanish gold?"

He chuckled at her excited voice. "Aye, like Spanish gold."

"I might have taken some," she admitted. "But only if you had a *very* large number."

He laughed then, the sound rumbling in his chest. "You are incorrigible."

"But honest," she replied. "Surely that's worth something."

"Aye, comfit." He reached out and cupped her face with a large hand, his skin cool and still damp from the storm. "'Tis worth something indeed."

She closed her eyes and leaned her cheek against his hand. She couldn't think for the passions that stirred through her, couldn't breathe.

He slowly slid his hand from her cheek to her neck, his thumb resting lightly on the base of her throat.

Fia shivered and gripped his wrist, holding his hand in place. "Sassenach, please . . ." She didn't know what she was asking for, only that it was more than she had now. More than he was really offering.

But she didn't care. She wanted his complete attention, every bit of it.

With a sudden groan, he pulled her against his chest.

She expected to feel the coldness of his wet shirt through the front of her dress. But the water that seeped through her bodice was as heated as he. It soaked through the thin wool, causing the material to cling to her peaked breasts. His scent came to her—fresh salt water mingled with a tantalizing dash of sandalwood, masculine and tempting.

He moved his mouth to her ear. "I am near desperate with wanting you." His voice dropped to a whisper, wonder mixing with passion. "I told myself I could do this— see you and keep possession of my reason—but I fear I was wrong. I just don't give a damn about reason when you're about. All I want is *more*. More of you. More of your scent. More of your taste."

The sweet warmth of his breath brushed across her cheek. It was maddening to be so close to those carved lips and not have them on her, kissing her, tasting her . . . She threw her arms around his neck and pulled his mouth to hers.

He stilled in surprise, but she tightened her arms and opened her mouth under his. The roughness of his unshaven face excited her. She slipped the tip of her tongue past his lips—he tasted of the sea and the heat of desire. She tangled her hands in his hair and moaned her passion into his mouth.

He gave a muffled groan and caught her against him. His hands slid over her back and lower, grinding her against the hardness of his desire. He molded her to him, refusing to allow her to part from him.

She was lost, spiraling in a world of pleasure. Threading her hands through his thick hair, she ran her tongue over his jaw, reveling in the scrape of his unshaven skin. She wanted him now and forever. They were meant to be. The signs were all there. She wanted the feel of him, the taste of him. He might regret this come morning, but she never would.

Hot desire ran through Thomas's veins like burning oil, sweeping thought away in a torrent. It was madness. He had come to the cabin worried that Fia was frightened by the storm, only to discover that she'd blithely rifled through his trunk. He should have been angry, even though he knew the contents of the trunk were naught, but then he made the mistake of touching her, and all else had fled before a sudden and thorough onslaught of hot, primal lust.

The smoothness of her skin, the delicate hollows of her neck, the silken mass of her hair, all lured him until he could no more quit touching her, tasting her, than he could think. She was his, and he would have her.

He savored the sweetness of her mouth, nipping and teasing the lush lips until they parted and welcomed him into their honeyed depths. He plundered her mouth again and again until she was moaning with unnamed need. He left her lips to taste the delicate line of her jaw, and she clutched at his arms.

Her head fell back, revealing the white column of her neck, and he was afire anew. Thomas trailed his mouth to her shoulder, then farther still, to where her dress pressed her breasts into a fascinating cleft. He was determined to free those lovely mounds from their prison of wool.

With eager fingers, he undid clasp after clasp. The wool parted slowly to reveal dazzling white skin partly covered by a modest shift. As the last clasp released, her dress dropped to the floor, its hem still firmly caught in the trunk.

Fia's plain linen shift clung to every curve, every hollow, and Thomas had never seen a more provocative garment in his whole life. He tugged on the ties and was rewarded with a satisfying ripping sound.

Within seconds she was naked, nothing between them but his wet clothing. Thomas ran his tongue around the delicate swirl of her ear as he let his hands roam freely, wildly, across her bared back. His mouth trailed down her neck to her shoulder and then to her breasts.

He laid her carefully on the bunk, his mouth never breaking contact with her breasts. Full, lush breasts tipped with rose-hued nipples that begged to be tasted. They were magnificent. They were perfect.

His mouth trailed farther down to the flatness of her stomach, to the tangle of fine, tight curls. She gasped with pleasure, her back arching convulsively as his tongue found her wetness. He worshipped her with his mouth as he frantically ripped off his own clothing.

He could tell from her gasps of pleasure and the clutching insistence of her hands that she was as lost in wonder as he was. Sweet Jesu help them both. They were drowning in this wild passion.

He wanted to take his time, to slowly initiate her in the pleasures of lovemaking, but the demands of his body and hers were too much. Within seconds he was positioned between her thighs. His body was tense with the effort to control his passion, since he knew this would bring her pain, but she surged up to meet him with eager hips and clutching thighs. She whimpered for a moment as he stroked into her, murmuring into the silk of her hair, lost in her wet warmth. Again and again he thrust into her, each stroke an agonizing, delicious exhilaration.

She gasped, and her hands tightened on his shoulders. He paused, taking in the sight of her on the crest of her pleasure. Her face was flushed, her eyes closed, the lashes fanning in thick crescents, her lips parted and swollen. His mouth covered hers and she tensed, gasping as waves of intense sensation rippled through her. A surge of exultation pulsed through him and carried him on a wave of passion.

Afterward, his breathing was loud in the silence of the room, only the faint howl of the wind and the lazy rocking of the ship reminding him where he was. He pulled her to him and wrapped her in his arms, refusing to think of anything other than how perfectly made she was for him. She was *his*. He would deal with tomorrow when it arrived. For once in his life he wanted to stop thinking and just *feel*.

As if she agreed with his unspoken thoughts, she snuggled into his arms, her cheek against his shoulder as her breathing slowly returned to normal.

After a few blissfully peaceful moments, he raised his head and looked at her. Fia was sound asleep. Thomas admired the faint flush on her creamy skin, the way her pink lips parted as she slept.

She was his, at least for now. As for the annulment . . . he closed his eyes and settled into the pillow. He'd think about that on the morrow. He's just spent four hours battling a storm, and combined with such lusty lovemaking, he was too exhausted to think.

Without another coherent thought, entwined around Fia, Thomas went to sleep.

Chapter Sixteen

ia awoke slowly, her back pleasantly warm from the sun. She smiled drowsily and snuggled deeper into the rumpled sheets, her bare skin gently abraded by the rough blanket.

Remembrance flooded through her in vivid detail. She trailed a hand over her neck, where Thomas's roughened cheek had left its mark. Her hand dropped lower still to the tenderness of her breasts. The sensation sparked a thousand memories of his roaming hands, the warmth of his lips, and the feel of his body against and inside hers.

Who knew lovemaking could be so glorious? A deeply contented smile curved her mouth as she turned over and pushed the blanket aside, stretching out in the sunlight like a contented cat.

Thomas had been so passionate last night. In his desire, he had murmured a thousand lies into her ear, each one sweeter than the one before. And she had let him. She had wanted him to say she was beautiful and perfect, that she was made for him.

Afterward she had fallen asleep in his arms, sated and happier than she had ever been. She wished he hadn't been called away from her side; it would have been pleasant to awake with his arms still about her. But his duties as captain of the ship couldn't be denied.

She smiled at the streams of sunshine flowing through the unshuttered windows. 'Twas a glorious day, the merry sea topped by a blue, blue sky, as if celebrating the fact that she and Thomas were now man and wife in the truest sense. The thought made her grin all the way to her toes.

Had this been one of her plays, Thomas would now return, throwing the door wide, his expression brightening on seeing her still in his bed. He would come to kneel at her feet and then, in the sweetest of words, he'd proffer his heart.

Fia's eyes grew teary. Every woman deserved such a scene. She loved so many things about Thomas. She loved how serious he was and how he took responsibility for everyone around him. She loved his quick sense of humor and the way his men cared for him. There wasn't a single one of his crew who wouldn't die for his captain.

She wrapped the sheet about her and scooted to the edge of the bunk, her eyes on the door. If this were one of her plays, Thomas would appear wearing a long, swirling cape of blue thrown over his shoulders, his black hair glinting in the sun and his white shirt unlaced to reveal his strong chest as it had last night.

Pure, hot desire would smolder in his velvety brown eyes as he knelt to place a lingering kiss on her hand. Then, gazing into her eyes, he would tell her of his love.

She heaved a deep sigh. 'Twas almost as good as when

Nicoli the Unruly had swept the lovely Rosalind from the bower in *The Lady of Ghent*. Fia stretched her bared legs and wiggled her toes in anticipation.

Almost as if on cue, a noise arose out in the passageway. Fia leaned forward, her breath caught in her throat as the door opened. Could it be Thomas? Was he coming to tell her that he—

Mary's red head appeared around the door. "Och, ye're finally awake!" The maid entered the room, her arms full. "Just look at ye, lyin' abed so late."

Fia hid her disappointment. "Aye, I overslept, but I'm awake now."

"Good, fer I brought ye some company, I did." Mary laid the gown and petticoats she was carrying across the back of a chair. Then she reached into the bag over her shoulder and pulled out a ball of brown fur.

"Och, you brought the wee rabbit!"

"Aye, fer he's drivin' the entire crew mad, hoppin' about and gnawin' on every rope he can find. Apparently some of them are too important to trust to a hungry rabbit."

Fia rubbed the rabbit between its ears before setting it on the table. He immediately hopped to the blue shoe that now sat upon it and sniffed suspiciously at the painted leather. "The animals are well after the storm?"

"They're better than Angus. He nigh broke his noggin."

"Oh, Mary, I'm so sorry. I didn't know he'd been injured that badly."

"Och, 'twas no' so bad; he has a head like a rock. He's fine now, though ye wouldna know it to hear him complain. The man's a nuisance when he's ill, refusin' to drink the possets I brought him and sayin' he's dyin'." Mary tsked as she busied herself about the room. "But men ne'er dinna deal well with illnesses."

"Aye, Duncan wasn't one to handle being confined to bed, either."

Mary lifted a gown off the chair. "I brought ye some fresh clothes. I even managed to iron the skirts, thanks to the cook, who heated me iron over his own stove in the ship's galley." The maid pulled a pair of slippers from her pocket and placed them by the bed, then went to shut the door. "'Tis good ye're still undressed, fer I ordered ye a hot-water bath. The rain filled all of the barrels on deck, so there's plenty of water to be had."

"A bath? On board ship?"

"Aye, I found a large barrel in the hold that will do the trick. The first mate complained when I confiscated it, o' course, but the ship's cook has been helpful. He's warming up the last o' the water right now."

"That's lovely! Mary, have . . . have you seen Lord Rotherwood today?"

"Aye, he's on deck bellowing orders. Angus said the captain is grumpier than a bear in a trap, and the men are tryin' to stay out o' his way."

Some of Fia's good mood slipped away. "He's in a foul mood?"

"Aye, snapping at everyone. He even snarled at Lord Montley and threatened to throw the man off the ship, though I dinna blame him fer that. I've oft wanted to— Och, I left yer special lavender soap in me cabin. I'll be right back." Mary scurried off and Fia dropped back onto the bed, her heart thudding.

Why is Thomas in such a bad mood? He couldn't possibly have been disappointed last night. Suddenly the grand scene

Fia had imagined earlier seemed woefully unlikely. *Does he regret what happened? Does our passion mean nothing to him, and he still wishes for an annulment?*

It was a lowering thought. Yet she had to admit that it was a possibility. Thomas was a sophisticated and worldly man; perhaps to him lovemaking was merely a pastime, while to her, it meant—

What? What *did* it mean? She didn't dare think about it until she knew how Thomas felt.

Her throat ached where a lump of emotion had lodged itself. No matter what happened, she wouldn't allow him to see how disappointed she was that he hadn't found their lovemaking an emotional experience, as well. *Montley told me that the court is rife with icy hearts and cold ambition. Though the signs were all there, I didn't realize he was warning me about Thomas.*

What was she to do now? When the ship docked, perhaps she should take Mary and Angus and the animals and set off on her own adventure. After a few months, she'd forget all about Thomas and their night of passion. In the meantime, she could find a sponsor for her plays on her own.

Or could she? Without the proper introductions to the right people, she might never find a sponsor. And where would she stay? She had limited funds and many to support. Perhaps she could sell the amber amulet. No, she'd promised Duncan she'd place it in Elizabeth's hands and Fia couldn't turn her back on her promise.

Ignoring the warmth of the sun streaming through the window, she lay across the wide bunk, her arms outstretched as if she'd expired.

She pictured herself huddled against the outside gates

of a huge manor, the wind and snow swirling about her as she tried piteously to start a fire with nothing but a broken piece of a flint and some damp twigs.

Her dress would be torn and shabby, her feet wrapped with dirty rags. Eventually she would die from the cold and they would find her wasted figure in the snow, her fingers clutching her brilliant plays.

Fia's head and arm hung dramatically over the edge of the bunk; she was the very picture of an innocent maid dying wrongly accused. She'd bet her best quill that Thomas would be sorry then. Aye, he would come to her deathbed and kneel, his head bowed over her lifeless hand as he realized that it was his cold heart, not the weather, that had frozen her to death and—

Mary bustled back into the room, halting at the door. "What are ye pretendin' now, lassie? Ye look as though ye've gone and died right there on the poor cap'n's bunk."

Fia's face heated as she scrambled to sit upright. "I was just thinking about a play I am writing."

"A new play?" Mary's eyes brightened as she bustled Fia into a robe. "Och, tell me about it."

A brief knock sounded on the door and Simmons nearly skipped into the room. "Good mornin' to ye, milady!" His ruddy cheeks stretched into a wide smile that grew wider when his gaze fell on Mary. "And to ye, too, Mistress Mary."

There was no disguising the admiration in his voice. Mary's blue eyes raked the first mate up and down, her mouth prim with disdain. "Och, now, and what do ye think ye are about, boltin' into her ladyship's room without so much as a by-yer-leave? Ye knock and *then* ye wait fer someone to tell ye to come in!"

"Sorry, mistress." Simmons regarded her rounded

frame with admiration. "I'm bringin' ye the tub, like ye requested." He stepped aside and waved in what seemed to be the entire crew, carrying pails of hot water and a half cask that must have been the washtub.

Mary watched as the men filled the makeshift tub with gently steaming water. "Dinna fill it too full. 'Tis a small tub and the water will splash out if ye do."

After Simmons and the men left, Mary dipped an elbow into the tub. "'Tis not much of a tub, but the water is hot."

Fia nodded. The small tub seemed to sum up her whole situation; she had to compress her unruly feelings into a smaller space than they wanted.

Mary shot her a quick, assessing gaze. "Och, dinna look so disappointed. 'Twas the best I could do and—"

Fia hugged the maid. "I'm very grateful for the tub. I'll fit, too. Just not all at once."

Mary chuckled. "Climb in, lass. Just think: ye might be meetin' the queen soon! 'Tis unlikely to be as soon as we'd hoped, though; the storm blew us off course a bit. But another few days will pass quickly enough."

Fia's heart sank. "We'll be longer at sea?"

"Aye. Now, in the tub with ye." Mary bustled to the door. "I'll fetch ye up some drying cloths." She shut the door behind her.

Fia sighed, tossing her robe onto the bed and settling into the small tub. It was ludicrously tiny and both of her legs hung out. "A bath," she said scathingly. "More like a puddle if you ask me."

Thomas the rabbit hopped to the edge of the tub and stood on his hind legs, sniffing the air.

Fia smiled reluctantly. "'Tis a paltry excuse for a tub, is it not?"

He apparently agreed, for he hopped back to the blanket, which had fallen to the floor, and flopped onto his stomach.

Fia sighed, trying hard not to succumb to the weight that pressed on her. "It appears that Thomas regrets what happened betwixt us, and it pains my pride. It's never nice to be regretted."

The rabbit's nose quivered as if he agreed.

"I need to stop thinking about his high and mighty lordship and pay attention to why I came to London: to find a sponsor for my plays." She picked up a cloth and rubbed Mary's lavender soap across it.

"I was foolish to think that just because my feelings for him have grown, that his feelings for me were doing the same." Fia rubbed her arms with the soapy cloth, using far more force than was necessary. "Perhaps if I act as if nothing has happened, he will do so, too. At least then I'll still have my pride."

The rabbit rolled to one side, presenting its back to Fia. "Aye, I'm fooling myself, aren't I? The man fascinates me as no other, yet he never seems as taken with me. I don't know much about relationships, but it seems poorly constructed to have one that is so lopsided. And I've a feeling that things will only get more complicated once we reach London."

The rabbit placed its head upon its paws and sat quietly, as if thinking.

"Aye, I shall have to put my mind to the issue, as well." Sighing, Fia rested her head on the tub's edge and closed her eyes, her mind whirling. She had to make it through the next week without allowing herself to fall even more under Thomas's spell. He was obviously upset that an annulment was no longer possible.

Perhaps *that* was the key. Perhaps if she showed him that *she* still wished for the annulment and would do what she had to in order to procure it, then he would be easier.

She sighed. It wasn't much of a plan, but for now, 'twas all she and her rabbit could come up with.

Chapter Seventeen

Thomas halted outside his cabin, holding the towel he'd wrested from a scandalized Mary, his other hand resting uncertainly on the brass handle.

All morning, he'd grappled with the cold reality of his actions last night. There was no longer a possibility of an annulment; they had crossed that line. Even now, Fia could be carrying his child. Taking the towel from Mary had been a bold move, for it had publicly announced that his wife was now his in more than name only, but he was feeling bold. Bold and determined to do the right thing, regardless of the cost to his happiness. A Wentworth could do no less.

Sweet Jesu, but it had been a short night. First the storm, and then finding Fia alone in his room. His blood heated at the memory. After hours of fighting the storm, he'd been so exhausted he'd barely been able to stand, but the second he'd pulled Fia into his arms, all that was forgotten.

This morning he'd been none too pleased to leave the

warmth of his bed to stand upon the frigid deck, knowing Fia was snug and waiting.

Fia . . . in his bed. He closed his eyes against the heat that instantly rose, astonished that he lusted for her still. Merely hearing her splashing in her bath through the door was an exquisite torture.

Thomas could almost see her white shoulders rising above the water, her hair floating around her like a mermaid's. His loins tightened painfully, and he scowled. By the saints, but he was as besotted as a stripling.

It was that thought that had sent him from her bed with such haste.

Being married to her would expose him to her charm all the more. He was already discovering that his original idea to see more of her and thus slake his hunger had done the opposite.

"Aye, look where that got you," he muttered. "Into her arms and more tangled than ever."

The truth was simple: there was a fierce attraction between them, one that made no sense and did not answer to any plans he'd made for his future.

He leaned his forehead against the door, a strange ache in his heart. Some part of him that had loosened under her sensuous touch had curled back into a tight knot when he'd realized how perilously close he was to falling in love.

And out of control.

His jaw set. If he had anything to do with it, such a thing would never, ever happen.

Yet what was he to do now? He'd compromised her; now he was cursed. But the time for complaining was gone. He'd made his choices and now they were his to live with. He gripped the brass handle and opened the door.

Fia sat with her back to the him, her arms and legs sprawled over the edges of a very small tub. Her wet hair hung in a curtain down her back and pooled into a puddle on the floor, strands clinging to her neck and shoulders. She looked more like a sodden puppy than the mermaid he'd imagined.

She turned at the sound of the door and Thomas caught a glimpse of her profile, her eyes tightly shut to ward off the soapy water dripping down from her hair.

"Mary, pray bring the towel. I've soap in my eyes."

If ever a woman had a voice that whispered of wanton pleasures, it was hers. Thomas tried to ignore the rise of her breasts as she reached blindly toward him. He was struck with an almost overwhelming urge to pull her into his arms and taste that bath-sweetened skin.

"Mary?"

Thomas dropped the towel into her outstretched hand.

"Och, thank you." Fia wiped her eyes and held the towel back toward him, never turning around.

He took it without saying a word.

"I can't believe this is all the tub that's to be had on the Sassenach's ship," she grumbled. "'Tis more like a tankard." She gazed at the steam that rose from the water. "Mary, do you remember the hot springs Duncan took us to see in Wales? The mist off the water curled into fingers, reaching up and up, only to waft away. I was fascinated and fearful yet I couldn't look away."

Every word drew Thomas in, feeding something thirsty deep in his soul. She was a conjurer, this woman of his, a magician who turned words into feelings and memories and thoughts he didn't want to have.

He found himself lost in a memory that had tucked

itself into a deep corner of his mind. He'd been young, maybe five or six, and his mother had come to the nursery and dressed him in a heavy woolen cloak and leather boots. He'd been excited, for it had rained for what had seemed weeks and weeks, and they hadn't been able to go outside.

He frowned, the memory slipping more firmly into place. His mother had loved to ride and would go in all weather, to his father's disapproval. She would come back flushed and muddy, her hair falling about her, her cheeks rosy, a grin turning up her usually somber lips. Those were the few times she'd really seemed happy.

Thomas always thought she looked so pretty then, but it somehow made Father angry, for 'twas not decorous to ride in such a manner. Yet Mother had refused to give up her riding.

This one day had been different, though. Instead of going out by herself, she'd come for him, whispered to him to be quiet, then they'd slipped past his father's study and outside.

A carriage was waiting and she'd taken Thomas to a clearing deep in the woods where the coachman unpacked a picnic basket. Then he and his mother had sat in the middle of the mist-filled woods, raindrops dripping from wet leaves all around, and had their luncheon. Mother had talked and smiled, but her usual somberness was never far away. Once in a while she'd look at the misty trees, her eyes dark with longing.

Had she wanted to get away even then? When he thought about it now, perhaps his mother had been as lonely as he, locked away in that house with no companions but his stern father.

There had been hell to pay when he and his mother had returned; Father was furious over their "unbecoming conduct" and had admonished the nursemaid not to allow Mother to take Thomas again.

Yet it had been worth it. For weeks afterward, whenever his mother and he would look at each other, they'd share a secret smile, remembering their enchanted time in the woods.

A splash from the tub recalled Thomas to the present. Fia had stretched a leg before her and was busily soaping it. "I feel the same way now that I did when I first saw that misty spring. I'm afraid, yet also excited. Those mist-formed fingers haunted me for weeks after, and I've always wondered if they were beckoning me forward or warning me away . . ." Her voice faded as her expression became distant. "Mary, do I go forward with the Sassenach, or away? I don't know which . . ."

Thomas's mouth went dry as he noted the seductive curve of her leg, and he wondered if she had any idea how appealing she looked. What thoughts had she become so lost in? He fished in his pocket for a coin.

A glimmer of gold flashed through the air, and Fia blinked, surprised as the glistening coin landed with a splash in the water, coming to rest on the curve of her stomach. Before she could speak, another coin glittered through the air and Fia gasped as it plopped onto the damp slope of her breast.

Behind her, a deep voice said, "Normally I'd offer a penny for a thought, but yours always seem to be worth more than most."

Thomas walked into her line of vision, a faint smile on his lips though his gaze was somber.

"My thoughts are hardly worth a penny, much less gold."

"Nay," he said with apparent disbelief. His eyes held hers, a disturbing flicker in their brown depths. Then his gaze wandered lower, and Fia instantly became aware of her lack of clothing and her ungraceful position.

With a mad scramble, she closed her legs and tried to cover her breasts and reach for the towel all at the same time. Her hand closed about the towel, but Thomas's booted feet held it firmly to the floor. An unexpected grin lit his face.

The most she could do was cross one leg over the other, fold her hair over her chest, and hope the soapy water hid the rest.

"I've already seen everything you're trying so hard to cover, comfit," he said in a dry tone.

He had, but that didn't prevent her cheeks from burning. "I know, but—" She'd been too distracted then to think about it. Now things seemed different. "What . . . why are you here?"

He leaned against the desk and lazily pulled the towel toward him with his foot. "I wished to speak with you privately."

She tugged on the towel again, but his foot remained firmly in place. 'Tis rude of you to deny me a towel. The water's growing cold."

His gaze flickered to her breasts, and his gaze heated. "So I see."

She glanced down and saw that her nipples peeked through her hair. Her cheeks burned brighter and she hurriedly crossed her arms over her breasts as she tossed about in her head for another topic—*any* other topic.

Her frantic gaze found the blue shoe on the table. "Thomas, the blue shoes from your trunk—who are they for?"

"The queen, if she likes them."

Relief, pure and lifting, washed through her. Suddenly feeling years younger and freer, she nodded. "The queen will love them. What woman does not love pretty things?"

"True."

"And men, too," she added.

"Nay. Men prefer things of use."

"Montley would beg to differ."

"Montley *does* differ," Thomas replied, "in every area you could name."

Fia didn't want to think of Robert right now. Thomas looked so handsome, and she was achingly aware of him. She wanted to press herself against him, pull his loose shirt from his broad shoulders, and run her fingers through the crisp hair on his chest.

Sweet Saint Catherine, I need to maintain some dignity! It took all her resolve to gather her wits, but she did. "Robert's a rare one. 'Tis as hard to teach manners to a pig as 'tis to get Robert to speak sensibly. I had a pig once who was said to possess some magic. I called him King Arthur."

"Of course you did."

"Duncan wanted Arthur for Michaelmas dinner. I tried to help Arthur, but no matter how wide I left the gate, he refused to leave his pen. I tried putting a lead about his neck to take him to a safer place, but he squealed enough to wake the dead."

Thomas tried to tear his gaze from her mouth long enough to follow her recital. "And?"

She frowned, and he was captivated by the slight crease between her eyes. What would she do if he kissed it?

"Och, well, I discovered that the problem was Arthur wouldn't leave his trough. He even slept in it, so attached was he. Duncan laughed and said 'twas a sure sign Arthur was meant for the table, but I don't believe in fate. Do you?" Black eyes fixed on him in silent appeal.

He heard himself reply with all of the assurance of a professional swineherd, "Nay. Many pigs sleep in their troughs."

"So I thought, too." Her brow creased again. "But Duncan was determined to eat him, for truly there was never so fat a pig as Arthur. So one night I bribed the kitchen maids to help me heft Arthur's trough onto an old wagon, then we coaxed Arthur into following it up a makeshift ramp."

"So you saved him."

"I *think* so," she answered cautiously, her even white teeth catching at her lower lip.

"But?" he prompted, wishing he could release her lip with a kiss of his own.

She shrugged, the moment causing her breasts to peek through the curtain of her hair again. Thomas gripped the edge of the desk with both hands and willed himself to look into her eyes.

Fia continued, blithely unaware of Thomas's struggle. "Several months after I helped Arthur escape, an uncommon amount of sausage appeared at the keep. I was suspicious that Duncan had found the poor pig, but he never would say."

As she contemplated the probable outcome of King Arthur, her lip quivered slightly, and Thomas hurriedly changed the subject.

"I hate to distress you, comfit, but we need to speak of something more complex than the fate of Arthur the pig."

Her dark eyes flew to him, and after a pause she nodded.

"Fia, 'tis obvious that we can no longer seek an annulment. Especially now that you might be with child."

She paled. "I hadn't thought of that."

"I should never have touched you last night. I'm not usually overcome by desire, but . . . there is something between us."

"Something," she repeated, disappointment coloring her tone. "That's what you think 'tis? Just *something*?"

She wanted it to be more—the realization froze his heart. He set his jaw. "Aye, 'tis passion and naught else. What else could it be?"

Fia forced her lips into a smile. "You may have changed your mind, but I have not. I have no wish to wed." It amazed her that she managed to say the words without a quaver, for her heart was jagged from his coldness.

"Fia, we have no choice."

"We do. We can wait to see if there is a babe, and if not, we can continue to pursue a dissolution of the marriage."

"But . . . your innocence. When you marry again—" He clamped his mouth closed.

"That is my problem and not yours," she replied coolly. "I came to London to procure a sponsor for my plays, not a husband, so my virginity was my own to dispose of as I wished." That sounded very far-thinking and strong.

"I cannot in good conscience agree with you."

"Och, don't be foolish," she snapped, her voice hard with the strain of holding back her tears. "'Tis not your decision but mine. And I want the end of this marriage." *Now more than ever.* How could she remain married to a man who saw their passion as something to regret? Something to wish he could undo?

Thomas raked a hand through his hair. "Fia, I don't think you—"

There was a knock on the door and Simmons said, "Cap'n, ye had best come quick. Lord Montley has been going over the charts and thinks we've been blown off course. We need to make a correction forthwith."

Thomas cursed but turned to the door. "We'll speak some more when I return; we must come to an understanding."

"We already have." She rubbed her goose-bumped arms, the water already cooling. "Last night was a pleasant interlude, that's all. There's nothing more to discuss."

Thomas realized that she was repeating his own decisions to him, her voice so distant that she might have been speaking of someone else. Somehow she made him feel deficient, as if he'd offered her a grave insult of some sort.

Irritation surged and he scowled. Damn it, this wasn't how he'd wished this conversation to go. Yet, looking into her cool, clear gaze, he couldn't find a single word to defend himself.

His chest heavy, he bowed. "I will leave you then."

"Thank you," she returned coolly, her eyes unnaturally bright.

She looked forlorn somehow, sitting in the too-small tub, her long, wet hair tangled about her slender shoulders and cascading across her proud breasts. Her chin was tilted high though her eyes were shining with unshed tears. The entire situation tugged at his heart in a way he couldn't bear to examine.

Thomas pulled his gaze from her and strode to the door, wishing he knew what words could untangle this moment. But none came, so with a short nod, he left.

Chapter Eighteen

The warmth of the sun settled upon Thomas's up-turned face as a light sea breeze flirted with the sails. While he welcomed the lack of storm clouds, the sunshine did nothing to lighten his mood.

The storm had blown them farther off course than Thomas had expected, the crew was restive, and worst of all, Fia had confined herself to her cabin.

A week ago, he would have paid for her to have made that decision. Now he found himself glancing about the deck, feeling as if something vital was missing.

He wasn't the only one; Simmons and some of the other crew members had wistfully noted her absence, a few wondering aloud if someone had offended her.

In all of his days on ship, and of the hundred or so lords and ladies he'd consented to carry, none had impacted his crew the way Fia had. Apparently he wasn't the only one bewitched by her presence. Surely that proved that he wasn't succumbing to some sort of odd magic after all.

With Fia's self-imposed banishment, Robert was free to wander about needling the hapless Simmons, who retaliated enthusiastically. Their bickering now took the place of the music and lighthearted banter, and Thomas hated all of it.

While his days were fully busy, he had long nights to lie awake and think. He found himself wondering if, in his zeal to reassure Fia that he would see to his responsibilities by her, he hadn't in some way lost something far more important—her respect.

Simmons hurried up to him now. "Me lord, we're ready to turn into the head of the Thames and there's a signal on the east bank." He handed his spyglass to Thomas.

Thomas held it to his eye. "A red flag—Walsingham's signal. They are waiting for us."

"That's good news, isn't it, Cap'n?"

"Good enough." Thomas closed the eyeglass and handed it back to his first mate. "As soon as we land, I must meet the minister. You will take Lady Fia, her servants, and our cargo to Rotherwood House. Lord Montley will escort you."

"If ye don't mind me sayin' so, I don't need Lord Montley's help."

"I know, but I don't wish him to follow me. He and Walsingham don't see eye to eye."

"Aye, Cap'n."

Thomas turned back toward the riverbank. In London he'd head to the tavern where he and Walsingham often met, away from the scrutiny and intrigue of the court.

The minister would be disappointed Thomas hadn't retrieved the letter, yet Thomas didn't really care. He had bigger concerns now.

He sighed and watched the bank as it slid by. Things would be better now that he was home. They couldn't possibly be worse.

The Blue Stag Tavern was like a hundred others along the waterfront. Its dark, dirty taproom held the stale odor of rotting timbers and unwashed bodies, while a jumble of uneven tables and broken chairs littered the room. Though the hour was early, several of the more hardy patrons already sat hunched with bleary-eyed hostility over bent pewter mugs.

Thomas made his way past the scarred tables. A gaunt dog bared his teeth, protecting a sliver of bone he had managed to steal from the kitchen. Thomas was glad Fia wasn't there; she'd no doubt have wished to adopt the beast.

He resolutely pushed away the thought. He couldn't afford to be distracted right now. As much as he respected and trusted Lord Walsingham, by the nature of the power the old man held, one would be a fool to take the association lightly.

At the very back of the taproom, leaning against a wall by a small door, sat an immense man, his boots worn and cracked with age, his black leather tunic marred by an array of unidentifiable stains. Small eyes glowered at Thomas from under heavy, scraggly brows.

"Hail, Goliath," Thomas said in greeting. "I come to see 'Leticia.'"

"What 'ave ye got to give fer it?"

Goliath was Walsingham's guard and "Letty" was the code name to gain entrance to the meeting room. Walsingham probably didn't know Goliath had taken to demanding gold along with the password, which amused Thomas, so he encouraged the practice by paying.

Thomas pulled a coin from his purse. "Here." He flipped it into the air. The coin was deftly caught and disappeared into the greasy tunic, but the giant remained blocking the door.

"What's this? Let me by; I've paid the toll."

The man shook his head, his gaze moving beyond Thomas. "It's two coins if Letty's to take on both ye and yer fancy friend."

"My fancy frie—" Thomas looked over his shoulder. "Damn you, Montley! What are you doing here?"

Robert flourished a bow that drew every eye in the dank tavern. "Why, I've come to see the wondrous Letty! I apologize for my lateness, but I found myself with naught but rags to wear." Robert was even more elaborately dressed than usual. His velvet doublet glimmered, the deep purple shot through with gold threads that caught the dim light and made him almost iridescent.

Thomas noted sourly that the gaze of every cutthroat in the taproom was now transfixed on Robert, their faces reflecting varying degrees of amazement and greed.

With a flourish of lace and grace, Robert tossed a coin to Goliath.

The giant caught it, held it up to the light, and then grunted. He lumbered to his feet. "I'll send Letty in to ye as soon as she's able."

Thomas threw the door open and stalked into the room, Robert's measured tread behind him.

As soon as the door closed, Thomas turned to Robert. "What the hell are you doing here?"

Robert tossed his cloak onto a chair. "I came to protect you from your own ambition."

"I don't need any protection."

"You do, and 'tis my right to provide it. I and my sisters owe you our lives and I'll not forget it."

"You owe me naught but peace. Now leave."

"I can't."

"Have you seen the street outside?" Robert lowered his voice to a whisper. "The alleys are narrow and fraught with dangers."

"You arrived without mishap," Thomas pointed out in a dry tone.

"I followed you. None would dare harm me so long as I remained within the safety of your shadow." Robert dusted off a rickety chair. "So here I remain until you leave, safe and sound." He sat down and stretched out his legs, the gloss of his black leather boots reflecting the weak blaze in the fireplace.

After sending Robert a hard glance, Thomas went to stand beside the fire. The room was little better than the taproom, the table greasy and the chairs broken and dirty. The only spot of freshness was a bowl of green apples sitting upon the table.

Thomas scowled at a small pot steaming over the gasping blaze as though in defiance of the chill wind that whistled occasionally through the plank walls. The chamber was cold, damp, and foul, and for once, he didn't appreciate Walsingham's turn for the dramatic.

He kicked at a loose ember, wondering what Fia would think of Rotherwood House. His father had won it from the estate of the Duke of Northumberland after that schemer had been sent to the Tower for treason. It was large and impressive, built of gray stonework set with narrow windows. It had been built to intimidate, not welcome.

After his father's death, Thomas had added a large fountain of warm yellow stone to the front lawn, ordered his gardeners to maintain flowers and topiaries for as many months as the seasons would allow, and added a portico crowned with flowers. The last had been Robert's suggestion, and Thomas had to admit that it helped.

He rubbed his face, feeling suddenly weary. *What do I care what Fia thinks of my house? She's not the woman for me, nor does she wish to be. She's still impulsive, opinionated, unconventional, and*—he closed his eyes—*completely adorable.*

It was madness, complete and utter. He didn't just want her; he craved her, yearned for her, day and night.

Was this the madness that drove my mother from our house? All these years, I've done what I could to be more like Father, but inside I always feared what I now know: I am as impulsive, impatient, and ruled by passion as my mother.

The door swung open and a barmaid sauntered in, her russet hair contained beneath a surprisingly clean scrap of lace. Her blue gown was torn and ill patched in a dozen places, but it was neatly pressed and fit her figure well. She flashed a smile and clunked two mugs of ale onto the scarred table, her overflowing breasts pressing against the inadequate scrap of muslin tucked into her bodice as she leaned over.

Robert drained his mug with startling quickness.

"I can see yer lordship is the thirstin' kind." The maid flashed a saucy smile at Robert, her eyes glinting hazel in the dim light. "Perhaps ye're wishful fer some more ale?"

He captured her hand, murmuring soulfully, "Forget the ale, sweet maid Leticia! Do but reside within mine heart, warming it until the coldness of death shall overtake it."

She pulled her hand free with a brisk tug. "Me name is Annie, no' Leticia. Letty's on her way, so I wouldn't waste no time if'n I was ye."

Robert clutched at his chest. "Fair cruelty! I seek but to please thee and instead I am sent away, sore and rejected as a beaten dog from the beckoning warmth of a hearth."

Anne sniffed. "Me duties don't include entertainin' the customers in no way other than servin' ale."

Thomas stirred restlessly. *God's blood, where is Walsingham?* The man had to be expecting him; the wily old fox knew every time a ship turned into harbor.

Suddenly a shadow darkened the doorway as an old man stood within the opening, his dirty face shadowed by a ragged cloak. "I've come to beg a word with me daughter." The voice cracked with weariness; the thin, dirty hand gripping the cloak shook with the palsy of age.

"Da!" The barmaid bustled to the door. "What are ye thinkin' t' be comin' down here? 'Tis in bed ye should be, not wanderin' about!"

"Let me be, daughter. Do I look t' be dead yet?" The old man began to cough, swaying dangerously.

"Come, Da." Annie pulled the old man from the doorway and fixed a pleading gaze on Robert. "Do ye mind if me da sits a spell here in yer room? He won't be no trouble, I promise. He can leave as soon as Letty comes fer ye."

Robert ignored Thomas's frowned warning. "Of course. Pray, bring the good man something to eat as well. He'll feel better once he's had some food."

The girl flashed a grateful smile as she pulled out a chair for her father and placed the old man in it.

Thomas's jaw tightened. Robert would adopt the girl's entire family ere they left.

The old man's wheezing lessened and he motioned to the girl. Annie leaned over and the man whispered into her ear. She nodded once, then said quietly to Thomas and Robert, "Knock upon the door when ye wish me t' return fer me da."

Robert frowned. "You're leaving him here? But—"

She lifted her brows, her expression suddenly haughty as the queen's. "Aye, I'm leaving him here." Her accent was now educated.

Robert gaped. "Mistress, you—"

Annie turned on one heel and was gone, quietly closing the door behind her. Outside they heard Goliath resume his position as guard, his chair scraping against the door.

The old man pushed the tattered hood from his head and said in a cultured, smooth voice, "And how fared your adventures, my fine young bucks?"

Robert scowled at the thin patrician face of Francis Walsingham, chief counselor to Queen Elizabeth. "You bounding knave," Robert said with disgust. "What a farce!"

Walsingham shrugged. "I've been followed every day for the last month. I had to take more precautions than usual."

"By whom?" Thomas asked.

"A man attached to the Spanish ambassador."

"The Spanish?" Robert leaned forward. "There are rumors of their armada."

"One day we will face them, but now they are merely fishing. Checking our strength, our capabilities."

"The queen knows?" Thomas asked.

"Of course. I don't know when they will come, but I

shall find out, and then—" Walsingham's mouth thinned. "Woe to King Philip." The counselor's gaze flickered to Thomas. "But that's not why you're here. Your venture to Scotland, was it profitable?"

"He asks not if you're well, but only about the mission," Robert said in a scornful tone.

Walsingham flicked a cold glance at Robert before he turned back to Thomas. "Why did you bring him?"

"He's here because I had need of him," Thomas said. "The streets are not safe, as you know."

Walsingham's lip curled. "Then ask a *man* to attend you, not a play actor."

Robert started from his chair, his fist about his sword.

Thomas threw an arm between the two. "Hold, Robert!"

Robert's eyes blazed, but after meeting Thomas's gaze, he subsided into his chair. "This man's tongue is as forked as the devil's."

Thomas turned to the counselor. "Cease baiting him. He's a good friend of mine. For that reason alone, he should be treated with respect."

Walsingham shrugged. "As you will." He leaned forward. "What of the letter? Did you find it?"

"Aye, but I was not allowed to return with it."

"Not allowed? But it was prom—" Walsingham clamped his mouth closed.

Robert's bright gaze locked on the minister. "The letter was *promised*? Is that what you said?"

"No," Walsingham snapped. "I meant to say something else."

"I think not," Robert said, his voice flinty, his blue gaze icy. "Who promised you that letter? Damn it, what devil's bargain have you—"

Walsingham slapped his fist on the table. "Leave it! I'll say no more, damn it!"

Thomas raised his brows. In the fifteen years he'd known Walsingham, he'd never heard the man curse.

His surprise must have shown, for the minister seemed to collect himself. He spread his hands upon the table and grimaced. "I apologize for my outburst, but I dislike being hounded. Now tell me more of the missive. Did you see it?" Walsingham leaned forward, his pale gaze locked on Thomas. "Was it what we thought?"

"Nay, 'twas vague. 'Twould not have held before the privy council."

Walsingham's face tightened with anger. "It was to have been more. *Much* more."

Robert paused in taking a drink. "You sent Thomas to risk his life for a letter of which you did not know the content?"

"I was given assurances—promises—that I believed."

"Fool," Robert spat.

Thomas held up a hand. "Leave it, Robert. I knew this before I left. 'Twas worth taking a chance upon."

"I doubt that. And this weasel shouldn't be so quick to toss your life before a mere possibility. Something about this situation smells like a two-week-old fish."

Thomas couldn't shake the same feeling.

Walsingham scowled. "Why must you persist in thinking I wish Rotherwood harm, Montley?"

"Because he knows everything there is to know about you."

"Oh, I doubt that, my fine friend." Walsingham picked up one of the apples, fished out a wicked-looking knife, and delicately peeled a long curl of skin from the apple.

"Elizabeth is much more likely to hang Lord Rotherwood than me if he tells the world how I have been protecting her vast interests. She *wants* her interests protected, at all costs."

"I wonder if she'd agree to that," Robert returned. "Something was odd about this entire venture. In fact, I think MacLean knew someone was coming for that missive."

"Nonsense. How could he?"

"He knew," Robert said stubbornly. "He raced home when there was no reason to."

Walsingham lifted a brow in Thomas's direction. "Do you think the same?"

Thomas considered this. Finally, he nodded. "MacLean wasn't surprised."

"Hmm. The information had to have come from someone close to you . . ." The minister sliced the apple into six neat pieces, his gaze resting on Robert. "But who?"

Robert clenched his jaw. "Don't even hint 'twas me. I didn't know of Thomas's errand 'til he needed rescuing."

"If I had thought you were to blame for Rotherwood's discovery, you would not now be in this room," Walsingham said sharply. "Don't underestimate my capabilities."

Robert began to answer, but Thomas held up a hand, his gaze on the counselor. "Well? Who do you think might have sold me out? I deserve to know."

"I have my own theories, but 'twill take some time to ascertain the truth. Of even more import, we must find out what the cunning Laird MacLean is up to. If he had that letter and then took it from you—" Walsingham's gray eyes gleamed, his hand tightening on his knife. "He is not to be trusted, that one. He's proven most recalcitrant."

"How so?" Thomas asked.

Walsingham's heavy lids slid down until his gaze was nothing more than slits of silver. "It matters not. Did anything else occur that I should know about?"

Now was the time to explain his marriage, but Thomas found himself reluctant to even mention Fia's name. Whether it was this new uncertainty about Walsingham's trustworthiness or the desire to protect Fia from this part of his life, Thomas didn't know. All he knew was that when he went to mention her name, his lips refused to move.

When Thomas's father had died, Walsingham had—in a vague way—taken the old earl's place in Thomas's life. It made sense, for his own father hadn't been a close, friendly figure. The excitement of the challenges Walsingham offered through his service to the queen had given Thomas a purpose for his life, something to challenge the famed Wentworth luck and prove it yet again.

At first he'd reveled in the assignments, but lately he'd found himself holding back. When all was said and done, Walsingham stood for Walsingham and the queen, and no one else.

Walsingham took a bite of his apple, his teeth showing briefly, sharp and small. "Thomas, perhaps you should—"

A sharp rap came upon the door and Annie whisked into the room. She crossed to Walsingham's side and whispered into his ear.

Robert's gaze met Thomas's. Thomas gave a small shrug to indicate he had no idea what was happening. Robert scowled and returned his gaze to the minister.

Walsingham's gaze widened and he gave Annie a hard look. "When?"

"The messenger arrived but a moment ago."

"Wait for me in the carriage. The queen must know, in case he decides to intrude upon the court."

Annie left immediately.

Walsingham placed the apple core in the center of the table. "Laird MacLean has become even more of a liability."

"MacLean?" Thomas frowned. "How so?"

"He is even now ensconced at Rotherwood House."

"At *my* house? But why would he come here—" *He's come for Fia.*

The thought slammed into Thomas's chest with an almost physical pain.

Robert frowned. "He must have left within a few days of our departure."

"Aye," Thomas said hoarsely. "With good horses, he could have beaten us as we were blown off course."

Walsingham's hooded eyes followed every nuance of Thomas's expression. "It's worse than you might think. Duncan MacLean didn't just bring his usual retinue; he brought an entire army."

Walsingham stood. "I must inform the queen. She will be alarmed to hear that a Scottish army has marched upon her land."

A dull roar swept through Thomas's head. Through a fog, he heard Robert say, "I don't understand. Why would MacLean bring an army?"

Thomas didn't hear anything else; Duncan's last words to Fia rang in his ears. *If you're not happy, I'll come for you.*

Duncan hadn't waited for Fia to send word. Had he changed his mind about the marriage? Had he come to take Fia back?

Thomas was faintly aware of standing, of his chair crashing against the wall, of the startled expressions on Walsingham's and Robert's faces, of Goliath's roar as Thomas yanked the door open and toppled the huge man over.

Then Thomas was out in the street, his blood pounding through him hot and furious as he ran. He was heedless of the damage he inflicted on those he pushed past and only dimly aware of Robert's steady footfall behind him.

All he knew was that Duncan had brought an army to reclaim what rightfully belonged to Thomas. Fia was *his*. And God rest the soul of the man who tried to change that.

Chapter Nineteen

Rotherwood House
Outside of London, near Somerset
May 31, 1567

*M*en in plaid kilts stood by the house and massed at the gate, their swords strapped across their shoulders with insolent intent.

Thomas ground his teeth and started forward, hand fisted about his sword. *By the rood, I will not let any half-dressed savage take my wife and—*

Robert held him back, the Scot's voice calm and purposeful. "*Mon ami*, we are outnumbered. If we walk straight into their clutches, we'll never reach Fia alive."

Montley was right. Thomas cursed a thousand times under his breath, even as he fought his own temper. *He will not hurt her. And he cannot have left and taken her with him, for his men would not remain behind. She is still here. She has to be.*

Thomas silently counted the Scotsmen. Already he and Robert had been noticed and the group about the gate had doubled. He cursed again.

Robert rubbed his beard. "We need a plan. Something to get us through this morass and into the house."

There was a side door that led directly to the major rooms. All he had to do was slip past the guard. Hmm . . . what would keep a Scottish army distracted for the time he needed to reach the door?

He cast a glance at Robert. "I have a plan."

Robert turned toward him, excitement lighting his face. "What is it?"

"We need a diversion to distract them while I slip into the house."

Robert's eyes gleamed as he stroked his beard. "And what for a diversion?"

"You."

Robert looked from Thomas to the men, and a slow grin spread across his face. "'Twill be the best sport I've had in a twelvemonth."

"Just don't win too quickly."

"I shall toy with the bastard, slash his clothing, and make him dance until he cannot lift that heavy sword from the ground. His companions will not be able to look away and no one will see you leave."

"Exactly. Let us proceed." Thomas strode toward the gate, Robert falling in beside him.

"Halt!" A red-haired guard stepped from the crowd and stood menacingly in his path. "State yer purpose, English dog."

Robert stepped between Thomas and the Scotsman. "Och, now, do my eyes lead me astray, or are you not a Douglas?"

Thomas hadn't heard Robert speak with so pronounced a Scottish burr since his first arrival in England years ago.

The man regarded Robert with a suspicious frown. "Aye, I am Kinnish Douglas. And who are ye?"

Robert swept an elegant bow. "Robert MacQuarrie, Viscount Montley, at your service."

An angry mumbling rose at the name but Douglas looked almost pleased, his yellowed teeth showing in a wide grin. "Well, now. So I have the pleasure of meeting the Coward of Balmanach. 'Tis a rare honor, that." Douglas called out, "What do ye think, men? Do I let the Coward of Balmanach pass unmolested?"

The men broke into a jeering mass of shouts and yells.

Robert seemed unconcerned, his eyes never wavering from Douglas. "Are you challenging me to a duel?"

"A duel with a white-livered traitor like yerself?" Douglas sneered. "Nay, MacQuarrie. Ye deserve no such honor."

Robert clicked his tongue as he regarded Douglas with polite disbelief. "If you're afraid, then so be it."

A dead silence fell.

Kinnish's face flushed red. "Fool! Foul pretender! I am no more afeared of ye than of a wee ant!" He threw his cloak to the ground and drew his huge sword, the steel flashing.

With no expression on his face, Thomas regarded the two-handed claymore. Robert's long, thin rapier would make mincemeat of this buffoon in no time.

Robert gave Thomas a quick wink and began to walk about, kicking loose stones out of the way, all the while taunting his foe. As he neared Thomas, he pushed Douglas's fine cloak toward him with a careless shove of his foot.

Thomas took the cloak and waited for the yelling to reach a fevered pitch. Every man crowded in a circle around Robert and Douglas, yelling taunts and exchanging money as the wagers began to flow.

No one paid him the least heed as he slowly melted into the crowd, the cloak crumpled in his hands.

Duncan leaned back in the chair and stretched his feet toward the fire. "Duart Castle is warmer than this even in the midst of winter. You'll freeze here, poppet."

Fia crossed her arms and frowned. "Surely you've not traveled all the way from Scotland just to compare your fireplace to my Sassenach's."

"I told you I came to see that you were well."

"I'm fine, as you can see. And yet you make no effort to leave. Duncan, what's toward?"

Duncan's dark gaze flickered over her, lingering on her face. "Are you truly well?" His voice was soft.

For a moment, the desire was strong to return to her childhood, when she could throw herself into his arms and weep for all that was or was not. But those times had passed. Now, if she wept, he would think she was sad, and she wasn't. She merely felt a deep sense of longing for what she didn't have—her husband's regard.

When she could trust her voice, she shrugged. "I am a wee bit tired from the voyage, perhaps, but that is all."

"A good nap will cure all, eh? Fia, I don't know if I—"

A sudden clamor arose outside and Duncan's brow creased. "Berwick!" he bellowed.

The door opened and a grizzled face appeared. "Aye, yer lordship?"

"What in the blazes is going on out there?"

"'Tis Robert MacQuarrie, me lord." Berwick's voice quivered with excitement. "He approached the front gate and challenged Kinnish Douglas. Ye can see them fighting from the window at the end of the hall." Berwick's eyes shone. "Robert MacQuarrie'll rue this day if'n he lives long enough. There's none like Douglas with a sword."

Duncan snorted derisively. "Fools! There's none like MacQuarrie with a rapier. Douglas'll not last a minute."

Berwick blinked rapidly. "Ye think MacQuarrie will win?"

"Aye, you fool. Where's the Sassenach?"

"I dinna know, me lord. There's naught but Mac-Quarrie."

"Like hell. Where you find MacQuarrie, you find that damned Englishman. Go now, and find him."

Though Duncan hadn't raised his voice, Berwick gulped and scurried from the room as if the hounds of hell pursued him.

"Coward," scoffed Fia. Thomas would have never been so quickly cowed. The thought made her chest ache. She and Thomas hadn't had another conversation since the morning after their tryst, for she could call it little else.

She didn't want to think that might be their last conversation, for they'd left on such a sour note: his less-than-romantic offer to confirm their marriage for all the wrong reasons, and her less-than-accepting answer for the right ones.

The truth was, she didn't know how she felt anymore. Every day, nay, every *hour* that she spent in Thomas's presence, the more muddled she became.

All she knew for certain was that she didn't want to be a part of his life if all they shared was physical passion, since it obviously meant so little to him. She knew she cared for him, but could he open his heart to her?

"This manse is well made, though you'd be hard-pressed

to defend the southern boundary." Duncan looked around the great hall with a faintly pleased air. "Still, the furnishings are rich enough for royalty."

Fia cast a glance about the great hall. It was of the new construction with heavy timbers crossing the high ceiling. Oak paneling covered the walls and an ornately carved mantelpiece was fastened above a huge fireplace. The heavy furnishings were covered in red and blue velvets that matched the drapes to either side of the multipaned windows, and the overall effect was one of grandeur.

When she'd first arrived, she'd been overwhelmed. Her husband was clearly a wealthy man—a fact she'd somehow missed in their short relationship.

She'd felt so overshadowed by the house that she'd been doubly glad to see Duncan, although she'd been appalled at how he had made himself at home, locking Simmons and the servants in the cellar.

She eyed her cousin now, wondering yet again what had brought him. His kilt was draped about him, a fur vest covering his broad chest, tall black leather boots strapped to his thighs. She stifled a faint smile. He and the men had done everything they could to appear less civilized than usual.

She watched as he stared absently into the crackling fire, noting the faint shadows under his eyes and the whiteness of his mouth, his almost haunted gaze.

What was causing him to look so bleak? "Duncan?"

He lifted his gaze to her with an obvious effort. "Aye, lass?"

"I know you've been concerned about the queen, but has something else occurred? I've never seen you so solemn."

He straightened in his chair, his lips curved into a false smile. "I'm fine, lass. 'Tis naught to worry your head o'er."

"But there's something about you, almost as if—"

"'Tis nothing." Duncan stood and moved beside the fireplace. "We should see that lackluster husband of yours soon."

If Duncan wasn't prepared to talk about whatever had upset him, he wouldn't, so she shrugged. "Thomas may be stubborn but he's definitely *not* lackluster."

Duncan's gaze darkened. "Fia, you're happy with him, aren't you?"

"I . . . I will be," she replied, knowing he'd sense the truth if she didn't offer an explanation. "We're still new to one another, but I've come to care for him." *Far too much.*

"And him for you?" Duncan's dark gaze didn't waver.

She lifted her chin. "Of course." It wasn't a lie so much as a hope expressed aloud.

Duncan sighed and rubbed his neck. "'Tis a beginning, I suppose. I wanted . . . but this will have to do. As much as I miss you, 'tis here you belong."

Something about the way he said it made her frown. "Duncan, what's happened? Something is not right." Fia regarded him for a long moment. "Ah! Did the White Witch come for her amulet?"

Duncan's mouth tightened. "She's not pleased with the MacLeans."

"You mean with you."

He shot Fia a hard look. "She won't bother any of us again."

Trepidation gripped Fia. "God's breath, Duncan! What have you done?"

"As soon as she arrived, I had her confined."

Fia clapped a hand over her eyes. "Duncan, no!"

"I had to do something; she threatened to put a curse on us all."

"You should never have taken that amulet!"

"I'm glad I did! She's done naught but torment our family, for no reason other than some ancient claim to our land that would never stand in a court of law."

"Have you examined this claim?"

"Why should I? Our holdings were granted from King Edward's time and are valid. She's done naught but threaten and—" He scowled. "It matters not. I have captured her and she's mine."

"Yours? You . . . you plan on *keeping* her?"

To her surprise, he flushed. "Aye. I cannot allow her to roam about, casting curses."

"Has she cast one yet?"

"Aye—I mean, *nay*! I don't believe in curses." Duncan raked a hand through his hair, the haunted look in his eyes stronger. "She's a charlatan and I'll prove her wrong. Besides, she can't act without the amulet."

"I don't know about that. She's a witch; can't she just make another one?"

"God's wounds, are you with me or against me?"

"Neither. I'm for the truth."

Duncan scowled. "I don't know what a witch needs. I just know she's a thorn in my side, and I've had enough!"

In the distance, thunder rumbled.

Duncan's head snapped toward the open window. He crossed to it and stared into the blue sky.

"What is it?"

"Nothing," he said tersely.

The rumble repeated, a bit closer now.

"That's odd. It was clear outside earlier." Fia started to join Duncan at the window, but he slammed the shutters closed.

Moving with a sharpness that bespoke his anger, he crossed the room, slamming all the other shutters closed as well. "I am *done* being told what I can and can't do," he growled. "Let it *be!*"

A crack of thunder ripped across the sky, so close that it made the floor tremble.

Fia stared at the closed windows as the unmistakable howl of a storm began.

Grim-faced, Duncan turned away, grabbing the poker and stirring the fire as if desperate for some heat.

Fia frowned. "How could a storm come so quickly?" She turned to go to the window, but Duncan threw up a hand.

"'Tis naught! Just . . . leave it."

"Duncan, you're pale. And your hand . . . it's shaking. What's wron—"

A muffled shout sounded in the hallway outside, then a voice she instantly recognized growled a command before something thudded against the wood panels. Fia was halfway to the door before Thomas stormed into the room, brandishing a sword, his face white lipped and grim.

His gaze found her the second he crossed the threshold. His clothing was torn and a thin trickle of blood dripped from the corner of his fine mouth. "Are you well?"

"I'm fine." Her voice quavered and he gave a muffled curse and stalked to her side to pull her close.

Fia sank against him, realizing for the first time how worried she'd been for him. She slipped her arms about him and hid her face in his neck, savoring his warmth. "I'm glad you're well," she whispered.

His arm tightened about her as he rested his chin against her temple.

"Well, if 'tisn't the Sassenach," Duncan reminded them of his presence.

"MacLean," Thomas sneered through his teeth.

Duncan returned the poker to its holder and turned to face Thomas. "You finally made it. I come to your house, and my cousin arrives by herself."

"She had an escort."

"Aye, of servants. Where were you? Shouldn't you have welcomed her to your home?"

Fia had been reveling in the feel of Thomas's arm about her waist, but Duncan's words reminded her that this warmth was not real. The closeness she shared with Thomas was temporary at best.

She tried to school her wildly beating heart as she gazed into Thomas's deep brown eyes. *Sweet Saint Catherine, why did I marry such a handsome man?* Just looking at him could make her body heat as though a fire were lit inside her. But pressed against him, his perfect mouth just inches from hers, she couldn't speak or even think.

Of their own volition, her fingers slid across his lower lip, her gaze locked on that perfect morsel. Her mouth felt swollen; it almost ached to be touched by his. Thomas caught her hand and pressed a kiss to her fingers.

"Stop it, the two of you." Duncan's voice rumbled over them like the cold sea. "'Tis a fine cloak ye have on, Sassenach. 'Twould be a pity to have to run my sword through it to pry you away from my cousin."

Fia's cheeks heated even as Thomas's arm tightened about her shoulders. "A pox on you, MacLean," Thomas said. "Were you not my wife's only living relative, I'd slice you in two."

Duncan eyed him for a long moment. "Rotherwood, you're fortunate I've been attempting to hold my temper."

"I don't care about you or your temper. Where are my servants?"

"Locked in the cellar. One or two are in the kitchen getting their broken heads seen to."

"You will pay for that, MacLean."

Duncan gave a mirthless smile. "I already have. You just don't know it."

"You are speaking in riddles," Thomas snapped. "What do you mean by invading my house with your accursed army?"

"Invade?" Duncan looked genuinely surprised. "I came in peace, as a relative."

"With over a hundred men?"

Duncan pursed his lips though his eyes gleamed with humor. "'Tis a bit much, eh?"

Thomas regarded him with a flat stare.

Och, they're going to keep this up until one or the other of them starts a fight, then we'll all lose.

As though aware of her thoughts, Thomas's hand slid beneath her hair to rest on her neck, warm and possessive, and she fought a shiver. He was merely letting her know he was concerned for her, that's all. It was a kind gesture, she told herself, nothing else.

As if to belie her thoughts, his thumb began to trace feather-light circles on her sensitive skin. She risked a glance up at him. His eyes locked with hers, and for a wild moment, she thought she could see into his soul. He was looking at her as if he *cared* about her. The realization gave her pause.

What if he did but was unable to show it? Maybe he wasn't sure how to act otherwise.

Hope flew through her and she leaned forward, lifting her face to his as—

Duncan gave a muffled curse. *"Cease that!"* Outside, a sudden wind rattled against the house, shaking the heavy shutters and puffing down the chimney to sputter the fire.

Thomas eyed the window with a frown. "I entered from the courtyard not ten minutes ago, and the sky was as clear as—" A crack of thunder rumbled outside. "Odd. Still . . . MacLean, you'd best leave before the storm hits."

"I wish I could." Duncan's voice seemed to carry the weight of the world.

Fia frowned. He seemed shaken, almost. She put her hand on Thomas's arm. "Thomas, Duncan is my cousin and guardian and I will not have him thrown out of the house when the weather's so dreadful."

Thomas scowled but he turned to Duncan and said grudgingly, "Fine. You may stay until the storm blows over. But *not* with such a large retinue, and *not* if you harm my retainers."

"You've a piss-poor bunch of servants, Sassenach. Not a bit of backbone in the lot."

"They were frightened, and who would blame them when you showed up with a bloody army?"

"I brought my men to protect me and mine. You never know what you might run into in this godforsaken land." Fia tried to warn Duncan with a frown, but he ignored her and continued. "In fact, we were viciously attacked just after we crossed the English border."

"No doubt some landowner took offense at your carousing through his lands," Thomas suggested.

"Mayhap." Duncan flexed his massive shoulders. "I

didn't have the time to ascertain the nature of his grievances. We trounced him right well and continued on here."

Fia winced at the sound of Thomas grinding his teeth.

A loud knock came at the door.

"Enter," bellowed Thomas and Duncan at one and the same time, their voices blending as beautifully as a chorus. They glared at one another, then Duncan said in a grudging tone, "Fine. 'Tis your house."

"Aye, 'tis." Thomas growled, then called, "Enter!"

The door opened and a disheveled Robert was shoved into the room.

"Robert!" Fia gasped.

He stumbled against a chair but forced himself upright as two men Fia recognized as Magnus Lindsey and MacKenna followed.

"Welcome, Coward of Balmanach," Duncan said.

"Go on!" Lindsey rudely shoved Robert toward the fireplace. Robert stumbled into a stool and fell to the floor. Smirking, Lindsey strode forward and shoved Robert with his foot. "The laird is wantin' to speak to ye, ye cowardly traitor."

"Enough," MacKenna snapped, his brow low. "The lad fought and fought well. He deserves better than to be kicked whilst upon the ground."

But the guard was too enthralled with his power. He lifted his foot to kick at his prisoner again, aiming for Robert's unprotected back.

MacKenna started forward, but Thomas was across the room in an instant, the flat of his sword slamming the Scotsman into the wall.

Fia went to Robert and slipped an arm beneath one shoulder, MacKenna assisting with the other. Together, they lifted Robert and gently set him in a chair.

Then Fia looked around for her cousin and found him standing beside Thomas, appearing every bit as furious. "Only a coward or an ass would kick a man when he is down," Duncan said with deadly quiet.

The wind picked up yet again, and hail pecked against the glass windows.

Fia shivered and rubbed her arms, glancing at the shuttered windows. The storm seemed oddly intent on punctuating Duncan's words.

Lindsey struggled to his feet. "I respect ye, me lord, but that coward—" The Scotsman wiped his bloody mouth, then spat toward Robert.

The hilt of Thomas's sword slammed into the Scotsman's stomach and sent him into a group of chairs by the wall.

Duncan chuckled darkly. "Let that be a lesson to you, Lindsey."

MacKenna nodded in agreement and went to the fallen man. "The fool's out cold. He'll have a hell o' a headache when he awakes, and he'll deserve every bit o' it." He lifted the inert body and dragged the man out the door.

Fia bent to examine Robert's battered face. "You poor thing!"

"*Sacre Dieu*," he murmured. "My head has a thousand needles sticking in it."

"I was sure you could take Douglas," Thomas said.

Robert winced. "'Twas not Kinnish but his brother. The filthy whoreson attacked me from behind."

Duncan's frown was sudden. "One of my men?"

"Aye, one of *your* men."

"That coward will be hideless when I finish with him."

"It seems your army is peppered with cowards," said Thomas.

"They're better than *yours,* which are all locked up in your cellar as we speak."

"At least *my* men don't—"

"Enough!" Fia yelled. "Poor Lord Montley needs his wounds seen to."

Thomas shrugged. "If Robert wanted a surgeon, he'd ask for one."

"That's true," Robert agreed, blinking unsteadily, blood running down the side of his head and soaking into his doublet.

Fia cast her eyes heavenward. "Heaven grant me patience!" She slipped his arm about her shoulders and pulled him to his feet. "We'll leave these fools to bray at one another like the asses they are." Casting a sweeping glare at Thomas and Duncan, she helped Robert across the room.

Thomas watched, both relieved and sad that she was leaving. It was difficult to pay attention to Fia's dangerous cousin while she was there, all flashing eyes and kissable lips.

Worse yet was her hair. He had almost lost control when he'd slid his hand under the silken mass to caress the warmth of her neck. Sweet Jesu, but he wanted to run his hands through her curls even now as they frothed about her shoulders and tangled beneath Robert's arm.

Thomas frowned. Had Robert been holding his wife a bit too tightly?

He walked to the door and peered into the hall, wondering if he should say something. But every time he tried to speak with Fia, he ended up sounding like a lackwit. Only when he held her did he get the response he wanted.

Hmm . . . maybe *that* was the key: less talking and more touching. As soon as they were alone, he would—

"By the holy cross, Rotherwood, leave her be." Mac-Lean's irked voice recalled Thomas to his senses. "She's safe with MacQuarrie. He barely has the strength to stand, much less make love to her."

Thomas turned from the doorway, managing a stiff smile. "You haven't yet explained why my household has been overrun by an army of Scotsmen."

"I came on an errand."

"Then perform it and be gone."

"With pleasure." He walked past Thomas to the door and bellowed, "MacKenna!"

The guard ambled back into the room. "Aye?"

"Bring me the casket."

MacKenna nodded and left.

Thomas turned to Duncan. "Casket?"

"Aye." MacLean returned to the fireplace, the heat stirring the bottom of his cloak. "I came to present you with a gift and to see if Fia is well."

"And?"

"She's not as happy as I'd like, but she's well enough," MacLean said in a grudging tone. "I wished to see how she truly fared, so it had to be a surprise. With forewarning, a clever man can hide a great many ills."

"As you can see, she is well." *And perhaps with child.* Thomas was surprised when the thought didn't settle into his chest like an aching weight. *I am getting used to the idea. That is something, at least.*

Duncan clasped his hands behind his back. "Sassenach, you've spent nearly a month with my cousin as wife. You're fond of her?"

"Fond" wasn't the word he'd have used. "Befuddled" was. "She's a beautiful woman."

"That doesn't answer my question."

MacKenna returned carrying a silver casket Thomas recognized, set it on the table, then left the room.

As the door closed behind him, Duncan said, "You saw this casket when you stole the missive from it, but you missed the most important part. There's a false bottom." He nodded toward it. "Look for yourself."

Thomas first opened the jeweled latch. Inside lay the missive, just as before. He removed it, then carefully examined the velvet-covered bottom of the box. Just as he was ready to give up, he saw a tiny thread. He tugged on it and the bottom of the box lifted to reveal several more letters, a silver cross on a chain, and a small miniature that he recognized as Lord Darnley, Queen Mary's dead husband.

Thomas opened the top missive and scanned it. The words seemed to leap from the page. "Sweet Jesu, if these are authentic—"

"They are." MacLean spoke with telling softness. "'Tis enough evidence of Queen Mary's trickery to warrant her execution."

Thomas swallowed against the dryness of his throat. Walsingham's final evidence. He carefully replaced the letter, closed the secret drawer, and set the casket back onto the table. *By the saints, I need some ale.*

"The Scottish queen has betrayed us all." MacLean's face was frozen and hard. "She married that treacherous fool Bothwell, who wants nothing more than to rule in her name. Such a foolish woman, to believe words of love. No queen can afford such."

"What's to be done?"

"Give these to Walsingham. He will know what to do with them. He's promised support for the prince, her only child, if she is deposed."

"Deposed? Good God. Where is she now?"

"In England. A group of lords rose against her and she fled."

"And Bothwell?"

"He escaped on a ship; we think he heads to France." Duncan crossed his arms over his broad chest. "Mary is in custody, but she must be removed from the throne before she plunges Scotland into a civil war. 'Tis but a matter of time."

Thomas whistled silently. "Walsingham has promised assistance?"

"He has. Now 'tis only a question of whether he'll honor his agreement. 'Tis for that reason I wished to deliver the missives through you. You will serve as more than messenger; you serve as witness, too. I was going to take them directly to Queen Elizabeth myself, but it can take weeks to gain an audience."

"You don't trust Walsingham."

"Nay. If he does not deliver those missives to the queen, then you must tell her of them yourself. You are a favorite; she would believe you." The laird absently stirred the fire, then looked up to meet Thomas's gaze. "You mustn't tell Fia any of this. I won't have her endangered."

"You may leave Fia to me, MacLean. I will take care of her." *No matter how we end.*

After a moment, the laird nodded. "Fine. I told my men we traveled here to bring that casket to Fia. They believe it holds the famed MacLean rubies. See to it that she is seen wearing her jewelry sometime soon."

"She has rubies?" It was difficult to imagine Fia wearing jewels.

MacLean looked surprised. "They're in one of her trunks." When Thomas didn't answer, MacLean chuckled. "Rotherwood, do not allow her fey ways to confuse you. Fia's born and bred to the purple; she's related to half the royalty of England and Scotland. She could call Queen Elizabeth cousin and not be committing a sin."

Thomas smiled faintly. "I wouldn't suggest such a thing; Elizabeth's quick to take offense."

"Aye, she's a stiff one, she is. I can only hope she does the right thing by Scotland and rids us of our foolish queen."

"Elizabeth is hard but fair."

"So I pray." Duncan rubbed his face as if to scrub away his thoughts. He dropped his hands and managed a faint smile. "Meanwhile, fetch Fia's rubies and make her wear the blasted things. 'Twill silence the wagging tongues regarding my journey here."

"And your men accept that they traveled here just to protect a small cask of jewels?"

"I brought the *MacLean* rubies, Sassenach. 'Tis enough for them. Though if you can get Fia to wear them, you're a better man than I."

"Was there ever a question?"

MacLean chuckled. "There's one more thing I wish you to do."

"Aye?"

"When you take that casket to Walsingham, tell the old fox we are now even. I've paid my part of the bargain."

"What bargain?"

Duncan's smile wasn't nearly so amused now. "The old fox hasn't told you yet, has he?"

"Told me what?" Thomas asked impatiently.

"'Tis not my news to spread; ask him yourself when next you see him. If I were you, I'd threaten to withhold those letters 'til he confessed the whole."

"Is it that important?"

"It might let you know your value. *That* is worth something, indeed." MacLean turned toward the door, then hesitated when he reached it. "You may not yet realize this, but you're holding Scotland's greatest treasure."

"Fia?"

"Aye. She's precious, and I couldn't love her more if she were my own sister." His voice was suspiciously husky. "You may not agree with all I have done, Rotherwood, but I did what I had to for Fia's sake. I wanted her out of Scotland and somewhere safe, somewhere she would be taken care of."

"What do you—"

"I must go. Tell Fia I will write. Good-bye, Rotherwood."

MacLean left, calling his men as he went. Within five minutes' time he'd collected them all and they were gone, leaving Thomas with more questions than answers.

Chapter Twenty

*S*weet Jesu! That hurts!" Robert said in protest.

The rabbit scrambled madly off the bed and skittered across the room, his fat stomach never clearing the floor.

Fia smothered a giggle.

"I die, and you play with that rabbit," Robert complained.

"Och, you're barely injured. You've a wee knot upon your head and 'tis scarcely bleeding now."

"*And* a black eye."

"If that's all it takes to kill you, 'tis a wonder you've lived this long."

Robert raised a hand to his right ear and gingerly touched the swelling. "No doubt if I lost an arm, you would call it a mere flesh wound."

Mary entered the room just in time to hear this. "Fie, Lord Montley. Here's the mistress a-tendin' ye as if ye were her own bamkin, and what do ye do but complain?"

"Let her be busy elsewhere," Robert said sulkily, eyeing with distrust the herb-soaked bandage Mary carried. "I would run and hide from you both, were that hideous animal not standing guard over the doorway."

Zeus lay sleeping on his back across the threshold, his legs splayed in an ungainly manner, drool dripping from the corner of his slack mouth.

Fia regarded her dog with a fond smile. "Och, now, don't make sport of the poor beastie. He's worn out from chasing all of the evil, villainous English cats from the courtyard. He was snarling and gnashing his teeth like a huge, terrible ogre."

Robert snorted his disbelief. "He possesses naught but gums, and he displays those only when you are present to protect him, in case any should take up his false challenge."

"Och, no. He can be strong and brave when he needs to be," Fia protested. "He must feel secure in your presence to sleep so soundly."

"Pathetic, mangy beast," muttered Robert.

Mary pinned him with a stern glance. "'Tis no wonder ye're out of sorts, but don't be takin' it out on the lassie. She's enough on her plate without ye addin' to it."

Mary wrapped the herb-soaked bandage about his head. "Ye took a mightly lump, ye did. I'm sure ye're achin' like a split gourd."

That seemed to console him. When she finished, Robert took Mary's rough hand and held it reverently. "Even angels would learn tenderness at thy touch."

"Psssht. Enough of yer foolery." She disengaged her hand but grinned as she patted his cheek. "Ye'll be feeling better in no time, me lord." She turned to Fia. "I'm off to the kitchen to see about supper. The servants are so upset o'er bein' locked in the cellar, that not one o' them is thinkin' about food."

Fia smiled. "You'd be upset if an army of Englishmen came to Duart and locked you in the cellar."

"As if they could," Mary said stoutly. "I dinna care what happens, ye still have to see to yer duties." Huffing, she left.

"How I wish I could witness that." Robert sighed wistfully.

Fia chuckled and perched on the edge of the bed. "I'd wager on Mary any day."

"Would you, indeed?" Robert's voice had unmistakable eagerness.

"Aye, though not with you! We still have a wager between us, and it doesn't suit me well at all."

"An easy wager, that. I've naught to do but transform you from a winsome Scottish lady into a winsome English lady. Then you will secure the queen's sanction, your plays will be the rage, and Thomas will see that you are the perfect wife."

"I never said anything about wanting to be the perfect wife. I think, instead, Thomas should work on being the perfect husband." *Or at least proficient.* Except for one area, he was sorely lacking.

Robert adjusted the bandage Mary had tied about his head. "I hope you are prepared to pay the fine when I win our wager."

"I don't even know what it is. All I know is that I may refuse if it includes anything mortifying."

"I dearly wish I hadn't added that caveat, but in a moment of weakness, I did."

"Perhaps you should tell me the forfeit now?"

"Nay," he said simply. "Though I will admit that you've already made excellent progress. Your dancing is impeccable."

Fia sighed. "It may not be enough, though. They say Elizabeth is capricious, and she dislikes it when her courtiers marry without permission."

"Aye, and she's like to resent your beauty, too." His expression grew somber. "Thomas is already known as the luckiest man in England, and his reputation will be set once you've been introduced to the court. Except, of course, with Queen Elizabeth."

"You're not making this any easier."

He placed a hand over hers. "She will rant and rail, but she will forgive him."

"And if she doesn't?"

"As he's committed no treason, the worst thing she would do is banish him from court. As he's not one to languish there anyway, he won't care. She will miss him anon and demand he return. And *then* everyone will know what good fortune he has."

"Poor Thomas. He's had to deal with many troubles lately."

"Strife is good for the soul. Thomas would be a better man if he'd had more of it in life."

"He wouldn't agree with that."

"Do not underestimate Thomas." Robert shook his head, and a flicker of pain crossed his face. "My poor head feels like an egg crushed beneath a boot. I'd like one good moment with that fiend Douglas."

"Aye, that would solve all. Then we'd have two broken heads instead of one."

His mouth curved sweetly. "Nay, you'd still have but

one. There wouldn't be enough left of him to bury, much less bandage."

Fia gave an inelegant snort. "Men. Fools and brawns, they are one and the same."

"A lovely sentiment," a deep voice drawled from the doorway. "Though hardly a welcome one to hear from one's wife."

Fia jumped guiltily off Robert's bed.

Thomas leaned in the doorway, one hand cupped about a bundle that seemed to be all rags.

"I would enter, but this thing"—he gestured at Zeus—"halts me."

Fia called sharply to the dog, who only twitched slightly. Sighing, she went over. With much shoving and tugging, she hauled the animal from the door.

Dusting her hands, Fia sank into a curtsy. "Your path is now cleared, your lordship."

"I thank you." Thomas deposited his bundle onto a table by her small writing desk, then pulled her up. A thrill ran through her as his large, warm hands slid down her arms to capture her hands, and he pressed a kiss to the back of each.

The backs of her hands tingled and burned, and her heart pounded so loudly she was sure everyone in the house could hear it.

He released her and grinned. "Lady wife, though I enjoy your wit, I find it much more humorous when 'tis pointed elsewhere. Why not sink your barbs into Robert? He is much more worthy of your scorn."

"And here I am, wounded nigh to death," Robert protested. "Surely I don't deserve such abuse!"

Thomas lifted his brows. "I'll cease abusing you when

you explain how 'tis that your bloodied head is upon *my* pillow and not one of the other twenty-two bedchambers?"

Fia whirled on Robert. "Montley, you said *this* was a guest chamber!"

"'Tis a guest chamber, as I am a guest and I am using it," Robert said impishly. "And as I am sore wounded . . ."

Thomas pulled Fia beneath one arm and lowered his voice to whisper conspiratorially. "See how he plays upon your sensibilities? Shameless."

"Aye, shameless," she echoed breathlessly. It felt so *right* standing there with Thomas, held against him. She wished she could capture this moment forever, to hold tight during darker moments. All she could do was savor the strength of his arm about her shoulders and inhale his scent of fresh salt water and sandalwood.

Robert waved a hand. "Rotherwood, you would refuse your bedchamber to the man who provided you with a tactical diversion?" He touched his forehead. "And at such cost, too."

"You enjoyed taunting those Scotsmen. Deny it if you can."

"It was enjoyable . . . until they attacked me from behind, the miserable spalpeens."

"Aye, there was no honor there. MacLean was mightily upset."

Fia looked up at Thomas. "We should prepare a bedchamber for Duncan, too. And what about all his—"

"He has already left."

"But . . . he didn't say good-bye."

"I think he feared he would be overcome. Say what I will about your cousin, he holds you very dear in his heart."

To her surprise, Fia's eyes filled with tears. Suddenly

she felt alone. She didn't know if it was the large house, or being in such space after weeks on board the ship, or standing here so close to Thomas and knowing it would not last—but whatever caused it, sadness suddenly pierced her heart.

Thomas pressed a kiss to her forehead and then turned to say something taunting to Montley, allowing her to collect herself. It was done with such quiet consideration that her tears welled all the more freely, and it took her even more time to stanch them.

Robert moaned loudly. "Thomas, leave me be. I'm too ill to move. Besides, this bed is softer than the one in the chamber you usually assign to me. The mattress must have been made of rocks, for I could sleep nary a wink."

"I don't believe it was the mattress that impeded your sleep as much as the enthusiasm of the woman you brought to that bed."

Robert reddened and cast a hurried glance at Fia. "I don't know what you're talking about."

"Of course you do. You met the chit at some tavern and brought her—"

"Thomas." Fia interrupted, feeling sorry for Robert. "I should assist Mary with dinner. I fear your servants were very poorly treated by my cousin."

He looked down at her, and she found herself unable to look away. He had the most remarkable eyes, surrounded by thick black lashes that would be the envy of any woman.

He smiled. "Very well, comfit. If you need aught, tell the housekeeper, Mistress Hadwell."

Thomas withdrew his arm from Fia's shoulders, feeling an instant loss. She looked like an angel, her dark hair a nimbus about her head, the curls caressing her cheeks and neck, her cheeks light pink with color. *Sweet Jesu, I would give all I have to take her right now and—*

Robert cleared his throat, and Thomas met his amused gaze. Thomas turned his back on the lackwit. "Thank you for seeing to our dinner. I'm sure even Robert will be grateful for something to eat."

"Actually," Robert said, "I'd just like some thin gruel and—"

"He will eat in the dining room with the rest of us."

Fia nodded. "Where are my trunks? I'll need to change for dinner."

"I had them delivered to the chamber next to this one."

The color in Fia's cheeks deepened, and she bobbed a quick curtsy and left.

Thomas followed her to the door and watched her walk down the hallway, her skirts swaying with each step.

"I die, and all the world falls in love." Robert's voice drifted out into the hallway. "'Tis a cruel, cruel world."

"What? Still in my bed? Get thee gone, lazy slug."

Robert gestured to the heavens. "Am I to receive no comfort? No care? No kind words?"

"None."

"I am sadly unappreciated, my genius wasted. I don't know why I even try. First I am attended by a beauteous woman who only showers her care on fattened rabbits and"—he gestured at the snoring Zeus—"*that;* then a warm and generous maid, who is too focused upon securing dinner to pay me the slightest heed; and now you, smiling like a besotted prince."

"I am just overjoyed that the Scottish giant has left us." Thomas crossed to a window where the sun streamed through, the final clouds resting on the horizon. Odd, he'd thought it would rain, but 'twas now as clear an evening as could be.

Robert sat up and slid off the bed with a surprisingly lithe move. "I think you're making a mistake to establish your wife in a bedchamber not your own."

Thomas carefully hid his expression. "Most married couples have separate chambers."

"Not all wives are as charming to behold as Fia," Robert tucked a pillow under each arm. "She's been good for you, too. You used to be the most ill-tempered man I knew, forever grumping and grumbling."

"I was not so bad as that."

"Aye, you worried constantly whether you could meet the impossible dictates of a man long dead."

Thomas frowned. "This is not about my father."

"Everything is about your father. Even now, you strive to please him." Robert's gaze softened. "You take everything too much to heart, *mon ami*. You always have."

"I take my responsibilities seriously. What man doesn't?"

"'Tis more than that. You have something to prove. Where other men stop, you forge on."

Over the years, Thomas had taken pride in that. Now he wasn't so certain. In fact, he wasn't so certain of anything anymore.

Over the weeks they'd spent on his ship, something had changed. For the first time in his life, he understood how his mother, as passionate and fanciful as Fia, must have felt married to his father, who had been so determined to control every aspect of her life, including her emotions. Before he'd met Fia, it had never occurred to Thomas to wonder what his mother had thought or felt.

"Robert, I appreciate that you are concerned for Fia and me, but we must set our own course."

"I cannot allow it when you're being such a fool. Give up this ridiculous idea of an annulment. 'Tis time you focused your energies on making this marriage work, rather than finding ways to tear it apart."

"If you've grown such a liking for wedded bliss, I'll speak with the queen. I'm sure she has a lady-in-waiting or two dying for the married state. Of course, they might be with child from another, but such is life in court, eh?"

Robert scowled. "I think I liked you better without humor." He turned toward the door, halting as he spied the bundle Thomas had brought into the room. "What's this?"

"Ah yes. I almost forgot. Open it."

Robert did so, blinking in wonder at the silver casket. "Thomas? Is this—" He reached out and ran a finger over the engraved "F" on the lid.

"It is for Francis II, Mary's first husband."

His eyes widened. "Queen Mary's?"

Thomas nodded. "'Tis the rest of Walsingham's proof. I'm to deliver it along with Duncan's compliments."

"Is it conclusive?"

"If the letters are real, they will seal her fate."

Robert yanked his hand away as if the box were a live coal. "By the rood, but you're a cold fish to stand there and speak so calmly! Men would die for this."

"I imagine they would. In fact, some might still."

Robert looked puzzled. "Why does MacLean provide so much for Walsingham?"

"I don't know. He spoke of a debt paid, but no more."

"I *knew* Walsingham was dealing below the table!"

"Aye, you did. I've already sent word to Walsingham and asked to meet."

Robert nodded, a cold smile on his face. "I shall look forward to that meeting." He placed the casket back on the dressing table beside Fia's small writing desk. He looked at her desk for a moment, then asked abruptly, "Thomas, have you read any of Fia's plays?"

"Nay, why?"

Robert flipped open the small desk and took out a sheaf of papers. He paged through them, selected a section, and held it out to Thomas. "This is my favorite. Fia read it to me while we were on the ship and it was vastly amusing."

Thomas looked at the sheaf of papers. What would Fia write about? Hopeless passion? Murder and mayhem? 'Twould be interesting to find out. He took the play and thumbed through it.

Robert was already digging back through the writing desk. "I vow, that's a beautiful jewel." He withdrew a large amulet, the center a large piece of the purest amber.

The stone gleamed, overshadowing the elegantly chased silver edging that held it in place. It was beautiful. Thomas held out his hand and Robert reverently placed it into Thomas's palm.

His fingers closed about it, the smoothness of the metal work hinting at its age. The jewel was oddly warm against his skin. "This must be part of the MacLean jewels, although the laird spoke only of rubies."

Robert lifted a strand of large rubies from the box. "Mayhap he meant these? 'Tis rare to see jewelry of such quality." He examined them a moment, then replaced them. "Shall I return the amulet?"

"Nay. I'll hold this a moment more." What was making

it so *warm?* The warmth was invading his thoughts, calming him, allowing him to see things—life—more clearly.

"Very well. Read that play. 'Twill impress you." Robert rubbed his forehead as if it ached. "Be certain you hide yon casket, too. 'Twill be difficult enough to sleep without *that* lying about."

"I'll hide it, never fear."

Robert's gaze brightened. "The secret hiding place?"

"I must have been mad to tell you about that."

"Nay, you were drunk on Michaelmas ale. I remember it well."

Thomas looked at the huge, black hearthstone that outlined the fireplace. "I hope I can remember how to trigger the latch. It's been years since I last tried."

Robert regarded him with a jaundiced eye. "Had I a secret hiding place in *my* house, I would keep all my silks within."

"'Tis not a closet, Robert. There's barely room for the box. I shall lock that away immediately, but first, pray replace my pillows."

Robert looked at the pillows still tucked beneath each of his arms, blinking as if surprised to find them there. "But you've many more. I count two, three, four—seven pillows still upon your bed. These would scarcely be missed. Besides, I need them for my sore head."

"'Twill make you even more sore if I have to yank them from beneath your slumbering head."

Robert sniffed. "Fine. Take your damned pillows." With a great show of dignity, he laid the pillows on a chair by the door. Then, after a slight bow, he quit the room, slamming the door in his wake.

Thomas tucked the play under his arm and hung the

amulet about his neck, then he quickly hid the casket, closing the latch and smudging the area with soot to make it blend in once again. As he crossed to wash his hands in the washbasin, he glanced up and caught sight of himself in the mirror. The sunlight caught the silver chain where it pooled on the dark wood and brightened a warm glimmer in the amulet. His gaze narrowed. The inside of the stone seemed to swirl like a mist washing over stone. Thomas shook his head and looked again. The mist still swirled, mysterious and beckoning.

Good God, what's this? He picked up the amulet, but in the direct light, all he could see was a faint outline of his own reflection, the center of the stone cold and still. Frowning, he dropped the amulet back to his chest and reached for the play, glancing back in the mirror as he did so.

The mist in the center of the amulet grew lighter, almost white, and Thomas was unable to look away or move. It was as if his entire body was frozen inside the amber, locked between times or places.

The mist in the amulet parted and there, in the center, was the ghost of an outline of a woman. He knew immediately who the woman was, her long hair tumbled about her, her feet shod in sensible boots as she made her way between the rocks, the mist alternately concealing and revealing her.

Thomas fought with all his being to look away, but the illusion was just as stubborn as he and it would not let him go.

The figure came closer and finally seemed to catch sight of him, for her face brightened. A glorious smile parted her lips and she said in her honey-rich voice, as clear as if she were really standing in front of him, "Thomas, I am your—"

Footsteps sounded in the hallway, and just as suddenly as he'd been pulled into this odd awake-dream, Thomas was released. All that was left was the strangely glowing amber amulet, warm against his chest.

For a long moment. Thomas merely stared, his heart thudding as hard as if he'd just run a race. Outside his room, a servant passed carrying a load of firewood for someone's bedchamber. As the servant's footsteps faded, Thomas forced himself away from the mirror. He yanked the amulet from his neck and threw it into the writing desk with the other jewelry, then slammed it closed. Heart sill racing, he stacked every book he could find on the top.

"Bloody hell, I'm becoming as fanciful as Fia!" He rubbed his face with both hands, his heart returning slowly to a normal pace. He forced a laugh. "Mayhap *I* should be the one writing plays."

Shaking his head, he pulled out the sheaf of papers and took a chair as far away from the writing desk as he could find. A sensible, straight-backed chair with solid legs that rested firmly upon the ground. Then, with only an occasional glance toward the writing desk, Thomas read Fia's play.

Chapter Twenty-one

"*O*ch, now, what might you be doing?"

Thomas jerked upright, slamming his head into the stone fireplace. A huge puff of soot billowed into the room and he began to cough, one hand wiping his streaming eyes, the other uselessly fanning the ashy air.

As he staggered away from the fireplace, one foot came down squarely on Zeus's tail. The dog yipped and Thomas spun away, tripping over a chair, his arms flailing uselessly.

For a second he tottered unsteadily . . . then crashed onto the floor in a cloud of soot.

Fia blinked in amazement. She'd just come to find her animals, who for some strange reason continued to migrate to Thomas's bedchamber the second she opened her door each morning. He was usually up and gone by the time she arose, so she had been surprised to find him still in his room. "I didn't mean to startle you."

He put a hand to his head but made no move to rise.

"Thomas?" Fia tiptoed closer, peering through the haze at his blackened face.

Thomas's hair was no longer gleaming black, but a dull, dusty gray. Black soot splashed trails across his head and shoulders, leaving only his neck and a small triangle under his nose the color of flesh. His eyes, which had filled with tears at the sudden fall of ash, were so reddened they could have frightened off the most stout-hearted of heroes.

Fia sank to her knees beside him, heedless of the ash dirtying her gown. "Thomas! Can you rise?"

"Aye," he choked out, rubbing his eyes with the back of a grimy hand. "Only . . . give me a moment to . . . recover my . . . breath."

Sweet Saint Catherine, if this is the luckiest man in the country lying here in the soot, then God help England.

She choked back a laugh, carefully wiping some of the soot from his face with the edge of her skirt.

He took a calming breath and shot her an irritated look. "God's breath, you scared me nigh to death."

"I'm sorry; 'twasn't my intention. What were you doing with your head up the chimney?"

"The flue was stuck," he answered shortly.

"Why would you worry about that? There's no fire."

"Aye, but 'twas making a breeze." He was thankful Fia hadn't come a moment earlier, or she'd have seen a place cleared of soot where he'd moved the lever to open the secret compartment. He'd been smearing it back over when she'd startled him.

Fia tilted her head to one side. "Do you think you can stand?"

Zeus shuffled over and sat beside Thomas, his tail thumping uncertainly, stirring small puffs of soot.

"Och, look at that. Zeus has come to see how you are."

"'Twas all his fault," Thomas grumbled, then sent a hard

look at Fia when she giggled. "Thank you, Mistress Mirth, but 'tis not a laughing matter. I was nigh killed."

Zeus tilted his head curiously at the familiar voice coming from the soot-covered face. He leaned over and sniffed loudly at Thomas's ash-blackened hair, then promptly sneezed in his face.

"Damn cur!" Thomas reached for Zeus, but the dog scrambled out of the way, his crooked tail wagging as he hid behind the high bed. "That mangy, good-for-nothing, ill-mannered, foul-smelling—"

"Half-eared," Fia added helpfully, still kneeling at Thomas's side.

Thomas favored her with a flat stare.

She bit her lip, knowing that to burst out laughing would be a grave error.

He saw her laughter anyway, for his gaze narrowed and without warning, he grasped her shoulders. "It has just occurred to me that I am so very, very dirty, whilst you are so very, very clean."

Before she could comprehend his intent, he pulled her against him and then rolled her under his long length. She was trapped on the dusty floor, soot rising in a foggy cloud around them.

His ash-covered face loomed above her, his white teeth gleaming as he grinned.

"You—you—" Words failed her.

His grin widened. "You must take your medicine." With deliberate slowness, he wiped the back of his hand on the front of her dress, lingering an unnecessary length of time on the swell of her breasts. "You owe me a forfeit, my lady."

A long smudge led down to where his hand cupped her intimately. Heat flared through her body, and she had to bite her lip to keep from pressing against him. "Laughing is not against our rules, so I owe no forfeit."

"Ah, yes. Our rules. I had forgotten them. What were they again? No dancing, correct?"

"In public—yes, that's one. And for you, no shouting."

"I hope my surprised yell when you snuck up on me doesn't count."

"Nay, not this time."

"That's generous of you." He traced a sooty finger down her cheek. "My other rule was 'No public displays,' I believe. 'Tis a good thing we're in private now. I find I'm rather fond of public displays here."

She had to laugh. He was so tempting when he was like this—mussed and smiling, charming and teasing. How could she resist?

And yet she must. The last three days had been difficult. She'd found herself staring at the wall that separated their bedchambers, restless and lonely in her bed.

Thomas shifted and winced, his hand going to his forehead.

"You're wounded!"

"I'll have a bruise or two. No more."

Duncan had always said that sometimes you had to grab fate by the throat to make it yours. She'd thought that was a rather violent way to do things, but perhaps there was something in it.

"Does it hurt"—she placed her hand on Thomas's chest—"here?"

His gaze went to her hand. "No."

Her heart thudded harder. "Good. But mayhap you hurt"—she moved her hand to his hard stomach—"here?"

His chest rose and fell faster, as did hers; the air about them suddenly charged.

"Nay," Thomas said in a husky voice. "It doesn't hurt there, either."

Slowly, so slowly, she slid her hand to his codpiece and rested it lightly there, her fingers curved around him. "Mayhap you hurt . . . here?"

She almost couldn't breathe. Never had she been so daring, so bold. Would Thomas reject her? Send her away? Tell her—

Thomas slipped an arm about her waist and kissed her, his entire body aflame. He needed to feel her against him, under him, *with* him.

She reacted as he'd known she would, with wild abandon. She strained against him, her arms about his neck, her tongue seeking his. Her hips lifted in an unconscious invitation. He had to steel his every nerve against the urge to immediately bury himself into her, so intense was the pleasure.

But this time he wanted to linger, to savor, to explore. He pulled back and looked into the smoky blackness of her eyes. "Easy, comfit," he whispered, then bent to gently nip her full bottom lip, laving the mock injury with his tongue. She moaned and closed her eyes, her thick lashes black crescents on her cheeks.

He smiled gently at the gray streaks that marred her creamy skin and whispered against her mouth, "I fear I've shared more of this soot than I intended."

She blinked up at him, comprehension rising slowly in her arousal-clouded eyes.

"I've always wanted to make love in front of a fireplace." She chuckled, the sound running through him like a rushing brook through a parched plain.

"You look more like you've been *inside* a fireplace, comfit." He placed small kisses along her delectable mouth and firm, rounded chin.

"As do you," she murmured, igniting him with the need to take her there, *now*. "Stop talking, please. Just kiss me."

He did so as he slid his hands into the luxury of her hair, instantly welcomed by the silky curls. He ran his hands past her waist to the curve of her hip and on to the firmness of her thigh.

With an impatient tug, he pulled her skirts up until he could cup the roundness of her leg in his hand. She was made for his hands, he thought possessively, kissing her with renewed passion.

Fia gasped as his hands began their ascent past her knee. Just as she tensed, his mouth was on hers, warm and demanding, his tongue questing. She threw one arm around his neck and placed the other on his back, running it up and down the hardness of his rippling muscles. When he touched her, she forgot everything else. Even all smudged with soot, he was still heart-rendingly beautiful.

"Take me," Fia whispered, the words wrenched from her secret heart as if he had placed her under a spell.

He slowly lowered his mouth to place an almost reverent kiss on her lips. She groaned and kissed him back, her whole body writhing with urgent passion. He plunged his tongue into her mouth in an insistent, seductive rhythm and she unconsciously ground her hips against his, her hands tugging at his clothing.

He began to loosen her dress. As her skin was exposed to the chilly air, her nipples hardened. He moaned and his mouth, hot and insistent, covered one taut peak as his hand cupped the other. She gasped, arching into him.

"Don't stop," she whispered.

Without ceasing to ply his heated tongue to her breast, he managed to free her dress and he stripped it from her, his eyes burning.

He lifted himself to look at her, his eyes moving slowly from her face and beyond, lingering on her body until she thought she would burst into flames from embarrassment. "You are so beautiful," he murmured.

She tugged at his shirt. "Undress."

He stared at her, a sensual smile playing across his lips.

"Undress," she pleaded again.

"Nay, sweet lady, I'll have you undress me," he whispered against her mouth, his hands never still.

She moaned and writhed as he nipped at her ear, his hand sliding up her thigh to brush ever so lightly against her moistness.

She began to pull on his shirt laces, crying out when they refused to loosen.

He chuckled and grabbed her frantic hands. "Softly, my sweet." His brown eyes glinted warmly into hers as he leaned forward to gently brush her lips with his. The kiss deepened and she felt his hand slide between her legs to thread gently through the curls.

Hot, molten liquid rushed through her veins. She was afire with want. She threw an arm about his neck and ran her other hand over his shoulders, down his back, and lower, kneading his firm muscles. She reached to cup his manhood and he groaned into her mouth—and moaned again as she stroked him through the cloth.

She tried to undo the lacing, cursing her trembling fingers, yet still he did not help her. Frustration made her bold. "*Undress,*" she demanded, thrusting her hips against him for emphasis. His eyes clenched shut as though he were in pain.

"Sweet Jesu, do not move!" he hissed, his face strained, a damp sheen moistening his lip.

For a second he lay still, his forehead dropping to rest against her cheek, his breathing rasping harshly through the room. Then his fingers were tugging and yanking at his own laces with satisfying desperation. In an instant he was naked, his skin warm against hers.

He pulled her legs apart and positioned himself above her, his eyes staring directly into hers as he lowered himself into her. There was an agonizing second of fullness as he ground his hips against her.

"By the saints," he whispered between clenched teeth. Before he could withdraw to sink into her again, she tensed and then threw back her head as wave after wave of pleasure rippled through her.

Her heat nearly singed Thomas as she clutched her legs about him, and he could not withstand the pressure of her reaction. Spiraling through heaven, she sent him over the edge without even moving.

For a moment they lay spent, legs intertwined as their breathing returned to normal. Thomas lifted himself to look down at Fia's flushed face and couldn't resist placing a kiss on the corner of her mouth. It looked like a dewy cherry, ripe for a taste.

She peered at him from beneath heavy lids. "I have soot all over my clothing."

He chuckled. "Aye, and your face as well." He kissed her nose. "Yet you manage to look beautiful all the same."

She smiled as her eyes drifted closed.

"What's this? 'Tis but midday, madam, yet you look to be asleep."

"I know," she murmured, not opening her eyes. "You've made me very, very tired." She shivered and a slight frown turned down the corners of her mouth. "I would sleep, but for the cold."

He laughed softly. "I promise to have a roaring fire awaiting you next time."

She grimaced drowsily. "Only if you get thicker carpets. I'm certain I'll have bruises."

"Witch," he said with a grin. He spread her skirt over her like a blanket. "I give you so much pleasure you nigh expire, and all you can do is complain."

She chuckled sleepily, the sound settling around him like a warm woolen cloak. He draped a leg across hers and pulled her to him.

She nestled against his chest, and slowly fell asleep. He watched her a moment before a noise in the corridor reminded him that some servant could knock upon the door at any moment.

He scooped her into his arms, then laid her gently on the huge bed. She snuggled into the mounds of pillows and blankets, then did not stir.

He tucked the cover under her chin, lingering for no reason. When he and Fia were alone, things seemed so easy and simple. Yet the second they parted, the doubts began, taunting him with dark memories.

But right now it was just he and Fia, and he could fight those thoughts. He bent and gently kissed her lips. She smiled in her sleep, a soft sighing smile that whispered of magical dreams, and for a moment, a flicker of regret washed over him that he didn't know those hidden thoughts.

Was she thinking of him? Or of her triumph if she managed to charm the queen into sponsoring her plays?

His smile faded. What if she smiled about something—or someone—else? Did he know her so well that he could swear there'd never been a man who'd held her heart before she'd met him?

He mentally shook himself. What madness was this, that he was even jealous of her dreams?

His own dreams were filled with her. The odd awake-dream he'd had from her odd amulet haunted him still, and he had dreamed it while asleep.

Yet another sign that he had to fight this attraction. He was becoming more besotted, more enthralled, drawn to her and yet afraid of what would happen when he lost her. Somehow over the last weeks, he'd stopped fearing the loss of his family dignity and feared instead for his own heart. He didn't want to lose Fia, no matter the price. He didn't know when the change had occurred, only that it had, and it frightened him more than anything in his entire life.

Was this how Father felt about Mother? Was this why he married a woman so obviously destined to leave him? Why he couldn't bring himself to allow her the freedom to enjoy life or even me, her only son? And am I now becoming that man? Oh God, please, no.

He forced himself to turn away and quietly left the room.

He didn't know how he'd do it, but he would regain control over his desires. If he could do that one thing, then perhaps he could also find a way to keep this marriage. Perhaps he could even be strong enough to forge this relationship into something that would keep the inevitable from happening. Because if he didn't, God help them both.

Chapter Twenty-two

$\mathcal{M}$ ary gawped. "Lord Montley! Why— Where did—" She pressed a hand over her eyes. "Lord Montley, why on earth are ye dressed as a *woman*?"

"I'm teaching Lady Fia the proper management of her skirts and petticoats." Robert held his arms out wide, the gown he'd loosely laced over his doublet and hose displayed about him. "What do you think of Mistress Roberta?"

As Mary tried to find her voice, Fia chuckled. Robert stood poised on his toes, in one of Fia's new dresses. The gown was uncinched to allow room for his much larger frame and the skirts barely reached his shins. The full sleeves tied but halfway up his long arms, his own shirtsleeves billowing below, and the gaping stomacher hung across his chest like embroidered armor.

Even more amusing was the huge red wig sitting precariously upon Robert's black hair.

The giggling maid shook her head. "I think ye need yer noggin examined."

Fia laughed. "Aye, he's mad, but he knows all of the tricks of walking and dancing with such monstrous layers of cloth."

Robert curtsied. "Thank you for such a gracious compliment." He held out a hand to Mary. "Come, mistress! What thinkest thou? And do not say I make an ugly woman, for I vow I would not believe you."

"Och, ye make a bonny lass, Master Robert, exceptin' yer mustache and beard. If not fer them, I'd-a thought ye one o' the queen's ladies-in-waiting."

Robert flicked open his fan and simpered over the top of it. "I vow, I am overcome! I know not what to say to such exaggerations."

Mary chuckled as she reluctantly turned to Fia. "I came to see if ye'd like me to bring yer luncheon here, or if ye'd like to eat in the dining hall."

"Has Thomas returned from his ride?" Fia tried to keep her voice light but could tell from the way Robert and Mary exchanged glances that she'd failed.

Robert lowered the fan. "I say we eat in here so we may continue our lessons without delay. The queen may send for you any day now, and you must be ready."

"Aye, that's a good idea," Mary said, bustling to the door.

Fia turned back to Robert. "I'm afraid I haven't been a very attentive pupil today."

"Your mind was elsewhere—mainly staring out yon window for the return of your husband." Robert pulled the wig from his head and tossed it onto the bed, winking at her. "Don't look so embarrassed, sweet. If you cannot stare at your own husband, whom can you stare at?"

Ah, there was the rub. Her husband was a complex man and she was never sure how he would react to her. Though

Thomas no longer spoke of an annulment, he still blew hot and cold—warm and laughing one moment, silent and brooding the next. She didn't know what to make of it, and it made her heart ache like mad.

Robert waved the fan. "Come, let's continue with our lessons. Your curtsy has grace, but you lack an imperial air. In court, style is everything."

He slapped the wig back onto his head and lifted the impossibly large fan. He tossed her a pouting smile and floated across the room in a surprisingly accurate imitation of a gentlewoman approaching royalty.

"You turn and bend and curtsy like so." His voice had an almost singsong quality to it.

"You belong on a stage," Fia said reverently.

He straightened and gave her a mock frown. "I just hope I'm never again forced to such lengths to keep the attention of a woman. If I didn't wear this garb, you'd still be plastered to yon window." He shook his head, the red curls bobbing. "You are ever hard on my pride. Now, come and see how easily such a commanding air can be accomplished."

She rose from her seat and was immediately aware of the stiff skirts and petticoats that bound her. She hated her new clothing. "'Tis too heavy, this skirt," she complained, kicking the stiff lengths out of her way as she went to his side. "I am likely to faint from the weight, and this stomacher is too tight. It presses my breasts up 'til they nigh overspill."

Robert assessed her rounded breasts where they bulged over the edge of her neckline. "The ladies of the court wear far lower and far more revealing bodices than yours, milady." He pursed his lips thoughtfully. "Though I must admit that there are few who show to such advantage."

"I shall probably catch an ague from such exposure." She tugged at the ruff around her neck. "This thing has been starched until it resembles a piece of wood."

"Do not touch it; you'll mar it."

"I want to do more than mar it. I want to rip it from my throat and toss it to the ground."

Robert appeared shocked. "You would not!"

"I would stomp it, too, except these shoes keep falling from my feet." She held up a foot, where a jeweled slipper hung precariously. "I wish I had my boots."

He shuddered. "Those boots look like something a farm laborer might wear."

"They are comfortable and allow me to walk where I wish without worrying about mud. *These* shoes are barely fit for walking."

"Those are jeweled slippers and worth a fortune, so cease your quibbling!"

"I am to be silent, though I am trapped by stiff skirts, a tight waist, and an overzealous ruff," she retorted, "while you cavort about in loose-fitting velvets and fine cambric shirts? Men always have the best of it."

Robert addressed the heavens, his wig sliding off onto the floor. "How can such a comely woman so hate the trappings of beauty?"

"Only the ones that pinch and scratch and bind."

"Come. Practice your curtsy again. You are so close to perfecting it."

She gritted her teeth but did as she was told, coming forward, then dropping into a deep curtsy. "Well?"

Robert tapped his bearded chin with the end of the fan. "You still lack the correct air. How can I convey that to you?" He pulled his gown off and laid it upon a chair, then took several swift strides about the room, hands clasped behind him. "Fia, suppose you pretend that this is one of your plays?"

She tilted her head. "My plays?"

He stroked his beard as inspiration struck. "Aye, pretend that you are the heroine from your play *The Beggar Prince*." He rubbed his hands together eagerly. "You will be the lovely, innocent Mirabella, come to ask the evil queen to release your beloved from the dreadful death she has planned for him."

He grabbed up the wig and planted it back on his head, going to stand by the fireplace. His chin rose to an unnatural height; his mouth pinched in vigorous disapproval. He stared down his nose. "Approach your queen!" His voice rose into the querulous whine of a displeased ruler.

Fia threw herself into her part, affecting an expression that was at once both brave and frightened. Lifting her own chin to match his, she swept across the room and sank into a deep and respectful curtsy.

"That's it!" Robert grabbed her about the waist and swung her around. "I trow, you are near ready to meet the queen."

Fia disengaged herself, his last words quelling her excitement.

"Do you really think this will be enough, Robert? Or do we play at a fools' game?"

He looked puzzled. "Fools' game? You think we'll fail?"

She sank into the window seat, dropped the confining slippers from her feet, and leaned against the cool pane. "When it comes to our interview with the queen, I suppose nothing and fear everything." She pulled her feet up and hugged her knees, looking out onto the garden.

"Fia, don't look so sad," said Robert bracingly. "You've made it to London; you have the benefit of a great position and the attention of a notable man—what more could you ask?"

Love. She gave Robert a brief smile. "I look forward to meeting the queen."

"I'm sure you do. 'Twill be a relief, in a way."

"More than you know." She toyed with the lace edge of her gown. "Robert, do you think Thomas might come to love me? Not now, of course, but perhaps in a year or two?"

"Lass, I'd say he is already wholly, completely besotted."

She managed a little chuckle. "I wish that were so. Once in a while, I think he's beginning to care, but then the next day . . . It's as if he pulls away every chance that comes his way."

"Aye, his heart and head are warring with each other." Robert sighed. "'Tis a gargantuan war, and I can't say which will win. He's a stubborn man and he paid dearly for his parents' lack of love."

Robert frowned. "Come! Such a sad face will haunt my dreams and I'll awake as hollow-eyed as a troll. Tell me what pretty trifle will lighten that brow. A silk fan? Another pair of jeweled slippers?"

Fia smiled and stood, determined to shake off the uncertainty that held her in its sway. "Nay. There's naught."

"Brave child. What you need is a diversion." He looked about the room. "What if I told you a tale of intrigue regarding a secret hiding place?"

"'Tis a true tale?"

"'Tis possible. This hiding place was a favorite of the family who lived here and hid their jewels and gold during less certain times." As Robert spoke, his gaze flickered to the fireplace and then away.

Fia suddenly remembered Thomas searching inside the chimney when she came into this room and a trill of excitement flashed through her. "Robert! This secret hiding place . . . is it in here?"

Robert's smile faded. "No, 'tis in another house. One on the opposite side of the Thames."

"Nay, 'tis in this house. I know it."

"Then 'tis somewhere outside—in the stables mayhap."

Fia went toward the fireplace. "'Tis here, isn't it?"

"No! I didn't say it was in here! How can you—"

She knelt before the fireplace and began to search about the stones with anxious fingers. "Where is it?"

"God's wounds," Robert protested. "Fia, don't! If you trigger the opening, Thomas will blame me for my loosed tongue and then—"

She turned from the fireplace. "So it *is* here!"

He grimaced. "Aye, but you cannot tell Thomas that you know."

"I'll not tell him a thing. What's hidden in there?"

"I cannot tell you."

"A *real* treasure?"

Robert groaned and collected his doublet, pulling it over his head and lacing it at the neck. "Forget I ever mentioned it. You, my lady, have a mischievous spirit that I cannot resist. You ask and I blurt out things like the veriest of fools."

Fia could see from Robert's expression that she'd upset him, so to calm his fears, she took a chair by the massive fireplace and twirled a strand of hair about a finger. "I promise not to tell who mentioned the hiding place."

"Good. Meanwhile, I left you a list upon the desk of all the members of the court and their titles. When you've time, you might wish to read through them, for 'twould not surprise me if the queen sends for us soon."

"I hope so."

He made his way to the door. "I'm leaving to visit my sisters. Call if you've a wish to try your hand at that new card game I taught you."

"I will. And, Robert?"

"Aye?"

"Thank you again. I can never repay you for your assistance, whatever the outcome."

His expression relaxed and he bowed, his blue eyes twinkling. "The pleasure is mine, lass." With a wink, he left.

Fia chuckled, watching him stride down the hallway until he disappeared from sight. The second he did so, she hopped up and went back to the fireplace.

The things she could do in her plays with a hidden treasure vault! And now she was able to see a real one, and note how it worked and how large it was, and any number of crucial details. All she had to do was discover exactly where it lay.

She ran her hands over the intricate stonework flanking the fireplace. Perhaps it was just a loose stone behind which things could be hidden, though that seemed rather pale. 'Twould be much more interesting if there were a release mechanism of some sort.

"Hmm. Where could that be?" Heedless of the soot, she bent over to look in the wide opening, scanning for an odd seam, a small lever—*something* that would indicate she'd found the hidden area.

Behind her, Thomas walked into his bedchamber carrying his boots, muddied from his ride. He saw Fia half-inside the huge chimney, her bare feet peeping from beneath her soot-embellished skirts. *She is looking for the casket. Good God, is she a traitor?*

Thomas scowled and tamped down his thoughts. *I have no reason to doubt her and I refuse to do so unless I'm given a reason. I am not my father. I will not take umbrage at the slightest veer in opinion or thought.*

"'Tis far too dark in here to see a thing." Fia's voice echoed up the chimney while she gripped the edge of the opening with a soot-covered hand. She sighed and pulled her hand out and then spied her dirty hands. "Och! What a mess! I'll—" Her gaze widened as she caught sight of Thomas, who was standing in the middle of the room, his arms crossed over his chest.

Instinctively she tried to cover the entire fireplace with her skirts. "I—I um, I was looking for . . ." She bit her lip and he noticed a wide smear of ash from her brow to the end of her chin.

"You were searching for more soot, mayhap? If so, you've found it. There's some on your cheek, your brow, your fingers, the bottom of your skirt." He tsked. "And those feet . . ."

She looked down at her skirt and scowled, then held up one black-soled foot. "Oh dear. I *am* a mess, aren't I?" She pushed back her hair and Thomas became instantly aware of her magnificent breasts, pushed into mounds well above the edge of her stomacher.

The sight inflamed him and irked him, as well. "You stand in danger of becoming unbound, milady."

Color stained her cheeks. "I was bending over when I

was searching the fireplace, and they must have . . ." She seemed at a loss for words.

"Spilled out?"

Her cheeks flamed anew. "They are not totally exposed."

"Not . . . totally."

She sighed. "Mary will have my head, for this is one of my new gowns, too."

Thomas had to admit that she looked lovely in it, even streaked with soot, her hair a tangled mess. Of green brocade, decorated with green and gold threads, the dress sparkled even under the smudge of soot. He supposed it was a grand gown, yet compared to the mouthwatering sight of her breasts, deliciously close to overflowing her stomacher, he didn't give a damn about the gown. At the moment, he didn't even care that she'd been attempting to open the secret vault.

He had once thought his lust for Fia would cool once he saw her in comparison with the other ladies of court; what a naive fool! Fia would stand out wherever she was, and he would find her appealing regardless.

"Thomas?"

Fia was watching him, her dark gaze assessing his expressions. He forced a smile. "What were you doing looking inside the fireplace?"

"Oh. That. Lord Montley told me a very interesting story about a house that had a secret compartment in the fireplace and I thought perchance he meant this one. But I cannot find it." She shrugged, looking disappointed. "I wonder if he meant there was one in his own house?"

Damn Montley; the man cannot keep a secret. Though it was obvious the knave hadn't told all to Fia, he'd obviously aroused her suspicions. Thomas sent a casual glance at the fireplace and noted that the area that hid the latch was still soot covered. *Good. She didn't find it, then.* "If there is a secret hiding place in Montley's house, I'm sure he has all of his best neck ruffs secured in it."

She chuckled. "I would not be surprised."

He returned the smile."I'm sorry if I startled you; my boots were too muddy to wear inside."

"Of course." She dusted her hands together to remove some of the soot, her breasts bouncing gently.

Thomas had to look away to keep from staring.

"Robert thinks the queen will send for us soon."

"I hope so." Thomas wished he knew what was occurring in the court. For the last three days, he'd been trying his damnedest to get another meeting with Walsingham, but the minister had been oddly silent. "She is not an easy woman to gain an audience with."

She nodded. "I think I'm ready. We . . . we are still asking for the annulment, aren't we? I—I'm certain I'm not with child."

Her soft words hung between them like a gossamer thread, tying them together by such a delicate strand that he had the impression that one misstep, one wrongly spoken word, and it would break.

An annulment was his first thought when he'd been forced to marry her, his most ardent desire. Now . . . he wasn't so certain. His mind told him it was the most prudent route, the one that guaranteed the safety of his heart and pride. But his heart . . . oh, how his heart lusted and burned, as did his treacherous body.

But what frightened him the most was the growing flare of feelings he had for her. When she'd admitted she was not with child, he'd felt a sharp pang of disappointment. Nothing had ever frightened him more.

He could see from the gentle question in her eyes that if he but took one step forward or reached out a hand, she would come to him. Within minutes they would be in his bed, their passion keeping the world at bay.

For the moment.

But each time he succumbed to her, he weakened yet more, and if he continued, he wouldn't be able to say her nay to anything, whether it was good for him or not.

With every ounce of control he possessed, he turned from her, ignoring the disappointment that flashed over her expressive face as he walked to the door. "I'll send Mary to you anon with a tub and hot water to wash away some of that soot."

Fia took a step toward him, her hand resting on the wardrobe that held her writing desk and that damned mysterious amulet.

The thought of the amulet made his temper flare even as his body tightened with a new wave of desire. "You're covered in soot; please do not touch the chair or stand upon the rugs unless you must."

She dropped her hand to her side, her face flushed. "Of course. I didn't mean to—"

He didn't hear any more, for he was gone, striding down the hallway, trying to calm his thundering heart. He'd send a hot bath to her along with her maid, but first he'd head to the stables to douse himself in buckets of icy well water.

Chapter Twenty-three

"*O*dd's bodkin, you are a difficult man to find." Robert's voice was sharp with impatience.

Thomas looked over from where he stood watching a stable hand groom a new gelding. "I'm in plain sight."

"Neither your beauteous wife nor any of your servants knew where you were."

Thomas shrugged. "Did you find that bastard? I've sent missive after missive to Walsingham's house, and he ignores them all."

Robert looked wounded. "But of course I found him."

"It could not have been easy."

"'Twould have been difficult . . . for a mere mortal."

Thomas shot Robert an annoyed glance. "Of course."

"We may intercept him this very afternoon."

Thomas turned toward his friend. "Robert, you were right about Walsingham; he is not to be trusted. I know he's received my messages, yet he refuses to return so much as a word. I've asked him to request an audience with the queen, too, which he assured me he'd do. This morning I saw Essex as I was leaving Walsingham's residence, and he said no request has been made."

"I wonder what darkness that spider is weaving now?"

"I don't know, but 'tis not to our benefit. Where will he be this afternoon?"

"He is to meet a spy from the French court at the tavern around two. If we go slightly afterward . . ." Robert shrugged.

"How did you discover his whereabouts?"

Robert looked pleased. "Through the elegant Annie, of course."

"The woman we saw with Walsingham? But how—" Thomas broke off at Robert's grin. "You seduced her."

"'Twas more a coupling than a seduction. It turned out that the icy Annie is not so chilled once she's been warmed by a proper introduction."

"I'm grateful for the information, however you discovered it. We'll leave immediately." He motioned for one of the stable hands to approach.

It was time to settle with Walsingham one way or another.

Goliath's eyes narrowed. "Whot ye doin' here?"

"I came to see Letty."

"She's no' here. No' fer ye, anyway."

Thomas dug into his pocket and pulled out a gold coin that glittered in the dim light. "No?"

Goliath eyed the coin, greed in his little eyes as he stretched his hand forth. "Mayhap, I—"

"Hallo, my large, smelly friend!" Robert grabbed Goliath's outstretched hand and pumped it eagerly. "Verily, I have been dreaming of this meeting."

A bemused look fell over Goliath. His shaggy brows lowered and he closed his massive hand about Robert's. His muscles bulged as he squeezed.

"How am I to reach for my gold if you crush my hand?" Robert asked through clenched teeth.

The huge paw slackened its grip and Robert pulled free. Perspiration beaded his brow. "By the rood, but I would like to see you take on a bear!"

Goliath grunted.

Robert wiggled his fingers before he dropped a coin in Goliath's hand. "You could have maimed the finest rapier hand in all of England. 'Twould have been a tragedy."

"Braggin' on yerself agin, Master Robbie?" Annie asked, opening the door beside Goliath. Her green eyes twinkled mischievously.

Robert grinned in return. "I don't know. Do *you* think 'twas bragging, mistress of mine heart?"

"Enough," Thomas said shortly. "Where's Letty?"

Annie answered quickly, "She'll be here soon."

Goliath frowned. "No one said nothin' 'bout these two."

Annie sent the guard a dismissive look. "Mind yer own, Goliath. Letty pays ye not to ask questions; ye'd do well to remember that."

Thomas walked past her into the room and dropped into a chair. "How long will we have to wait?"

"Not long." Annie placed three mugs on the table.

Thomas noted that while her cheeks were artfully smeared with dirt, her neck and hair were remarkably clean.

"How did you get the knave to join us?" Robert asked.

"Walsingham just met a messenger from the French court. He walked to his carriage but will return for me soon." She shot Robert a humorous glance. "He won't be pleased to see the two of you."

"Will you be in trouble for assisting us?" Thomas asked.

Annie shrugged. "I doubt it. I've my own uses and Walsingham knows them well."

"Thank you, *ma chère.*"

Annie sent Robert a saucy look before she slipped out the door, her skirts swishing.

"Sweet Jesu, I find that woman intriguing," murmured Robert. "I wish I—" A noise arose outside. "A-ha. He comes."

The door swung open and Walsingham entered. "Annie, pray make haste, for—" He broke off, the door closing behind him.

"Surprised?" Thomas asked, his irritation rising now that he faced the old man.

The minister pushed back his hood, his mouth tight with displeasure. "What do you want?"

"Don't say you didn't get any of my messages, for I know otherwise."

The older man's lips thinned. "In case you have forgotten, I am under the queen's command and my duties are vastly important. I've been very busy this week."

"Oh?" Robert affected surprise. "Weaving more webs? *You?*"

Walsingham sent the Scotsman a chilly look. "I've been busy protecting this country." He turned to Thomas. "Since you are here, you might as well tell me of your visit with MacLean."

"I didn't come to be your informer. I came to ask you about something MacLean left me."

Walsingham frowned. "What?"

"This." Thomas opened the bundle he'd tucked under his cloak and laid the casket upon the table.

Walsingham regarded the casket as one might regard a holy relic. "Queen Mary's casket." Walsingham sent him a hard glance. "MacLean sent it? Did he say why?"

"Nay. Only that 'twas a payment of sorts."

"Ah! Good." Walsingham looked pleased. "So he didn't say anything else."

Thomas leaned back in his chair, crossed his boots at the ankles, and placed them upon the table. "What should he have said?"

"Nothing. I was just musing aloud." Walsingham reached for the casket, his eyes glittering as he opened the box and looked within. His smile disappeared. "Thomas . . . the letters."

"Aye. They prove Mary's perfidy in Darnley's death."

"But they're not here." Walsingham turned the casket toward Thomas. " 'Tis empty."

"What?" Robert snapped.

Thomas's chair slammed onto the floor. "Damn it to hell, they were there, in that casket, not a week ago!"

Walsingham's brows drew down until they almost touched. "So you saw these letters for yourself? Read them?"

"Of course," Thomas answered shortly.

The minister gave a muttered curse and slammed the lid shut. "By all that's holy, we've been tricked." Walsingham's hands curled into fists. "Tricked by a Scottish bastard! After all I gave him! After all of the chances I took! I should have known better than to have—" The minister halted and closed his mouth, seeming to think better of his words.

Something rang false about this entire episode. "You *knew* MacLean brought me the casket and letters."

"I've never seen them until now."

Robert made an impatient noise. "That doesn't answer the question."

The minister sent Robert a hard glare, but after a moment, he shrugged. "Fine. I knew MacLean had at least one letter. I had no idea there were more, though it doesn't surprise me."

Robert leaned forward. "You are still hiding something. Tell us all."

Walsingham's lips folded into a frown. "There is nothing more to tell."

"I disagree."

"We have both been duped. Me for trusting a Scottish infidel, and you for . . ." The reedy voice faded into silence.

Some shadowy fact lurked on the edge of Thomas's mind. Slowly, he said, "You knew what was in the casket because MacLean had already told you. Because you had already *paid* him for it."

Walsingham licked his dry lips. "I have not—"

"You said 'After all I gave him.' And MacLean said 'twas for a debt owed and now paid." Thomas remembered Fia blithely explaining that Duncan had enough gold and silver tucked away to replace any trifling candelabras she might steal. He pinned Walsingham with a frigid glare. "But MacLean did not seek money."

The bony hands closed into fists. "Nay. He did not."

"The truth," Thomas said dangerously, coldness seeping through his bones and chilling his heart. "I want the truth."

Robert scowled. "The truth and this man have ever been strangers. I wouldn't believe him were he to swear upon his own blood."

Walsingham flicked a contemptuous glance at Robert. "There is nothing left but the truth."

Robert leaned across the table. "Then speak quickly, old man, else I will slit your gullet."

Walsingham shoved the casket to the center of the table. "My association with MacLean began the week after Queen Mary's husband, Lord Darnley, was murdered. As you know, rumors began almost immediately, implicating her and her lover, Lord Bothwell, in the death. However, Elizabeth would not hear of Mary's involvement without conclusive proof. I had to find that proof."

"So you approached MacLean?"

"Aye. Repeatedly. At first he resisted, but eventually he came to see how advantageous this arrangement would be. He offered to provide the letters, stolen from the queen's lady-in-waiting, and I—" Walsingham flicked a nervous glance at Thomas. "I compensated him."

"How did you buy him? Land?" Robert demanded.

"Nay," the counselor said. "There are few things the MacLeans holds of value. It would have made our negotiations much simpler had he wanted land."

Thomas leaned forward, not recognizing his own voice, so harsh and distant. "What was his price?"

Hooded gray eyes flickered for an instant. "I did what I thought was best. What needed to be done."

What did you trade MacLean for the letters?

The minister said nothing.

Robert's rapier lifted, the slender point resting directly under the counselor's chin.

Walsingham swallowed, the sound echoing throughout the room, and a trickle of blood dripped down his neck.

"Speak!" Thomas commanded, his fists clenched.

"A bridegroom," answered Walsingham, gulping air. "I sold him a bridegroom."

"*Mon Dieu!*" Robert's sword arm dropped, his eyes wide as he turned to Thomas. "'Twas you!"

The truth struck Thomas with the solidness of steel against bone. *He had been sold like a bull at auction.* He felt as though his soul had been shredded. Anger, pure and hot, poured through him.

Trust no one, his father had said. *No one.*

Thomas took a deep breath. "What of the letter I was sent to retrieve from Duart? What of that?"

Walsingham wiped the blood from his throat with a cloth. "'Twas fabricated. MacLean was desirous of meeting you before he sealed the bargain. He swore to deliver the casket to me here, at the inn, the week after you married his cousin. It never arrived. Instead, MacLean showed up at Rotherwood with that damnable army and refused to see me. I didn't know he had left the casket with you."

"I was a fool from the beginning."

"Nay, Thomas." The minister leaned forward and placed a hand on his shoulder. "Not a fool. Just loyal. The queen will—"

Thomas shoved the hand away. "I was a *fool*. A blind fool." *How Fia must have laughed at me.* The thought burned through his soul.

Walsingham sighed. "Thomas, I know you don't see it as such, but 'tis a compliment of sorts. He could have asked far more and I would have paid. Title, lands, anything. Instead he asked for a noble bridegroom to wed his cousin and take her from his war-ravaged home." He shrugged. "All in all, 'twas easy enough to arrange."

The rapier flashed up again, the tip hovering but a hairsbreadth from the pale skin. "Sweet Jesu, Thomas," Robert cried, "let me slice this evil whoreson!"

"Nay," Thomas answered, and Robert reluctantly lowered his blade, his visage black with fury. A multitude of images swirled through Thomas's mind, foremost among them the picture of Fia calmly telling him she intended to go to London whatever the price.

Whatever the price.

It had seemed coincidental that she had been fleeing the very castle he had stolen into. It had seemed equally fortuitous she had been on her way to London as well, he thought bitterly. As was the fact that his horse had been chased off by her dog, leaving the two of them with Thunder, whose slow pace had ensured their capture. Then the chit had stolen his boots and lured him into the hall right in front of her cousin and his guests.

The damning memories piled up, one upon the other.

It had all been planned. All of it. He could still hear Duncan thundering of Fia's honor and virtue, and how 'twas Thomas's duty to wed her. But it had been no coincidence that they had been caught in such a compromising position. Duncan and Fia had planned the entire miserable episode.

The minister placed a hand on Thomas's sleeve. "Thomas, I never intended for the wedding to stand, I knew the queen would grant an annulment. You would have been freed as soon as you set foot in court. I should have arranged for that already, but I've been busy dealing with the French and— I vow that before the week is out, you will have your annulment."

"Thomas, don't believe him."

"'Tis true," said Walsingham. "The Queen will be furious when I tell her how MacLean forced you to wed that little Scottish doxy, and—"

Thomas stood. "Did Fia know?"

The minister hesitated. "From what MacLean said, your lady was aware of all."

"He lies!" Robert ground out, his fist whitening about his rapier. "Don't believe him! Fia would never—"

"I have no reason to lie, you fool," Walsingham snapped. He turned to Thomas. "We were betrayed, you and I. They betrayed us both."

The words hovered in the air like rank perfume. *Trust no one.*

"But Duncan had arranged a marriage for her," he heard himself say. "Malcolm Davies and his clan had come to Duart Castle."

"Do you honestly think Duncan MacLean would welcome a marriage with a sniveling whelp like that? He and Fia had to have a justifiable reason for her fleeing the castle so you would be caught with her. Duncan had thought to catch the two of you together in the outer bailey, in front of a host of witnesses. I hear you made it even easier than he had hoped."

Thomas looked at the empty cask. "But where are the letters now?"

"Perhaps your lady could tell us that," said Walsingham carefully.

Fia had stolen the letters? She'd crossed, double-crossed, and crossed him yet again.

Robert made a disgusted sound. "Thomas, I cannot— This cannot be right. Fia couldn't do this."

Thomas sat silently. It made too much sense. He remembered Fia's face when he had discovered that she had broken into his trunk on ship. And then, when she had convinced Robert to show her the secret panel within the fireplace. Seemingly innocent actions now fraught with meaning.

The minister closed the empty casket. "I can't pretend I am not shocked by this latest turn of events. I need those letters. Thomas, you must get them from her."

Thomas had heard enough. He stood up so suddenly, the room spun. With a shuddering breath, he leaned on the table, his head low, struggling against the roaring in his mind.

"Thomas?" Robert's voice echoed through a long, deep tunnel. "What will you do, *mon ami*?"

Thomas looked into Robert's concerned eyes. What *was* he going to do? He met Walsingham's pale, considering gaze, hatred burning within him at the detached curiosity in those eyes.

"Damn your rotten, filthy soul," Thomas said with quiet intensity. The emptiness of fury burned through each word. He kicked his chair across the room, then slammed his fists onto the table, splitting the wood. "Damn your soul *and* that little Scottish slut's," he snarled.

Chapter Twenty-four

If innocence had a face, it would have been hers. Curled on her side, her hand tucked beneath her cheek, she looked as untainted as a child. The rabbit snuggled against her, curved against her warmth.

Thomas took a long drink from his mug and closed his eyes against the burn of the whiskey as it slid down his throat. He welcomed the pain, savored it. If he did not feel pain at this moment, he would feel nothing.

Nothing but emptiness.

He leaned his forehead against the smooth bedpost and stared at his sleeping wife. Silently, he toasted her sleeping form and gulped down more whiskey. He frowned into the empty mug, then turned to the fireplace, where the bottle rested on the mantel. Zeus raised his head and lumbered to his feet, approaching Thomas with a wagging tail. Thomas growled at the dog, showing his teeth in a feral gesture. Zeus's ears flattened and he slunk across the room, wiggling under Fia's bed until only his hind leg showed.

Thomas felt a little shamed at his display. The dog had

done nothing. He tried to coax the dog back to the hearth. "At least one of us should be warm and happy this eve, eh?" he asked the dog.

Zeus wagged his crooked tail hesitantly.

Thomas refilled his mug and returned to the bed, inordinately proud that his steps wavered so little. They could accuse him of having been duped by a Scottish wench, but he could handle his whiskey with the best of them.

He stared into the amber liquid and wondered why he had even bothered to drink. The agony of Fia's betrayal had disappeared late in the night, leaving a forlorn numbness, as if some part of him had been ripped asunder.

Fia stirred in her sleep. Her hair flowed across the pillow. How he had loved to sink his hands into those silken strands. His loins tightened at the thought and he smiled bitterly. Sweet Jesu, he burned for her even as she poisoned him with her lies. His father had been right. Believe no one. Trust no one.

After storming out of the tavern, he had ridden to his house as though the very hounds of hell were at his heels. Snarling at every servant who stood in his way, he had stormed through the house and thrown open the door to his chamber.

He had wanted to rant and shout and drive her into the street, but she had been asleep. And for some reason, he could no more wake her than he could leave. He felt a wave of disgust for his weakness.

He turned from the bed. It would be light within the hour. The time was swiftly approaching when he would have to speak with her. But what could he say to a woman who had purchased him like a pair of shoes?

Fortifying himself with a swallow of the fiery whiskey,

he threw himself into a chair, willing the creaking of the wood to awaken her. She didn't move, and he scowled. He smacked the mug on the chair arm, heedless of the whiskey spilling over the sides. She stirred and his chest tightened painfully.

"When did you return?" Her voice, heavy with sleep, had the consistency of honey. He stilled the urge to cover his ears to block out the sultry sound.

He took a gulp and wiped his mouth, staring at his hand with bleary concern when he saw how it shook. *Do not look at her. You will never be able to get through this if you do.* He forced himself to answer, "Before midnight."

Fia sat up and shoved her hair from her face, wondering at the curtness of his tone. His meeting must not have gone as well as he had hoped. "'Tis late. You said you'd be no more than an hour."

Thomas flicked a glance at her, his eyes almost black in the shadows. She wondered at his stillness. He slouched in a chair, legs sprawled in front of him, his shirt loosened to his waist. His unshaven face seemed to have aged overnight.

She felt the first flutter of fear. With a concerned glance at the mug he held so tightly, she asked, "Are . . . are you well?"

He laughed, a bitter, self-derisive sound that chilled her. "Perchance *you* should tell me the answer to that, madam wife."

She scooted to the edge of the bed. He was different. "What has happened? You seem angered."

He exploded to his feet and crossed the room like a raging storm. He wrenched her from the bed, his fingers biting cruelly into her arms. "Am I not to be allowed even that?"

"Wh-what are you talking about?" She could only stare up at him, her mind racing furiously.

He sneered. "You and Duncan greatly mistook the matter if you thought I was a man of even temperament. Or wasn't that one of the qualities you sought in your bridegroom?" His breath was laden with whiskey.

"Thomas, I don't understand. What did you—"

"Lies!" he spat, and shook her roughly. "All you speak are lies! I saw Walsingham tonight, you scheming wench!" Through gritted teeth, he hissed, "Tell me the truth ere I kill you."

Fia began desperately, "Sweet Saint Catherine, you're mad! I don't know—"

"Cease this pretense." His eyes shot amber sparks, and Fia feared he would catch afire with such fury. Yet in a voice as cold as ice, he bit out, "I am tired of your deceit. I met with Walsingham. I know everything."

"What's Walsingham have to do with anything? I don't even know him or—"

He threw her from him and she fell against the mattress. Though she was not hurt, she cried out in her fright.

He winced. "Sweet Jesu," he muttered, his voice twisted in anguish. "You have but to cry out and I suffer." He stumbled to his chair and took a shuddering breath. "How am I to deal with you when I cannot even stand to see you bruised? How am I to send you away when I . . ." He closed his eyes, a spasm of pain washing over him.

Fia gathered the blankets to her, staring at him with concern. Whatever had happened, Thomas was suffering the torments of hell. "Thomas, pray explain what has happened."

He regarded her with haggard eyes. "I am ill, lady wife.

I am sick unto death at the sight of every lying, manipulative inch of you."

"Thomas, please stop speaking in riddles and just tell me what's happened."

"Tell you?" He turned red-rimmed eyes on her. "Tell you what? Tell you that you have brought your ill fortune into my house and I am now cursed with it?" He shook his head. "Nay. We have discussed enough. You will sit there until I have decided what to do with you."

He stood and crossed to her desk, pulled a parchment from a cubbyhole, and held it out. "You see here our contract, Lady Wentworth. Let me show you the worth I place on your word." He wadded the paper and tossed it into the fire.

As Fia watched the flames lick hungrily at the parchment, her heart hardened. Whatever ailed Thomas, she was not about to accept his vile temper. "I know not what demons possess you this eve, my lord, but I will not stand for your wretched manners."

She gained her feet shakily and crossed to the door. Grasping the handle, she threw it open. "Leave my chambers immediately. We will speak when you have slept through your ill humors."

He laughed, a low, taunting laugh. The sheer ugliness of it made Fia shiver. "Aye, you would love to write Duncan of how you threw me out of my own bedchamber, wouldn't you? How amused he will be to see how well his plan has worked."

"Plan?"

His grin thinned into a bitter snarl. "You may think you have purchased a gullible, manageable bridegroom, but you are wrong, madam."

She frowned in confusion. "You make no sense."

"Determined to play an innocent to the last, aren't you?" He shrugged. "And why not? It has been amusing thus far. So let's continue this charade a bit longer. Allow me to recount my discovery. This very eve, I found 'twas no coincidence we were thrown together at Duart Castle."

Fia thought he looked like an avenging angel, beautiful yet dangerous. She clutched her hands tightly together.

"You and MacLean may have purchased me outright from Walsingham like a side of beef in a butcher's shop, but no more. I have cut my fetters and I stand before you a free man." His gaze bore into her before he turned away, as if he could not stand the sight.

"Who told you such nonsense?"

"Cease your playacting, madam," he snapped. "You know it all! I was traded for a packet of letters proving Queen Mary's guilt."

"You have been misinformed. Neither I nor Duncan would do such a thing."

"Duncan delivered those very letters into my hands and bade me carry them to Walsingham." Thomas chuckled harshly. "But then, you know about the letters, don't you, comfit? After all, you stole them, did you not?"

"I haven't stolen anything!"

"What happened, Fia? Did you and Duncan think you could make a deal with the devil and not pay?" His eyes raked her body with insulting intent. "Wasn't I worth even that? Didn't I meet your expectations? God's wounds, I made you cry with pleasure. Surely *that* was worth payment of some kind."

Heat washed through her and then receded, leaving her cold and shaking. "I don't know anything of these letters, but if you mean to suggest that Duncan or I had any kind of dealings with Walsingham, you err. I've heard Duncan mention Walsingham before and he holds no faith in him."

"There is little trust on either side of that fence. But I am far from mistaken in my beliefs." Thomas spoke with a quiet, merciless certainty that chilled her. "I will never forget the duplicity of your behavior. Never. Even if we remain married for all eternity, I will hate you every minute of every day. I will despise your breath, your laugh, your love—I will hate you, madam. *That* is what your perfidy has purchased you."

Fia almost gasped from the pain. "*No more.* I will not hear this! I am tired and confused and . . ." She pressed a trembling hand to her head. This was a nightmare. She wished with all her heart she would awaken to find the Thomas she loved nestled in bed beside her. Anything but this bitter, angry stranger who stared at her with such virulent hate. "I-I cannot bear to hear this. Please stop."

Thomas stared at her quivering lips. Pure desire, hot and immediate, raced through him. He cursed himself that she still had the power to stir his blood. "Don't bother to act so tragic, madam. There is no need."

"There has been some mistake. If I could but speak with Duncan, I could—"

"Did you not hear me? Duncan asked me to deliver those damn letters to Walsingham myself. I had the casket from his own hand." His mouth curved into a derisive smile. "Sweet Jesu, he even told me to tell Walsingham that they were now 'even.' How he must have laughed, to have me deliver the payment."

Fia wrung her hands and took a step toward him. "Duncan would never do such a thing! Walsingham must be telling a lie and—"

"Do you think I have not considered that?" he snapped. "But what has he to gain from such a stratagem? What reason would he have to speak falsely? Meanwhile, Duncan and you gain all. Duncan found a fool to wed his cousin and take her safely away from war. And you, sweet, were ever loud in your demands to go to London."

"Nay!" She took a step toward him, her hand outstretched. "Thomas, you must listen to me—"

"Silence!" His eyes hardened. "I know you for what you are: a liar and worse. There is nothing you could say that would make me believe otherwise."

Her hand fell to her side. "Then there is naught left." Her voice was hollow with disbelief and loss.

"Oh-ho, a playwright *and* an actress!" He clapped loudly. "Excellent! Such unexpected talents!"

She stiffened. "Enough! You barge in here, calling me names and accusing me of vile crimes; then you refuse to believe me no matter the truth. Well, I've had enough of your nonsense."

"So have I, madam. I have been made a fool a thousand times since we met." He threw himself into the chair, his face contorted in fury. "I even asked Essex to give the queen one of your plays, hoping she would sponsor you."

Her lips parted in amazement. He had never said a word. Through the pain came a thrill that he had thought her plays of a quality to have risked giving one of them to the queen. "I . . . never knew you had read them."

He stared at her, his eyes lingering on her mouth. "I have read every word that has ever come from your pen." He met her surprised gaze and a bitter smile curved his mouth. "I thought 'twould please you if the queen took you to heart." His laugh was full of loathing. "A romantic lackwit, was I not?"

A smile trembled on her mouth. No matter what he said, he loved her. But Walsingham had led Thomas astray. *Why?*

"Well, madam, you will have no chance for fame and fortune now." He stared into the fire with bleak eyes. "'Twas all a lie, and I shall inform the queen of it first thing tomorrow."

Fia's throat tightened painfully. She wanted to tell him that she loved him now and forever, but he would just use the words to wound her more. Whatever poisonous lies Walsingham had told Thomas, she must find the truth. Find the truth and cure him.

Fia struggled for breath. "You are just angered. In the morning we will talk, and this misunderstanding will end."

He smiled, his mouth a grim curve. "Oh ho, but I have barely begun. I will spend the rest of our time together reminding you of your trickery and deceit."

Fia gathered the last vestiges of pride she possessed and said tiredly, "Then there is no more to be said." She turned and went to the bed. Grabbing up the blanket and a pillow, she headed for the door.

Thomas reached it first. He kicked the heavy panel closed and leaned against it. "Nay, madam. You will not leave this room until I have decided your fate."

"Decided my *fate*?" Her brows drew together. "I vow, sirrah, you test my temper. I want nothing more to do with you."

"You no longer desire my presence? Is your purchased husband too base, too loud for you?"

"Aye, and boorish and rude as well. I will not listen to any more of your false accusations." She lifted her chin, her hands clutching the blanket and pillow like a shield. "Move."

He pushed away from the door, and for a heart-stopping moment Fia thought he meant to grab her. She backed warily away.

He smiled, satisfaction curling his mouth. "Finally, you begin to realize your danger. But 'tis too late. I know you well and true now."

"And I know you," she replied evenly. "There is no more to be said."

The dull pain in her eyes gave him pause and suddenly, his anger disappeared, leaving him hollow and aching. He was silent for a long moment. "You're right," he said wearily. "We will wait until tomorrow to continue this. By then I will know what to do with such a beautiful, willful little liar as you."

"There will be no tomorrow," Fia snapped. "Don't expect me to be here when you return."

"Oh, but you will." He reached into his pocket, pulled out a key, opened the door, and inserted the key into the outer lock.

"Don't!" she cried. If she wasn't free to find out the truth, how would she ever be able to prove Walsingham's base lies?

"Do not think, Mistress Deceit, that Angus or Mary will come to help you, either. I will have them closely guarded. I will leave you here to think on your sins. Come morning, you will have one chance—only one—to confess your sins and return the letters."

"And if I don't have them?"

"Then you will be banished, my lady. Banished where the sound of your voice will cease to torment my soul. Locked away and forgotten."

"You wouldn't dare!"

He gave her a mocking bow, then slammed the door shut.

The sound of the key grated in the room.

Fia sank to the floor, despair filling her. "What will I do?" she whispered. "What will I ever do?"

Chapter Twenty-five

A shaft of sunlight streamed directly into Thomas's face, the bright light blinding him. He groaned and closed his eyes against the glare, vaguely aware he lay atop a sack of grain in his own storehouse.

"Oh-ho! It awakes!" Robert announced.

Agony pounded through Thomas's skull. The memory of the previous night wavered to the fore. Clamping his jaws against a wave of nausea, he struggled upright.

Fia. The pain left him panting and retching. *How could she? How could she?* The thought echoed over and over.

"Easy, Thomas," Robert murmured, handing Thomas a rough cloth that had been hung on a peg by the door.

Thomas gratefully wiped his face, squinting against the sun. 'Twas a beautiful day, and he cursed every gleaming beam, twittering bird, and dewy morning flower.

Robert shook his head. "The Earl of Rotherwood, most fortunate of men, asleep atop sacks of moldy grain. You have come to a sad pass, *mon ami*. You are fortunate that

Cook sent a boy for some wheat this morning or no one would know you were here."

It pained Thomas too much to glare. "I feel as if I died sometime last week," he muttered through the foul taste in his mouth. He peered into the gloom and found his mug on the floor behind him. Grabbing it up, he gulped the remaining whiskey, welcoming the acrid burn.

"Similia similibus curatur," Robert murmured.

"Aye," Thomas grumbled. "Hair of the dog. A foul cure for a foul illness." He wished he could just vomit and be done with it. He stood and slowly made his way to a pail of water that stood by the door.

"I planned on dumping that on your head, but you awoke before I could do so."

Thomas regarded Robert sourly. "And you call yourself a friend?"

Robert quirked a cool brow. "You are fortunate I didn't do more. Your behavior is unacceptable. I tell you this *as* a friend."

Thomas rinsed his mouth and then dumped the rest of the water over his head.

"A foul illness for a foul temper," Robert returned.

Thomas dried himself with the rough cloth, wondering if anyone had brought Fia her breakfast. The idea of her locked in her room was painful; the thought of her going hungry was agony.

He immediately pushed the traitorous feelings aside. It would serve her right to miss a few meals. It would serve her even better if he locked her up for the rest of eternity, as he'd threatened.

But he knew it had been an empty threat. He covered his eyes wearily. He should send her away and be done.

Duncan would take her back, and Thomas would be free to return to his life as it was before he had met that saucy, conniving little thief. His life would be orderly, with no unexpected twists and turns.

The thought ripped new agonies in his chest. He could no more send her away than he could cut off his own arm. Pressing his hand against the ache in his chest, he wondered if he should take her to his estates in Northumberland until he could decide how best to deal with her. Time would lessen the hold she had on him. It must.

He leaned his forehead against the cool wall and tried to force his swollen brain to reason.

Robert sat on a barrel. "I spoke with Mary. 'Twas difficult to hear through the locked door, but we managed well enough."

Thomas closed his eyes.

"She says she and Angus are confined by your orders. I hear Fia is also locked away." He waited for Thomas to respond, then asked, "You trust Walsingham before you trust Fia?"

"I do now," said Thomas shortly, wishing Robert would have the decency to at least lower his voice.

"Had I known what you were about, I wouldn't have spent near an entire evening tracking a certain fat, bumbling oaf to his filthy lodgings in an effort to discover the truth."

"Robert, let it go. There is nothing more to be said. She lied to me," he whispered.

Robert bared his teeth. "You know, *mon ami*, I never before realized how greatly you resemble your father at times. It ill becomes you."

"My father was right. Look where trusting has put me."

"How can you speak of trust when you locked away a beauteous maid who has done nothing but love you and honor you? When you take the word of that spineless maggot Walsingham over the word of your own wife?"

Thomas rubbed his forehead. "My head aches."

"Because it is filled with rocks," Robert said coldly. "She loves you. It shines from her every time you enter a room, though you are too blind to see it."

"I have never known love," Thomas scoffed, wondering how anyone could bear the pain.

"You do. You were a man changed this past month."

"Whatever I felt for Fia is no more. It must be so."

"I can't believe you! You meet with the most incredible good fortune! You find a woman made for you, a woman who loves you, and you throw it away. You—"

"Silence!" Thomas roared, shuddering as the echo pounded through his head. "I will hear no more."

"Sod you and your festering anger! I have tried to help, to be a friend when no one else would." Robert stood and stiffly turned toward the door. "I have wasted my time."

"Nay, you have not," Thomas said dully, rubbing his neck with an unsteady hand. "I am a lost cause, Robert."

Robert leveled a steady gaze at him. "No one is a lost cause, *mon ami*. You showed me that."

"Then I was wrong. Before you leave, see to it Fia is fed well. Take Mary to her." He drew a shuddering breath. Somehow he would find a way through this agonizing madness.

Robert's face lit up. "Oh-ho! So you can't even bear for her to miss a meal. There is hope for you yet." He returned to his barrel and leaned forward. "Listen to me. You should know this: Walsingham—"

"Let it die, Robert. Walsingham told the truth."

"Some of it was true. But as usual, he didn't tell you all."

Thomas stilled. "You've mistrusted Walsingham from the start. What would he have to gain by telling such a foul tale about himself?"

"Lying is mother's milk to that pox-ridden pig's bladder. There *was* a deal between Walsingham and MacLean, but neither you *nor* Fia knew of it. You were both manipulated. MacLean deliberately chose Malcolm the Maiden as a bridegroom, counting on Fia taking action, enlisting you to help her escape."

Thomas took a deep breath. *Sweet Jesu, what if Fia . . .* He refused to finish the thought. "Who told you?" he asked harshly.

"Goliath. Since he sits so near the door, I thought he probably heard many interesting things, and I was right."

"What else have you learned?"

"Goliath overheard all of the negotiations between MacLean and Walsingham. One part of the bargain was that Fia was never to know."

Suddenly, the memory of MacLean saying to Fia that he'd done what he could to help her, to keep her safe, flashed through Thomas's brain. *She didn't know.*

Joy, pure and sweet, coursed through his blood. Walsingham had used him, sold him, but Fia was blameless.

"She's innocent," he said wonderingly.

"Aye." Robert crossed his arms. "A pity she's locked away in her room, else she could breakfast with us in celebration."

Guilt hit Thomas and he sagged against the wall, seeing Fia's pale, desperate face. "God's wounds," he whispered. "I accused her of so much."

Robert frowned. "Surely you said nothing that can't be unsaid. Once she realizes how Walsingham used you—"

"She tried to tell me, but I wouldn't listen." He could barely stand, remembering the anguish he had seen in Fia's eyes. He needed to go to her, to tell her what happened, explain everything.

Then he would deal with Walsingham. The idea of exacting vengeance gave his thoughts a more positive focus. He pushed away from the wall. "I shall beg her forgiveness."

"Good!" Robert said. "Go on bended knee. Surely she will listen if you woo her with flowers and sonnets."

Thomas looked around the room. He couldn't afford to think what he would do if he had killed Fia's love. "There was a key . . ."

Robert slid his hand into his pocket and withdrew it. A large iron key lay in his palm. "'Twas on the floor." His eyes were somber. "Was it so necessary?"

"She would have left," Thomas said. "Even furious, I couldn't let her."

"You love her," Robert said quietly.

Thomas took a deep breath and held out a hand. "Give it to me."

Robert idly swung the key on one finger. "Perhaps *I* should release the sweet Fia and assist her in escaping such a tyrant."

"Do, and I will kill you," Thomas growled. "Sweet Jesu, Robert—if Goliath speaks the truth, we don't know anything of what Walsingham is about."

"I have been saying the same to you these past five years and you would have none of it. 'Tis time you saw the dark side of that conniver."

"Nay, I knew of it. His motives were to strengthen England, as were mine." Thomas closed his empty hands into fists. "But there is a limit. I will not have him near Fia. After I have released her, we will find him and explain how things will be." He stared at his fists, trying to grasp some elusive fact, some cloaked truth that lingered just out of sight. He raised his head and looked at Robert. "Why did Walsingham say Fia was involved in the trade if she wasn't?"

Robert's brows lowered. "Does he need a reason? He makes mischief to amuse himself."

"Nay, everything Walsingham does is for a purpose, usually cloaked in some intrigue to benefit Elizabeth. He told me Fia was involved to gain something." He walked to the window and stared out. *What is the old fox trying to accomplish now?*

"Perhaps," Robert said slowly, "he told such vile lies because he thought he knew how you would react."

"Like my father."

"Aye. And never again speak to her or of her." Robert smirked. "He didn't know you cannot even bear to see her miss her breakfast."

Thomas rubbed his forehead. "I am weaker than he thought."

"Nay, you are infinitely stronger. Love requires strength of mind and spirit, *mon ami.* You have both." Robert frowned. "But why did he try to break you from her? What purpose does he have?"

"That's what we must discover." Thomas held out his hand for the key.

"Release her quickly, *mon ami.* Fia is not the type of damsel to languish in a tower."

Thomas closed his hand around the cold metal. "I'll release her now and—"

A long wail rose through the morning air and then dropped into whimpering silence. Thomas locked gazes with Robert.

Zeus.

A stab of fear ripped through Thomas. He grabbed the key and his boots, and raced outside and across the courtyard, his bare feet cold on the hard stones. He took the stairs two at a time and soon slid to a halt in front of Fia's door.

The horrible moan rose again. Thomas dropped his boots outside his bedchamber door and unlocked it with hands that fumbled in haste.

The room seemed cold, empty. Trailing from the bed, knotted end to end, were the bed curtains. The makeshift rope trailed to the open window and disappeared over the sill.

Zeus sat staring out the window, his face mournful. Nose quivering, the brown rabbit regarded him from the bed.

Fia was gone.

Thomas's throat tightened in fear. He crossed to the window and leaned over the edge. No broken body lay in the garden. A heavy sigh of relief escaped him, and he sagged against the windowsill.

"What's happened?" Robert spoke at his shoulder.

"She escaped." He was amazed he sounded so calm, for his heart was lodged in his throat.

"What?" Robert leaned over the sill, then turned a stern face to Thomas. "Damn your temper!"

Thomas stared blindly at the sky, his brow creased in concentration. "Where is she? We must think; she—"

Below them, a servant appeared carrying a basket.

Robert leaned out the window. "Hold!"

The man halted and looked up, shading his eyes with his hand.

"Have you seen the countess this morn?"

The servant shook his head. "Nay, yer lordship. I jes'..." he trailed off as he noted the makeshift rope hanging from the window, his mouth gaping in surprise.

Thomas pushed Robert out of the way. "Go on, man! What did you see?"

"I've been picking apples here in the garden all mornin', yer lordship, and I ne'er saw hide nor hair of the lady."

"Did you leave at any time?"

"Only when th' basket was filled. I was gone but a moment."

"When was that?"

"About a half an hour ago, yer lordship. It couldn't have been more'n that."

Thomas felt a stirring of hope. "Then she can't be far."

"Or perhaps she was long gone before this man arrived in the garden. We've no way of knowing," Robert said.

"Pardon me, yer lordship," the servant said eagerly, "but I did hear of two horses missin' from the stables jus' ten minutes ago."

"Which horses?"

The man scrubbed at his ear. "That be the strangest thing. Of all the horses in the stables, the thieves took a pretty mare, a large bay, and then the ugliest and meanest horse alive." He held up his hand. "The blasted thing bit me yesterday."

Thunder. Thomas nodded his thanks, then strode to the door, grabbed up his boots, and tugged them on.

Robert leaned against the bedpost. "She doesn't know anyone in London."

"Nay, she is alone." Alone and lost, looking for God knew what.

A cold, wet nose nudged his hand. Thomas looked into Zeus's eyes and rubbed the dog's good ear. "We'll find her, Zeus, I promise. She couldn't have just . . ." His voice trailed off.

Wherever she was, he would bet she was concocting a plan to overcome Walsingham's scheme. A thought settled. *Sweet Jesu, surely she wouldn't . . .*

He looked at Robert. "Go see if Mary and Angus are still locked in their quarters."

"You think she took them with her?"

"Aye, which is why she needed three horses. If she's gone to do what I think she has, she'll need their help. I only pray it is enough."

Robert's eyes widened. "Walsingham," he breathed. "Good God, she's gone after Walsingham."

Chapter Twenty-six

"I've come to see Letty," Fia announced. Garbed in a coarse brown dress that reeked of stale onions, she looked like one of the dubious patrons of the tavern.

Beady eyes glared at her. "Letty'll not see th' likes o' ye." The giant stuffed a huge slab of meat into his mouth, red juice dripping onto his stained shirt.

Fia repressed a shudder. *A play. 'Tis just a play.* Across the room she caught Mary's frown and shook her head. She could deal with this. "Tell Letty I've somethin' of hers she'll be wantin'."

The guard removed a cleaned bone from his mouth, wiping away the grease with a dirty sleeve. "Ye do, do ye? Suppose ye tell me what ye have t' sell?" His little eyes lingered appreciatively on her low neckline.

Fia crossed her arms. The dirty gown lacked fastening of any kind, and the stained leather girdle did little more than push her breasts up into the ragged opening. Perhaps trading her new gown and cloak for this garment hadn't been such a masterstroke after all.

But it was too late to think of that. It was too late to think of a lot of things. She was committed to this venture, however it turned out. At least she had had the forethought to bring Mary and Angus with her.

Mary wanted to charge up to Walsingham's fine house and demand the truth. Fortunately, Angus had known about the tavern. "'Tis a fittin' location fer such vermin."

"How do you know of it?"

"The laird told me. He said to go there and ask fer 'Letty' if we ever needed to return to Scotland."

Now Mary sat by the door, keeping her eye on their horses and ready to run for help should anything go awry. Angus stood stoically by Fia, one hand resting on his claymore.

Looking at Goliath, Fia was glad for their presence. She forced herself to grin. "Well, now, I might have a lot to sell. Ye ne'er can tell. Me name is Kate." She reached out and squeezed his arm. "Fine an' brawny, ye are, like a bull. And what be yer name?"

"Most calls me Goliath. I am very strong," he replied with pride. Throwing the bone over his shoulder, he flexed a massive arm.

"My! What an arm ye have!" Fia wondered to see the giant grinning like a lad.

"I can lift three barrels at once." He beamed at her. "I bet I can lift a lil' wench like ye wi' but one finger." Goliath reached out with hands the size of platters.

Angus stirred uneasily as Fia skipped out of the way. "Not 'til I've seen Letty, ye don't." She lowered her lids, hoping she could keep this lumbering romancer at a distance without resorting to her knife. "Perhaps afterward, if yer still of a mind, I could be persuaded to serve ye."

"Ye can't git in. Ye might as well spend the time wi' me."

"I might, if ye've got the proper coin," Fia replied, noting with relief the dimming of his enthusiasm.

"I has t' pay, do I? How much?"

How much? Fia blinked. She wondered what Kate was worth for a brief pleasuring.

She was still involved in her calculations when Goliath leaned closer to rumble in her ear, "Ye know, Kate, I could get ye in to see Letty if ye were nice wi' me." His foul breath seeped through the gaps in his lecherous grin.

"Goliath, let the chit be." Fia turned and met the green gaze of a tavern maid. The woman held a mug of ale in one hand, the other resting on her hip as she surveyed Fia from head to foot, her critical eyes assessing every detail.

"What are ye doin' here?" the woman asked, her reddish hair curling from beneath a dirty scrap of lace.

"I came to see Letty. This lout was tryin' to charge me," Fia returned, frowning sternly at Goliath.

"Here, now, Annie!" Goliath seemed to cower before the bright green gaze. "I wasn't doin' no—"

"Let her in," the woman interrupted.

"But I was told not t' let no one in but the coun—"

"Let her in."

With a great show of reluctance, the huge man opened the door. Fia scurried past, Angus close behind her. Annie lifted her brow at the burly Scotsman, who positioned himself in a chair by the fire and crossed his arms, clearly intending to stay put.

"I'll go an' get ye a drink," the maid announced.

As the door closed, Fia gave a sigh of relief. She tested a rickety chair and sat on the edge, then waited, shivering at the dampness of the room.

The door swung open and Annie returned. "Here," she said, plopping a mug on the table. Water sloshed onto the dirty surface.

"Thank you. I'm very thirsty." Fia offered a tentative smile.

"Aye, ye were so thirsty ye have forgotten how to talk," returned Annie, her own mouth curving in response. "Ye've lost yer accent, Katie."

"I don't suppose you would believe *this* is a fake accent and the other my real one?" Fia asked hopefully.

Even Angus smiled at that.

Annie's mouth twitched. "I'm no' such a fool as that."

Fia sighed. "Then I suppose I'll have to tell you the real story. You see, I'm hiding from the unwholesome regards of my evil uncle, the baron."

"You're an heiress, no doubt?"

"Och, now you've lost your accent as well." Fia sniffed the air. "There must be an evil wind as sneaks up and steals them."

Annie grinned reluctantly. "'Tis difficult to remember, isn't it?"

"Aye, though you do it quite well," Fia said with an admiring look, wishing she had thought to smear dirt over her hands and face.

"I've had more than my fair share of practice, milady." Annie took a chair and regarded Fia with calm green eyes.

Fia sipped her water. "I have a message to deliver to Letty." She looked about the small room. "Do you work here? I mean, with Walsingham?"

Annie's frown was as quick and sharp as a strike of lightning. "Hold your tongue if you wish to keep it!"

"Is he so fearsome?"

"He can be."

Fia shrugged. "Then leave."

Annie's face reflected a moment of hope before she shook her head. "Nay, I'm of no account here. 'Tis you who should leave."

"I'm of no more worth than you," Fia returned.

"I know exactly who you are. He's been expecting you. For that reason alone, you should go quickly. There are other ways to discover things. I'll help you."

"He knew I was coming because I sent a message for him to meet me here. Walsingham and I have a thing or two to discuss."

"I don't know if you're brave or foolish. He leaves nothing to chance. He knows *everything.*"

"My dear Annie," said a dry voice from the doorway, "you make me out to be a mystic. Lady Fia will run in fear if you continue."

Fia studied the man she suspected of attempting to ruin her marriage. He was tall and slender, with silvered hair and a sharp face. In the tattered cloak, he appeared like an evil magus. A shiver slithered up her back.

Annie flushed and stood. "I was just—"

"Leaving," he said, finishing her sentence, and draped the cloak across a chair. "I will speak with you later." He dismissed her with a curt wave of his hand.

Annie exchanged a level look with Fia and slipped silently from the room.

Walsingham sighed and crossed to close the door. "Servants. You can never train them properly." He looked at Angus, who stared back with an impassive gaze, his hand resting on his sword. "But I err. Mayhap yours are better trained than mine."

He pulled a chair near to hers.

Fia wished he hadn't moved quite so close. Her knife was tucked inside her boot, but it suddenly seemed too far to reach. She shot a glance at Angus and was reassured when he winked.

She returned her attention to Walsingham. "There are so many servants at Rotherwood that I don't know them all. But I am sure you are familiar with at least one."

"Why would I be familiar with any of the servants at Rotherwood House?" he asked.

"Because you needed someone who knew the house well enough to know about the secret hiding place."

He raised his brows. "My, this sounds very dramatic. Why would I need to know the location of this, ah, secret hiding place?"

"To steal the letters."

He gave a dry laugh. "You've a wonderful imagination. Tell me, child, do you think this is one of your plays?"

"You had better hope not, for the villain always dies at the end of my plays."

"I'm no villain—not any more than your cousin."

"My cousin. I have been thinking of him all morning. You know how 'tis when you behold a puzzle. It lingers, annoying and teasing your mind until you are nigh sick of it."

A politely bored expression settled on his thin face. "We are wasting time, my dear. I hear your husband locked you away and has all but cast you out. Perhaps you should return to Scotland. I could arrange passage for you on the next ship. You could leave today if you wished." His sympathetic smile encompassed Angus. "And your servant, as well."

"I've not come here to seek your help in leaving. I could do that on my own."

"Even though your husband wishes it?"

"Thomas loves me," she returned calmly.

"And he shows it by locking you in your bedchamber and accusing you of lies? A strange love, if 'tis love at all."

"That is my concern and not yours. Why did you steal the letters Duncan so freely delivered?"

The sharp, steely eyes flickered briefly. "You are in no position to accuse me of anything. Your husband has already branded you a liar and worse, milady. You have no recourse but to return to Scotland."

"I'm not going anywhere. 'Twas Thomas's anger speaking, not his heart. Now tell me of this bargain that was struck between you and Duncan, or I'll go to the queen."

Angus stirred. "I have a letter fer the lass that will get her to the queen, e'en without yer help. The laird gave it to me afore we left Scotland."

Walsingham regarded them both with the incurious gaze of a serpent. "So tell the queen. Who would listen to a half-wild Scot? No one. Go home, milady."

"Nay, Duncan wanted me here. 'Twas that very thought that kept occurring to me this morning. I remembered how happy he seemed when Thomas and I finally wed."

"'Twas a wedding he'd planned himself. Of course he was pleased."

"Aye, he wished me out of the country in case there was a war. 'Tis one reason why he bargained with Queen Mary's letters."

The minister lifted a brow. "There were other reasons?"

"Duncan wants Elizabeth's help to keep Scotland from war. He thought of a way to accomplish all of his objectives at once." She smiled proudly. "There are few men who have Duncan's genius at scheming."

Walsingham frowned. "This is foolish—"

"Nay, 'tis not. You thought to outwit him by stealing the letters and sending me home disgraced. Duncan would be furious, but there would be naught he could do. And you'd have it all: the letters, the proof of Queen Mary's perfidy, and—"

A crash sounded in the outer tavern. The minister came to his feet, a small short sword appearing in his hand. Angus stood as well, his sword drawn and ready. Another crash followed and then another, until Fia wondered if a single table remained standing upright.

The door creaked open slowly. Goliath stood in the entry, a thin line of blood dripping down his cheek.

"Speak, fool!" Walsingham snapped.

The giant swayed, his face pale, and Fia noted his blank expression. With a gusty sigh, Goliath toppled facedown on the floor.

Walsingham stiffened. "By the rood, what is the meaning of this?"

Thomas stepped over Goliath's slumbering body, and his eyes found Fia's. "I came as soon as I could."

She lifted her chin. "I am not—"

"Comfit," he said softly. "I was wrong. So, so wrong."

The simple words released a torrent of emotion in Fia. "Aye, you were."

He held out a hand. "If you will give me the chance, I'll never doubt you again."

Fia instantly placed her hand in his, wondering when she had forgiven him.

"Very touching," said Walsingham. "You have come just

in time, Thomas. Your wife was just telling me the most wondrous tale."

"If my wife says 'tis so, then 'tis so," Thomas answered quietly. "She never lies." He slid his sword into its scabbard and flashed Fia a quiet smile. He looked like a tousled hero, his shirt undone and his doublet left behind. "I've a lamentable temper. I should have believed you."

Robert lounged in the doorway, his rapier ready. "Don't give him quarter, Fia! Make him sing for you!"

Thomas scowled over his shoulder. "Perchance you should secure the door. I wouldn't want any unpleasant surprises."

Robert chuckled and turned to Angus. "Mary has hit some poor man over the head with a tankard, and I fear there's to be a good brawl. Would you like to assist me in cleaning up a bit?"

Angus nodded and left.

With a brief salute of his sword, Robert disappeared back into the tavern.

Thomas sniffed the air, then looked down at Fia. "I see you've managed to be authentic in odor as well as garb."

She wrinkled her nose. "I thought I'd be less obvious if I came dressed as a tavern wench."

He pulled her closer. "You'd need more than a dress that reeks of onions to appear like a tavern maid."

Walsingham gestured impatiently. "Have you forgotten she betrayed you? Think of the whispers, the laughter." He leaned across the table. "Think, Thomas, of your father and all he suffered. 'Twill be the same for you."

"If all I ever have to bear is the laughter of the court, then I am indeed the most fortunate of men." To Fia's astonishment, Thomas clutched at his heart. "There are many things worse than the laughter of fools. There is loneliness and lost love. There is sadness so deep it wrenches your gut into a thousand pieces and you bleed with every breath. Worse yet, there is life without sun, without warmth. Life without Fia."

Fia stared at him. "Thomas! That was from my play, *Duke's Paradise!* You sound just like the hero, Sanctus."

Laughter twinkled in his brown eyes. "I liked the heroine, but the hero is sadly lacking in certain virtues."

"Then I'll rewrite it." Her smile was blinding.

Thomas caressed her hair. She was more precious to him than life. "Let's finish this." He lifted his gaze to the minister. "Speak now."

The minister sank into a chair. "I suppose it doesn't matter," he said with weary resignation. "The chit will get the whole story from MacLean and you will believe every word."

"Aye," Thomas answered. "I will."

"As you know, MacLean wanted a noble bridegroom— and he chose you. When he came to me, he knew everything there was to know about you—your title, lands, everything. All I had to do was deliver you. In exchange, he was to send the letters."

The minister shook his head. "Though you might not credit it, I tried to talk him into choosing someone else: Essex, Hatton, anyone. But he was adamant. 'Twas you or none. I was at a loss."

"Not for long," said Thomas.

The counselor smiled tiredly. "True. I thought I detected an error in his thinking. He didn't know Elizabeth. *I* knew the queen would never let the wedding stand once she discovered it had been forced."

"I suspected as much myself."

Walsingham nodded. "So when MacLean delivered the letters, I decided to make certain you were granted an annulment."

"You planned to trick Duncan from the beginning," said Fia.

"I had no wish to sacrifice your freedom, Thomas, but MacLean was a step ahead of me the entire time. He had already thought of that possibility. That's why he arranged for Malcolm Davies to come to Duart."

Thomas frowned. "I don't understand."

Fia touched his arm. "I think I do. Malcolm Davies may be the biggest maw worm to ever grace Scottish soil, but as a witness, you could ask for none better."

Walsingham's thin smile appeared. "Aye. As a jilted bridegroom who would sneer about his betrothed's sordid behavior in the hallways with an unclothed Englishman, Malcolm had an important part to play. As soon as we tried to arrange an annulment, MacLean would step forward with his witness to refute any claims of your innocence. Queen Elizabeth is not a prude, but even she would not accept such behavior. Your marriage would stand."

Thomas blinked. "MacLean planned all along to claim that I'd taken Fia's innocence in Scotland and to use clan Davies as witnesses?"

"Exactly. Unfortunately I didn't realize this until it was too late."

"That doesn't explain why Duncan gave the letters to me." He looked at Walsingham. "You were surprised by that move, too, weren't you?"

"Very. They were supposed to be delivered to me here,

within two days of your wedding. Instead, he showed up protected by an army and refused to see me."

Fia nodded. "He gave the letters to Thomas because he suspected you would try to secret them away and say you had never received them."

"I had thought of it," Walsingham admitted.

"By giving them to me," Thomas added, "and making sure I knew what they were, MacLean had arranged for another creditable witness."

Walsingham spread his hands upon the rough table. "I had no choice. If the queen had discovered the trade, I would have been severely discredited. I had to get those letters. More importantly, I had to separate you, Lord Rotherwood, from your bride."

"Why?"

"As protection. If you sent Fia away in disgrace, 'twould make anything MacLean said look like the ranting of an injured guardian. 'Twould merely discredit him with the queen."

"I would never have sent her back to Scotland," said Thomas.

"I erred. I thought honor was all that held you to the marriage, that you had been compromised by passion."

Thomas caught Fia's gaze. "I worried you would miss your breakfast this morn."

She laughed softly. "I ate on the way here. Mary insisted."

Thomas wanted to lift her in his arms and kiss every last inch of her. He turned back to the minister. "Where are the letters now?"

"Safe. Queen Mary's existence puts Elizabeth in danger, though she won't hear of it. The letters will give us enough information to convince Queen Elizabeth to keep Mary locked away for years to come."

"You do everything for Elizabeth."

Walsingham nodded. "Everything that she will allow. She has far more qualms than I do; 'tis quite tedious at times." He heaved a sigh. "Well, my friend, we are at checkmate. I can't tell the queen the truth, for fear she would send me to the Tower or worse. You dare not tell her, for fear she will cast aside this marriage you have come to value."

"She wouldn't do such a thing," said Fia hotly.

Thomas looked down at Fia's hand resting in his. It fit perfectly, the graceful fingers spread across his rough palm.

As much as he hated it, Walsingham was right. Elizabeth's pride was legendary. If she knew how a renegade Scottish lord had purchased a titled English bridegroom, she would demand an annulment forthwith.

Walsingham stood and gathered his cloak. "I had best be on my way. The queen has yet to see the letters. I was waiting until I could tie up these few loose ends." He looked from Fia to Thomas. "Such passion. Had I known there was such a bond betwixt the two of you, I would have approached this in an entirely different manner."

Thomas crossed to Walsingham and hauled the older man forward with a hand bunched in his velvet doublet. "One last word. If you ever attempt to meddle in our lives again, there will be no bargaining. Just you and my blade." He released the minister.

Walsingham stumbled slightly, then righted himself. Though his face was red, he managed a wan smile. "Let's hope the need never arises."

Fia crossed to the doorway and looked out, motioning

to Angus, who was picking up the few unbroken chairs in the taproom.

He came at once. "Aye, lass?"

"Lord Walsingham requires an escort to his carriage."

Angus nodded, looking pleased.

"Well, that is that." Walsingham gave a bow and disappeared into the taproom; Angus silently followed.

Thomas looked down at Fia. A mischievous smile curved her lips.

"What?" he demanded suspiciously.

"I'm thinking of all the ways I am going to make you suffer for your lack of faith."

He laughed and swung her into his arms. "Are you, now?"

"Aye. Some of them cannot be played out in public." She placed her hand on his cheek. "Perhaps we should retire."

"Fia, I don't know if you can ever forgive me for—"

She placed a finger to his lips. "Do you love me?" she whispered.

"With all of my heart," he answered fervently.

"Then I promise to be easy on you."

He laughed. "And how do you propose to do that, my lady wife?"

Robert stormed into the room. "Thomas! You can't allow that poisonous bastard to just walk away!"

"We have to," said Thomas. "If the truth ever came out, Fia would most likely bear Elizabeth's wrath."

Robert cursed. "I will at least make sure that scurvy hag-seed doesn't lurk about to cause more problems. What of Fia?"

"She stays as my wife. I shall ask the queen to bless the union as soon as I can."

"She will not like that you married without her permission."

"Aye, but once she realizes my wife wrote the play she cannot get enough of, I think she'll soften."

"She likes it?" Fia asked breathlessly.

"Aye. Essex sent a messenger just as Robert and I left. She asked if you had any more, and when she could see them performed."

Robert gave Fia a brilliant smile. "As soon as you're presented at court, I will have won our wager and you will owe me."

"What exactly *will* I owe you?"

He threw back his head and laughed. "As soon as I have chased Walsingham back to his lair, I will return and we can discuss it." With a quick salute with his rapier, he was gone.

"I warned you not to wager with Robert," Thomas said.

She chuckled. "Whatever the cost, 'twas well worth it. You never could have taught me to curtsy with such grace."

"Before I give you the kiss you deserve, comfit, we need to talk about your propensity to climb through windows. I almost died of fright when I saw your bedsheets hanging over the ledge."

Fia peeped at him through her lashes. "Did I ever tell you about my uncle Donald? He used to dream about things before they happened. One time he—"

"What does that have to do with bedsheets?"

"Because one time he dreamed—"

"Never mind," Thomas said, kissed her soundly, silencing her the way he knew best.

Epilogue

$\mathcal{S}$heets of rain obscured the muddy streets, yet the horse galloped onward, urged by the steady hand of its rider.

Thomas cursed the rain, the mud, and his own lack of resistance. Why had he let Fia talk him into attending the play? It was her sixth in as many years, each one vying with the others for success, each one widely acclaimed as brilliant.

Though not published under her own name, since her position at court made that an impossibility, 'twas well known that Fia Wentworth, the charming Countess Rotherwood, was a successful playwright. Thomas was unable to keep from bragging to one and all of her talents.

Queen Elizabeth had taken a surprisingly keen interest in Fia, frequently calling her to court to discuss various books and plays, although Thomas suspected that the lonely queen enjoyed Fia's fanciful stories more than the plays.

Of course, the gift of the amber amulet had helped to

pave that road. The queen loved it well and rarely went without it, although of late, Thomas had noticed the queen staring into the depths of the stone as if seeing something enchanting.

He'd thought of asking her about it, but when he remembered the personal nature of the images the amulet had shared with him, he'd decided that some secrets should be the queen's alone.

He slowed the horse when the lights of Rotherwood House glimmered in the night. After he jumped down, he tossed the reins to a waiting servant and bounded up the steps, water streaming from his cloak.

"Milord," Mary greeted him, her face wreathed in smiles. "'Tis a boy! Saints be praised, but ye've a bright cherub of a son with black eyes and the blackest of hair!"

"Fia?"

"Is restin' as easy as ye could expect." Mary took the wet cloak from his nerveless fingers. "The vicar is with her now."

"The vicar?"

Mary's smile faltered a bit. "Aye, I warned her ye'd be none too pleased about that, but she insisted on naming the wee one as soon as he arrived—"

He ran up the steps without waiting to hear more. The vicar stood over the bed, a small infant in his hands. His angular face beamed with pride. Fia opened tired eyes, breaking into a smile as soon as she saw Thomas.

He went to her immediately. "You, madam, are impatient."

"'Twas little Robin who would not wait."

"Robin?" he asked, a sigh in his voice.

She chuckled. "Aye." A giggle at the door announced

the arrival of their other children. "There they are! Bring Roberta and Robbie here," she told the vicar.

The cleric held out the babe to Thomas, who wondered how the wee one could sleep so soundly with all the noise his brother and sister were making.

The vicar brought the children to the bed and was rewarded with a beaming smile from Fia. The old man's face suffused with color; he was like bread dough in Fia's capable hands.

Thomas looked down at his other children and noted they each held an incredibly fat rabbit in much the same way he cradled the new baby. He grinned. Heaven help them, they were all puppets to Fia's bidding.

"Let us see the baby!" demanded Roberta, her brown eyes sparkling with excitement. "We brought Prometheus and Mercury to see him."

"I get to see him first," replied Robbie coolly. "I'm older."

"I'm four and I can see him if I want to," retorted Roberta with a mutinous toss of her red-brown curls.

"You can both see him at the same time," Thomas said as he lowered the babe to their level. "But keep those animals away from him."

"He's wrinkled." Roberta scrunched her nose in disgust. "And all red."

"Aye, and too small to play with." There was no hiding Robbie's disappointment.

"He'll grow," Thomas said. "I promise."

The vicar said, "I know you would both like to visit with your newest addition. Perhaps the children can show me the new baby rabbits? I hear they are a fine brood indeed."

"Aye," Robbie stated. "A fine, rollicking brood."

Roberta grabbed the man's hand, her rabbit hanging

over her arm like a pillow. "We always have new baby rabbits," she said seriously. "Mama says 'tis because we are blessed." She turned to Fia. "Isn't that right, Mama?"

"Yes, dear. We are very blessed," Fia answered, exchanging a warm, laughing look with Thomas.

"Too much so where those rabbits are concerned." Thomas tried to scowl but could not.

Fia chuckled as the vicar allowed the children to lead him from the room.

Thomas ran a finger down the infant's soft cheek. "Robin, eh?"

"A wager is a wager, Thomas," Fia defended herself. "I never thought we'd have so many children—else I'd have made Robert settle for naming only the first after him." She looked at the door. "Where is he, anyway? Robert never misses my plays."

"He was at all of the rehearsals, but he missed this eve. He said to tell you 'twas important business." Thomas lifted his brows. "He says you've inspired him to take his life in his own hands. Do you know what he was babbling about?"

Fia smiled. "Aye. 'Tis time he did."

The baby yawned widely, showing Thomas toothless gums that reminded him of Zeus. A twinge of sadness washed through him. He missed Zeus, though the dog's innumerable sons and daughters were in the barn, making life miserable for the old, decrepit horses Fia had collected to keep Thunder company.

Thomas sat on the edge of the bed and laid the baby in Fia's arms. "I suppose Robin was the best name you could think of."

Fia's mouth twitched. "We can call him by his middle name. 'Tis from one of my plays."

"I'm almost afraid to ask."

Her face lit with laughter. "You should be. 'Twill be a trial for him to spell."

He laughed and placed a gentle kiss on her forehead. "I suppose he'll get used to it."

She smiled shyly and threaded her fingers through the baby's wispy black curls. "You know, Thomas, I just thought of another."

"Another what?" he asked with alarm.

"Another name. For our next baby." She peeped up at him as mischievous and irrepressible as when he had first met her. "What do you think of Robertina?"

"I think, dear wife," he said as he kissed her nose, "that you are perfect."

Turn the page for a sneak peek
at the next delightful book in
New York Times bestseller
Karen Hawkins's
Hurst Amulet series,

One Night in Scotland

coming soon from Pocket Books

As snow swirled across the white-covered road and piled in high drifts to either side, the carriage creaked around the final bend of the cliff road and passed through the large stone gates of the castle. They bumped and swayed as the dirt road turned into cobblestones.

Mary lifted the leather curtain and stared up at the huge stone building. It was an amazingly beautiful castle, more of a palace. Several stories high, it soared above them, the large multipaned windows sparkling in gray-mortared granite walls. The building was impressive and appointed with rich details about the windows and the huge, wide oak doors. Yet, it was the fartherest wing that caught her attention. Blackened with soot, the roof completely open to the falling snow, it was a complete ruin. Black-streaked walls were framed by thickly smeared lines where wood shutters had once rested, while half-charred timbers stuck up from the snow like giant bones. Though the damage was not new, no attempt had been made to fix it. The only effort made was that someone had boarded up the windows and chained closed the charred doors.

The sight of this damaged and neglected wing was in odd contrast to the smooth gray perfection of the rest of the castle, the overall effect ominous. Mary shivered a little at the sight.

A moan pulled her back into the carriage. She patted Abigail's knee. "Are you still feeling ill?"

Abigail leaned forward, her arms crossed about her stomach, her face pale and pulled. "Gor', tell me we've reached the castle, miss!"

"We have. We should stop any second."

Abigail looked past Mary to the castle walls outside, her pained expression brightening a bit. "I've never been in a castle afore, miss. It's so big, isn't it? I—" She peered more closely out the window as they passed a window streaked with soot. "Why, it's naught but a ruin! It's done burned down."

"Only one wing. The rest of the castle appears to be in good shape." She wished she could ask about the circumstances that had led to such destruction, but their escort had offered little in the way of explanation. Once he'd practically shoved them into the carriage, he'd said not a word, but had climbed upon the coach seat with his assistant and they'd set off immediately.

The carriage turned sharply and pulled up to the wide oak doors, the carriage jolting as it stopped. Abigail sighed with relief. "Gor' miss, I've ne'er been on such a horrid road."

"It was very narrow and bumpy, wasn't it?"

"Aye, and straight off the cliff in places." Abigail drew a shuddering breath. "Thank goodness we're here."

Mary couldn't agree more. Between the dangerously winding road, the rapidly deteriorating weather, and Abigail's moaning, the trip had not been pleasant. It would have been even more unpleasant if they hadn't been in such a surprisingly luxurious carriage, complete with well-sprung leather seat backs, a foot warmer, and red velvet trim on the thick cushions.

Their coachman must work for a very wealthy family. She didn't know his name, or why he'd agreed to help them, or what his connection was to New Slains Castle—if he even had one. Perhaps now her questions would be answered.

She waited until the door swung open and the dark stranger appeared, large and imposing, his coat covered in snow, his muffler wrapped about his neck and covering the lower half of his face until only his green eyes showed.

His cool gaze flickered across Abigail, taking in her pinched expression, and then on to Mary, who met his indifferent gaze with an interested one of her own. He reached down and unlatched the steps, making sure they were in place before he stepped back to allow them to alight.

As Mary gathered her cloak, the front doors to the castle creaked opened and several impressively liveried footmen rushed down the stone steps toward the carriage. The stranger turned to speak to them, his voice muffled by his scarf and the wind.

The footmen halted, looking uncertain. He snapped another order, and two of the footmen rushed forward to take the trunks, while the rest moved respectfully out of the way.

Their coachman/guide turned and held out his gloved hand to Mary. "This is New Slains Castle."

His voice washed over her like the brush of dark velvet. "Thank you," she returned, aware of how mundane her own voice sounded next to his.

She knew very little about Scottish accents, but his was different from the ones she'd thus encountered. It was fainter, more hidden, rounding out a word here and there. It was also far more attractive, and she had to suppress an inane desire to make him speak more.

He lifted a brow and she realized he was still

holding out his hand. She gathered her skirts and finally placed her gloved hand in his.

Though their hands were separated by their gloves, she still felt something odd, as if she could almost access his thoughts. She withdrew her hand as quickly as she could, her face heated.

She couldn't shake the feeling that she somehow knew this man, or of him. The idea was preposterous. She'd never met him before and would likely never see him again. Her reaction was simply a combination of exhaustion and gratitude that he'd assisted her.

As she took a step toward the castle entryway, her boot hit a patch of ice. For a second she wavered, struggling to catch her balance, when a strong hand grasped hers once again, an arm slipping about her waist.

Instantly, the world steadied. Mary found herself staring up into the stranger's eyes, aware of her heart thundering madly in her throat. It was a heady feeling, whatever it was, and she allowed her fingers to tighten over his. His green gaze locked onto hers, heating with an intensity that let her know that he, too, felt that tingle of awareness.

Heat flew through her and she was aware of how her shoulder pressed against his broad chest, how strong his arm was where it encircled her waist, warming her the same way a cup of delicious hot chocolate might.

Just as suddenly as he'd caught her, he released her and stepped away. "The stone is icy. Watch your step."

She nodded mutely, wondering at how her skin prickled with heat. *Good God, what is this? I have never been so affected.*

She had to know what it was. Without a word, Mary reached out and took his hand once again and waited. It took less than a second for her body to tingle again. Amazed, she looked up at him and tightened her fingers on his.

His brows snapped down as his gaze flickered to where her hand was swallowed by his larger one, and then back. "You shouldn't—"

"Miss?" Abigail called weakly as she stood in the doorway of the coach. "I think I might be sick after all."

With a muffled curse, he released Mary's hand and reached out to assist an obviously weak-kneed Abigail to the ground.

Mary rubbed her tingling hand, her heart beating irregularly. Goodness, that was certainly interesting. She didn't know what it meant, but she hoped she'd find out.

"Lud, miss, I'm done fer." Abigail shivered miserably as their rescuer handed her over to the nearest footman. "I'd give me left teat fer some hot stew and a fire to sit beside."

The stranger's firm mouth quirked—had that been a smile? Mary couldn't be sure.

"Abigail didn't enjoy the winding road," Mary explained.

"So I see. You look well enough, though."

"I'm an excellent traveler. I just wish I had the opportunity to do more."

He sent her a curious glance.

"La, miss!" Abigail shivered. "If me left teat ain't enough fer a cup o' stew, I'll offer me right one as well, and—"

"Abigail, *please!*" Mary pretended not to notice the astounded gaze of one of the footmen.

Their rescuer's eyes blazed with humor. "I'm sure the earl is at least hospitable enough that you'll find yourself before a warm fire *and* some hot stew and still keep your, ah, personal possessions."

Mary murmured, "We can only hope."

He shot her a quick glance, his face warmed with laughter.

Mary's breath caught in her throat. *Good God, he's beautiful when he smiles.*

There was no other word for it. His stern face relaxed, his fine lips curved from their harsh line into a warm and generous smile, and his eyes crinkled in the most amazing way. He was like two different men.

Their rescuer turned to the waiting footmen.

"Take these trunks inside and escort the ladies to the library. They wish an audience."

There was a scurry of activity as his requests were fulfilled.

Mary raised her brows. He was certainly cavalier in how he spoke to another man's servants. Though he hadn't been any less cavalier in his treatment of her and Mary, really.

The closest footman bowed. "My l—"

"I will return to the stables with the coach." He favored Mary and Abigail with a faint bow. "Good evening, ladies." With that far-too-brief farewell, he turned and proceeded to the carriage.

"Wait!" The word sprang from Mary's lips before she knew what she was about. Standing in the courtyard, surrounded by the exquisitely outfitted footmen in the shade of a massive castle, her only companion a coach-sick maid, the awkwardness of her mission came crashing upon her.

She was about to enter this forbidding abode to ask a desperately needed favor from a man she'd never met. For a moment, she wanted to somehow borrow some of the easy strength that seemed to sit on their coachman's broad shoulders.

She hurried up to the coachman, who stood beside the front wheel, and gulped at the cool curiosity in his gaze. "Pardon me, but . . . will you wait for us? We shouldn't be long, for I only need to ask the earl a question, and then we'll wish to return to—"

"No."

"I will pay—"

"You may keep your money."

Her shoulders sagged. "But how will I get back to our carriage at the inn?"

He shrugged. "If you request it, the earl will arrange a return ride to the inn."

"Very well." The snow drifted between them, the wind tossing their cloaks around their ankles. There was less than two feet between them, yet it seemed as wide as the North Sea. "I-I wish you'd stay."

His brows lowered. "Me?"

Her face heated. "I don't know anyone here, and it would be nice to have one friendly face."

"You think *I* have a friendly face?" His voice could not convey more surprise.

She looked directly at him. No, he didn't have a friendly face. His expression was too cold, his gaze too piercing. "You do when you laugh. Right now you look—" She tilted her head to one side. "Rather sour, as if you'd just eaten something you didn't like."

His lips twitched. "You don't pull your punches, do you?"

"Should I?"

"No. Not with me." He regarded her for a moment, then said abruptly, "You are afraid to speak to the earl."

"No . . . yes. I mean, I— I don't know him and I must have his help."

"For what?"

She shook her head. "It's a complicated story and I— Please, if you could just stay until I've had a chance to speak to the earl. It would be comforting to know we had a way back to our carriage." She wondered at her sudden lack of spirit. *I'm just tired. I need to collect myself; Michael would never be so foolish.*

"I told you that I must go. Erroll will see to it that you're taken to your carriage." He turned away to climb into the seat.

She placed a hand on his arm. "Wait. Please."

He looked down at her gloved hand before turning to face her. "I am not staying."

"I know, but . . . perhaps you could help me in another way. What do you know of the earl?"

He shrugged. "Just what I've heard."

"Is he *kind*?"

The coachman's expression hardened. "No."

"Oh." That was too bad. "I don't suppose you have any hints as to how to best approach him? It could be difficult, as I've never met him before."

The green eyes narrowed and she wished he would remove that muffler that hid so much of his face. "You should have thought of that before you came."

"I didn't have a choice," she returned, her tone sharp. "It's very important."

The green eyes assessed her head to foot. Finally, he said, "Just tell him the truth . . . if you can."

"Of course I can," she said with a touch of asperity. "I'm not a storyteller, Mr. ——" She waited expectantly, but all he did was shrug.

Her jaw tightened, a flash of irritation making her snap, "Fine. Thank you for your assistance in making the trip here. I suppose it's too much to expect you to offer to do more." She spun on her heel to march off.

"Hold." The softly spoken word halted her in her tracks.

She turned back to face him.

"I know one thing about the earl."

"What?"

"He cannot stand a woman who is anything other than meek."

She curled her nose. "Meek? How archaic."

His eyes seemed to twinkle, though she was certain it was a trick of the pale light. "The Hays are an old family. Perhaps he's merely acting as he was taught."

"That makes sense."

"Yes, it does. Now, if you'll excuse me, I must be off."

"Of course. Oh, wait. I almost forgot." She dug into her pocket and pulled out her purse to fish out two shillings. It was a dear sum, but a bargain was a bargain. She grasped his wrist and turned his hand palm up, ignoring the way her heart immediately began to gallop as if yearning to run straight toward him. *Such a curious reaction! Am I affected by green eyes? I've certainly never seen any that color.*

She placed the shillings in his gloved hand. "Your payment."

His long fingers curled over the coins. "Of course. I would have hated to have hunted you down and"—his gaze flickered over her in a way she was totally unused to—"demand payment."

For some reason, the thought of being "hunted down" by this man did not raise a feeling of alarm, but of shivery pleasure. "I am not a woman to avoid paying what is due."

"I didn't think you were." He glanced over her head toward the castle, then bent low. "One more word of caution: the earl has a temper. Do not cross him."

"No! I have to be meek *and* watch for his temper? What a termagant."

"You can't say you weren't warned. Now, I must be off." He turned and climbed into the coach seat beside his assistant, his cloak flapping damply in the snow.

Mary watched the coach jerk into motion and cross the courtyard toward the stables. No doubt their rescuer desired to rest his horses before he continued home.

Where was his home? Was it close by? Would *he* be close by? An unsettling sweep of yearning swept over her. His presence had made her feel safe, which was utter nonsense. *I don't even know his name.*

"Miss? May we go in?" Abigail called. "I'm chilled to the bone, I am."

"Of course." Embarrassed she'd forgotten her maid, Mary hurried to the woman's side. "Good evening," she said to the footman. "We would like to see the earl. 'Tis a matter of grave import."

True love
is timeless with historical romances from Pocket Books!

A Malory novel

Johanna Lindsey
No Choice But Seduction
He'd stop at nothing to make her love him.
But should she surrender to his bold charms?

Liz Carlyle
Tempted All Night
When deception meets desire, even the most
careful lady can be swayed by a scoundrel....

Julia London
Highland Scandal
Which is a London rakehell more likely to survive—
a hanging, or a handfasting to a spirited Highland lass?

Jane Feather
A Husband's Wicked Ways
When a spymaster proposes marriage as a cover,
a lovely young woman discovers the danger—and
delight—of risking everything for love.

Available wherever books are sold or at www.simonandschuster.com

POCKET BOOKS
A Division of Simon & Schuster
A CBS COMPANY

POCKET STAR BOOKS
A Division of Simon & Schuster
A CBS COMPANY

20472

Delve into a *passion* from the *past* with a *romance*
from *Pocket Books!*

---◆---

LIZ CARLYLE
Never Romance a Rake
Love is always a gamble....But never romance a rake!

JULIA LONDON
The Book of Scandal
Will royal gossip reignite her husband's passion for her?

KARIN TABKE
Master of Surrender
The Blood Sword Legacy
A mercenary knight is bound by a blood oath to reclaim his
legacy—and the body of the one woman he desires.

KATHLEEN GIVENS
Rivals for the Crown
The fierce struggle for Scotland's throne leads
two women to courageous new destinies...

**Available wherever books are sold
or at www.simonandschuster.com.**